The Cleansweep Counterstrike

THE CLEANSWEEP COUNTERSTRIKE

A Matt Tremain Novel

By Chuck Waldron

The CleanSweep Counterstrike
© 2018 Chuck Waldron

All Rights Reserved. No part of this book may be reproduced or transmitted
in any form or by any means, electronic or mechanical, including
photocopying, recording, or by any information storage and retrieval
system, without permission in writing from the publisher.

This book is a work of fiction. Characters, names, places, and incidents are
fictious or used fictitiously. Any similar to real persons, living or dead or
events, is coincidental and not intended by the author.

Distributed by Bublish, Inc.
bublish.com

ISBN-10: 1-948543-07-9
ISBN-13: 978-1-948543-07-1

Other novels by Chuck Waldron
The CleanSweep Conspiracy
Tears in the Dust
Remington and the Mysterious Fedora
Served Cold

As with all my novels, this is dedicated to Suzanne first, last, and always. You have made this wonderful writing journey possible. Your support is invaluable, your encouragement priceless, and your unconditional love beyond measure.

I owe a huge debt of gratitude to some amazing beta readers. You picked the story apart until the tricky bits, were tamed. Thanks: Michael, Kathy, Joanne, Neil, Robert, Jon Dixon, and Marty. The work was hard, the pay was low, but you're all loved.

Thanks to Mike, a great editor, helping me make up for sleeping through high school English.

A final thanks to Kathy Meis. I found my author's best friend, the founder of Bublish. Pay a visit to www.bublish.com and see why.

CHAPTER 1

BULLSEYE

Matt Tremain trained his eyes on the gun barrel, waiting for the shot. Charles Claussen smirked, aiming the silver 9mm Luger. Matt watched Claussen's finger slowly increase pressure on the trigger and braced himself for the blast.

• • •

Jolted awake, Matt struggled to untangle the sweat-soaked sheets. *Another panic attack, the same nightmare. Charles Claussen with that weapon,* he thought. Matt tried to hold on to details, but the images floated away as soon as he opened his eyes. The acrid taste of stale alcohol was a reminder of self-medicating, desperate to stop the recurring night-time terrors.

He cringed, throwing off the sheets as a siren penetrated the quietness. *An ambulance?* he wondered. The city sounds of pre-dawn Toronto replaced the fading siren's wail.

Matt stumbled to the bathroom to rinse the fuzz from his mouth and was alarmed to see the water glass quivering in his hand.

Returning to his bed, Matt tried to rub away the hammering pain, but it didn't help. He tried to ignore the clock display as he drifted between awake and sleep. *It's no use,* he thought.

Matt walked back into the bathroom. He didn't recognize the face in the mirror. Murky bloodshot eyes looked back at him. Matt splashed his face with cold water. It didn't help. *Time to face the world. It's the best I can do.*

Matt had a world-class hangover, like someone tapping on his skull with a hammer. He'd hoped for a free day, no appointments nor commitments. Matt wanted to be left alone with his panic as he opened the door at the Beanery. He needed his go-to hangover cure, a robust Sumatra blend and three extra-strength pain tablets. *At least I'm not puking.*

• • •

The crowded coffeehouse was noisy, the aroma thick and curative. The barista handed Matt his coffee. He noticed a couple leaving and walked to the empty table then powered on his laptop. He took a deep breath as he faced the blank screen. Matt felt his skull throbbing. He lowered his chin, rotating his head to ease the pain.

"That's him." Matt heard a young woman at the next table whisper to her companion.

Shit, Matt thought. He wanted privacy. He looked at them until they turned back their conversation.

Matt looked at his computer screen. *It's no use. Who can focus on writing with a hangover like this?* He wanted to go back to the way it was, hiding behind his computer. He knew the clock couldn't be turned back. Matt's life changed forever when he helped blow the whistle on Operation CleanSweep.

Why am I afraid? Matt thought. *Charles Claussen, the man behind CleanSweep, somehow eluded capture. Claussen's a coiled snake, ready to strike without the warning rattle.*

Matt knew it wasn't his imagination. *With Claussen on the loose, I'm not safe. He's after revenge. He has the resources to carry out his threat.*

His phone vibrated and skidded toward the edge of the table. He grabbed it before it dropped to the floor. Matt opened the message and stifled a scream as he examined at the photo. "My face. A sniper's target superimposed, the bullseye centered on my nose, between the eyes.

Matt shuddered at the words. "I'm coming for you."

"Damn!" He slammed his phone onto the table. Coffee sloshed over the rim of the cup, covering the table and the back of his computer.

Customers turned. The barista rushed around the counter with a large towel in hand. "Matt, what's wrong? You look like you've seen a ghost."

"I have." He looked at the table. "Sorry for all this, Marsha."

"Claussen?" she asked, using the towel to soak up the coffee, first on the table, then the floor. "People are always claiming to have seen him. There's more sightings of Claussen than Elvis. I had the radio on yesterday. A woman called in, claiming Claussen's living in some rinky-dink town in Florida. Another nutty caller."

Matt didn't reply, keeping his phone display hidden.

"How can it be Claussen? The police said he killed himself—" Marsha was cut short.

It's too much. Matt felt the walls closing in. His face blossomed dark burgundy. "Sorry, Marsha. Sorry, I have to get the hell out of here." He stuffed his computer into his backpack, grabbed his phone, and ran to the door, unsure where to go.

Outside, he punched some numbers and held the phone to his ear. *Voicemail, damn,* he thought. "Carling. It's Matt. Call me. It's urgent."

Matt read the text one more time. "I'm coming for you." *This arriving today. After I had that nightmare.* He didn't welcome the coincidence. *It's Charles Claussen. He's alive.*

Matt was on edge—gripped by fear, paranoia, and sense of doom.

Two young men around nineteen walked toward him. One had a ball cap pulled down to cover his eyes from view. His companion pulled something from his pocket, swinging it upward. They had a 'gangsta' strut, twisting their hands and flashing what could be gang signs. They walked directly toward Matt.

Claussen. You bastard!

The two approached quickly, then brushed past, nudging him, staking a claim to alpha male status.

He wouldn't send punks, Matt thought, trying to shake off his intensifying sense of alarm.

The streetcar approached, clattering to a stop. Instead of getting on immediately, Matt spotted a park across the street. It was a small, grassy area flanked by two apartment buildings that stretched from the road to the lake. He changed his mind, motioning the streetcar driver on.

A bench faced the water. Matt leaned back and tried to relax. A shaft of light sliced through spring-fresh leaves, and he felt like an actor captured in the spotlight. He tilted his head back, wanting to absorb the warmth, but his body couldn't shake off the dread.

Matt removed his laptop from the backpack. His anger grew as he scrolled through the files. He felt something else: a wave of sadness. He located a blog post. Matt started rereading the blog he wrote after Charles Claussen and CleanSweep were exposed.

● ● ●

The Evil of CleanSweep, by Matt Tremain

Looking back over the past months, I keep asking myself one question, a single word. How? How does evil like this grow and fester among us? The evil of CleanSweep wasn't imported. It grew on the inside like cancer.

We are distracted by speeches and tweets about terrorism, losing sleep, thinking hooded men are standing poised, ready to behead us. We've been shown the launder list of people to keep out, immigrants who don't speak our language, people who worship differently. We want to build walls, physical and virtual. What about the hate creating domestic terrorism?

Now, we have a poster boy for hate—the face of Charles Claussen.

Norman Rockwell created four paintings representing what our country stands for: Freedom of Speech, Freedom of Worship, Freedom from Want, and Freedom from Fear.

Claussen's versions are a perversion.

Speech? The first to go was Freedom of Speech. Anyone not agreeing with him would be heckled, threatened, or worse.

Religion? Sanctioned churches only. No Jews, Muslims, nor new age meditators need to apply.

Want? He claimed hard work and determination would free people from want. Those left behind needed to be gradually eliminated. Costly social programs will no longer suck the budget dry, thanks to a Clean-Sweep administration.

Fear. What about Freedom from Fear? Claussen's manifesto stated that people with nothing to hide from the government have no reason to fear.

I wonder how Norman Rockwell would paint Claussen's CleanSweep vision. A friendly janitor CleanSweeping away grit and grime, along with the great unwashed.

A text ringtone interrupted his reading and his gaze shifted on the screen of his cell phone. "In court now Got UR message We need 2 meet 10-8 @ 3."

Matt smiled and tried to relax. Talking to his best friend would help.

Matt looked at the glass-like surface of the water as the wind vacuumed waves away. He watched as a fish broke the surface and disappeared as quickly, spreading rippling concentric rings. Matt shuddered.

• • •

Hidden in the shadows of a nearby building, a young man pulled back his hood, raising a phone to his ear.

Matt couldn't shake the feeling of rising panic as he walked back to the streetcar stop.

CHAPTER 2

THE 10-8

Matt read the text again. *"10-8."* *The cop bar*, he thought, *Of course.* Matt was twitchy and arrived early. He never felt welcome at the 10-8 as he knew he didn't fit in. He wasn't a cop, and the 10-8 didn't exactly hang a welcome sign on the door.

The bar wasn't crowded, so Matt sat there, collecting his thoughts and flinching whenever the front door clattered open. Since the Clean-Sweep riots, Matt jumped at loud noises.

A large man stormed through the doorway. Many angry cops failed to damage the door. However, Detective Wallace no-middle-initial Carling, head of Police Services counter-terrorism bureau, came close this time.

His rage filled the 10-8 bar, and two cop groupies sitting at the bar looked like they wanted to be somewhere else, anywhere else.

"Seriously," Matt said, trying to calm his friend. "Watch your blood pressure." Matt looked at the big man wedging into the booth. "Where's your fedora—"

"Shut the fuck up," Carling said, his words squeezed through clenched lips. "I'm assuming we all got one of these from Claussen," he said as he held his phone out.

The photo on Carling's phone also a sniper's bullseye superimposed on Carling's face.

"The ghost of CleanSweep future," Carling said. "Susan and Remy each got one for sure. You can count on it. We have to call and find out to confirm."

"They're still in New Zealand," Matt said.

"I know. Remy told me they're filming a documentary about Maori culture, sacred buildings, or some such. Maoris are something like our Indians."

Matt decided to ignore the insensitive reference to aboriginal cultures, realizing it was Carling's anger speaking.

"I talked to Remy before they left," Carling said. "Will a wireless phone work there?"

"I'm sure New Zealand has wireless communications. Although it might be a bit primitive, using drums and smoke."

Carling didn't take the bait. "Let's talk about this," he said. He pointed to the photo on his phone, and his voice shifted from anger to fear. "We knew this was possible, didn't we? If he's out here, we aren't safe. Claussen got away, and I'm convinced he's planning to get even. How the hell did he even avoid arrest like that?" The question floated over the table before Carling answered his own question. "He had some ingenious trick up his sleeve."

Matt cringed at the cliché.

"We're ready now," Carling said. He signaled to the bartender, holding up two fingers. "Beer, mate. Make it Keith's." Matt and Carling sat without talking as they waited for their drinks. Matt enjoyed how comfortable they could be with silence.

Holding his bottle to cool his face, Carling broke the silence. "I was a wreck in court today, mumbling like a rookie. I couldn't keep my concentration. All I could feel was anxiety—thinking about that text," he said.

"You're afraid? You have a gun," Matt said. "Imagine me. I'm armed with a laptop. I never retreat; I backspace." *So much for humor,* he thought.

"Claussen's dangerous. He's had a long time to plan revenge." Carling took a long drink. "We have no idea where he is, what resources he has."

"What do you hear on the job? You must have access to some kind of resources with your new job." Matt tried to sound calm, but it wasn't working.

"Some rinky-dink town in Florida," Carling said. "I've never heard of it. To me, Florida is Miami or Orlando. Everything in between is nothing but swamp."

"What did you say?" Matt said. "You said a rinky-dink town in Florida. The barista used those same words this morning."

"I wouldn't have my new job if I didn't know how to ask the right questions," Carling said. "There're some good people on my team. It took Janice, one of the techies, less than sixty seconds to ping the origins."

Carling opened a notebook. "The first message came to my phone. It bounced from a tower in... Wewahitchka. Helluva name, eh? I checked Google Maps. It's in the Florida panhandle. The service provider leases antenna space on a tower near there. The second ping came from a tower halfway between Wewahitchka and Port Saint Joe. That tower transmitted one to you. He sent out one each to Remy and Susan," Carling said before taking another swig of his drink.

"You think Remy and Susan have seen theirs yet?"

Carling tipped his mug to finish. "No idea. How soon can you be packed? We'll need something for a couple of days. I put my stuff in the car already," he said.

"Won't take long. I don't need much, but what if it's a trap?"

"We went after Cleansweep, didn't we? I have a team and resources now that can help. The feds wanted to take control when I told them about the threat and photo," Carling explained. "They're not going to wait long."

Matt glared at him in annoyance. *Why did he call the feds already?*

"I see that look. Relax. They've given us a forty-eight-hour head start."

The front door opened, and the light flared like a camera's flash. Two men were talking as they walked toward the bar. "Hey, Carling," one said as he started to make a detour to the booth the friends were sitting at. He saw a look on Carling's face and stopped. "Guess you guys want to be alone."

"Where was I?" Carling said. "Oh, yeah, I bought tickets to Panama City, first class on Delta. We can stop by your place on the way," he said. "That's closest to the town where he's supposed to live. Let's find out if he's there."

Matt watched him take a breath and asked, "Do you really think I'm up to this? What help will I be?"

"Matt. Who knows this creep better than the two of us, four if Remy and Susan were here? If it weren't for you and Susan, CleanSweep would have—" He didn't finish.

"Something just occurred to me. With Claussen's background, he must know you can track him. Is he doing this on purpose, giving these clues to his location? He's waiting, his ambush prepared, ready to feed us to the alligators," Matt said.

More cops in uniform began to walk in. "Shift change," Carling noticed, easing Matt's discomfort. He stood and motioned Matt to follow.

Matt almost smiled at Carling, who still drove the same battered sedan. "By the way, when did you start texting?"

Carling grunted something unintelligible, then grinned. "What made you think I didn't know how to text?" he said.

● ● ●

Cyberia inhaled, then puffed out a cloud of cigarette smoke. *It's been awhile. What are you doing, Matt?* he wondered. *I saw Claussen's text to you. Be careful, my friend.*

Cyberia, Matt's online friend, used his ability to hack into the Operation CleanSweep computers. He had provided Matt the edge needed to avoid arrest—and likely worse.

Cyberia continued to run his CleanSweep program, even though it was no longer needed; he enjoyed monitoring Matt. The SIM card in Matt's phone gave the Russian hacker all he needed to track his location. Poking around Matt's computer was simply child's play to Cyberia.

Cyberia was a ghost, part of a sub-culture of people with superior hacking skills, who existed in one of the darkest corners of the darknet.

He watched the screen dedicated to Matt Tremain until it went dark again.

CHAPTER 3

GETAWAY

Charles Claussen despised the heat. He placed a high value on appearances and considered sweating distasteful. As he sat in the shade of an enormous live oak tree, he was angry; it didn't provide cooling relief. A light breeze from the bay scarcely moved warm air around. Claussen felt wetness collecting under his arms. He looked at the barrier island in the distance. Two-Mile Channel separated Apalachicola from the island. A line of trees looked like a serrated knife, the heatwaves stirring in the afternoon sunlight.

I hate this place, he thought. *I won't be here much longer. I can taste it. I'll get my revenge. I'm so close now.* He focused his rage on four targets: Matt Tremain, Wallace Carling, Susan Payne, and Carl Remington.

I'm coming for you. No, you're coming to me. The trap is set. My texts will put everything into play. Matt and his friend won't be able to resist.

The day his cherished program was exposed, Claussen began planning his revenge. *They took away everything*, he thought. He remembered every detail about the day Operation CleanSweep came crashing down.

Claussen thought back to his narrow escape, the police banging on his office door, shouting his name. In a split second-decision, his double was on the floor bleeding and Claussen made his escape. Faking a suicide was his escape plan, but he never thought he'd have to use it.

It was over in less than a second. Brain matter, blood, and cartilage sprayed a grisly pattern. The floor-to-ceiling window looked like an appalling display of abstract art.

The memory of that moment was a tape running through Claussen's mind playing the scene in ultra-slow-motion. Did he imagine it? Did he really see the Parabellum bullet spiraling from the business end of the 9mm Luger he held?

Impossible, he thought. It was invisible, traveling at a velocity of 1,300 feet per second. He convinced himself he saw it. Either way, he did see the aftermath. The bullet entered below the chin, traveled upward, and fragmented as it tumbled a path through the skull. He watched, amazed at the catastrophic damage that practically demolished the cranium.

When it was over, a man's body splayed backwards, remnants of the head still attached. There wasn't anything left of the face of the man who was once counting money. Claussen saw the surprise when the man realized what was about to happen, submerged in thought. Claussen assumed he was planning on how to spend the stack of the twenties and fifties.

Earlier Claussen made the man an offer. "I have a proposal. How would you like to make a thousand dollars, tax-free?" Claussen smirked.

Watching Claussen, the man's eyes conveyed acceptance; money never came readily to the likes of him. He knew the cash would never be spent, more money at once than he'd ever dreamed of.

Claussen watched him hold his hand up as if to stop what was coming when he saw the gun. He looked at Claussen, holding the Luger in his right hand and a large white towel wrapped around the left.

The next movement was swift and practiced. Claussen rehearsed well, as he did with everything. Holding the towel with his left arm, he looked like a matador. The Luger in his right hand had been engraved by Georg Luger himself.

The banging on the door grew louder. Then he heard shouting.

When he pulled the trigger, he was deafened by the sound. Planning didn't prepare him for the carnage created in less than that second.

He tasted his own vomit, embarrassed. The treasured family Luger was carefully placed in the man's hand, making sure to place it in the right hand, to stage it better.

The police wouldn't be fooled for long; he knew that. DNA and other forensic evidence would uncover the truth. It simply had to look like a suicide. He needed time—two hours at most. He'd already established a rigid timetable to pull off the escape. Now he just had to do it.

He took final inventory, trying to avoid looking at the bloody stump where a head used to be. Claussen wasn't squeamish, but this was another level of gore. His only regret: the damage to the suit on the body, a Brioni Vanquish II. He'd paid $43,000 for the ensemble splattered with detritus.

• • •

"That's a gunshot," he heard someone yell. "Kick the door in, now," someone said, immediately followed by the sound of shattering wood.

Claussen stepped back and squeezed through a narrow open panel of the wall. Inside, he touched a keypad. The panel closed, concealing the exit. He stood for a moment, hearing splintering wood. He listened to police breaking into his office and someone shouting adrenalin-infused commands.

"Damn, he killed himself. Fucking coward," a man said.

"No, no, no," a woman cried. As he listened in, he recognized the voice of his head of security, Angela Vaughn, from the other side of the door.

He can't get off that easily," someone shouted.

His ruse was working. Claussen set a two-hour countdown clock using the timer on his smartphone. He programmed it to make a reminder beep every ten minutes. *I never imagined making use of this plan. Still, something told me to prepare for all contingencies. Hah. I choreographed my disappearance. Now, I execute the dance.*

The shouting from his office grew faint as he walked down a narrow passageway. The people who knew about this secret panel and passageway had been paid well to forget it ever existed.

His eardrums throbbed from the detonation of the gunshot.

He reached an alcove at the end of the passageway. A single bulb overhead provided enough light. He opened a locker. Claussen undressed, taking time to hang his suit with care, a slave to habit. He took off his tie and placed it on the shelf. When he stripped off his white shirt, he frowned at the traces of vomit. He carefully placed his dress shoes on the floor of the locker with precision.

Looking into a small mirror, Claussen used his handkerchief to wipe away flecks of blood. He had to pick away two pieces of bone fragments stuck to his right cheek.

• • •

Claussen was putting on a pair of jeans when the alarm beeped. *Ten minutes are gone.* He looked at the plaid shirt with contempt before putting it on. A light tan photographer's vest jacket came next. It was a snug fit. He was lacing his boots when he felt an electrical shock of anxiety. *I can't afford that,* he thought, *I have to get moving.* Claussen put on a baseball cap and listened at the exit, his ear to the door.

He didn't hear anything and stepped onto the landing. There were two brushed aluminum elevator doors. The one to his left was narrow, marked private. The special elevator sat unused, preset for this moment. He glanced at his watch. *Only fourteen minutes elapsed.* He was about to step into the elevator when he heard voices.

"Did you hear that? They say he shot himself," a man said.

"The loser's way out," another said.

"Yeah, for sure."

"Nothing for us to do now."

Two men talked on the landing above. Claussen froze, his panic wrapping his chest like a boa constrictor. Letting his breath seep out in a long, controlled sigh, he heard their voices fade. They walked toward the top, away from his direction.

Too close, he thought. His willpower took charge. Claussen paused to send a text message to the operations manager at Calluden airport. "Have the plane ready."

One hour and forty-eight minutes to go—more than enough time.

A smart-card gave him control of the elevator. The car made a heart-stopping plunge to the lowest parking level. He anticipated the police would be watching his designated space on the executive level.

When the door opened, a newly-dressed Charles Claussen stepped out. He scanned left to right. Two police vehicles sat empty, their doors open, the flashing blue lights strobing off concrete walls. There was no sign of the officers who had abandoned them.

Claussen listened for footsteps or shouting, but he didn't hear anything out of the ordinary, so he walked three levels to street level. A police officer stood at the top, to the right. The officer had his back to the garage, intent on watching the activity at the building entrance.

Sirens came from the left, with more police cars filling the street. Claussen watched as a television truck parked across the street, the transmitting antenna telescoping above.

It's the Channel 12 Action News logo. Is Payne covering this? he wondered. *That bitch. I'll get even, whatever it takes. You and your cameraman. Then, Matt Tremain and Detective Carling. I'll be coming for you all.*

Claussen eased past the preoccupied officer and blended in with the crowd of nearby looky-loos drawn to accidents, death, and excitement.

I can't run. Claussen maintained a steady pace down the street. People rushed past him in the opposite direction. He reached the next corner unnoticed and turned into a deserted street. It was eerie; all the cars were abandoned by their drivers in their eagerness to see what was happening at Claussen Towers.

Claussen felt his temples throbbing, his pulse rate off the chart.

The howl of sirens echoed like electronic coyotes, bouncing from concrete and glass urban canyons.

Claussen walked toward a sign for a public parking garage. *This next step needs to be complication-free. Forty-five minutes to get to the airport,* he thought. His watch beeped—another ten minutes gone. *Enough time? Am I cutting it too close?* This wasn't time to second guess. He had to continue the plan.

The parking lot attendant barely looked away from a magazine as Claussen hurried in. Claussen noticed the magazine was mostly pictures of women in various stages of undress.

He approached a dark blue Range Rover parked on the upper level, and Claussen used the fob to raise the rear door. A strongbox was welded to the floor. He opened it and took out a driver's license, pilot's license, pilot's logbook, and passport. He almost smiled at his new name: Charles Hunter.

I will be hunting those responsible. That German was a master forger with a sense of humor, Claussen thought.

There was another set of documents for the alias Ralph Porter. "Just in case," the forger had said. "I've provided everything you ordered. I've even included library cards. Whatever you do," he forger warned, "don't use your own credit cards."

Claussen scoffed. "No need to tell me. I'm not stupid. I made a fortune scooping records and personal information from unsuspecting credit card holders. The way I did it was even legal," he had said.

Claussen set aside the identities and opened an envelope of cash. He looked around to see if anybody was watching before he divided the money, stuffing bills into various jacket pockets.

The only thing left in the lockbox was a black velvet bag fastened with a drawstring that held a fortune in diamonds. Claussen slipped the gems into an inner pocket, zipping to make sure it was secure.

The only thing remaining looked like a television remote.

"Place anything that can identify you in the box. Then make sure you are at least ten feet away when you push the button. In fifteen seconds, everything inside will be reduced to ashes. No putting anything back together," the forger said.

Claussen placed all traces of his old life into the box and closed the lid. He stepped back until he was far enough away as he was told. When he pushed the remote, a small eruption sounded like a gun with a silencer. Claussen almost laughed. *The detonation sounded like a loud fart*, he thought, weird coming from a man not predisposed to making a joke. Smoke seeped from the box. When it stopped smoking, he opened the container. Nothing remained except a fine layer of carbon black powder, as promised.

Charles Claussen was now a phantom.

• • •

Sixty-seven minutes to go, Claussen thought, forcing himself to resist panic.

Exiting the garage, he turned right, away from his former office building, Claussen Tower. He drove on the sidewalk to get past abandoned vehicles. A woman with a shopping bag gestured her displeasure.

This roadblock is eating into the redundancy built into my plan. He approached the ramp to the Gardiner Expressway and calmed down. The Range Rover, with 834 miles on the odometer, glided smoothly over potholes and bumps.

I squandered eighty-five thousand dollars for a thirty-five-mile drive, he thought. Claussen turned on the thousand-watt, twenty-nine speaker audio system and scrolled to his favorite album, German Military Marches, to play "Horst Wessel Lied."

Perfect, he thought, accelerating.

Heatwaves radiated from the hood as he drove the Range Rover through the airport gate and onto the tarmac. He held his hand to shield the sun backlighting the waiting jet. He had researched corporate jets carefully; Claussen needed something he could fly solo.

His choice was a we ork of art, a Spectrum S.33, with twin turbofan engines nestled at the base of the tail.

Claussen drove to the man standing by the boarding ramp and braked. *One hour and three minutes. I'm falling behind. It's only my nerves. I'm precisely on schedule.*

"Mr. Hunter," the man said, sounding like a question. I'm Richards, the airport manager. Your people gave clear instructions. Everything is ready. The international flight plan to Marsh Harbour on Great Abaco Island, is filed. I used the 800-WXB-REIF phone number."

The manager paused, looking as if he was scrolling through a mental checklist. "Don't forget, you have to radio and activate the flight plan when you're in the air."

Claussen bristled but nodded his understanding.

"All necessary charts are on the starboard seat. The Bahamas Customs Form C7a is on the top of the charts. Your outbound flight is cleared, ah, Mr. Hunter. You should contact Miami Flight Service Station by radio when you return the US, just to be on the safe side."

Claussen watched the man examining paperwork, still not speaking.

"All I need now is to see the necessary ID," the man said.

Claussen handed over his new identification. *This is the first test,* he thought. He watched Richards scrutinize his license and logbook. *The man is taking too long examining the authorization letter.*

"What's the latest weather," Claussen asked. It was just enough to distract the scrutiny.

"Turbulence over Savannah, but clear after that." The manager said and handed the documentation back.

"Is it still the same, merely fly in, check with customs when I land?"

"Correct. I double-checked, Mr. Hunter. You're not required to contact Bahamian authorities before arriving."

"Well, I'm ready," Claussen said.

"Blue side up, mate. I'll pull the chocks when you give me the sign, and I'll take care of the Rover, as directed."

Looking at his watch, Claussen almost smiled at the meticulous timing. *I'm well under the two hours I needed for my escape.* Shaking hands with the manager, Claussen climbed the boarding steps. He smiled at the sound of the stairway folding into the door behind him. He made sure the door was secure and stepped into the cockpit.

Sitting at the controls, Claussen relaxed for the first time since his escape. He set the onboard guidance system, but reworked calculations in his mind to make sure. Flight distance was 1,493 miles, at 475 mph.

Claussen scrolled through the options. The computer blinked wheels down at 3:42 pm. He listened to the whine of the powerful turbines, waved at Richards to pull the chocks, and eased the plane forward. He taxied to the turning point at the head of the runway, turned the nose of the small plane down the runway, and waited.

"Tower. Clear for take-off,"

"Roger that." Claussen pushed the throttle and released the brakes. Two Williams FJ-33 engines roared with 1,750 pounds of thrust each. When the nose lifted, Claussen pulled back on the controls. When the jet was out of the traffic pattern, he gave one last look around for other aircrafts. Satisfied, he pushed the throttle to full position and started a steep climb.

The nose stabbed into a cloud layer, wrapping the plane in cotton. Climbing at 5,000 feet per minute, Claussen was momentarily blinded when the aircraft soared through the cloud stratum. He reached for his aviator sunglasses. *Hawkeye Tortoiseshell, by Barton Perreira, a deal at $549,* he thought.

Two hours after his suicide and under ten minutes from takeoff, Claussen was traveling at nearly 500 miles per hour at a breathtaking altitude of 45,000 feet. His watched beeped the final ten-minute warning.

CHAPTER 4

ON THE FLY

Claussen looked at Apalachicola Bay, smooth as a glass table. Sitting in the shade of a Live Oak tree, a whisper of air skimmed his face. His hope for a cooling breeze vanished as the wind fell off. He closed his eyes, remembering the fresh, cool onshore winds wafting from Lake Ontario.

Claussen heard the hum of car tires on the flyway to the bridge, a screeching fight between two seagulls, and the diesel motors of passing fishing trawlers.

A droplet of sweat formed on his brow, but he refused to acknowledge it. He thought about the next part of his escape.

• • •

Why is my leg cramping like that? Claussen thought, rubbing his right leg. *I've only been at the controls for two hours.* Claussen decided pain helped keep him remain alert.

Through a break in the cloud cover, he saw the Savannah River snaking its way past its namesake city. It matched the image on the GPS screen.

The strain of his escape had been intense. Now he had time to reflect with clouds layering below and a dazzling cobalt canopy overhead.

Claussen took pride in self-control. He liked to keep his emotions on a tight leash. His prized Operation CleanSweep was in ruins before it could be implemented.

Rioting in the streets would have people needing protection. They would be begging for safety, he thought. *With my teams of agents, we would create a new city-state. Toronto would be rid of criminal once and for all. Refugees would be identified and detained. The homeless and other vermin would be dealt with. Every detail planned, with internment centers funneling detainees to facilities where they would humanely eradicate. Nothing like the excesses and cruelty of Nazi death camps.*

The blogger and TV reporter somehow found out, he thought, unable to contain his rage. He snarled and pounded on the instrument panel. "I'll get my revenge, no matter how long it takes, or how much it costs," he yelled to no one in particular.

He had his list of those responsible for its downfall: Matthew Tremain, Wallace Carling, Susan Payne, and Carl Remington. It wouldn't end well for them, especially Tremain.

He vowed to get even with the bitch TV reporter Susan Payne and her cameraman, Remington.

Claussen thought Carling was a traitor. The police forces, above all, were expected to embrace the principles embedded in CleanSweep. Liberal judges would be replaced. There was to be no more throwing criminals back into the faces of hard-working police officers. *Yes, Detective Carling's a traitor. That man undermined me at every step.*

But Claussen didn't want revenge to be a dish served cold. He wanted the dish to come out of the oven, hot to the touch. He hurled curses, vowing payback, even for Angela Vaughn. *Why did she betray me?*

He turned his attention back to his escape plan. Flight was his only option for now. He needed time to regroup.

Running away like this tastes like biting into a lemon, he thought, cursing the need for an escape. CleanSweep was working. The rioting went as planned. The government legitimized the plan. "What if?" he screamed. Seething with rage, the coastline and Tybee Island went unnoticed.

Thirty minutes later, Claussen saw nothing but water, except for the wake of a container ship, far below, creating a V-shaped wake. Pushing the transmitter button, he contacted Grand Bahama Island airport. With the latest weather report for the Abaco Islands, he smirked. Claussen had no intention of landing at Marsh Harbour.

He contacted Miami Center, asking to be passed to Nassau approach. Permission granted, Claussen waited five minutes, then asked for a change. "I'm requesting a course, adjusting the navigation system, to Providenciales International Airport. The airport on the island of Providenciales in the Caicos Islands didn't raise any red flags with Bahamian authorities.

Five hundred and forty-three miles, Claussen thought. *The shit-storm will begin as soon as I land.* He planned the next step to take place so quickly that officials wouldn't have time to react.

Close to Providenciales airport, he turned off the automatic guidance system. He started a dive, plummeting from over 35,000 feet before leveling at 2,000 feet. He snickered, roaring toward the runway at Providenciales. Two men ran out of the terminal building, looking at the Spectrum S33 approaching at top speed. Passing over at 2,000 feet, the plane left an ear-piercing roar in its wake. The two men disappeared behind him holding their hands over their ears.

Before an alarm could be raised, Claussen was heading toward his planned destination. Soon, Cooper Jack Bay Settlement flashed below. Heading over the water, Claussen forced the plane even lower. He felt the exhilaration of flying close to the wavetops at over 400 miles per hour, knowing one slip-up and it would all be over.

Claussen made a sharp turn to the right, then another to the left. He smiled, imagining panicked radar operators trying to understand then sounding the alarm once they couldn't understand.

He set a course to the southwest and the smaller airport at Matthew Town. He selected Inagua Island for its strategic location, ideal for the next part of his escape route.

Sixteen minutes later, he pulled back sharply on the controls, soaring to 5,000 feet. He saw the airport on the port side and turned slightly to starboard. He hugged the north coast before looping away from the coast at Farquharson Beach. He finally lined up with the runway at Matthew Town.

Clearing the beach road, the wheels contacted the tarmac seconds later. Applying the brakes and using reverse thrust, Claussen steered to the far end of the runway. Two men stood waiting beside a dust-covered Toyota FJ Cruiser.

Claussen allowed himself a deep breath. *I made it this far,* he thought, *no time to relax now.* He knew his plane was tracked by radar and satellite. He didn't care. He expected it. This last maneuver was planned to happen so quickly, any adequate response would be too late.

This next part is the most dangerous and decisive. I can do it.

CHAPTER 5

A Home in Apalach

"Look for an FJ cruiser," a man said. "Your contact will wait at the east end of the runway, farthest from the administration building."

Claussen didn't shut down the engines. As they idled, he set the brakes, lowered the boarding ramp, and sprinted down to the tarmac. The temperature on the tarmac was oven-hot, but he wasn't about to take off the photographer vest. Sweat pooled as he carried a backpack over his left shoulder and toted a duffle bag in his right hand.

He looked back, hoping the aircraft shielded him from observation by anyone at the administration building.

"Hurry, they're heading this way. We don't have long," a man said, holding his straw hat in the wind.

Claussen raced to the FJ Cruiser. He watched as another man sprinted from the cruiser. Claussen's look-alike walked around so people in the control tower could see him. Then, he boarded the aircraft in Claussen's place.

When the airport security officers write their report, they're going to describe a crazy pilot landing and taking off. It will likely be written off as drug-related, Claussen thought.

Without waiting, Claussen sprinted to the open passenger door of the Rover. His boots kicked dust as he stepped off the pavement. He turned to watch the Spectrum turning around on the runway, revving to take-off speed yet again.

Emergency vehicles raced from the administration building, lights flashing. They swerved to the side of the runway when they saw the Spectrum accelerating toward them. The pilot lifted off at the last moment, clearing their vehicles by mere feet as it roared out over the ocean.

The man at the controls had Charles Hunter's identification, taking over that identity from Claussen. What a simple switch.

Claussen patted the pocket with a passport and documentation for his latest identity, Ralph Porter.

The pilot was paid well to take the heat for any investigation and possible jail time, Claussen thought as his former life disappeared as quickly as the Spectrum did, now a small dot vanishing toward the northwest. He grabbed a handhold as the FJ Cruiser shot over the runway. It was a one-and-a-half-mile drive on a sandy road to the small bay that served as the harbor, which they covered quickly.

● ● ●

Claussen saw three boats tied alongside a concrete seawall. The FJ cruiser skidded to a stop next to a small weathered building with a wind-swept harbormaster sign hanging at an angle. The shack was boarded up, its roof sagging. The driver pointed to the lone boat off to the left. "That's it," was all the man said.

Sirens grew louder. "They love to use their flashing lights," the driver said. "This is the most excitement than this place has seen in ages. Stories about this will be told for years."

Claussen looked where the driver pointed. He saw a boat built for speed. Manufactured by Statement Marine, the Passion 50 looked fast with Marine Turbine T-55 engines. *What about the weather?* he thought. *Storms come and go quickly in this part of the world. How will the boat handle in heavy weather?* he wondered. He saw the outline of sinister clouds, backlit by the orange sunset display. The clouds were billowing to an alarming size with the shade of a bad bruise.

"Miguel," a short man said as he jumped onboard. "*Mi Inglés no es muy Buena.* English no good," he said. He handed Claussen a flotation vest. Claussen stored his bags inside and secured the hatch behind. There was no way he was going to stay inside that cabin in rough seas.

Claussen sat next to Miguel at the control panel. The large screen video and GPS display were impressive. Miguel expertly scrolled through the choices and finally set the course he wanted.

Once clear of the harbor, Miguel pushed the power controls forward. Claussen felt pushed back and grabbed a handhold for balance. He had no idea a boat could reach speed this quickly. Claussen turned and tried to catch his baseball cap as it blew off, only to watch it disappear in the wake behind. He watched flashing red and blue lights fade into the darkness.

A few minutes later, Claussen grew concerned about storm clouds gathering strength to the north and west. Miguel skillfully kept the boat to plane. Claussen knew this was an ocean-going craft, capable of high speed. It was the building waves converging on the forward starboard quarter that worried him. Despite the challenge, the boat was like a race-horse, leaping forward, with Miguel in command.

The sixty-six-mile run to Cuba didn't take long. Miguel pointed to a ridge of hills as they approached the shore. "Parque Nacional Alejandro de Humboldt," he said. "I stop Paso de Tao. You walk two hours. Find the airport at Baracoa. Only a fool would take off into that weather," Miguel said. Massive dark clouds seemed to gather energy with each minute passing.

"Jump when I get close. Take everything with you," Miguel said. "You will soon meet the fool crazy enough to take off in such weather. You're going with him back to the Bahamas."

Claussen heard Miguel laughing above the sound of the motors and roar of the wind.

● ● ●

That's all in the past, he thought. He sat under his favorite tree in Apalach, the local's name for Apalachicola, Florida. Claussen pondered the twisted route since his fake suicide and escape. *I'll never forget what happened or who to blame.*

He muttered a curse when a black woman walked by, four young children tagging behind. *Person of color, I'm supposed to say. CleanSweep was designed to rid us of people like that,* he thought, momentarily distracted from the heat.

My escape was carried out with precision. I can hardly believe it worked. Cuba, to Eleuthera in the Bahamas, then on to Fort Lauderdale. I handed over my new identity. I got my printout from the kiosk and waited in line. The Customs and Border Patrol agent waved me back to the United States. "Welcome back, Mr. Porter," the agent said. Can you believe that?

A few weeks in Marathon, in the Florida Keys. After that, working my way north along I-75. How many weeks did I spend checking reflections for small clues of someone watching? I altered my daily activities, avoiding a predictable pattern.

"You should be safe now," a muffled voice said. Claussen used a throwaway phone, as directed. He rented a car in Sarasota—the first time he used his new, secure credit card. He drove west from Perry, following directions on his mapping app. Tall pine trees lined the highway liked soldiers standing guard.

He thought the forest would never end when he reached a bridge, and the water of Apalachee Bay looked as if someone had sprinkled it with glitter. From there, it didn't take long to reach Apalachicola. The coastal highway had little traffic.

If I can be safe there, this might be the place to set a trap for my four targets. Claussen drove through the small village of Eastpoint, crossing a long bridge. Stepping from the air-conditioned car, he was surprised. He liked it. *If it wasn't for the heat and blood-sucking mosquitoes...*

Apalach did indeed turn out to be an agreeable place. It was a small town, but he felt at home. He loved hearing some talk about hating the government, the liberals, and blacks, not necessarily in that order. They were up-to-date, even adding Muslim and Mexicans to their hate list.

When Claussen asked one man if he'd seen a Muslim in Apalach, the man admitted he'd never seen one and had no idea what *those* people were really like.

Apalach was a close-knit community of locals. Their commercial fishing industry was being replaced by gaping tourists, now the town's main source of income. "Damned government won't let us fish. They say there's too much pollution," one man said.

"The water still looks clean to me," another added.

Claussen kept mostly out of sight. When he did go out, he went to the Up the Creek Raw Bar, his favorite watering hole. He listened to shrimpers and heard stories from men trying to make a living by raking for oysters. *Their disenchantment with the government is fertile grounds for an idea like CleanSweep.*

The parking lot was usually packed with trucks with rifle racks hanging on the back windows. He stopped to admire a high-lift truck fitted with Super Swamper tires. The trucks were also covered with bumper stickers and decals exhibiting the stars and bars, the former Confederate battle flag.

Inside, Claussen listened as men bragged about concealed weapons. "One of these days, we're going to need them," one man said. "There's gonna be a race war, for sure."

"I ain't prejudiced," a man said to Claussen. "I'm protecting my heritage."

Yeah, Claussen thought. *You would make a good recruit for me.*

Charles Claussen felt a kinship here. He was almost sorry when it was time to set his trap and send the text messages. *Matt Tremain will get the first one. Carling, you're second. Maybe I can even get that TV bitch and her cameraman at the same time.*

He took great pleasure in photoshopping a personalized photo for each of them. He created a sniper's target overlaying each of their faces.

Wiping the sweat from his forehead, Claussen smiled. His phone touchpad chirped as he sent each text. He smiled even wider when he saw the confirmation that each message was on the way. Smiling didn't come naturally for Claussen.

The trap is set. It's all falling into place. Time for a settling of scores, he thought, turning off the phone. "Raw oysters and a cold beer," he ordered. Claussen didn't notice the heat quite as much walking home. For once, it didn't feel so oppressive.

● ● ●

Cyberia watched his tracking system that was programmed to flag any anomalies in Matt Tremain's messages. He didn't do this out of any concern; it was like a game he couldn't stop playing.

He lived with his computers on the outskirts of Moscow.

Tonight, he sat at his console, staring at the photo on the far-right monitor. It was a picture of a sniper's target superimposed over Matt Tremain's face. Three other similar messages followed, one each to Carling, Payne, and Remington.

Cyberia tapped the keyboard and tried to identify the origin of the text photos. He narrowed it down to the southeastern part of the United States, a location in Florida.

What's going on, my friend? This has Claussen's fingerprints on it, he thought.

Cyberia moved the photos into a subfolder and dragged that subfolder into a Matt Tremain folder.

I need to contact Matt first thing in the morning, his time, he thought.

CHAPTER 6

CURIOSITY KILLS

San Diego, CA 92121

Michael Young read the text from Vladimir Švajgel, SER1n. Michael rubbed his eyes, and then he read it again. SER1n was code for a crisis, to arrange an online emergency meeting.

When everyone was logged in, he clicked a link to notify them their video conference was secure. The text meant something highly extraordinary and urgent. The four members were in a situation his favorite fictional detective, Harry Bosch, called high jingo.

It sounded straightforward when he was hired. It also sounded too good to be true. "Your job is to coordinate all communication between four clients. Nothing will go directly from one to the other. It will all pass through you. We insist on your discretion," the man wearing a gray suit said.

The salary exceeded anything in his college fantasies.

All I must do now is… he thought. His concentration took a detour. *What's so unusual about this meeting? If I screw this up… I can't.*

Michael Young leaned back. Stretching, he turned from his desktop computer screen. A seagull soared, wind currents providing lift.

Why don't I take the time to enjoy the ocean view? he wondered. The ocean looked calm, living up to its the name. Ferdinand Magellan called it *Mar Pacifico*, Portuguese for peaceful sea.

Michael knew better than Sir Magellan. It was an ocean of typhoons and polar storms. He stood to stretch and walk around.

My instructions were clear-cut and simple. If the threat code is sent, it required three things. First, arrange a secure online video conference. Second, confirm the invitees are logged on. Finally, click out, guaranteeing absolute privacy.

Michael developed the prototype in grad school. He devised a cryptographic key based on a sequence of intertwined computing photons that allowed messages to be sent using any email service. After an unauthorized attempt to decrypt a message sent through Michael's program, the photons would be destroyed, along with the message. He came up with a name for the protocol: Virtual Toast.

He used the darknet, far below the internet radar. Specifically, he used *Tumma Pilvi*, Finnish for dark cloud. Michael's friend in Espoo, Finland maintained the server in the darkest corner of the darknet.

Michael was satisfied, today's emergency conference was completely hidden from view.

"We never expect to use it," a man said. "But if you get an email with SER1n, it requires immediate attention. Only you can link all four personal satellite computers at the same time."

Why did I listen in?

Michael met that strange man for the job interview. Sitting at an outdoor café table, he thought the man's accent had a trace of eastern Europe. He told Michael they were negotiating, but in truth, Michael was given a brief job description. Then, the man handed him a note that said how much the pay would be. Matt was too stunned at the amount of the pay offered to bicker.

The man took back the job and salary. "Flash paper," he said, holding them over a match. The notes flared before vaporizing.

"My name is Vladimir Švajgel," the man said. "We demand absolute discretion. You will arrange everything, but never, ever, listen in." Michael thought maybe the man had a Slovenian accent, but discerning the subtleties of dialect wasn't Michael's strength.

"We will pay you well, yes? We pay you for technology, yes? If anyone deciphers our communication... Well, you don't want to know. That's why we pay you. We pay you for your virtual secret darknet network. It is the only one that all experts agree can't be penetrated. You will arrange it so our conversations never existed. Do you know what I mean?"

Michael nodded. He understood perfectly.

Vladimir smiled, but his tone was icy. "*Ne zdrsne na banano olupite,*" he said. "That means don't slip on a banana peel." The man paused before continuing. "You are the weak link. Other than me, you alone will know the identity of the four members of The Brotherhood. We pay you well," the man said, aiming his finger like a pistol, "To make sure the weak link remains connected."

● ● ●

Michael never listened in to one of their video conferences... until today. Today, Michael slipped on the banana peel.

He was in free fall.

Curiosity is a powerful narcotic, more compelling than heroin. When it reached Michael's ears at hypersonic speed, he couldn't keep from listening.

I'm not going to listen to the whole thing, he thought.

He watched as each member logged onto the video conference. Vladimir was first, as usual. Michael watched Vladimir's image appear. Michael was afraid of Vladimir. He felt unsettled, seeing him in hi-def, the large screen covering an entire wall.

Michael swiped his hand across the screen, using touch technology. Rudainah Saja Basar appeared next, sharing the screen with Vladimir. Neither spoke nor gave any indication of recognition. Michael looked at her IP address. She logged on in from a location in Iceland. Michael found her Arabic features attractive. A striking woman in her late sixties, she wore a turquoise caftan dress with a black silk scarf covering her head.

Julina Souza Alves signed in from his office in Sao Paulo. He sat in a wicker chair, wearing a white guayabera shirt that matched the color of his hair. Senor Alves had the blackest eyes Michael had ever seen—dark inky pools that gave nothing away.

The master screen split into four parts when Hsin Shen Logged on, the last member to join. Michael smiled. The obese man could double for a statue of Buddha. Michael wondered how the man squeezed into a seat in his private jet. Instead of China, he logged on at a villa in Canada.

Michael thought it was a cool address; 625 Rue St Jean Baptiste, Causap-scal, Quebec.

Vladimir was Slovenian, Michael discovered shortly, but he currently lived in Portugal under a different name as he had been declared a war criminal in 1991.

Vladimir said he was merely following in his father's footsteps. A minor police officer, His father sided with the Nazis during the invasion. That led to his assassination when debts were settled after that war.

The screen was split into ultra-high definition images, with Michael's head bubble in the lower right corner. "The network is secure," Michael said, clicking the icon removing his image from the screen.

Then, it went sideways for young Michael. He continued watching and listening.

What's so damned important, anyway? Michael wondered. His question was soon answered.

"Vladimir, my friend, what's the urgency," Julian asked.

"Yes, I wondered the same," Rudainah added.

Hsin Shen sat with his hand on his stomach, simply waiting.

Vladimir looked down at some notes in front of him. "We've got a lot at stake. I believe our faith in Charles Claussen was ill-advised."

"I've always had doubts," Rudainah's voice added, cold as dry ice. "Not the concept. CleanSweep was a good template. When it was put to the test, however, it turned into a disaster with Claussen's inability to deal with what happened. He was an excellent engineer. He built a business empire on skill and cunning. Was he really up to the leadership of something like CleanSweep?"

"Noted," Vladimir said. "His plan for CleanSweep was magnificent. Hubris was his downfall, however. What happened was unfortunate. Maybe the blame wasn't entirely his. How he failed to deal with the aftermath, however, is a different story."

"What about us? What's our exposure look like?" the Brazilian asked.

"Nothing can be traced back to us. Claussen eluded capture. I must say, staging a fake suicide was spot on."

"If he'd come directly to us after his escape, we would've helped," Hsin Shen said. "Not doing so makes me uncomfortable."

"We'd have given him the resources to remain out of sight until we arranged a second, follow-up test, learning from mistakes," Julian added.

"And that's," Vladimir said," why we're talking now. We all agree on the value of CleanSweep, but you asked about exposure, Julian. If any, it's Claussen's obsession with revenge. It's a distraction we can't afford."

"CleanSweep was Claussen's plan. He deserves another chance, don't you think?" Rudainah asked.

Nobody answered.

When they resumed talking, Michael watched each member express their opinion. They soon reached a consensus. Claussen's fixation on revenge was problematic. Without resolution, it prevented moving forward.

"Who do we have to manage another test?" Julian said.

"Claussen, without his thirst for revenge, is still the only one," Rudainah's said.

Vladimir looked visibly uncomfortable as tugged at an earlobe. "I think we have a problem," Vladimir said. "When CleanSweep went down in flames, Claussen didn't come to us for help."

"What are you saying?" Julian said.

"He's gone to ground. We have no idea where he is," Vladimir said.

"How did that happen?" Hsin Shen said. "You never told us that."

"What?" Rudainah shouted. "Why didn't you inform us? We can make sure he doesn't have a fake death this time."

Michael stared at the screen, catching his breath at their conversation. Charles Claussen and Operation CleanSweep were both very much alive.

Michael felt an unfamiliar tug of emotion. Patriotism? *Who can I contact?* he thought. He'd never considered ethics before.

He watched the rest of the meeting. When he got the text from Vladimir that the meeting was over, Michael erased all evidence. He stared a blank screen and shuddered as if something evil caressed him.

• • •

Vladimir trusted no one, and Michael wasn't an exception. Like Michael, a woman was well paid to report directly to Vladimir.

She lived in Ossining, New York. All she needed was a modest laptop to monitor Michael's actions. Lacking access to the content of the video conference, she knew Michael eavesdropped, listening to The Brotherhood's conversations.

The woman lived in an apartment overlooking the wall of the prison with a familiar name. It made her hometown legendary—Sing Sing.

A text message alerted her that a video conference was about to begin. She powered on the laptop to observe Michael's computer. She dished out cat food and returned to the computer, sipping on soda as her computer connected to the internet.

Connected to Michael's computer, a large icon pop-up appeared on the screen, the skull and crossbones symbol for minefield. Clicking the image, she read the report and sent a text to Vladimir, *"Violation of Protocol."*

Gladys also sent an email, marked urgent, to vladimirSvajgel@rhyta.com.

Report: Mr. Young stayed online during the teleconference.

• • •

An electronic tone sounded on Cyberia's computer. The email security wasn't as secure as promised. Cyberia couldn't read it all, but he connected some of the dots as he used a program to access a Russian database. The email address was linked to the Fraternité des Aigles. Cyberia didn't know what the connection meant yet, but he made a note to look more closely when he had time.

For some reason, he sensed it had something to do with his friend, Matt Tremain.

Cyberia yawned, turned off the lights, and went to bed.

• • •

"Good morning and welcome. In today's news, a police spokesperson reported the body parts washing ashore along North Beach were possibly linked to the latest rash of shark attacks. DNA analysis revealed the victim was Michael Young, a graduate student at..."

CHAPTER 7

WEWAHITCHKA

"Ladies and gentlemen. Welcome to Atlanta, where the local time this morning is 8:48. Flight attendants, please prepare final cross-check."

Matt held his breath until he felt the plane shudder from the wheels contacting the runway. The airplane bounced once and settled for good. He didn't release his grip until the brakes and the engine's reverse thrust slowed the plane to taxi speed. He let out a long sigh.

"We're on time," Carling said. "Don't you love first class? First on, first off."

They walked toward the center of Concourse C. The escalator led to the automated people mover, the Plane Train. They got off the train at Concourse B.

"Gate 10," Carling said, "No need to hurry."

They sat near the boarding gate. "I should've stopped for some coffee," Carling muttered, looking like he was falling asleep. Matt knew otherwise. Carling was alert, thinking about next steps.

Matt heard a phone ringing and looked. The gate attendant wore a dark blue uniform, her straw-colored hair pulled back into a tight bun. He could see her name on a Delta badge—Cassandra. Matt watched her turn to the man next to her. "That's good news. It's an on-time departure. In fifteen minutes, we can begin boarding. Wheels up, right on time."

"Blue eyes, five seven," Carling mumbled. "I guess the weight at 122."

Matt looked over. Carling's eyes appeared closed.

"How do you do that?"

Carling motioned. "We have time. Let's grab a coffee, find a table, and look at the map again," he said.

"I'm 123 pounds," Cassandra corrected, smiling as Matt and Carling walked past.

The two carried their cups to a table where Carling opened a map. "I don't know anything about this part of Florida," he said.

"Same here," Matt said. "I checked online. Mostly timber. Apparently, lumber and pulp is the main industry. My laptop's in my bag," he said, reaching under his chair. When it was powered on, he clicked on the map tab. "How do you spell the name?"

"W-e-w-a-h-i-t-c-h-k-a," Carling said, looking at his notes. "I have no idea what that name means."

Matt read the search results. "Seminole, for 'water eyes.' If you look at the map, those lakes are shaped lie eyes."

"Huh," Carling said. "How'd Seminoles know how it looked from the air?"

Matt drew an imaginary circle on the map with his finger. "We land at Panama City. That area to the east and south is nothing but a national forest, sliced in half by the Apalachicola River. The river empties into that bay," he said.

"Hmm," Carling said, "Wewahitchka sits right in the middle. There're way too many places to hide. Look at that," Carling said. "Dead Lakes. Sounds creepy. I close my eyes and see moss-draped trees, dangerous things slithering in the water."

"Sweet," Matt said. "The area's famous for Tupelo honey."

Carling ignored that, squinting at the map. "I don't have a plan yet," he finally said.

"Ladies and gentlemen, Flight 1403 to Panama City is now ready for boarding. Any passengers needing special—"

• • •

Matt was grateful for a smooth flight. He was more relaxed in a smaller plane, not strapped in with nothing to see but the rows ahead and buckle-your-seat belt signs. He sometimes imagined they were about to smash into a mountainside.

"What about a car?" Matt asked, pulling his luggage like it was a dog on a leash.

"Let's ask those Feebs," Carling said. Two men wearing matching dark-blue suits were waiting at the gate. "Their FBI badges got them through security," Carling whispered. "Watch out, they're armed," he said, laughing.

"They don't look welcoming," Matt said. He was right.

"Here's the key fob. A full tank of gas. Parked in the security lot," the one on the right said.

"A man of many words," Matt said. The two agents walked away.

"They're pissed off. I didn't want the feds in on this, Matt. I think they're still smarting from the way they dropped the ball with CleanSweep."

The automatic doors opened, and they walked into bright sunlight.

"It must be over ninety degrees," Carling said. They walked through the parking lot, looking for their car. Frustrated, Carling pushed the alarm button on the fob. The horn blared, and lights flashed. They were standing next to it. "It figures," he said. He took off his fedora and wiped his forehead with a shirtsleeve. "Let's hope it has A/C. I doubt they gave us one of their best cars, even if it does look pretty new."

"Can't you guys work together?" Matt asked.

"They're definitely wound tight. I told them if they wanted my information, they'd give me forty-eight hours. After that, the case will be in their hands. Let's get moving, *vamanos*. Damn, this is some serious heat, even for Florida."

"Where to?" Matt asked.

"Use your navigation app. The feds didn't give us GPS," Carling said, leaving the parking lot.

"Take a left ahead," Matt said. "We don't have many choices. Highway 388 east, then south on Route 77. That takes us downtown. Wait… This takes us around to the east. It connects with Highway 22. From there, it's thirty minutes to We… wa… hitch… however, you say it."

"That's a hard name to pronounce," Carling said. "We should be there by dinner time. I could use something to eat."

* * *

"Nothing except trees and these damned logging trucks," Carling said, his impatience showing. They followed a truck hauling logs that looked like they were ready to slide off the trailer.

"It shouldn't be long now. Some company owns all this forest. It must feed that pulp mill we saw back there." Matt said.

"Finally. Something besides pine trees," Matt said, now passing farms. "There's the sign—Wewahitchka."

"I don't see a place for dinner," Carling muttered, waiting for the traffic light to turn green. A sign warned, 'No right turns on red.' "Not another vehicle in sight, and here we sit, waiting." Carling tapped the steering wheel, his Morse code for irritability.

Matt looked at his phone. "According to this, two restaurants are out of business. There's a bar-slash-restaurant, a Subway franchise, and a Chinese restaurant. I don't know," he said, "But Chinese, in this town?"

"Bars serve booze. I vote for bar-slash-restaurant. Give me enough to drink, and the food doesn't have to be gourmet."

"Turn right. It's around the corner." Matt said. "Whoa, Carling. We nearly missed it. It's a former gas station. You can still make out the Sunoco sign." Carling turned into the parking lot.

"Five pickups and a car," Matt said. "You wouldn't know it was open if it wasn't for that neon sign."

"That sign says AYCE shrimp or frog legs. Any idea what an AYCE shrimp is?"

"None," Matt said. "But I'm not about to order frog legs, either."

As they walked in, Matt leaned into him. "I expected country and western music. That's a Nora Jones ballad." Conversations in the room stopped. Everyone, including the bartender, turned to see who walked in.

"The natives look restless," Matt muttered.

"It's the car, Matt. Someone made us as soon as we parked."

"You don't suppose it's anything to do with our wardrobe? I don't see anything except jeans and plaid shirts here. You're wearing the only fedora."

The stares weren't exactly hostile, simply the way people stare at outsiders. Drama over, they turned back to their meals and drinks. Conversation resumed, and Nora Jones was replaced by Enya.

"Not the music I anticipated," Matt said to the bartender as he and Carling took chairs at the bar.

"What's an AYCE shrimp?" Carling asked.

"You're kidding, right?" The bartender laughed. "Did you two come from another planet? It's shorthand for 'all you can eat.'"

Matt watched his friend's face flush crimson. It wasn't often he saw Carling embarrassed.

The shrimp turned out to be gigantic. Matt ordered his steamed. Carling decided on breaded lightly. The man behind the counter, who said his name was Bryan, smiled when Carling said, "This is really good."

That's not the first time Bryan heard someone say that about his food, Matt thought.

"Look at the time," Matt said. "Is there any place to stay?" He stammered trying to say Wewahitchka.

"Y'all aren't from around here, that's for sure," the bartender said. "We call it Wewa. Makes it a lot easier. You might want to try the Dead Lakes Sportsman Lodge."

Matt saw Carling flinch.

"Your only other choice is to drive back to Panama City or head to Port Saint Joe—the same distance either way."

"Thanks," Carling said, wiping his chin with a napkin. "I'm not staying any place with dead in its name." He nudged Matt and whispered. "No sense in snooping around tonight. We need to figure out a different approach tomorrow."

Ten minutes later, they were driving back toward Panama City.

"Have you ever seen a sunset like that?" Matt said. "Bright ginger-orange, and look how it's framed by trees along the highway."

Carling sat as if he was thinking deep thoughts. "Isn't it odd how we think the sun is moving when it's our Earth spinning around like a top?"

A deer munched grass at the side of the road, paying no attention to them as they passed.

· · ·

Bryan wiped his hands on his apron and pulled out his phone. "They're driving a 2016 Dodge Charger, light blue. Florida license plate 759-3BJ," he said before disconnecting the call.

• • •

With only the light from computer monitors, the Russian, Cyberia, scrutinized a map program. He watched the icon tracing Matt's phone, starting in Panama City over to a place called Wewahitchka. *What an odd name*, Cyberia thought.

Cyberia felt like he touched a live electrical wire. A warning flashed on the screen tracking the phone belonging to Charles Claussen. It pinged from a town called Apalachicola. *That's close to Matt. Too close.* Cyberia didn't believe in coincidence.

He began typing a text to send to Matt when he came under attack of a hacker attempting to break into his computers.

CHAPTER 8

TARGET PRACTICE

What? No. Who's trying to break the door down? Matt thought. He bolted upright, trying to focus. *Where am I? What's that banging?*

A beam of light flickered around the edge of curtains. Matt shook his head. He looked at the phone—Comfort Suites, Panama City.

"Stop pounding like that. I'm awake," Matt said. He unlocked the door, squinting at Carling, who was framed by bright sunlight. He, then, closed his eyes to slits. "What's your hurry?"

"It's after eight. This is our to-do list. Get ready." Carling said.

Matt waved him into the room. Carling yanked the curtains apart, and Matt used his hand to shield the light.

"I need water and a painkiller," Matt said. He walked to the bathroom sink and turned on the tap.

As soon as Matt walked back through the door, Carling began crossing off his list. "First," he said, "we need to change wheels, something that won't stand out in Wewa. I went for a walk this morning. There's a place selling cars dirt cheap. It's two blocks from here. It opens in twenty-seven minutes," Carling said, looking at his watch. "I found the perfect—"

"Whoa, I need a coffee first," Matt said. He opened the one-cup package, inserted it into the small coffee pot, and added water. He smiled at his friend's irritation. "You were saying?" Matt said.

"It's perfect for us, a 1999 Ford Ranger. If you look past the rust, I think it's red. We need to find out how it runs. Second. We need different clothes. There's a Goodwill store nearby." Carling looked ready to kneel for a hundred-yard dash, waiting for the starter's pistol.

"Three," he said, "I got a call from my tech team. They're smart. They didn't let the Feebs know. Sanderson sent an address of a woman claiming to know where Claussen is living. She's in a trailer on the Apalachicola River, close to where we had dinner last night. We turn left at that traffic light instead of right," he said, looking at his note. "Drive until we see the sign for Dead Lakes Sportsman Lodge," Carling grimaced. "I still don't like that name. Once over the river, past the lodge, we make the first, second, or third right after we pass the lodge." Carling narrowed his eyes at the piece of paper in his hand. "I'm not sure, maybe the fourth right. We'll figure it out when we get there. I still don't like the sound of that name—Dead Lakes Lodge. Superstitious, I guess."

"Hearing banjos?" Matt said. "I have to tell you, I'm nervous too. The locals didn't exactly roll out the welcome mat last night."

Carling wasn't listening. He mumbled as he turned a page in his notebook. "If she doesn't talk, we have another contact on..." he paused. "On Red Bull Island, wherever that is. You should be able to get it on your phone."

Matt finished packing. "Ready if you are."

"Four. There's one final stop. I couldn't shake the feeling last night. Finally, I got out of bed. It was shortly after two. In all the time we were chased and the close calls with the CleanSweep agents, you weren't armed."

Matt drew in a breath. "What are you saying?"

"You need to be armed."

"Brick, I'm not against guns, but I've never touched one. Don't I need some training?"

"You always use my cop name when you're wound-up. You decide, Matt. You've heard the expression," he said, "about taking a gun to a knife fight."

Matt nodded.

• • •

Carling watched Matt hand over a credit card at the hotel desk and stabbed at his phone with a finger.

"It's the feds," he told Matt. "Your car's in the hotel parking lot. The fob's in the console. Best get the car before somebody nicks it, although why anyone would want that piece of crap?"

Carling's face turned a bright red as a voice barked at him from the other end of the phone.

"And the horse you rode in on, asshole!" he said, disconnecting before there was any reply.

"You're a class act," Matt said as he shook his head at his friend.

"Remove the SIM card from your phone, Matt. The feds don't need to know where we're going. How do people stand this heat? It's still early, Matt. Ninety plus. What's it going to be at high noon?"

They walked south until Carling said, "That's it. USA Motors, deep discounts for the military. The air base nearby explains the flags," he said. Faded red, white, and blue flags sagged in anticipation of a breeze.

"That 2001 Honda is the newest car on the lot," Matt said. "What a bunch of rejects. Some don't even have paint. You're not serious, are you?"

Carling pulled Matt along to the back, stopping at a truck.

Matt looked at the piece of junk in front of him and said, "You must be kidding. No way."

"What do you expect? It even has two extra lights attached to the front bumper. One points to left, the other aiming upward. All bases covered."

"The hood is caked with mud," Matt said. They haven't even bothered to clean it. And, what's with that radio antenna? It's artistic with that sharp bend partway to the top."

Matt ran his hand along the fender. "Whoa, hot to the touch. The passenger door's obviously a replacement. They didn't even try to match the original color."

Matt walked around the truck. "That emblem on the side's missing a letter. What used to be Ranger is now R—nger. How do you pronounce that? That final r is hanging on for dear life."

"Why so picky?" Carling said. "It's just a car."

A short, balding man ran from the office, sunlight reflecting beads of perspiration where his hair used to be. He clamped the stub of a cigar firmly in the left side of his mouth and wheezed like a man inexperienced at moving faster than a walk.

"What can I get you gents into?" The man said. Matt expected a name like Billy-Bob, but it turned out to be Stan.

"Did he actually say gents?" Carling muttered to Matt before addressing the shop owner. "You can get keys to this truck, Stan."

• • •

Matt was amazed when the truck started. It sounded to his ears, well, better than adequate.

"I was hoping for this," Carling said. "I've been told folks in these parts may not care what their trucks look like, but they take care of what's inside."

"Look, Stan. Here's the deal," Carling said, placing cash into Stan's waiting hand. He stopped. "Is that enough, Stan?"

Matt was amazed at how quickly the money disappeared into Stan's pocket.

"We're in a bit of a hurry, my good man," Carling said. "I don't want to stand in line for plates and paperwork. Get my drift?"

"Another hundred," Stan said.

Money in hand, Stan raised a hand. "Wait here, gents." Matt watched him walk to what passed for an office. When he returned, he handed over a license plate with enough dents and dings to match the truck.

While they waited for Stan to get back, Carling turned to Matt. "Get ready to move, I don't want to hang around here—or this guy—any longer than necessary," Carling whispered. Matt didn't need prodding.

"I think it may have a good motor," Carling said as they drove off the lot. "The brakes may be a bit dodgy, though."

Matt didn't like the dodgy part but sat back. They passed the hotel and turned into the parking lot at the Goodwill store.

"You could have picked something with A/C," Matt said, tugging at his shirt collar.

"You ever heard of WD60?" Carling said. "Stands for windows down and sixty miles per. That's our A/C."

The Goodwill store was uncrowded. They walked toward the overhead sign saying men's clothing in peeling letters. Matt didn't feel right picking through the clothes. "I'm not comfortable with second-hand. Are you sure they sanitize them?" Matt said.

"Feeling snobby, my friend? Whenever I went undercover, I got my wardrobe from Goodwill," Carling said. "It's a great organization, and they can put our money to good use."

They paid and asked if it was okay to change before leaving.

"No problem," the clerk said.

Walking back to the truck, Matt saw his reflection. "We do fit in now. Everyone at the bar last night was wearing these," he said, tugging at a baseball cap.

"Do your shoes fit?"

"Sort of," Matt answered.

"We make do, partner."

Matt liked that word, partner, especially coming from Carling.

• • •

It was almost noon, the temperature steadily climbing. The heat approached the predictable Panama City level for this time of the year with a dash of humidity for spice. They were sweating, leaning their heads out the window for relief. The phone kept slipping from his hand as Carling attempted a call. "Damned sweat," he muttered. After listening, he slurred a "Thank you" and disconnected.

"North. Then left on 11th Street," Carling said. "Look for Chestnut Avenue, a sign for Truesdell Park." A block later, he announced, "There's a blue Mazda," and pulled alongside the car. "Wait here."

Matt watched Carling walk over and get into the car. Carling heaved his bulk into the front seat and pulled the door closed only after scanning the area with his eyes first.

When Carling got out of the Mazda, he cradled a large brown shopping bag in his right arm. Before Carling got back to the truck, the Mazda backed out and sped away. "I guess he didn't feel like joining us for lunch," he said, handing the bag to Matt.

Matt didn't anticipate the weight and almost dropped it. He looked at the metal inside as he opened the bag.

"Not here. We don't know who's watching."

Matt dropped the bag between his feet, making a loud clunk. Matt's paranoia meter registered code red as Carling drove, staying carefully under the speed limit. "No need attracting attention," he said.

Right, Matt thought. *An old pickup's really an unusual sight in these parts.*

• • •

On the highway toward Wewa, Matt relaxed. *WD60 doesn't help,* he thought as the truck rattled over a pothole. He looked left and saw a sign for Callaway Parkway, a water tank with 'City of Callaway' painted on the side.

"I remember that tower from yesterday," Carling said. "There's a side road coming up." Part way in, he turned the truck around, ready to head out quickly.

"Let's see the groceries we bought." He motioned Matt out of the truck. "Put the bag on the tailgate."

"This thing weighs a ton," Matt said.

"This's a beauty," Carling said, pulling out the first handgun. "What do we have here? Sig Saur 45. It's old." He pulled the stainless-steel slide back, checking the mechanism. "Decent trigger pull and a healthy weight. Eight Mag semi-automatic. Not bad. It's been well cared for."

He then showed Matt a Beretta 92FS and a Walther. "The Beretta's military issue. I bet the inventory at the Tyndall Air Force Base is short at least one semi-automatic 380 caliber weapon." Carling scowled. "I was hoping they would all be the same caliber, but we can't be picky."

Looking at the Walther, he handed it to Matt. "It's a 45mm, same as the Sig. This's the runt of our litter here. It may as well be yours," Carling said. "It's reliable and makes a lot of noise," he said, laughing at his friend's look of discomfort.

"When we were on the run from the CleanSweep agents," Matt said, "I held your weapon once. You'd left it on the front seat of the car. I don't know what I felt. It was a strange feeling—cold and power mixed together. I didn't like the contradiction then, and I feel the same way now."

"Don't be afraid," Carling said. "Take it in your hands, Matt."

Matt slid his fingers along the side of the Walther, surprised. It felt different. "It's almost sexual," he commented. "I read how power and sex are related. I have no idea how to use this."

"Our grocer made sure we have plenty of ammunition," Carling said, pulling out several boxes, opening one to examine the contents. "I paid him well enough. Close the tailgate. If I remember, there's another side road in the direction of Wewa."

They drove two miles when Carling saw the road he wanted to take. He drove the truck until the bumper touched a padlocked gate. He looked both directions, checking for traffic. "I don't think anyone saw us." He nudged the truck ahead. The chain snapped, and the gate pushed aside. He drove down the logging road to a turn-off. "We're hidden from the highway now," he said. "Those trees are good for something."

It was so quiet that Matt didn't realize birds made so much noise. They hardly heard a logging truck passing on the highway.

"This's perfect for target practice," Carling said. Walking to the back of the truck, he spread the handguns and ammunition on the tailgate and showed Matt how to load the magazines. "You need one magazine loaded and locked into place. You'll also need to have two more loaded, ready as a backup. That's the safety," he said. "We don't want a stupid accident."

Carling showed Matt how to stand when shooting.

"Like the movies," Matt said, holding the gun sideways like a wannabe gang member.

"Don't joke around. Hold it straight if you want to hit something," Carling said. It's not about looking like a wise guy. It's more accurate like this," Carling said, showing Matt how to aim. "Look down the barrel and point in the general direction of the target. Start shooting. The object of it all—besides shooting someone—is making as much noise as possible. Even if you don't hit anyone, it will rattle them. Shock and awe," he said.

"I feel queasy, Brick."

"You're nervous," Carling said. "That's expected. If you aren't, well, you should be." He took the Walther away from Matt. "When the bullets run out, push this," he said, indicating the magazine release. "The magazine will fall out the handle," he said. "Let it drop to the ground and insert a new one. Look at that fence post."

Matt watched as Carling held the trigger, firing bullets until the clip emptied. Carling used his thumb to push the release. The magazine fell to the ground. Carling, in a practiced move, shoved a new magazine into the slot and commenced firing again.

Matt sniffed at the cloud of cordite enveloping them. "You're right," he said, "that makes a lot of noise. More than I expected."

"Wait until you hear the Beretta," Carling said.

Matt took his turn at target practice, surprised at how natural the Walther began to feel in his hand. The ergonomic handle was comfortable. After some shots, he turned it sideways. "Gangsta style." He said, "You're right, Brick. It feels awkward."

"No kidding around," Carling said, slapping Matt on the shoulder. "Like I told you, hold your arm out and point as if you're using your finger."

An hour later, Carling said, "That's enough. Let's get going." Back on the highway, he turned right, toward Wewa.

"I guess you aren't closing the gate?" Matt said.

By mid-afternoon, they'd reached the city limits. "See that Jeep Grand Cherokee?" Carling said. They drove by the same truck parked in a driveway. "I saw it parked at the bar last night. Those two men were at the first table on the left as we came in. One wore a hat with John Deere on it. Go figure. They left before we did without paying."

"How did you —?"

Carling waved his hand. "It's a cop thing, he said. "We're trained to observe and remember details like that. I had a bad feeling about them last night. I sure don't like the idea of them sitting there now."

• • •

The two men sat in the Jeep Cherokee, watching for any vehicles that looked out of place. "Damn, all this waiting for what? Nothing. Do you think they'll show tonight?" one said.

"We're here as long as the boss says so."

They watched a beat-up red truck passing them, heading toward Wewa. "Couple of good-ole-boys and their cracker truck," the driver said.

"Something ain't right," he started to say to his partner.

A ringtone sounded like someone burping, and the driver pushed his uneasy feeling to the side. "Nothing," he said in reply. "The only vehicles we've seen are locals." The driver couldn't quite get that rusty-red pickup out of his mind as he listened. "Sure thing, boss."

• • •

When the phone burped a second time, the driver jumped as if a mouse had crawled into his pant leg.

"We fucked up," he said to his partner. "That's the boss again. He's furious, saying the crazy lady called him. Two men were knocking on her door."

He pushed the ignition button, the wheels spewing gravel as he pulled onto the highway. "I knew it. That truck. There was something hinky about that pickup."

• • •

When Matt removed the SIM card from the phone, Cyberia temporarily lost the ability to track his movements. Cyberia, however, always built redundancies into his programs.

After CleanSweep was exposed, they all celebrated. Matt's online friends sent congratulations. Cyberia sent a gift by Fed-Ex International. It was a watch and fitness device—with a tracking chip secretly installed. Now, Cyberia switched to the alternate monitoring program, and Matt's icon reappeared.

The new icon began to flicker. *Something's not right. That shouldn't be happening. Something's wrong. That's most odd*, Cyberia thought, as his monitors went dark.

Cyberia was frantic, typing commands to restore the system when his phone chirped. It was a text. "You're under attack. Is there anything I can do?" He looked at the name. It was Lake Devil, calling from her location in Florida.

"It may not be all that bad," Cyberia said, knowing it was.

CHAPTER 9

A RIVER CRUISE

"**D**id it *not* occur to you they might change vehicles? You came recommended. That's why I put you in charge." Charles Claussen was furious, but he knew resentment was a needless distraction.

"It won't happen again, sir. They're trapped. There's only one way out." Daryl Woods disconnected the call. He frowned, concentrating on the next move and irritated by his rookie mistake. However, Daryl was anything but a rookie. He'd fought in both Iraq and Afghanistan, first in the military, then later under contract with an international security company.

Daryl Woods knew it would be wrong to apologize. His mantra for a mistake: "Make it right and move on."

A ringtone interrupted his thoughts with news. "My guy spotted them in town, boss. We're heading there now." It was his second in command.

Daryl drove while listening, holding the phone tucked between his shoulder and right ear.

"Hold on, Daryl, I see the rest of my squad now. Give me a sec."

"I'm on my way." Daryl looked at the GPS display. "I'm eight minutes out."

"I sent two men toward Port Saint Joe, boss. I don't think it's necessary, but I'm not taking any more chances."

When he arrived, Daryl dialed Claussen. "I want to bring you to speed, Mister Porter," he said, putting it on speaker. He wanted the team to hear. "They turned onto Lakegrove Road. They're almost at the crazy lady's house, and they've made a tactical mistake. There's no way out. We have them blocked."

"I want them alive," Claussen said. "Hold them until I get there. I want to take care of them myself. I'm almost at Saint Joe now," he said, clipping his words as he disconnected.

"We won't screw the pooch again," Daryl said. "Take two men. If they turn onto Byrd Parke or Lakegrove, keep going to where Heyes Road turns. Then we have them trapped for sure."

The men gave a mock two-finger salute. Daryl was assured the team was well armed. "They only have one option. They must come back over the bridge at the Dead Lakes Lodge. It's the only way."

Daryl looked at the men. *Is it enough?* He wondered.

"What about McCabe Island Road?" someone asked aloud.

"It's a dead end," his number two said. "No big deal, nothing but swamp, snakes, and gators."

"That guy, Mister Porter, said he wants them alive," one of the men said.

"Screw him," Daryl Woods said. "These two made fools out of us. Terminate on sight."

"Roger that, boss."

• • •

"It's a trap!" Carling said. He slapped the side of his head. "What was I thinking? There are certainly more than the two guys in that truck. Have you seen anyone following us?"

Matt rested his left hand on the Walther. "I don't have cop eyes. How would I know? A green Camaro was following us, almost to the bridge, but it turned off."

"There's a blue pickup following," Carling said. "It was closing on us, fast, before turning into a parking lot. I've never trusted coincidences," Carling said, rechecking the mirror. "I trust my instincts, and right now they're sending SOS signals. The pickup was expensive—a high-end package. I don't think neon green Camaros are common here."

He shrugged. "How close are we to that lady's address?"

"Turn right," Matt said. He looked at the navigation app on his phone. "Past the first road until it curves. She lives seven houses down. It should be on the right-hand side. There it is," he shouted.

Carling let the truck coast to a stop. It was a double-wide trailer with a green shed attached to the side. They sat listening to the engine pinging. "I'll bet this truck's dripping oil," Carling said.

"See that?" Matt said. "I saw a curtain move. I don't see a welcome sign." Matt looked around. "No neighbors in sight, either."

Carling eased the door open, but it still made a loud squeal in protest. The trailer porch looked like a do-it-yourself project gone wrong. Five uneven steps led to a small platform at door level.

Carling was halfway between the truck and the porch when the door opened. A woman stepped out. Her face was a roadmap of a life lived hard.

That's someone who's paid a lot of dues... To the wrong kind of people, Carling thought. He made mental cop notes. *Gray hair with a streak of what likely started out as black. She wore a straw hat that shielded her eyes. Jeans tucked into boots and wearing a plaid shirt hanging loose, tail out,* he noted.

The double barrel 12-gauge shotgun held his full attention. The woman held it pointed down, but Carling had a feeling that could change quickly if she had the mind to.

Carling held his hands to show he meant no harm. "I'm looking for Dora, Dora May Kelly. Is that you, by chance?"

Matt watched, uneasy. On instinct, he slid over to the driver side and started the truck.

The lady raised the gun enough to make Carling stop.

"I know why you're here. I ain't got nothing—"

In the distance, sounds of revving truck motors and squealing tires covered her words. Dora May Kelly pointed the gun as Carling raced back. "It's a trap. She's in on it," he yelled as a shotgun blast shattered the rear window of the truck cab.

Carling jumped into the passenger seat as Matt sped away. They sped past trailers and houses until they came to a T-intersection, hoping it was a way out. As the road curved back to join Route 22, they saw the ambush two blocks ahead. Carling yelled, "Stop the truck, let me drive."

"I see at least three trucks," Matt said, not concealing his panic as he switched seats. He held the Walther in shaky hands. "I don't know if I can do this."

"You're about to find out," Carling said, steering left but slowing as they approached the bridge. "That's what's been bothering me," he said. "Our only way out is back over that bridge." He drove slowly until they had the lodge in sight. "They have the bridge covered. We're in a pile of dog poop."

The first shot came from the right, behind a nearby cabin. It was a glancing shot, skimming off the hood. "There goes the paint job," Carling yelled, slamming on the brakes. "I don't see anyone, do you?"

Matt could barely stutter an answer. "No. Wait. Someone ran to that house on the left."

The next shot took out the windshield, covering them both in a snowfall of glass. Carling put the truck into reverse, the rear tires spinning so fast the truck bucked like a bronco, and the smell of burning rubber filled the cab.

"Three men, maybe four," he shouted to Matt. "Look. One on the left, two on the right." As he said that, they heard another shot, but louder. "Damn, that's a rifle." The shot hit the front of the truck, steam spouting from the radiator. They both knew the truck wasn't going anywhere.

"Quick, follow me," Carling said. He sounded out of breath. "If we get back to those trees, we have a chance. See those trailers behind? We need cover."

Matt forgot to limp as they ran. He was gasping for air, hanging on to the Walther, the loaded magazines bouncing in his pocket. He stopped when Carling raised his hand.

"Stay behind this tree. I'm going to the other side. On my signal, don't worry about aiming; just point the gun and shoot," Carling said before dashing across the tarmac, taking cover behind an Airstream trailer.

Matt saw Carling mouth something and point at a man crouched, crab-walking toward them at a steady pace.

Carling spotted two others. He saw the one with the rifle, a danger at this distance.

He saw Matt looking at him, eyes wide. He held his hand and gave the signal. Matt began shooting. Carling couldn't tell if any of Matt's shots were accurate, but the noise caused the chase team to pause. Carling chose the Beretta, taking careful aim. He was familiar with the weapon and was counting on it now.

He steadied his hand on the rear bumper of the Airstream, took a deep breath, and squeezed the trigger. Three quick shots, and the man with the rifle went down. He'd emptied the magazine. After reloading, he pointed downrange and held his finger on the trigger, providing continuous firing as he ran back across the tarmac.

Carling stopped behind the corner of a trailer, his head down, hands on his knees, gasping for breath. He watched Matt changing magazines and firing again. He tapped him on the shoulder, and Matt swung the gun around, his finger still on the trigger.

"Whoa, stop," Carling yelled. "Follow me," he said and started running.

Matt was on a maximum overdose of adrenaline. He lowered the Walther and followed. They ran between two trailers. One had a dock behind it. The stream was a branch of the Apalachicola River.

Carling stopped and raised his hand. "There's a man crouched in that boat," he said. "I don't think he's part of this."

As they edged closer, Carling whispered. "It's an old man—looks to be in his eighties."

"He's so scared he pissed himself," Matt said, realizing he'd done the same.

The old-timer looked like he was pleading for his life until Carling showed his police badge. "Can you help us? He asked the man. "Police business. Will that motor start?"

The question freed the man from his inertia. He waved them onboard and untied the lines. The motor started, and he backed them out. Turning downriver, the old man twisted the throttle wide open. The skiff and motor responded in time. As they reached the first bend, the spitting sound of bullets filled the air. Four men stood near the dock, firing everything they had. It was a useless exercise, no shots coming close as the boat pulled out of range.

"How far can you take us?" Carling asked.

"How far do you want to go? I have extra fuel, a stable boat, and a good motor. I haven't been shot at since Korea," he stammered, talking the way people do when they are nervous.

"We owe you big time," Carling said.

"My name's Butler, Sidney Butler," the old man said. "Would you mind showing me that badge again? My wife's never going to believe this."

With Sidney Butler's steady hand on the motor, the skiff snaked between low-hanging tree branches. Birds took to the air, screaming their disapproval as the speeding boat disturbed their fishing. They entered the flow of the Apalachicola River. Matt heard Sidney Butler talking, but he wasn't paying the slightest bit of attention.

"This river starts north of Atlanta. It's called the Chattahoochee there."

Matt didn't really care, his adrenalin spent. Chattahoochee was just another strange-sounding word to him. He was still holding the gun tightly, his arm resting on his thigh. He knew it was nerves, but he couldn't help smiling.

"Way to go, partner." For once, Carling didn't sound sarcastic when he called him a partner.

That's huge, coming from Carling. He thought. Matt suspected they were only at the beginning of the middle of this story. Still, he couldn't stop smiling. *We're alive,* he thought.

CHAPTER 10

SNAKES AND ALLIGATORS

That's cutting it too close, he thought. Matt pulled the sweat shirt away from his body, the wind rushing past provided no relief from the heat. He watched the wake, spreading in a V, small wavelets barely disturbing the shoreline. He watched the old man pilot the skiff with one hand and hold the brim of his cap with the other. Finally, the man gave in, turning the cap backward, shielding his eyes from the sun with his free hand.

Matt found Sidney was a talker, nervous or not.

"I'm Sidney Butler, but everyone calls me Sid except for my wife. She calls me to dinner," he said and laughed until he snorted. His two passengers smiled politely. "I've recently turned 84. That gunfire reminded me when the Army sent me to Korea. I was drafted in fifty-one. I got this a week into the Battle of Bloody Ridge," Sid Butler said, lifting his shirt to show a scar. "Yep, 1951, August 25th. I never made it past the first month. It wasn't all that bad. The docs patched me up, and I was back on the line. I spent a lifetime there," he said, his voice fading.

Matt noticed Carling showing the old guy respect, nodding as if he was interested. *Perhaps he is*, Matt thought.

"Kids today never hear about that war. Most grownups don't remember, either. I wonder. Was it worth it?" He glanced at a large egret soaring above the water. "This ain't my only scar, only the one you can see," he said.

Matt realized Sid had quite a story. *When this is over*, he thought, *I'll arrange an interview*. Matt jumped at a loud splash he heard over the racket of the motor. He turned and saw ripples spreading out in circles. Something reappeared, and Matt realized it was an alligator—a large alligator.

"Hey, guys," he shouted. He saw the head at first. Then the spinney ridges on the back came into view. With a loud tail slap, the alligator vanished.

"Carling, Sid," Matt yelled and pointed.

"That's a big one," Sid shouted. "She must run close to eighteen feet. Who wants to go swimming?"

Matt looked at his watch. "Damn, it's broken," he said. "My nerves are fried."

As if reading his mind, Carling tapped him on the shoulder. "Where's that coal chute when we need it?"

Matt appreciated the jab. Once, they were both trapped in a basement. The only way out was crawling through a concealed coal chute. Matt thought about that cellar often. When he remodeled his basement office, he discovered an unused coal cellar behind a door. He nailed a sheet of plywood over the opening. *A piece of plywood that saved our lives...*

"I'm thankful the coal chute was there," Carling said. "We would have been toast. Do you think Claussen would have kept us alive?"

Matt shook his head. "Operation CleanSweep would be in total control." He looked at the phone in his hand. "May I put my SIM cards in now?"

Carling shook his head. "I'll say when."

"I gotta piss," Sid yelled, interrupting. He steered to a bank on the right. "God's joke on old men, the prostate."

"How do you stand this heat?" Matt said. He stood, feeling the boat rock, and quickly sat back down. *That alligator? Are they all that big?* he wondered. He took his shirt off and knew, right away, it was a mistake. Taking it off didn't help. Besides being hot, he was swarmed by blood-sucking mosquitoes. "Hurry, old man," Matt said, trying to swat them away.

Carling was also cursing the insects, flapping his arms like out-of-control windmill blades.

Sid stepped back into the boat with a practiced move that barely moved the skiff. "These baby skeeters?" He scoffed. "Wait until you see the grown-ups." They pulled away from the riverbank, leaving a cloud of swarming mosquitoes behind.

"Where are we now?" Carling asked.

"Apalachicola River, main channel," Sid said. "How long have we been going now?"

"Almost half an hour," Matt yelled back, checking the time on his fitness watch.

Sid rubbed his chin, thinking. "It's a guess. We're making twenty miles per, maybe more, maybe less. He closed his eyes in thought. "We have the current in our favor. It's about five miles from my dock to where we are, Louisa Bend. See that fish shack on stilts?" he said as they glided past. "This river looks like a snake, viewed on a map."

"What about snakes?" Matt said. He looked at distended branches, sure there were poisonous water moccasins draped from branches, ready to drop on him at any moment. "This place gives me the creeps."

"What are the options, Sid?" Carling said as he tried to come up with a plan. "I know cities. This is your world."

"We can make it all the way to Apalach. That's about forty miles from my dock," the old man said. He increased the speed as the river widened. "The river straightens out a bit after this next bend. That helps. It's only an estimate, but I think we're at least another two hours from there."

"What about fuel?" Carling asked.

"We're okay on gas. I have plenty. This motor isn't very thirsty. What the—"

Matt heard the opening movement of Beethoven's *Fifth Symphony.* Sid took out his phone, a dented flip-phone.

"I haven't seen one of those—" Matt started to say, *in years,* he finished in his head. Carling raised his hand. They saw it on Sid's face. Something was wrong.

"Bastards," he said. Sid listened again and yelled, "Damn you to hell!" He closed the phone as Matt and Carling waited. "They have no idea who they're messing with," he said, twisting the throttle to full speed.

He was trying to shout over the sound of the motor when his phone rang again.

Matt whispered to Carling. "Sid turned white."

The old man listened then pressed the phone to his chest. Sid turned off the motor, the boat drifting in silence.

"That first call," the old man said. His voice was low and steely hard. "They told me if I didn't bring you two back... They were going to pay a visit to Rosalie, my wife."

Sid took a deep breath. "This call is from her phone." He listened again and covered his face with his hand. "She says there's a gun to her head." He held the phone to his ear. Whatever he was hearing, his face gave nothing away. The skiff drifted like a leaf in the powerful current.

Sid's words came in fragments, his voice cracking. His voice turned stone cold. "Do what you have to do," he said. He listened for a long time, holding the phone to his ear, staring at something Matt and Carling would never see.

Suddenly, Sid's body jerked. It looked like a movie scene, a man twitching in the electric chair. Sid wiped an eye with his shirt sleeve and slipped into a thousand-yard stare. He had the limp, blank, unfocused gaze of a battle-weary soldier.

Sid closed the phone, and when he started talking, his words were clipped. "Was coming on to sixty-three years, Rosalie and me."

Carling raised his hand to stop Matt from saying anything.

"They covered her mouth. Not until she had her say, though. My Rosalie told me to keep going, no matter what. Hell, I knew what she meant," he said, wiping tears away. "If they had half a brain, they would have noticed her head. Shaved! No hair! None! That's what chemo does." Sid pulled on his shirttail to wipe his eyes. "The docs told us we had hours, maybe a day or two. Her case was packed for the move to hospice. She never let on, but I'm told her pain must have been awful."

Matt watched Sit begin to sob. "That's why I was sitting in the boat back there when I heard all the shooting. I was trying to imagine what it was going to be like without her—"

His voice broke. "Rosalie's said goodbye to me... On her terms, not theirs," he said. His sorrow wrapped around words now. "She said to keep going. 'Don't come back,' she said." Sid Butler sat straight. "She called them fucking cowards to their face. Sixty-three years, and I never heard her say that word once."

Matt tried to say what he was thinking, his own tears streaming. "Why did we drag him into this, Brick?"

"They had no intention of taking us alive," Carling said. "They don't have any regard for collateral damage. He understands that."

A loud keening came from the back of the boat. "They've killed my Rosalie. I heard the gunshot before they cut off the call. I know she didn't have long. Still, I wanted to share it with her. It was always..."

He began sobbing. When it subsided, he displayed no sign of embarrassment. "In a way, we did share the end," the old man said. Matt saw Sid's grief turn to raw fury, rage. "I *heard* the shot."

• • •

Matt stared at snowy white birds taking flight, disturbed by the boat's passing. Alligators were no longer a novelty, but none were as big as that first one. He made sure to keep his feet and hands inside the boat.

Carling sat with his chin on his chest, deep in thought. His eyes were closed, but anyone who knew him would never mistake that for sleep. He was all ears when Sid spoke.

"I thought our best bet was to make it all the way to Apalach," the old man said. Sid's words were clear and sharp now, calm with a sharp-edged sound.

"I may have a better idea. Someone's checked and knows we're headed to Apalach. What if they're waiting for us there? You told me you don't know how many there are. I think we should stop at the Fort Gadsden landing. It's only ten, maybe twelve miles ahead. I never measured it. Didn't have to until now. I used to think it was a real fort? Maybe it was once. It's a state park now, but I heard it used to be a colony for free blacks and runaway slaves back in those days. Nobody in these parts wants to talk about stuff like that anymore. It's a state park, inside the Apalachicola National Forest."

Sid's words were camouflage, hiding what he felt. He made a sudden turn to avoid a floating log, Matt grabbing the gunwales as Sid kept talking.

"I doubt if anyone's there; hardly ever is. There's a small, tight-knit community behind some trees, but not too close. It takes a tourist, or someone with a lot of curiosity, to drive from the highway to Fort Gadsden. Won't take us nearly as long," he said as he flipped his phone open. "This thing may not be smart, like yours," he said, looking at Matt. "But it gets damn good reception. How many bars do you have?"

Matt looked at his phone. "None."

"Your phone's not so smart, now is it? Sorry. I'm only jerking your chain." He paused. "I used to tell Rosalie that a lot, you know, jerking her chain, teasing her." Sid was quiet for a long time, resting the phone on his leg. He let out a sigh and flipped it open.

"Craig." Sidney Butler said, describing what happened. It was a clear, unambiguous report. He described the sudden appearance of Matt and Carling. Drawing a breath, he explained what happened to Rosalie.

"Thanks, Craig. Now, here's what I want."

He asked Matt and Carling some questions and returned to his call.

"Here's the number for Kyle Mendez. He lives west of Panama City. I think he knows where Santiago's living now. Ron Silva's in Tallahassee. You have his phone number? Good."

Sid swatted a mosquito away.

"Great, Harper. Yeah, he's perfect. What about Hughes and Barker? Don Hughes knows his explosives. Barker, I can never remember his first name. Dexter, Dexter Barker. You're right. I don't need any Sergeant Butler shit from you," Sid said.

Matt and Carling stared at Sid as he closed the phone.

"What, you two don't want any geriatric help? Hang on, that's the landing for Fort Gadsden," the old man said, slowing the boat. The current carried them sideways until Sid powered them to a boat launch ramp. Lush green trees draped their limbs into the water as if testing the temperature before diving in.

CHAPTER 11

RAW OYSTERS

Up the Creek Raw Bar was uncrowded. *Perfect,* he thought. *I should get the call soon. Tremain and Carling, in custody.* Claussen forced himself to act as if unconcerned, here to enjoy the house specialty.

He discovered a fondness for fresh-from-the-boat oysters. Sitting at the raw bar, he sprinkled hot sauce on his order, only a dash. "I saved this one for last," he said to the woman behind the bar. "It's the crown jewel of the dozen," he said, tipping it to his mouth and swallowing the treat.

She smiled. "I picked it out special for you."

He knew she said that to all the customers for working tips.

One day, she told him about learning to shuck oysters. "When I was a kid, Daddy brought me a step-stool to reach the counter."

Sitting at the counter now, Claussen couldn't think of a next step. He watched her pick an oyster shell, deftly slipping a blade into the opening and twisting slightly. She scraped meat to the side, dropping it into a steamer, then raised her arm to brush a strand of hair away from her face.

Jennie noticed him watching.

"You have to cut the muscle. We used to have shucking contests. Not so much anymore. It isn't the same since the water quality got so bad." She turned away, working on another oyster.

Pretending interest in watching a passing boat, the net towers spreading like wings. The skipper headed out, hoping for a load of shrimp.

He watched as the server, Jennie, leaned over, her t-shirt rising to expose the skin above the top of her jeans. Claussen, appreciating the view, decided this was a splendid day, indeed. He smiled at the tattoo revealed of a skull and crossbones.

When his phone chirped, Claussen's day took a decidedly different turn. He scrambled to tug it from a pocket, smiling in anticipation. He'd expected a message from Daryl Woods that Matt Tremain and Detective Wallace Carling were in handcuffs. He answered, "Speak to me."

Three women sitting at a nearby table glared in his direction when he began cursing. Claussen shouted into the phone as he stomped onto the deck for privacy, swearing even louder. He looked back through the open door and saw the shock on the women's faces. Jennie even stopped working, watching him pace. She saw his face contorted in rage.

Charles Claussen listened to Daryl Woods. "They escaped how?" He asked. "You assured me they were trapped, there was no way out."

"There was no way to predict—"

"All you've done so far is react," a furious Claussen said.

"They only have one way to go," Woods said. "They have to go downriver."

"You know that how?"

"I sent two men to the Gaskin Park boat ramp in case they went upriver. They saw the boat turn south, downriver. We got a plane up. They entered Hitchcock Bay before cloud cover made sighting impossible. The pilot turned off the motor. He said he could hear the boat's motor heading south. The pilot had to restart the engine and return to Wewa."

Claussen was about to push the button to hang up when Wood said, "There's more, boss."

Claussen tensed.

"I killed the old lady." Daryl Wood recounted his actions to lure the old man back. "It didn't work. She spat in my face before I pulled the trigger."

"Are you out of your mind?" Claussen didn't know what else to say. He looked at the screen and pressed the red icon to disconnect the call.

Jennie raised her shucking knife in a defensive stance when he stormed in, his face blossoming blood red. She knew that look—like her husband before he battered her.

"Can someone get here by boat from... Wa... Wa... Wewahitchka?" he said, spittle flying.

Jennie held the knife at the ready, even though she was behind the bar. "Sure, that's where this river comes from," she said, concealing the blade.

"How long does it take somebody in a rowboat or whatever you call it with a small motor?"

"If you unbend the river, it's almost forty miles," a man said. The cook came from the kitchen, wiping his apron. "It depends on boat speed and currents. The wind can change things."

"But they would come past here, right?" Claussen demanded. "Is there any place they can stop in between?"

"Hardly any places to stop. Yep, they have to come right past here. No towns along the way. Nothing but swamp."

"How long, damn it?"

"I don't know. Maybe two hours. I ain't a boating man."

Claussen's face was a dark red as he left.

"Thanks, Charlie," Jennie said as they watched Claussen walk to the door. "He scared me," she whispered. "I've seen that look on a man before." She took a deep breath, "You could have told him. You know how long it takes by boat."

"Yeah, I know," the cook said.

• • •

A woman saw his look and crossed the street. He'd left the raw bar, walking north on Water Street, then Fulton Street, where it became Dr. Martin Luther King Drive. He pushed the gate on the chain-linked fence hard enough to make a loud clang. Claussen stomped to the door. He'd rented a shotgun house that may have once been turquoise.

He was an oddity when he moved in. "Never heard of a white man living in this neighborhood." After the first week, nobody paid him any mind. They had no idea what he really thought about people of color. *Who would think to look for me here?* he thought.

His anger abating, he walked down the hallway. The second bedroom served as an office with two card tables and chairs. He called it the war room.

A dented filing cabinet leaned to the right on uneven flooring. Claussen opened the top drawer, took out a folder, and carried it to the kitchen. He opened a cupboard, getting a bottle of single-malt whiskey. "Only tourists can afford that brand," the clerk had said.

He sat at the table, reaching into his shirt pocket for a packet of extra-strength aspirin, he downed four of them. Rubbing his head, he leaned back, thinking. *I can't talk to Woods until I have a plan. If only I had the time to find someone else.*

"What are my options?" he thought aloud.

He took a mental inventory of his resources. Far from running out of money, he couldn't finance his private army much longer. His rage came to the surface again, realizing how much he paid Daryl Woods. *Look how that turned out.*

As if on cue, Daryl Woods called. "My men are on the way. I told them to ignore speed limits. I'm keeping two men here, in case. But the only escape route is Apalach by boat. Carling and Tremain didn't have time to plan any other way. They can't get past us now."

"That's what you told me earlier," Claussen snapped.

After the call, Claussen looked at a map pinned to the wall. *What if they make it here before Daryl and his team gets here?*

He talked out loud to focus his thinking. Claussen stood, pacing while he talked. "A setback leads to opportunity," he repeated this mantra until he came to a decision.

I don't need anyone else. I can do it myself, up close and personal, he thought. Claussen clapped his hands. *The old man? Collateral damage.*

Claussen opened a cabinet. He removed a three-foot long steel box, carrying it to a table. Admiring the well-cleaned assault rifle, the HK-Mp7, he lifted it from the protective foam support.

He pulled back a part that acted as the buttstock. Extended, he tugged it to his shoulder, lowering a front handgrip. He inserted a full clip, feeling prepared. A Keckler and Koch, with a firing rate of 950 round per minute. Can empty a clip in less than four seconds, set on full automatic. "Best of all, it's German," he whispered.

Even with a silencer, it's accurate. I'll get you now, he thought. Claussen strapped on a leg holster and practiced drawing the gun.

"Bang," he said. "That's for you, Tremain. Another for you, Carling. Bang. One for the old man helping them."

Claussen folded the gun. In the holster, it would draw little attention. The holster was custom designed. With one clip in the weapon, two additional clips were in pockets on the side of the holster. *Nearly twenty thousand rounds should be enough,* he thought.

Back in the kitchen, he looked at the map. He put his finger on the location of a train bridge. *Their boat has to pass under it,* he thought. *That's where I'll be waiting.* He loaded his backpack and started walking. He looked at his watch. *I'd better hurry to make it to the bridge in time.* He walked past the high school. *Some student may start boohooing, but this gets me there faster,* he thought as he broke the lock and pedaled toward the bridge.

Claussen reached the railroad crossing, the bridge to his right. He dropped the bike, hiking between the rails leading to the bridge.

The bridge extended several feet from the bank, stopping at a piling near the middle of the river. Claussen walked to the end. A swing bridge stood on another concrete base in the center of the channel. The bridge was turned in the up and downstream position, ready to swivel, aligning with the rails on either bank. Claussen hoped a train wasn't coming. *That's all I need,* he thought. *All the time I've lived here, have I ever seen a train?* Claussen gauged the rate of the current. Water raced past the piling at a ferocious rate, water rippling downstream like a string of pearls.

He walked as far as he could and knelt. He decided to stretch out on the piling, risking splinters. *The perfect spot for an ambush.* Taking a breath, the only sound was water rushing by and a whopping water bird on the opposite bank.

● ● ●

Two boats passed, both going upstream. Claussen rolled over to keep out of sight. A splinter poked his leg, and both legs started to cramp. He twisted his arm to see his watch. *Over three hours, close to four now. No sign. What's going on?* he wondered. *Something is wrong, and I'm losing daylight.* Shards of lightning outlined fearsome-looking clouds to the southwest. *It's pointless to stay,* he decided.

He pushed the buttstock back into the fold-up position. He turned the front handle and ejected the magazine from the rear grip, then put everything into his backpack and started walking.

The bicycle was where he left it, but he chose to walk. *The owner and friends are looking for it,* he thought.

He kicked off his boot, cursing the blisters he gained from the two-hour walk back. *Maybe I deserve it. I didn't really have a plan.*

• • •

At a picnic table near the Fort Gadsden landing, Matt and Carling told Sid about CleanSweep.

"We were up against armed agents who believed they had more police powers than Homeland Security," Matt said.

"I heard," Sid told them. "I never figured that story would touch me here. Rosalie and me," he said as he choked back tears, thinking about his wife. "We moved here to get away from the ugliness of the world."

"It would have touched everyone," Matt consoled the older man. "It's touching us now. Still, you didn't deserve to be involved in this."

Carling nodded his agreement.

"I fought in Korea, doing my part to put an end to Commie expansion," the old man said, then poked at the ground with his toe. "I figured I was fighting for my country, standing for what's right. It didn't make a difference, did it? The bastards at the top keep pulling strings, making us little guys dance like puppets. What did it have to do with reality?"

Matt and Carling waited for the long-winded Sid to continue.

"I always wondered if the Commies didn't feel the same way about their bosses," the old man said. "Whoever's responsible for this shit storm we're in today crossed the line. First is the one who pulled that trigger. He took everything I have to live for. I don't give a damn about anything except getting even. This is for my Rosalie now. I don't give a rat's ass what happens to me. That's my advantage, you see; I don't care what happens to me. My other advantage? It's been a long time, but the army taught me one thing: how to kill people."

He couldn't stop talking. Matt watched Sid cough, wiping small drops of blood from the corner of his mouth.

"You tell me this guy–Claussen—is behind it all? That's enough for me. Let's go after him. Where is he?"

Carling looked sheepish. "We don't know. He's in this area. We came to Wewa to find someone who claimed to know," he said and told Sid about the woman at the trailer.

"You two were damned lucky. That's Kelly Flowers. Rumor has it she's behind at least three men who went missing. All the water around here is a pretty good place to get rid of a body."

Matt thought about that big alligator and shivered.

● ● ●

Carling told him it was okay to put his SIM card back in, but he still couldn't get reception. "No bars. None," he said. It irked him when Sid's phone started to play Beethoven again. "You and that old relic."

They waited while Sid talked. "That's Ron Silva," he said. "Ron left Tallahassee an hour ago," looking at the time. "He should be here in a few. We all rendezvous in Apalach after that."

Matt thought Sid now sounded like one of those tough sergeants in an old black and white war movie. "What do you mean, 'we'," he asked. Matt had to turn away from Sid's wicked looking smile.

CHAPTER 12

FORT GADSDEN

Matt paced while thinking and didn't want to hear any more of Sid's stories about the history of Fort Gadsden. He looked back; the old man and Carling sat together talking. Matt sprawled on the grass under an enormous live oak, dripping Spanish moss like green tinsel.

A piece of lumber floated by, swept by the current. "How about a bet?" Sid asked. "How long will it take the wood to reach that massive tree limb arching over the water? See, where the river makes a slight bend to the west?"

"You're on, old-timer."

Surrounded by tall slash pines, Matt listened to them make the wager. He walked to a lonely looking flagpole. "That marks the site of the fort," Sid had told him.

Matt rubbed the side of his leg, massaging the discomfort. "Your limp's more apparent," Carling noticed aloud. "The past few hours have been quite a strain."

It'll be dark soon, Matt thought, trying not to think about the pain in his leg. *It's not getting any cooler with the sun gone.* Humidity draped in the air like the Spanish moss on trees.

He joined Carling and Syd. They all stood in silence, waiting for the man from Tallahassee.

How did this happen so quickly? he thought. *I've lost track of time. Has it only been two days? Is today Thursday?* he thought, trying to figure it out.

"Carling! We flew down Monday, right? We stayed at the hotel in Panama City that night, didn't we?"

"No. We came down Tuesday. Drove over to Wewa and back to Panama City for the night. We drove back to Wewa this morning. I know. It's surreal," Carling said.

"It's like a machine is compressing the story into a small package," Matt said. "That, or bent time all out of shape."

Sid didn't say anything. His thousand-yard stare had returned.

"He's thinking about his wife," Carling whispered.

Matt shook his head. *Was it only yesterday, the Claussen text? Claussen laid this all out like a trail of breadcrumbs. He has his team herding us into a kill zone. We got away this time, but—*

He started to shake, swatting at yet another mosquito as the rustling tree leaves and animal noises began to sound quite sinister.

Crickets? He wondered although he had no idea what a cricket sounded like. There were occasional bird calls. It was like listening to a soundtrack to a jungle scene. He couldn't stop shaking despite the heat. With the fading light, he still guessed the temperature was in the 90's.

He saw Sid looking. "Heatstroke," he said. "This Florida heat can kill you if you're not careful. I think I still have a bottle of water." Sid walked toward the boat.

Matt conceded the battle to the mosquitos. He was sure more worrisome creatures lurked in the dark, visions of malaria, snakes, spiders, marauding panthers, and alligators. Matt was a city boy. *I need to stand on concrete, not this fetid grass and clay I'm standing on now.*

Matt thanked Sid for the water. It was tepid but tasted good. Off to the side, he heard his friends talking. He was the first to hear the car. Limping, he hurried over to Carling and Sid. Then they heard it, too, and Matt thought Sid got to his feet pretty darned fast for someone his age.

Matt looked at Sid, who shrugged as if to say, "Maybe; I don't know." Moonlight was casting soft light onto the grass. Matt strained his eyes. "The road's at least a hundred yards away, or more," the old man said. Matt heard the engine but didn't see headlights. He was afraid to ask who it might be.

Sid remained calm. Despite that, Matt noticed Carling holding the Sig alongside his right leg. They all jumped. A spotlight pierced the darkness, outlining pine trees. Three short flashes of light, two short bursts, then three more; then dark again.

"SOS. Damn. It's Ron Silva. It took him long enough," Sid shouted. "As soon as I saw that old shit on a shingle code... I knew who it was."

A man stepped into view and waved. *Shorter than me*, Matt thought. Ron Silver wore white hair pulled back into a long ponytail. His leather vest was covered with military patches. Matt also noticed something else. *This is a man with firm steps, who walks on the balls of his feet, at the ready.*

"Sorry, Top," Ron said, saluting.

"That's sergeant major to you," the old man said. The two men embraced.

"It's been awhile, Sarge. No matter. Screw the small talk. It's time for payback. That thing about Rosalie... Bites, big time," Ron said.

Matt felt a sharp stomach cramp, a reminder how long he'd gone without eating.

Introductions over, Silva led them back to a Nissan Pathfinder. "I'll leave the lights off until we're back on the highway. No sense waking anyone back on Brickyard Landing Road. Locals live to the left," he said.

Nobody spoke until they were on the blacktop, heading south.

"Something didn't feel right about going to Apalach," Sid said. "I pulled in at Gadsden to do some thinking. There're too many places for an ambush if we'd stayed on the river."

"What do you mean?" Carling asked.

"You asked me back there how long it would take us. Something bothered me. They could've easily made it ahead of us. It's less than fifty miles."

Matt and Carling leaned forward to listen.

"Besides, we don't know if someone's assigned to be in Apalach. Like I said. It ain't right. What do you think, Ron? Too many variables," Sid Butler said.

The Pathfinder was a smoker's truck, complete with overflowing ashtray, and Ron had the voice to go along with a sixty-year habit. "You're right. They're there for sure. How long have you been here?"

"Two hours," Matt said.

"The guys are on their way," Ron said. "After your call, we got our old unit telegraph going. Craig has a good suggestion. This road T-bones onto the highway to Eastpoint. Take a right, and it's not far to a burger place Craig told me about. Oh, I have some stuff in the back," Silva said.

"What'd you bring?" Sid asked. They all knew he meant weapons.

"Enough to hurt them, and then some. This is gun country, Sarge. We're gonna make some serious noise. How're your friends fixed for ammo?" he asked.

"We could use some more," Carling said. "We had to leave some behind."

"You have some training?" Ron asked, his interest piqued.

"He's a cop," Matt said.

"The kid here had his first taste this afternoon. Turns out he's pretty good. Fought through his fear. We wouldn't be here otherwise."

Matt colored at the compliment, as he watched Ron push the Bluetooth button on the steering wheel.

"Talk to me," someone answered.

Sid almost smiled.

"I have Sarge with me," Ron said.

"Sarge," a voice said over the speaker. "We're almost ready here. New location. Look for sign. Red Pirate. Eastpoint, on your left. Past Chevron on the right. Some of us here. The others will be along shortly." The call was disconnected from the other end.

Sid turned to Matt and Carling, who were sitting behind him. "He's our communications guy—always clips his words when he talks. He can sure put away the beer, though."

"He'd be great on Twitter," Matt said.

Ron snorted. "I never thought about that. We aren't far... Be there in fourteen," he said as he accelerated.

Matt almost expected someone saying asking to coordinate their watches.

The Red Pirate Grill sat behind a putt-putt golf course. It was dark as Ron drove into the parking area. Matt counted three pickups. A Harley was parked to the side of the lane, next to a red railing, protecting a narrow sidewalk and a latticework fence on the other side.

"They take care of their trucks," Carling said.

Matt saw him giving a long look at the bike. "That's some bike."

Five men walked out of the shadows. A large man dominated the view. "Six-six," Ron said. "He weighs in at 280 pounds. That's all muscle, not an ounce of flab, even after all these years."

"And beer," Sid said.

Matt looked at the man's vest. *That and the bandana wrapped around his shaved head leaves little doubt as to who owns the Harley.*

Carling still hadn't taken his eyes off the motorcycle. "That bike started out as a Fat Boy®," he said. "See that? Custom Reaper wheels—"

Carling was interrupted when two young men and a girl walked by. "We're closed," one boy said. "The boss said it was okay for y'all to use the fire pit out back. You won't bother anyone there. We let officer friendly know, just in case."

Sid turned to Matt and Carling. "The guy who wants to look like he belongs to a dangerous biker gang. In real life, a retired lawyer—only slightly crooked," he said. "The skinny guy is a dentist. Next to him..."

When Sid finished the introductions, he looked at Ron. "Where's Tommy?"

"Tommy's on recon, Sarge. He's over the bridge in Apalach, nosing around. He'll call when he has intel," the large man shouted, a habit a biker develops yelling over the road noise.

"We're talking about Tommy Hughes," Sid explained to Carling.

Matt asked what the man was doing in Apalachicola.

"He's a ghost," Sid told Matt. "You'll find out."

Now that's mysterious, Matt thought. *These men talked a good game, but one looks like he needs a walker, or at least a cane. I must admit, there's steel in their voices.* As they gathered, Sid waved Matt and Carling to join them in a circle.

"I'm the odd man out," Matt whispered to Carling. "Look how old they are."

"What about him," someone asked about Matt.

"He had my back when it counted," Carling said, telling them about the shooting in Wewa.

The rest of the older men listened, nodding their approval. Carling told them about Matt's part in uncovering CleanSweep.

"Matt didn't know what to do when he uncovered the conspiracy. I had my doubts at first, but this guy has good instincts. All we went through, then and now, I never cut him any slack," Carling said. "For a journalist, he's got some brass ones, I tell you. The man's a pit bull."

Matt felt embarrassed, but he heard sincerity in the praise coming from his friend. Matt then realized Carling accepted him. He always hoped Carling would like and respect him. It felt good.

He turned to Carling. "You haven't contacted the feds yet," he whispered.

"Screw 'em. This is personal. It's you and me, isn't it?" Carling said.

Matt nodded and leaned back. He needed something for the pain, his head throbbing. He closed his eyes. *Was really it only yesterday morning I was sitting at The Beanery enjoying a coffee?*

CHAPTER 13

THE GHOST

The Ghost had a unique skill set. He could walk unnoticed, hiding in plain sight. He could be deep in a jungle, the middle of a desert, or standing on an icecap in Greenland. Apalach was merely another place to apply that singular talent.

People didn't give Tommy Hughes a second look. Rail thin, he carried himself in a permanent slump, a slight hump between his shoulder blades. His doctor told him osteoporosis, but Tommy knew it came from carrying sixty-eight years' worth of worry.

Tommy was unlucky at marrying. His third wife was no improvement on number two, but both topped wife number one. He woke one morning in an alcoholic fugue state, terrified he'd married wife number two for the second time. Tommy had also learned to shrug a lot. Pretending to listen seemed to work when it came to women. Keeping a bottle of bourbon handy also seemed to help.

Tommy once told a friend, "The only thing I'm actually afraid of? Women."

When asked about his children, he snorted. "I don't like 'em, and they feel the same about me. I haven't spoken to them in years. We seem to prefer it that way."

He wasn't thinking any of that now. Walking around Apalach, he went unobserved. Passers-by only saw an old man—if they noticed him at all.

There was a time when he noticed women glancing in a secretive way. He wasn't Hollywood handsome, yet something about him was magnetic.

He was hard-pressed to explain it; that's just the way it was, but he didn't get those glances anymore at his age. He was now one of the invisibles.

Few called Tommy Hughes by his nickname. In truth, he scared anyone who didn't know him well. He was The Ghost. He told the Marine Corps recruiter in Meridian Mississippi, he was eighteen. A fake birth certificate sealed the deal. He celebrated his sixteenth birthday on some remote island, the name of that coral atoll long-since swept into history's dustbin. Tommy was self-taught at disappearing into the jungle, returning with accurate and timely intelligence. He also brought the occasional trophy from an unsuspecting enemy who was no longer alive.

Tommy was comfortable being alone. If he were to admit it, he liked it better that way. It helped explain alienated children and a string of disenchanted wives.

• • •

On the northeast corner where Avenue E met Commerce Street, Tommy stood under an awning, looking for anything that stood out.

What is it? He thought. He tried to focus his thinking. Standing under the awning, he rubbed a shooting pain in his left shoulder. *Nothing happening.* Then it came to him. *This is off-season.* There weren't many vehicles parked near bars and restaurants, except for one. That made them stand out. He observed pickups parked at a weathered building standing on stilts, five concrete archways frowning below. It didn't appear to have a name until he read the sign that pointed to a restaurant with an observation deck.

"Give it a try. That's Up the Creek Raw Bar," a woman said as she rode past on her bicycle. "Great place if you like oysters," she said over her shoulder.

A pickup parked, and its brake lights flashed red. Two men got out, walking toward the steps. He knew this was what he'd been looking for. They were armed and looks like pros.

The Ghost sent a quick text message before taking the stairs.

He was at home in a bar—a perfect place to nurse a drink, look, and listen.

"What'll you have?"

"Draft, Stella sounds good," he said.

She turned away as soon as he nodded yes to a tab. Tommy grinned. *She follows the money, smiling for tips.* He didn't mind; he had his reasons for being here and getting noticed wasn't on the list.

Another man sat at the end of the bar, wearing a hat decorated with a stars & bars Confederate flag. The Ghost watched the man tilt his glass, spilling some beer over the edge. *The guy spends afternoons here until Jennie sends him home. I don't respect someone who spills booze. Even less for wearing that cap with that repulsive symbol.*

The man tried to say something and got a look sending him back to nursing his beer; Tommy was the grand master of stink-eye. Tommy signaled for another beer, then walked to a table at the back of the room, next to the door to the deck.

It was perfect for eavesdropping, unnoticed by the men on the deck. *Professionals, for sure.* Tommy recognized the look, ex-military or trained, high-level security agents.

The loud, insistent voice belonged to the man they called Daryl.

Discussions stopped when a man standing to the side raised a hand. Graying hair and ramrod straight back, the man they called Porter sounded dangerous, his voice cold, expressing authority with quiet words. The Ghost knew that despite Porter's soft words, he was seriously pissed off with the men around him.

"Tell me again how it happened," the man said.

"They showed up in Wewa. We had them trapped, boss," Daryl said. "It turns out they were armed. I figured the big guy, being a cop and all, was armed and knew how to handle himself. Your intelligence said the other one was only a writer of some kind. We didn't expect him to be armed, too."

Porter looked at Daryl with undisguised anger.

"When Reid got hit," one of the men said, "that split us. It went wrong."

"I don't need any help telling this," Daryl snapped.

"Go on," Claussen said.

Tommy saw Daryl unbalanced on his feet.

"We rushed them," Daryl said. "They were cornered. We worked our way in when they ran to the old man in his boat. Our targets jumped on board. We were too far away, and all we could do was get off pointless shots. They were too far and moving fast. All we did was waste ammunition."

Porter listened, his face crimson.

"We learned the old dude's name, Sid Butler," Daryl said. "We... I decided to use the wife to put pressure on the man. She gave up the guy's phone number. When I called, he told me to fuck off. He wasn't bringing the targets back. Using her for bait didn't work. It was almost like she asked me to kill her," Daryl said. "I lost it when the old man cut me off. When I shot her, I made sure that old man heard it."

Porter then sat for a moment. "I thought I'd hired professionals. Killing an old woman was stupid. I expected discipline."

Daryl understood it wasn't a time for excuses. He shrugged, making eye contact with one of his men, but didn't give anything away to the man they called Porter.

Unnoticed, Tommy typed a text message until a man from the deck glanced at him. "Look. Trying to figure out how to use a smartphone," he said. His friends joined in the laughter.

The Ghost finished his report, "Enemy headcount twelve/two in Wewa/not amateurs/guy named Daryl killed Rosalie/let Sarge know," and pressed send. Deciding to have some fun, he carried another beer back to the table.

"Gotta piss," he heard one say. Tommy managed to get his foot out far enough to trip him as he walked in from the deck.

The Ghost made a great show of apologizing. He slurred his words, spilling beer down the front of his shirt. He saw two men run in from the deck to help their buddy from the floor.

"Watch it, old fart," one of them said.

Tommy raised his glass, trying to look sorry.

"Listen up," Porter said, calling his men together. "I'm making the decisions now. They haven't come down the river yet. That means they're still between Wewa and Apalach. Do we have eyes at that end? They've had enough time to call for help. If Carling's calling in reinforcements, it's likely police. Does anyone have a problem with going up against cops?"

None of the men raised objections.

"How many do we have in Wewa?" Porter asked.

Daryl replied, "Two, boss. I'm sending two more to make sure it's covered."

"I was at the swing bridge earlier. I want two men there. "They're not getting away again. Not again," he said and stormed out without saying goodbye.

CHAPTER 14

TWO SIDES OF THE BRIDGE

Matt woke, squinting at the light from his phone. *Friday, 4:45 AM.* He had one of those wondering-where-am-I moments, his eyes adjusting to the light. He rubbed the pain at the back of his neck, a burning sensation. He remembered thinking he'd never sleep, sitting in the Pathfinder.

The other three had drifted to sleep, but Matt was still on an adrenaline rush. "Cops and doctors, grab sleep when they can," Carling said. Seconds later, he was snoring faintly. The other two men joined, creating a trio of wheezing and snorting. *How can I sleep with htat?*

Four hours later, Matt was awake, in a panic at what awaited them. He imagined scenarios, all bad. Swiveling his head and lifting his shoulders, he couldn't ease the intense burning pain.

Matt drifted back into a stage somewhere between sleep and awake. He gave up when Carling, Sid, and Silva synchronized their snoring. Joining together, the sounds of inhaling and wheezing air filled the vehicle. *This must be what it sounds like in a steel mill,* he thought.

Matt opened the door, the overhead light winking like a spotlight. Nobody stopped snoring as he stepped out, quietly closing the door. His night vision was momentarily disrupted by the door light. When it returned, he saw pickups parked in a group. It reminded Matt of circled wagon trains in old western movies.

He looked up and was astonished by a breathtaking display of stars, free from city lights. *Where are the zodiac signs embedded in the pat-*

terns? He thought. *What are some of them? Orion? Cassiopeia? I should be able to find the Big Dipper, showing the way to the North Star circling Polaris.*

I feel so insignificant looking at all that.

Matt stretched his arms behind his back, straightened, and walked toward a street behind the Red Pirate. His shoes crunched on the oyster shell driveway as he took slow steps to minimize noise.

He walked past a parked truck, no driver in sight. Matt came to the narrow street. In the distance, he saw a sagging banner draped from the town's water tower urging Matt to root for the FC Seahawks. A warm wind brushed his face, and details from last night rushed back. *They seem so confident about tomorrow,* he thought. *They're so old. How can they?*

His thoughts were interrupted by a deep voice behind him that almost caused Matt's heart to stop beating. "Change of weather, for sure."

Matt wheeled around toward the voice.

"Sorry. Didn't mean to startle you."

Matt took a deep breath, trying to bring his pulse rate back to normal. A man stepped out of the shadows. Matt tried to remember his name but couldn't. "I'm jumpy enough about tomorrow, today, now. You could have given a heads-up."

"Looks like we're the only two who can't sleep," the man said. "I needed a smoke." He used a match to light a cigarette and inhaled.

Matt decided this wasn't the time to point out the perils of smoking.

"Feel the wind," the man told Matt. "It's shifting. This afternoon, it was coming from the east, and now it's turning from the southwest. Cold front coming for sure. It'll be storming soon, the wind blowing like stink soon. That makes this morning even more interesting."

• • •

On the other side of the bridge, Claussen couldn't sleep either, so he walked to settle his nerves. He called the lookouts posted on the railroad bridge. "Nothing," one of them said.

A wind gust blew a candy bar wrapper past his foot. He walked to the parking lot when it occurred to him. The wind had a cool feel.

Claussen borrowed a truck. He drove to check on the two men sent to observe the highway coming from Port Saint Joe, who were parked at the airport road intersection. The driver signaled thumbs up.

They're not coming from there, Claussen thought. Claussen was micromanaging, inspecting, making sure everything was in order.

Returning to Apalach, Claussen walked the town. A saw a man sitting on the porch at the Gibson Inn. "I'm checking on anyone coming over the bridge from Eastpoint, boss. Just in case," the man said.

Now we wait, Claussen thought. He decided to walk to the park.

Priding himself in his knowledge of the stars, he sat, head tilted, making out shapes in the stars. *The Big Dipper,* he thought, *Too easy.* He located the alpha star, Dubhe. An imaginary connected it to the beta star, Merak. The line led to Polaris, the North Star. For some reason, it caused him to shudder. *That star reminds me of all I've left behind.*

His resolve for revenge surged to the surface.

A gust blew debris past his face. He looked to the southwest. A slim line of irregular lightning flashed on the horizon, the leading edge of a storm front.

Adding an exclamation mark, a strong bolt blazed over his right shoulder, followed immediately with a bone-jarring boom. In the darkness, Claussen saw a bank of rolling clouds closing rapidly from the north and west, as if drawing the curtain to end the theater of the stars.

Claussen looked at his watch, 4:58 AM. "I have a good feeling about this day," he yelled into a powerful blast of colder air.

CHAPTER 15

WATCHING IT WON'T HELP

Matt couldn't concentrate on the plan. He knew what he had to do but was distracted by the pain in his right leg, the one he called his limping leg. He forgot about the stars and constellations when they heard Sid.

"On me, now!"

Matt raced back to the wagon-train circle of four pickups, one Pathfinder SUV, and one Harley. He noticed that none of the men gathered looked tired. *These are men who know how to awaken fast; Carling, too.*

"I heard from the Ghost," Sid said, looking around to make sure everyone was listening. "They're well-armed professionals. The thing is they've got youth and firepower, but they've made two huge tactical mistakes. First, they split their force in three directions. Second, they don't have intelligence. They're complacent, thinking it's only our two friends here and me. They don't know about the rest of us," he said, looking around. "We may be rusty, but we're trained. They won't see us coming. These men may have youth on their side, but their long game isn't as smart as ours. That's their blind spot."

Matt almost laughed when Sid used a stick to draw a map in the sand. He started to say something when Carling gave him a glare.

"Four men left, heading toward Port Saint Joe. Two others," Sid said, aiming the stick at his sand map, "Were dropped off on the edge of Apalach. Two are posted at the train bridge upriver. One is on the porch of the Gibson Hotel." He read the text. "It'll be on your left as you come off the bridge."

"He sounds like a job for the Ghost," someone said. "What do you think?" Everyone laughed except Matt.

"First, he'll let the man at the hotel sound an alarm," Sid told them. "When he does, Tommy will have another trophy. This one for Rosalie."

The men were silent, each with their own thoughts about why they were there.

Sid continued. "Their main force is stationed at an oyster bar. When they rush the hotel, we'll be ready. Counting Claussen, there are six, maybe seven. They don't know about us. That's their big mistake, a lack of intelligence. 'Know your enemy' is the first rule in Sun Tzu's *The Art of War.*"

Carling asked to speak. "Charles Claussen is nobody's fool. If he's using these guys, they're pros."

"That may be, but we may have one more edge," a man at the back said. "Feel the wind? It's coming south-southwest now." As if to emphasize his point, a low growl of distant thunder provided backing soundtrack. "It should hit at the same time we get there. It's going to provide a distraction. "

"We've been through these cold fronts and know how disorienting they are," Sid added. "It'll confuse the hell out of someone inexperienced with it."

"I'm worried about the two on the far edge of Apalach. They can get back in a hurry," Ron Silva said.

"I checked the map," Carling broke in. "We can cover it. If Matt and I get to the corner of—" he stopped. "Ron, drop us at the hotel. The two of us will head west two blocks, then take a right on Sixth Street.

"Listen up!" the biker said, his commanding voice causing Matt to stand at attention. "Remember what these guys did to Rosalie. I ain't one for a speech...."

The men shuffled around trying their best to conceal emotions. A strong gust washed words away.

"Fuck 'em. Let's do it," someone yelled.

"First light's in a bit over an hour," Sid said. "That's when we go. I'm in the first truck over the bridge." Nobody even thought about disagreeing. "I'm sending Tommy the text now."

"We're riding with Ron," Carling told Matt. "Checked your ammo?"

Matt nodded yes, his mouth too dry to talk.

Walking over to the Pathfinder, Ron raised the rear door, Matt and Carling standing off to the side.

"Remember, one clip seated and three for backup," Carling said. He started to ask a question when Matt stopped.

"I'm not afraid, Brick."

I know," Carling said.

• • •

Matt thought his phone was out of order. Every time he looked, it seemed as if no time had elapsed. Frustrated, he put the phone into his pocket. The digital clock on the dashboard also changed at a snail's pace.

"Watching it won't help," Ron said over his shoulder.

Matt turned. Carling stared ahead, giving nothing away. "We shouldn't have done this to Sid," he said.

"His life ended with Rosalie's diagnosis," Ron said. "In a strange way, this may be merciful. We knew Sid was devastated. He tried overly hard not to let it show, especially to her," he added, almost whispering. "Hell, she knew all right. The last thing she told me? How worried she was about Sid. Can you believe that? Close to dying, and she worried about him."

"I know only too well," Carling said. "When my wife was diagnosed, I was sure I would never...."

Matt jerked his head around to look. Carling had never talked about a wife. Matt was about to ask him a question when Sid yelled. The trucks lined in a row roared to life.

"When Ron stops on the other side," Carling said, "Get out and follow me. We won't have much time. Run like hell, and stay on me, got it?"

Matt wasn't afraid. *There's something fatalistic about it now. It'll turn out well, or it won't. Either way,* he thought, *I won't have to worry about Charles Claussen anymore. One of us isn't going to make it through the Battle of Apalachicola.*

• • •

Up the Creek Raw Bar was officially closed, but men sat at tables. This wasn't a time for alcohol. Jennie walked around, refilling cups with strong coffee. She heard enough to know they meant harm.

She wanted to ask what Matt Tremain and a Toronto police detective named Carling had done to earn their wrath but knew better than to ask. They, sure enough, were hopping mad about something to do with a clean sweep, but this Porter was the angriest.

She rarely watched the news, as reality shows were her choice. She didn't read newspapers, and CleanSweep meant nothing to her. She did know her men, though. Her former husband was ex-military and would have been right at home with this group.

Jennie saw one of them casually lift an automatic weapon and walk over to the door. "I'll head back to the hotel. Comm check as soon as?"

"Count on it," Daryl Wood said. "It's time for you guys heading to Saint Joe. Drop those two by the Red Top Café," he said and watched them nod, gathering their weapons and ammo.

"Who do you have assigned to the boat?" Claussen asked.

"Roosevelt and Norm," Daryl answered. "You two, stay on your toes. If you hear shooting, get back as fast as you can." He turned to Claussen. "That leaves us, Mr. Porter."

Claussen looked around the room. "Six; counting me, seven." He looked at Jennie and signaled for more coffee. "Don't let me down again," He added to Daryl.

He didn't have to say, or else.

CHAPTER 16

THE BATTLE OF APALACH

Matt was unafraid, his anxiety lifting as they started toward Apalach. He closed his eyes. *Fatalistic,* he thought. *Yes. That defines it, resigned to the outcome.*

Earlier, the pressure felt unbearable. Wind from the advancing cold front rocked the truck as he mulled over the plan. It was a simple one, without subtlety. Sid had sounded sure of himself. *Who am I to question a man with Sid's experience? After all,* Matt thought, *how many shoot-outs have I—?* Memories of yesterday, the sounds of Wewa gunfire, came rushing back. *I remember reading somewhere, a German military planner who wrote that no battle plan survives first contact with the enemy.*

He turned to Carling. "If you want to make God laugh, tell him your plan."

Carling was about to reply when lightning was followed by a burst of thunder.

"Sid's plan is a good one," the front passenger said, as rumbles of thunder ended. "Keeping it simple is the key."

Matt wanted to ask about backup planning when Ron said, "Third truck in line. You guys know what you're supposed to do."

Carling looked at Matt. "We need to be fast, running on the double as soon as we're out of the truck. All we've been through this past seventy-two hours—" After a pause, he looked at Matt. "Will you be able to keep up?"

"Right behind you, old man," Matt said. "Locked and loaded." *When did I start talking like that?*

The lead truck flashed headlights from low to high beams. Husky mufflers belched out deep bass rumbling. "A convoy of macho trucks," Carling said. "Look at it. Except for the Harley, nothing but heavy-duty pickups and SUVs. It doesn't get any better than this."

A throat-clearing squelch on the handheld radio was followed by a single command. "Roll."

Matt gulped in a large breath of air, closed his eyes, and muttered what may have passed for prayer.

The convoy started slowly, each truck struggling to keep pace. Reaching the peak of the bridge, the first sheet of rain swept across the windshield. "Damn, that's a lot of rain," Ron said, his voice revealing a smidge of anxiety.

• • •

Storms were living things to Tommy. He called them beasts. He knew this beast would be helpful. He'd spent the night crouched a stairway behind the Owl Café on Avenue D. He was used to waiting until it was time to act.

The Ghost stretched his arms, shifting from one leg to the other as he stood. He ignored any lingering aches and stepped from under the roof.

The waterfront was barely visible as Tommy turned away from the water, walking toward the Gibson Inn. Shards of lightning scattered the darkness, but Tommy kept walking casually, nothing that would draw attention.

He almost laughed aloud when he saw the lookout on the porch. *The jerk's lighting a cigarette, shielding the flame from wind. These guys are too sure of themselves. Too cocky,* he thought.

Approaching from the west, Tommy stepped between a plumbago hedge on his left and a small sago palm to the right. Inching up the steps, he listened for creaking floorboards. He needn't have worried; the storm covered his footsteps.

He stopped at arm's length from the lookout. The man's posture showed tiredness, boredom, and indifference. The lookout was about to pay the price for sloppiness.

When Tommy felt his phone alarm vibrate, it was time. With the speed of a striking cobra, he grabbed the man's shoulders. He twisted the unsuspecting man around, registering disbelief.

"The old fart. What the—"

The guard didn't have time to finish. With one leg stretched behind the knee of the guard, the man ended on the floor before he finished speaking. Tommy straddled the guard, a knee on each forearm.

The man was enraged. He struggled but was helpless. The man on top of him didn't weigh more than a hundred pounds and was old. The lookout sagged, conceding the struggle.

"Not a word. Listen carefully," Tommy said. "Your decision will determine whether you live to tell this story, or—"

The man spat, missing as Tommy turned his face away.

"That wasn't nice," Tommy said, barely above a whisper. Tommy grabbed the man's radio that dropped to the side. "All you have to do is report that everything is okay. You can do that, can't you?" He watched the man's face closely.

He'd planned it, knowing what the other man would do. When the transmit button was pushed, the man began shouting, alerting his team. He started to add something but was cut off. That shouted warning was exactly what Tommy hoped for, listening to follow-up traffic. *They're taking the bait*, he thought, the sliver of a sneer appearing.

The Ghost had never intended leaving the guard alive. The lookout could have chosen a quick, painless death. Instead, the man spat the wrong words. "We laughed when we killed that bitch back in Wawa."

The man's dying screams over the noise of the storm began waking guests at the Gibson Inn.

● ● ●

At the oyster bar, Daryl grasped the radio. "That's our man at the Inn," he said, hearing the guard's shouted warning. "They're here," he shouted. "Coming across the bridge." His men were dozing but woke instantly with Daryl's orders.

"If they're coming that way, I'm calling the men back from the Red Top Café," he said. He keyed transmit. "Targets coming from the east.

Downtown. Now. No time for a car. On the double," Daryl said, pocketing the radio.

He then turned to the men around him. He pointed to a tall, bearded man, and ordered. "Head to where the highway makes that turn west, the seafood grill on the corner."

The man nodded and slipped out the door.

Daryl identified two more men and barked, "You two. Water Street. The rest down Commerce." Then he turned to Claussen.

"We're ready. The men are in place. You and I can head to Avenue G, covering the road toward the main intersection." He looked satisfied with himself. "The team's in control."

Claussen tried to ignore his growing unease, the sense something wasn't right. It was like a photograph slightly out of focus. How could Carling and Tremain be coming from that direction? He disregarded the feeling and followed Daryl.

• • •

Tommy sent a message to Sid. "They fell for it. Look out for the two on the west side. They've been called back."

"Copy," Sid answered.

• • •

Three pickup trucks, an SUV, and a Harley raced down the bridge where it sloped past the courthouse. They braked on the signal at the Gibson Inn. The motorcycle flew past, heading to an assigned position.

Matt and Carling jumped out. Matt saw the convoy stop at Avenue C, the red brake lights flashing.

"Let's go," Carling shouted above the wind.

Matt followed, pausing. A body was sprawled out on the porch, the head and torso draped down the steps. Both ears had been severed, and Matt saw lots of blood pooling.

Running until it felt like he wore lead weights for shoes, Matt followed Carling as they turned toward the intersection with Highway 98. *I'll never let Carling,* he thought, gasping for breath, *know how exhausted I am.*

At the intersection, Carling motioned. "There's no cover," he said. "I didn't take that into account. We make do. I don't think we have much time—look."

Matt saw two men, shoulders down, running hard. "I'm cramping," one shouted. They stopped at the next intersection to the west. The other man leaned over, hands on his knees, looking out of breath.

"We don't have time for cramps," one said.

"Matt," Carling whispered. "We need cover. There's no place except—"

The two men were running again, but one was limping, in obvious pain. "Go ahead," he cried.

"I don't like it," Carling said, "but we may have one chance for some cover." He pointed.

Matt realized they were next to a church. There was sign perched on a brick base, First United Methodist Church across the top. The foundation supported seven layers of weathered red bricks.

"Let's hope it's enough," Carling said.

They each hid behind a corner, crouching behind the bricks.

Zig-zag lightning, like a photographer's flash, exposed their position. "See them? Behind that sign," one of the men shouted. Professionals, their training took over. They acted on instinct, one running to the far side of the street. The other crouched behind a large hedge next to the house on the southwest corner.

"Splitting up," Carling shouted.

Bullets shrieked past Matt, a chip of brickwork stinging his left cheek. He was surprised how quickly blood flowed. He resisted the urge to call out and wiped the blood with a shirtsleeve.

"Shoot for the bushes," Carling yelled. "Don't bother aiming. Finger on the trigger. Keep shooting."

Matt rested his elbow on the bricks, aiming at shrubs, and fired. Red flecks shot back, bullets sounding like wasps as they hissed by.

The man on the north side of the street stepped into the partial light. It was enough. Carling took deliberate aim and let off one shot. The man tumbled to the ground and didn't move.

Carling and Matt both aimed at the hedge at the house on the other corner. Matt quit counting. He used two magazines, and about to insert the third, when he realized it'd fallen silent, no gunfire. All Matt heard now was wind.

"Stay here!" Carling dashed to his left, then turned right before crossing the street. Matt watched him move closer to the hedge, holding his breath until Carling reached the shrub. Carling stuck his leg in and kicked something out to the side.

Matt realized it was a leg. Carling gave a thumbs-up signal.

Unaware he was holding his breath this long, Matt let out a whoosh between partially closed lips, his cheeks puffed out. Gunshots from behind startled him.

• • •

A bullet shattered the window next to Claussen's head, and he ducked, cursing his reaction. He realized immediately why their planning was wrong. Carling and Tremain shouldn't have been coming from that direction. What was totally unexpected was the people with them. *How did they manage to come from that direction?* He thought. *There are more. Where did these other men come from?* But he didn't have time to think about it.

His team was facing a force they hadn't anticipated. Initial shots came from the direction of the Gibson Inn. Then, Claussen heard gunfire to the west, sounding close. He heard one of his men scream, realizing someone was taking advantage of the shards of lightning to aim.

"Who are they?" one of Claussen's men yelled.

"Where did they come from?" It was Daryl Woods, directing men into new positions. "Take cover, boss."

Claussen glared. "How did this happen?" he sneered, his words swept away by the wind and rain. "It happened because you went into this half-cocked."

"Where are the two men coming back from the Red Top café?" someone shouted. "Tell them to swing around behind."

"No answer," Daryl said.

There was a flurry of gunshots from three blocks away, then quiet returned.

"Status report," Daryl shouted over the wind as he squeezed the radio, his face contorted with rage. He didn't get a response. Two separate shots rang out. The man on Claussen's right took a hit, seriously wounded and bleeding. The man to his left was on the sidewalk, half his face turned into a red mush.

Two other men threw down their weapons, running into the darkness of the storm. "We're not paid enough for this," one of them said.

Daryl turned to Claussen with a shrug. "It's not worth it." The ground seemed to shudder. A shaft of lightning hit a nearby radio tower, the thunderclap less than a second behind.

The wind was building to gale force, blowing a trash can into a parked car. That distracted Daryl. He was slow to react when an apparition stepped out of the rain squall.

Sid walked with slow, steady steps. He had Daryl's description. "You're the one who shot my wife, Rosalie," he said. Sid stood as if he was inviting death, ready to join Rosalie.

Daryl raised his weapon and pulled the trigger, hearing a click.

Claussen stood, frozen, unable to formulate a thought. All he could do was watch this old man as he walked up to Daryl, shoving him back against the window. The glass didn't break. The younger man cowered, wondering how this old man could be so strong.

A flash of lightning lit the scene. Daryl saw it in the old man's eyes, knowing a killing look when he saw it. Sid held Daryl against the glass with one hand, reaching to pull something from behind. A bayonet. Sid plunged it into Daryl's belly, under the rib cage, and yanked upward, using muscle memory from his Army training.

The force of the stabbing pushed Daryl through the glass pane. A blizzard of tiny flecks of glass fell to the sidewalk. Sid made sure his victim heard three last words: "That's for Rosalie."

Matt was running when he saw what Sid was doing. Shocked, he saw Claussen's movement too late to shout a warning. Claussen placed a gun to the back of Sid's head. The wind dropped in time for the silence to make the shot sound louder.

Sid's head flopped forward, then snapped back as he fell on top of Daryl's body. It was nothing like it's shown in the movies or television. It was a macabre ballet.

Matt looked around. It felt like the storm had swallowed his friends. He couldn't see or hear anyone.

He was exhausted; his weapon felt like a thick piece of iron. He didn't have the strength to raise it again. All he could do was watch as Claussen aimed at him. Matt remembered his nightmare, Claussen holding a gun. Matt simply closed his eyes, accepting his fate.

A shot came from his right, and Matt opened his eyes. Claussen looked surprised, his weapon spinning as it fell. Matt saw red blossoms spread across the front of Claussen's shirt.

The scene blurred again as rain squall blew as if trying to sweep the street clean.

He felt Carling's touch. "I think I hit him."

"In the stomach," Matt nodded.

"Gutshot," Carling said. "That's a painful way to go."

There was a break before a curtain of rain blinded Matt.

"Damn," Carling said, running ahead, disappearing into the rain. Matt followed and saw Carling looking down. "That's his blood, but where the hell is Claussen?"

Ron Silva and the others gathered around, Ron taking charge.

"We'll take care of Sid. We know what to do."

Tommy came running to join them, looking down at the body of his friend. "We don't have any time—the sirens."

Ron turned to Matt and Carling. "We need to get you two away from here. The cover of this storm won't last." They headed back over the bridge.

"Another Claussen disappearing act," Carling said. "I know I got him though, gut shot."

"You did," Matt said. "I saw it."

"Where did he get to this time?"

CHAPTER 17

TEDDY ROOSEVELT

Clutching his stomach, Claussen managed to start running. It felt like someone was holding a blowtorch to his abdomen. He ordered his brain to ignore the pain. It didn't work. *Is this how it ends?* he wondered, realizing he couldn't go on much longer. Slashing rain hounded him as he ran, reaching the oyster bar. The man who valued quick thinking now stumbled, his hand stretched in front, groping for unseen dangers.

Claussen heard shouting from town. A change in wind direction brushed the shouting away from his hearing.

Where is it? I must be getting close, he thought, clutching his wound with his left hand. The weathered siding of the bar came into view. Built on a concrete base with five arches, the center archway was an open path to the dock behind it. *I just need to get to the dock.*

Claussen's eyes filled with tears from the excruciating pain. Blood leaked through his fingers as he pressed the front of his shirt.

"Boss! Over here!" He saw two men standing between boats on trailers. "We'd been keeping watch on the river and heard shooting, so we hurried back."

Claussen stared in disbelief. *These are the two men I sent upriver. I remember how big the black man is.*

"We knew something was wrong and headed back as quickly as we could. What's happening?"

Claussen squeezed his words out through clenched teeth. "Daryl's dead... The others—" Claussen cried out in pain. "The two from... We heard shots. What's...your names?"

"Pickett, sir. This big guy here's Roosevelt. Teddy we call him."

"That old man...from Wewa. It was his...wife...Daryl killed. He came at...Daryl with a knife... I had to...shoot the old man," Claussen said. His words came between sharp pains stabbing at his stomach, but he tried to finish. "There were more. Where the hell did they come from? I can't—"

They heard the throaty exhaust of a pickup truck.

"Sounds like a Dodge Ram 3500," Teddy said, "coming this way, fast."

Claussen dropped to the ground. Pickett said something, and the large man knelt, hoisting Claussen.

• • •

Partway to the boat, Claussen started to waken, but it didn't last long; a final jolt of pain knocked him out cold.

"Hurry. We have to get him into the boat," Pickett said. "More headlights coming on Water Street."

Roosevelt carried Claussen and motioned to Pickett who'd stepped down into the Carolina Skiff. When Pickett had his footing, Roosevelt handed down the limp body of Claussen. "Damn," Pickett said. "We banged his head."

"Don't guess he's feeling much anyway," Roosevelt said. He held a finger to Claussen's throat. "Strong pulse. Push hard on his stomach. I think the bleeding stopped but keep the pressure on."

Pickett cradled the boss's head, pushing on the shirt, blood still oozing between his fingers. He felt the boat rock as Roosevelt jumped from the dock, surprisingly agile for a man his size. Roosevelt untied the lines, and the stern swung away from the dock. He started the motor but kept it idling to keep anyone on the street from hearing. Roosevelt waited for a gust of wind to let go the front line and steered upstream.

He last saw a woman looking down from a window overhead. The oyster bar seemed to be swallowed by a rain squall. The first light pierced the darkness, the storm gradually surrendering to another sunrise.

Roosevelt steered upstream. Outgoing tide combined with a powerful current made headway difficult. He didn't want to increase speed and sound of the motor. He allowed the boat to drift back. Timing his next move, he throttled up, making a sharp turn to starboard. He aimed toward the calm waters of Scipio Creek Channel.

The storm eased, and it was growing light. Roosevelt took the risk, passing a hotel and marina. Hugging the far bank, he hoped it was difficult for anyone to see them from the other side. Luck held until he reached a two-story structure on stilts, located at the entrance to the commercial marina.

A truck raced from the south, headlights sweeping the river as the driver turned toward the boat.

Roosevelt held his breath. "I don't think they've seen us, Pickett," he said. "This is far enough. Once the skiff was through a narrow opening that widened, they were out of the main channel. I'll squeeze past that small island and the bank."

In the protected water beyond, Roosevelt steered toward a boat at anchor.

Anyone looking would think it was abandoned or neglected. Roosevelt liked it that way.

He pulled alongside on the starboard side of the boat, away from view. Even with his strength, it was a struggle lifting Claussen from the skiff. Claussen started to wake and look around. With another stabbing pain. He went limp again as the two men lowered him down the companionway.

"Where am I?"

"It's okay, boss. We have you hid away."

Claussen almost corrected the man's grammar but thought better of it.

"How long?"

"Three days now. They've turned Apalach upside-down," Picket said. "Roosevelt used to be a medic in the Army. He slipped into town for some first aid but had to be extra careful. Everyone was talking about the fighting, on the lookout for anyone with a gunshot injury. He knew better than to get bandages. All he could manage was some towels and some extra-strength pain pills."

"I could use some pain relief now," Claussen said, tasting copper in his mouth from the blood.

"You're shot through and through. You lost a lot of blood. We didn't think you were going to make it," Picket said.

"Police don't know anything," Teddy said, his voice thick. "They counted seven dead on our side. There was some old man too. They didn't know who it was." He walked over to look out a porthole. "They learned it was his wife found murdered up in Wewa. They found out where you were living. It was in my neighborhood. You had some serious hardware stored there." He appreciated the irony of a man like Claussen hiding in the hood.

Claussen tried to sit up. It hurt, but he forced himself to get out of the berth. He swung his legs to the deck, his head spinning.

"How'd you two like to make some real money?"

· · ·

The battle of Apalach was still the main topic of conversation on the news. Detective Waldron from the Franklin County Sheriff's Office did his best to put the puzzle pieces into some order. "No success," he said. "We know there's ties to the woman who was killed in Wewahitchka. The other victim's been identified as one Daryl Wood. After that, all leads evaporate."

· · ·

Roosevelt waited a week, keeping a close watch on Claussen's injury. "I think we can move you now," Roosevelt said. He told Picket to pull anchor and started the diesel engines. The boat wasn't abandoned nor was it neglected. In fact, it was a functioning commercial craft, a common sight in Apalach, and the boat didn't look out of place when it pulled into another harbor a few hours later.

It wasn't the Panama City Marina with all the fancy boats, though. This was the commercial harbor, with working boats coming and going as they pleased.

Pickett and Roosevelt watched as Claussen climbed the ladder, trying not to show pain. When Claussen got to the top, two men helped him into the back of a high-top van, an expensive touring coach. They watched as brake lights flashed, and the van pulled away.

"What are you going to do with your money?"

Teddy Roosevelt simply smiled.

• • •

Cyberia listened from an apartment in a Moscow suburb, trying to make sense out of what happened in Apalachicola. He didn't know much; he only knew that Matt was involved. Using an emergency back-up server, Cyberia lost contact before he could help. He could disrupt some police radio signals, trying to shield Matt's GPS coordinates, but that was about it. He looked at the manifest of Air Canada flight leaving Atlanta airspace. Matt was heading back to Toronto.

Something was disrupting his emergency system; his computers started acting quirky, flickering on and off.

He heard a car braking to a stop, car doors slamming, and people shouting.

There were loud footsteps on the stairs of heavily booted men in uniform. They stopped at Cyberia's door, one stepping forward to pound his fist on the door. "Open the door, immediately!"

CHAPTER 18

EVEN IN PITTSBURG

Charles Claussen cringed, pressing on his abdomen, feeling lucky to be alive. *All this time, and my stomach still hurts,* he thought. A wiper blade splashed rain from the front window of the trawler. The seas ahead looked ominous, dark, and dangerous, each wave seeming to grow larger.

Apalachicola, Florida to the mid-point in the Sea of Japan—the East Sea as South Koreans call it—is 8,174 miles in a straight line. The journey was anything but straight for Charles Claussen.

I could have hired someone to kill them. But no, it's something I need to do in person, Claussen thought. *I need to think ahead, now. I need a long game.*

Of course, he wouldn't hire someone else to do the job; this was personal. He wanted to be face-to-face when he pulled the trigger. Now, staring through a rain-splattered windshield, his uneasiness had him wrapped in an emotional straitjacket.

I had the trap set perfectly in Florida. How did it go wrong?

He thought back, knowing he shared most of the blame. His blindside—an obsession with revenge—was a craving he couldn't satisfy.

How long have I been on the run, constantly looking over my shoulder? Fear of exposure is my constant companion, he thought. *My capture often feels moments away. Every footstep will be the last before I can get my revenge.*

His vision, his prized Operation CleanSweep, was in ruins. All because of those he blamed the most—especially Matt Tremain. Thinking about that caused him to clench his fists. He squeezed a fist so tightly his fingernails drew blood, his rage unrelenting.

Shaking his head, he tried to remember all the warnings. *Where? Was it the Bahamas? The last warning came in Florida, Panama City,* he thought. *No, Atlanta was my next stop. Another warning sent me from there to Pittsburgh.* The places all melded together. As he relaxed and unpacked at each place, another warning call told him to move.

"They're getting close," the caller would say, the voice loaded with hesitation. It became Claussen's form of torture. He knew that the 'they' the caller mentioned referred to The Brotherhood.

• • •

Claussen was living in a squalid apartment in Pittsburgh when he got the warning call. Claussen's smartphone chirped a perky ringtone. "They're closing in." With those words, Claussen was on the run, avoiding pursuers. He cursed. *My fake suicide worked at first, didn't it? I knew it might fool the police. Not The Brotherhood, though,* he thought. *They want me to pay back the money I don't have.*

In Florida, he thought enough time elapsed, and it would be safe to set a trap for Tremain and his friends. He'd lure them into the noose. *It should have worked,* he thought again.

Staging a fake suicide by gunshot made good his escape. After a cursory investigation, the police closed the case. The Brotherhood, his real danger, hid behind a scrim, and they were far more ominous and fearsome than the police and exposure to public ridicule.

Like Faust, Claussen made a deal with the devil. Four Devils, in fact. They called themselves *La Fraternité des Aigles*, The Brotherhood of Eagles. *Brotherhood of Vultures more like it*, Claussen thought.

Now, they demanded payment in full. "Cash would be nice," the text from the chairperson said, "but, if not, well." Claussen knew it was that damned Vladimir behind the text, the last contact he had with the group of predators.

• • •

The Brotherhood contracted with a private security company who only had one client: The Brotherhood. The head of the security company wasn't fooled by Claussen's fake suicide stunt. He knew Claussen was very much alive. His only job was to find him.

The Brotherhood didn't need the police, and preferred to deal with such matters privately. This was a group used to handling such things in their shadow world. They unleashed a highly-skilled team of elite agents to find Mr. Claussen.

The text was simple. "Find Charles Claussen." Nothing more was needed, but they weren't happy with the reports they kept getting.

"We followed his trail to the Bahamas. He chartered a boat and headed to Cuba. We couldn't track him from that point. Our next sighting was Sarasota, Florida. We were close, but he was gone by the time we got to his address. We were tipped that he might've moved to the Florida Panhandle.

"Before the team could get there, there was a gunfight in the small town, Apalachicola. A field agent described talked to someone who said Claussen had been seriously injured. The trail led to Panama City, Atlanta, possibly Pittsburgh."

The four members of The Brotherhood read copies of the report. "That business in Apalachicola is all about his misguided revenge," one said. There was a brief discussion.

"Terminate?"

"Not yet. Let us wait a while longer."

"I agree. Let's get back to the report."

• • •

Since Florida, Claussen had managed to evade capture, constantly changing places, ending in Pittsburgh, but he was always looking over his shoulder. He'd set up a man to protect him. It operated like a blind trust, arranged by an intermediary. He'd entrusted his protection to a man he didn't even know. Far from bankruptcy, Claussen knew his resources wouldn't last forever. If he ran out money, how long would his trust in them last?

Then, this latest warning call, and he was packing to leave Pittsburgh.

Did it come in time? he wondered. *I'm tempting fate…if I believed in chance, that is.*

"They know your location, they're close," the caller said. "You have one choice, one way out." The words were still fresh in his memory, and Claussen was irate. He was asleep when the rough words clawed him awake. "Get out, now," the voice said. "They're only minutes away."

• • •

Now, Claussen was standing beside an Asian man piloting the trawler. Claussen widened his stance, clutching a hand grip for balance. A sudden change in wind direction funneled diesel fumes into the pilot house, adding to a stubborn, disgusting odor of fish. He pulled a capsule of Dramamine from his shirt pocket, looking at it. Despite his nausea, Charles Claussen put the tablets back into his pocket, determined to hide any discomfort from the others.

Claussen watched the bow rising as if being lifted by a giant crane. Reaching the highest point, the boat paused before yawing to starboard, finally plunging down the far side of a wave.

"Crackers, eat crackers... good for sick... eat more," a man said in a singsong rhythm, his English pronunciation coming with difficulty. The skipper, Choe Sang-Hun, was the owner of the fishing boat. "Same name as a famous South Korean journalist," he said when Claussen came aboard. Now the skipper repeated, "Eat crackers, they good."

Claussen looked at the ink black sky merging with an inky black sea. Silvery white crowns bleached the tips of the waves, the wave tops folding back toward the bow of the boat.

What was that about some journalist, he thought.

Claussen forced another cracker down, determined to battle nausea. He looked at the seas ahead, cursing the man standing directly behind him.

"Do you have any idea what you're doing, getting me into this?"

The man stood expressionless in the shadows at the back of the pilot house. He seemed unperturbed. The butt of an automatic weapon was visible as the lapels of his jacket parted.

Standing farther back in the shadows was an enormous man. Claussen was 6'4" and didn't look up at many others. *This bodyguard's at least five, maybe six, inches taller than me,* he thought. The man's massive shoulders spread over a muscular frame. The right side of the bodyguard's jacket was pulled back, revealing a dangerous looking automatic weapon. His name was never offered. He was someone who knew his job and did it without words.

How did I get here? Claussen wondered not for the first time.

• • •

"If you were spotted, they have the airport covered. You can count on it," the man said, urging Charles Claussen on the boarding ramp onto the boat. "We've used this escape route before. Choe is someone we trust."

Stepping over discarded fish entrails, Claussen looked at the outline of the vessel, unimpressed. He followed the gunwale line from the square stern, making a slight curve before rising to the pointy end, the bow. The pilothouse rested amidships, a metal roof extending back, shielding the after deck from sun and elements.

Touches of faded blue paint were reminders of how the vessel may have looked when first launched. The name on the stern in Korean lettering was meaningless to Claussen.

Still, Claussen sensed, the boat looked seaworthy, and that's all he could ask for.

Approaching, he watched the ship rise and fall to the waves caused by the wake of passing vessels. A jet-black cormorant splashed into the water nearby. A dog, bold as anything, sniffed the heel of Claussen's right shoe. As it seemed ready to lift a leg and mark his territory, the dog turned away, indifferent.

Onboard, he was introduced to the captain. When the skipper's hand was offered, Claussen barely touched it, averting his eyes from the dirty hands and closing his nostrils to the peculiar stench common to commercial fishing boats.

The skipper spread out a nautical chart. "Call me Choe," he said, drawing a line with his fingers, saying something in Korean.

Claussen's guide translated. "This port Ulleung, the Island is Ullengdo. We're well off the east coast of Hanguk; we call it South Korea. That route he's indicating is our way out to Vladivostok. With luck, it should take less than thirty-five hours. There's a lot of history in the Sea of Japan, a lot of it disreputable."

"What about the weather?" Claussen said.

The guide turned to the captain. After a machine-gun staccato exchange in Korean, he turned back to Claussen.

"When we reach open water, seas will run over one and a half meters, with an SE wind of 15-20 knots. The wind will be shifting to WNW, waves increasing to over four meters. After that, we can expect winds WNW at 25-30 knots and waves topping five meters."

Five meters, Claussen converted in his head from metric as he looked at the chart, *waves close to sixteen feet, and a strong wind blowing almost bow-on.*

"Are you sure this is safe?"

"The captain says so," the guide said, nodding over his shoulder. "This kind of weather means nobody will be bothering us. And we don't have much choice, do we?"

• • •

All that behind him now, Claussen studied the waves, growing higher to create the look of a snarling beast, foaming whitecaps forming what looked like fangs. He hardened his will, fighting both nausea and panic.

The skipper, Choe Sang-Hun, said, "Rough weather... Not too bad... Be there..." He turned and spoke to the guide in rapid-fire Korean.

"He says it will be okay soon," Claussen's guide said. "We'll have smooth water soon, and it's better to make land in the dark. He'll have us on dry land by midnight. He knows the good places, no officials sniffing around. He's done this before. Relax. He's good at this. He knows who to pay off on both ends."

Claussen looked at his expensive watch. Eight more hours. Once more, he wondered how he ended here, then it came rushing back to him. It's been a long way from Florida and Pittsburgh to here.

CHAPTER 19

Technical Malfunction

A monitoring analyst for the Aviation Security Services reached the end of his shift when he heard the alarm. He looked at the screen. The alarm, a persistent ringtone, reminded him of a scanner beep at his supermarket checkout. He took pride in screening travelers passing through Christchurch International Airport, New Zealand.

He was tired and daydreaming, his chin touching his chest. He was planning the approaching weekend. The tepid remains of coffee sat at the bottom of a mug next to his keyboard. His supervisors ignored the rule about keeping liquids at a safe distance from electronics; it was more important for operators to stay awake. Plus, keyboards were easy to replace.

Knuckling his eyes, he'd been staring at the bank of television screens, eleven large LED displays, streaming video images of deplaning passengers. *Do they know they're on TV?* he wondered. Monitor number seven caused the alarm. He turned off the ringtone and looked at the monitor. The screen was in frame freeze, displaying a man's face.

The analyst adjusted the toggle and zoomed in. There was nothing remarkable about the face. He keyed a program and waited. *There's nothing on the no-fly list. Why was the image captured by the software program designed for facial recognition?*

The computer sounded a different warning, nudging Larry into further action. He looked at the main computer screen. A three-dimensional model of a man's head looked surreal, lines and dots adding to the appearance, and he pushed a button to alert his supervisor.

Who is this guy? The analyst wondered, pushing the question aside.

The system was designed for super-fast and accurate facial recognition, combining eye measurement and other features that would be matched to a massive database.

Connecting to the central Five Eyes server through a satellite uplink, he relied on the database to, at least, make a broad match. Using a process called morphing, information was converted into an image that could be rotated sideways, as well as up and down.

The door banged open. "I heard the alarm. What is it?"

The analyst pointed at the overhead monitor first, then at the split-screen display.

"Monitor seven has something," he said. "I'm running a database scan now. My shift's about over, and I—"

A soft chime sounded. The computer had stopped scanning, a single face was displayed, filling the monitor. At the bottom of the screen was a name: Charles Claussen. The display indicated a link to verify the data with the Five Eyes database.

The analyst clicked on the link, reading, "Deceased. No additional information." He and the supervisor leaned in as if to find a footnote in small print.

"That's impossible," the supervisor said. "According to the database, the guy's dead." Then, he reached over the analyst's shoulder, whacking the edge of the monitor with his hand. "It may be the digital age, but sometimes it helps to give it an old-school spanking."

"It says he's been dead," the analyst interrupted, "almost three years now. He committed suicide. Has something like this ever happened before?"

The supervisor gave a shrug. "No. We have enough to worry about people tracking those still among the living," the supervisor said, a feeble attempt at a wisecrack. "The computer is never wrong."

"Either this guy managed to rise from the dead, or we're looking at software error," the analyst said, stifling a yawn. "As much as I like zombie movies, I'm betting on a software glitch."

"Report it," the supervisor said. "Let the techies sort it out. It's been a slow night. The only person we caught tonight was that Australian guy, the one with his eye candy hanging onto his arm. He left a wife and three kids behind. That wouldn't have been so bad if he hadn't packed all his company's money into a suitcase to finance his little escapade. He's in custody now."

The supervisor turned back around and returned to his office.

The analyst was reporting the Claussen anomaly to the Five Eyes support team when his replacement walked in. "Anything I should know?" his replacement asked.

"There was a software glitch. I'm glad this shift is over," the analyst said. He stretched and rolled his shoulders. "See you."

● ● ●

The police interrogation wasn't as bad as Cyberia expected. *All they had was their suspicions. In the old days, truth or innocence wouldn't matter. I would be rotting away or dead,* he thought.

At his safe house, Cyberia powered on his reserve computers. He started a special program to guard against other attacks. Cyberia was unnerved by the police raid, but far more upset by the electronic assault on his systems.

He was a hacker, not the one hacked.

Finally, the computer was ready. He entered the command to follow Charles Clausen and CleanSweep. There was a flicker, then a report came onscreen. *It doesn't make sense. Some computer glitch concerning Claussen,* he thought. *New Zealand?*

Cyberia established another layer of protection for his computer systems, just in case.

CHAPTER 20

TOGETHER AGAIN

Matt felt like he was in free fall, falling through the air without a deployed parachute. Back in his apartment, Toronto wasn't far enough away from Wewa to suit him. Dog tired, he wanted Florida in the rearview mirror.

"I tell you, Brick, I'm still overdrawn at the adrenaline bank."

'It's been months now, Matt," Carling said on the speakerphone.

"I know. I'm still experiencing a letdown. Talk later, good-bye."

Sprawled on the sofa, Matt scrolled through TV channels, finding nothing of interest to watch. He was half asleep when his phone vibrated. He looked at the caller ID to see the name Susan Payne.

"It's him, I tell you. I'm sure, Matt. He's still alive," she shouted.

"Hello to you, too," Matt said. *Him?* He thought. He heard uncertainty hiding between Susan's words. He also heard something else: fear.

Matt didn't have to ask who. "Claussen," he said, hissing the name between compressed lips as he gripped the phone. "Where?"

"New Zealand. The airport at Christchurch," she said.

"New Zealand? Get real. Why would he be…?" He said. "Susan, it's been…" Hearing the name Charles Claussen sent Matt into a panic.

"Are you still there, Matt?"

"Sorry… uh… Susan. Chalk it up to brain freeze. What're you talking about? The last time I saw him, he'd been shot, likely bleeding to death," Matt said.

"We wrapped up our work here. We were on our way home when I saw him. I yelled at Remy, oops; Carl likes to be called Remy now," she explained. "The two of us were in the main terminal lobby, heading toward international departure. The airport was crowded. Something, I don't know what exactly, caused me to look to my left." Susan Payne's voice escalated in pitch and volume as she continued, "Thinking it *might* be that man."

"What would he be doing there? How in the world?" Matt said. "He was in Florida, bleeding from a stomach wound. How would he get…?" Matt didn't finish.

"I know, Matt. I saw a sign for coffee, about to suggest stopping, when I saw him. Claussen. I couldn't believe it. 'What's he doing here?' I asked myself."

Matt listened. He didn't know what to say.

"Remy was ahead of me. I yelled at him to turn around. I pointed and shouted over the crowd noise. Matt, I swear it was Claussen. He even glanced around and looked in my direction."

Matt held the phone under his chin while he walked to the kitchen. He poured coffee and waited for Susan to continue.

"Matt, I'm a journalist," she said. "After years of observation, I've developed sixth sense, scanning everything around me for some future use. I can't help it. I do it on autopilot."

"Take a breath, Susan."

"Sorry. Where was I? Oh… I saw people sitting, the same faces you see at any large airport. I saw a young man wearing a striped shirt. He held his chin, staring into the far distance. At another bench, a young couple sat. The man's head tilted to his right. He ignored an open laptop resting on his lap. His companion rested her head on his shoulder, buffing her nails. A woman sat by a window. She was reading a real print-version book, a rare sight these days."

"Get on with it, Susan. Back to the point." Matt's impatience was palpable.

"I looked at the overhead sign for international departures. When I turned, I couldn't believe my eyes," she said. "I saw a tall man walking in our direction. He was in a line of passengers heading to baggage claim and exit. I had to shake my head to unlock the memory. It was Charles Claussen. This Claussen was tall, well over six feet. That matched. This man had a beard and looked unkempt. Claussen never looked like that. He wouldn't be caught dead in a brown leather jacket with a torn sleeve. And blue jeans? Never." She finally took a breath.

"I couldn't shake it," she said. "There was something about the man. He walked past on my right. Did I see the smallest flicker of recognition? No. He didn't even look at me. Still? Claussen? No way!"

"You're sure he didn't notice Hurricane Sue?" Matt said. He used her nickname to slow her down. It didn't help.

"I yelled to Remy. 'Did you see that man?' I said. 'What man?' Remy asked. He knows when it's code red on my curiosity meter, he calls it. 'I swear it's him,' I yelled at Remy. 'Claussen, Charles Claussen.'" I looked back over my shoulder. Was it my imagination?" she asked and paused. "Matt, it must be over 9,000 miles from Toronto. We looked at the stream of passengers heading toward baggage claim. If he's still alive—and that's a big if—what would he be doing in Christchurch? New Zealand is thousands of miles from home. Besides, we all have a doppelgänger, a double, somewhere," Susan said.

There was something about that man," Remy admitted. He grabbed his camera to run after me, his camera bag slapped against his right leg as we ran. We chased after the line of passengers heading to baggage claim. Remy had his camera ready," she said.

Matt listened without interrupting.

"Look, I told Remy. A man passed baggage claim and fast-walking to a waiting shuttle van. Remy lifted the camera, his thumb nudging the zoom for a close-up. He told me he wasn't sure. Crap, I heard him muttering. I didn't have to ask; I know his frustration when I hear it. He didn't get a clear shot. Remy looked at the skylight and headed to some shade. He squinted and said he could tell. We needed a full screen to be sure. How could it have been Claussen, here?" she said.

Matt didn't remind her she had already asked that question—a lot.

"This is the first time I have thought about CleanSweep in months, Matt. Now, with that business in Florida, it all flooded back. What if I'm wrong? Should we stay?"

"I don't know what to tell you," Matt said.

"Remy's telling me we need to get home. If we know something certain after enhancing the video, that will help. In the meantime, we're committed to finishing our film project," she said.

"I'll call later and let you know, when Remy and I get home."

• • •

Susan and Remy cleared security and looked for a place to take a closer look at the video, but they needed something more robust than their tablets. Showing VIP cards, they entered the Quantas Club lounge and located a computer terminal.

Remy removed the media card from his camera as if it was unstable nitroglycerin. He inserted it into the laptop, and the screen flickered a small, whirling hourglass symbol. When he clicked the file folder, a video image appeared. "Before anything else, I'm making two copies and sending one to my home email account," Remy said.

Susan leaned over his shoulder when he replayed the video.

"I was afraid of that, Susan. You can't see anything with his back turned liked that."

"Remy, you're a master of the obvious, she said.

They examined the video of a man turning to board the shuttle van. Then, they re-examined and re-reexamined it.

"You can't make a face out?" Susan asked.

"Take a deep breath. You're too excited."

"Remy, can you enhance it when we get home? For a micro-moment, we can see a profile, but we can't tell...for sure, using this computer. Should we cash in our ticket and check the story out here, Remy?" she said, sipping a glass of Harrington's and sounding like she was trying to convince herself.

"What can we do if we stay?" Remy said. "The official report states he's dead. We both know how that fake suicide worked. Still, New Zealand? We need to get home. We're also looking at a lot of money circling the drain if we don't finish the documentary on time."

"We were going to suggest a get-together when we get back home, you know, for old times' sake. Now, this." Susan used her smartphone and started a text, typing in Matt's screen name: wordster.

"This is far too much for a text," Susan said and started to cry as she dialed Matt's number.

• • •

Matt clicked off his phone when the call from Susan ended. He sat hunching his shoulders together. *A text with the sniper's target, followed by the episode in Florida. This story began with a text, like the first warning about CleanSweep,* he thought. All this time, he still loathed the reminder of that ringtone. "Why don't you change it?" Carling asked. Matt didn't have an answer.

The second text wasn't a warning. It was a threat, he thought. *I need a walk to clear my head.*

Matt walked to an outdoor table, tugging his jacket tight against the chill. His phone rang again. This time, the caller ID showed it was his editor. He let the call go to voicemail, watching shadows racing past; a flock of sprinting clouds skimmed overhead, interrupting the sunlight. *The clouds are like messengers in a Greek play, running in from stage left to proclaim an approaching storm, then exiting stage right,* he thought grimly.

He watched a gust of wind push a discarded coffee cup to the curb, prodding it along, and a passing tire barely missed crushing it. *Why this sense of impending...* the thought was unfinished as Matt pulled the front of his jacket tighter still, trying to assure himself that this recurring sense of alarm was only his imagination. *But the call from Susan wasn't imagination,* he thought.

Matt felt dragged into a continuing story not of his choosing.

He contemplated Susan's call. His first thought, seeing caller ID was that he hadn't heard from her in ages. *She was frightened now,* Matt thought.

Now, Matt sat at the outdoor table, sunlight chasing away a lingering chill. Nobody sat at the three other tables, clustered in a small area enclosed by an iron railing. Sun umbrellas were tightly wrapped around their posts as if trying to hug themselves. If the coffee shop intended to transform the sidewalk into an outdoor café, it didn't work. *Who would honestly think they were at a bistro on a Paris boulevard*? he thought. Matt looked around at his Toronto neighborhood of small stores with apartments above. *Nope, not Paris.*

He watched a butterfly acting confused. *Aren't we all?*

CHAPTER 21

Twisted Sister

"What if she's right, Brick? What if it is him? How the hell did he end up in New Zealand, of all places?"

Matt held the phone to his ear. He stood and stretched, rubbing his right leg, the one that gave him his trademark limp. It was something he did when he was anxious, without thinking. The call from Susan fired a synapse, his nerves stretched taut on high alert. He walked toward the streetcar stop, ready to call Carling, but Brick beat him to it.

"Detective, I was just about to call you. Is the Claussen sighting a grotesque coincidence?" Matt said, trying to sound more cheerful than he was.

Matt stopped talking briefly with a suspicious look from a woman passing on his left. He pointed to a Bluetooth device over his ear. She walked on, tossing a tsk-tsk expression over her shoulder. At least it sounded like that to Matt.

"First Susan, now my favorite detective calls," he went on. "At least she didn't roll her eyes."

"What are you talking about?" Carling sputtered.

"Some lady was staring at me like I was talking to myself," Matt laughedd. "What do we do, Carling?"

"What are you talking about?"

Matt told him about Susan's call and the sighting of Claussen.

"We need to talk. Lunch, the Twisted Sister. Two o'clock!"

Matt held the phone out. He hadn't heard Carling's clipped cadence in...three months. *Has it really been that long since Florida?* He thought.

"I reserved a table at the back," Carling said. Look for me. Noon rush will be over. It'll be slow by then."

"Funny you should call. I was writing an anniversary piece about you know who. Then, Hurricane Sue called."

Matt heard the click of Carling ending the call. *Screw you too*, he thought. *But Carling's not someone to be thin-skinned about. Besides, it'll be great seeing him again. Some time with my friend will help.* Matt couldn't help but feel a growing sense of dread from in the pit of his stomach.

Coincidences are piling up, he thought, *Too many*. Matt tapped his headset again and said, "Vaughn." He listened to the phone click through his contacts, finally arriving at Angela Vaughn's name. Waiting, he almost disconnected when she finally answered.

After a long pause, she greeted him. "Hello."

"This is Matt, Matt Tremain."

"I know. Caller ID," she said briskly. "I can't talk now. Give me five minutes," she said before a soft click in Matt's ear.

Everyone's hanging up on me. Matt squinted, raising a hand to shield the glare. *My favorite time of the year,* he thought. *Crisp nights and warm, bright days.* He absorbed sunlight, storing the memory for a cold season coming. *These are days of cloudless skies, a blue impossible to describe with words, and no rain.*

A gust made a sudden, unscripted appearance. Matt came up with impetuous to describe the wind shaking tree overloaded with leaves of red, yellow, and brown. Some began to spiral, ending in a small pile at his feet. *I do love this time of the year*, he thought, pinching his collar together at the sudden drop in temperature. His earpiece chirped at the sound of an incoming call.

"This is Vaughn. I can talk now," the woman said, sounding out of breath. "How did you get this number?"

"It took some digging. It's been over two years now," Matt said as if she didn't know. He cringed, grateful when she chose a more direct approach.

"I don't give interviews. I don't know where Claussen is. I don't know anything about the remnants of CleanSweep. I've already told everything I know about Claussen's operation and plans. It's all on record. I've served my time. What do we have to talk about?" He tried to ignore the reproach when she added. "And I definitely won't be interviewed by you!"

Matt started to respond in kind but veered away. "We're coming onto the anniversary of the rioting and aftermath. My editor hinted that I should write a 'remember when' piece. We can talk off the record, purely background. I've always wondered about his motives."

"I thought all you did was write a blog. I don't watch the news or read newspapers anymore. And we both know there's no such thing as off the record."

I have a question, he thought. "You've been out of jail for seven weeks now. Then, you dropped out of sight."

"Do you think it's by chance, dropping out of sight? That's why I'm wondering where *you* got this number."

Matt danced around her jab. "You aren't hanging up on me. Does that mean you might be willing to meet with me? Do you think it's possible that Charles Claussen...." Matt asked another way. "Did he ever mention New Zealand to you?"

The pause lasted so long he wondered if she was still on the line, but he didn't hear a disconnect.

"If we meet, it will be on my terms. My time. My location. If you can't handle that, let me know."

"Your time and location. Your terms," he said.

"I haven't talked to anyone—" Her sentence was left unfinished. "I'll text you the place."

The call ended. Matt weighed the defeat he heard in her voice. *Angela Vaughn's a frightened woman, but we should all be worried.* Looking at his phone, Matt felt an icy blast of air.

· · ·

Stretching an arm out for balance, Matt walked to the rear exit and off the streetcar. He checked the time. *Enough time to get to the office, the bank, and make it to the Twisted Sister,* he thought.

Office? Matt laughed. *Room dividers on the third floor, two rows of workspaces jam-packed together. Some office.*

Entering the building, Matt walked toward bronze elevator doors only accessible to persons with the correct five-digit code. He'd been told the lobby was designed to impress and intimidate people. What the public saw as they entered was fingerprint-free glass and polished granite floors. Perky clerks smiled through the glass, handling payments, want-ad submissions, and, hopefully, new subscriptions; the lobby housed one of the few newspaper boxes remaining in the city.

Wood-paneled executive offices were on the second floor, and it worked. Anyone managing to get to the second floor was greeted by a forbidding receptionist, standing guard to the executive's sanctuary. No reporters ever went to the second floor. Only a privileged few passed her scrutiny, gaining access to the inner sanctum, and nobody did that without an appointment. The executive floor foyer was paneled with Dalbergia wood, imported from Madagascar and considered one of the ten most expensive woods their money could buy.

Sitting in the break room, a reporter said, "Newspapers are like the Titanic refusing to believe in icebergs. At least our board and executives will go down with a whiskey in one hand and a Cuban cigar in the other." Nobody thought it was amusing.

Reporter's cubicles were hidden on the third floor, out of public view. It was even harder to get access to the third floor, Matt's level. There was no receptionist. One needed to pass three levels of security. First was the elevator keypad code in the third-floor foyer. A code to another keypad and a retinal scan opened the door.

Inside looked nothing like a newsroom on TV or films. Matt walked past a honeycomb of cubicles. Worn, dirty gray carpet was a nice decorating touch he'd once noted. He no longer noticed. The third floor was a place of work, filled with noises, excitement, and a scent that Matt could never identify. It wasn't pleasant by anyone's definition.

The internet was the way to reach subscribers now. A handful of die-hard print newspaper readers remained, and hardly anyone bought a paper at a newsstand anymore, even the one in the lobby. Digital was hurling online news and opinions to readers at warp speed.

• • •

Matt knew the mounting loss of readers meant squeezing into smaller work areas.

An exception was the area behind the glass panels at the rear with modern furniture and the latest in computer technology supporting the evolving electronic news department. Matt didn't envy reporters behind the glass. He didn't care about appearances or where he worked. His target was access to the newspaper's database. He loved the archives. Over twenty-plus years of stories were digitized, but real paper copies were stored in an annex, a warehouse containing issues of *The Toronto Gazette*, stories the newspaper had covered for the previous ninety-five years.

An office in the annex granted access to microfilm files. "You're the only one who asks for microfiche anymore," the newspaper's librarian told Matt. "I doubt if the kids even know how to use the reader."

Matt's editor blamed it on television. "That started it all," he told Matt when they were discussing his contract and salary.

Matt knew it wasn't that simple. The internet helped shape a tectonic shift in the print landscape; the earth under the publishing industry was still shaking. Despite some old-timer's longing for a return to the old days, Matt knew it would never turn back.

"Matt, what's up?" someone called to him.

Matt turned. Kathy was one of the few reporters treating him with any degree of warmth.

"Kathy, hi. Only checking emails," Matt said as he headed to his workspace. "Anything going on, news-wise?"

"You'll have to wait and read my story," she said. "It's even making the print edition."

At his desk, Matt waited for his computer to power on. Working from home, he only came to this workspace when necessary. He mainly was drawn to the floor above, the database. Matt loved the feel of print editions, the paper feel of stored editions. Today, he wanted to access information above, the heart of a contemporary newspaper. "That's where the computer servers are at," his editor said. Matt resisted the urge to point out the peril of ending a sentence with a preposition. *Even if the Grammar Girl says you can,* he thought, *doesn't make it alright.*

Matt looked forward to using his access the database, the heart of *The Toronto Gazette*. The company was obsessed with security so much that they didn't allow online, wireless access. The only way to get into the system was the hardwired computers on the third floor.

Matt looked at Kathy, leaning over her keyboard. He appreciated her friendly competition. She was an exception from the rest of the people there, who ignored him, or worse, bad-mouthed him. It stung, knowing they considered him an outsider. "He doesn't even have a degree," Matt heard someone say behind his back.

I have a degree, Matt thought. Two, in fact. The University of Perseverance and On-the-job Work Hard University. They just can't get over the fact that I was instrumental in bringing down CleanSweep. All I get now is a cold shoulder.

When he griped to his boss, he was told, "They're all jealous as hell. Screw 'em. Keep writing."

Matt didn't easily make friends anyway. He wasn't changing now. He knew the difference between being a friend and being friendly. He counted few of the former, not many of the latter.

Matt, enclosed by the fabric walls of his cubicle, tap-tapped his way through e-mails and spent a few minutes searching for the information he wanted. Tapping the print key, he waited for the message that his print copies were ready.

Killing time, he thought about the place Carling mentioned, the Twisted Sister Bistro. He laughed out loud reading the website. It's nothing to do with a heavy metal band. It was named after the owner, Rosanna Selina. "Yeah, I'm twisted. My friends and family, especially my sister, have said that for years," her online post said.

Matt decided instantly that he liked Rosanna Selina.

• • •

Matt nearly missed the hand-made sandwich-board sign touting specials of the day. *Talk about laid-back*, he thought, pushing the door open. The lunch rush was over, the room uncrowded. Conversation buzzed like a swarm of bees. Carling was the only man in the room. Women traded tidbits of chit-chat while sipping white wine.

Matt was pleasantly surprised by the music in the background, John Coltrane's haunting rendition of *Naima.* Matt regarded Trane's set-piece to be four-and-a-half minutes of pure soul. He paused, listening to the solo part played barely above a whisper. The melody weaved past conversations into his ear.

Matt noticed a woman angle her head, apparently absorbing the John Coltrane riff. *She's caught in the sophisticated musical web Trane was weaving. Trane. Didn't everyone call him that?* Matt thought. *A woman who appreciates real jazz.*

They gave each other the upturned chin nod, one aficionado to another. Matt took extra care to minimize his limp.

His vision adjusted to the inside lighting when Matt spotted a fedora hanging on a wall fixture. It was indoors after all, but the white summer weight straw version was out-of-character for Carling. "Didn't anyone ever tell you not to wear white after Labor Day?" Matt said.

The two men danced through an awkward man hug. Carling gave Matt a sharp punch to the shoulder as he stepped back.

"It's great to see you, too," Carling said, his smile matching the words. However, the look on Carling's face turned dark quickly. "Matt, we have a huge problem."

"I like small talk, too," Matt said, closing his eyes to the elephant in the room, John Coltrane and the attractive woman forgotten.

CHAPTER 22

ELEPHANT IN THE BISTRO

Wiping beads of moisture on his glass, Matt took an unhurried drink, savoring the taste. He held out the mug in a half salute to show he was pleased to be sitting across from his friend.

Easing into small talk, they both knew there was the elephant in the room. Hell, it was on the table. Neither wanted to mention it, but small talk was a way to ease toward its presence.

"I need to ask a question. Why did you turn down the promotion? You earned it. You were offered a plum job, chief of detectives. Wow. Why'd you turn it down and choose counterintelligence?" Matt asked.

"I was holding out of Chief of police services," Carling said, adding a sly grin. "But they offered me COD, chief of detectives. I'm only an old-style gumshoe." He drew words out to imitate a private detective in an old black and white movie.

"'Old-fashioned gumshoe'? You've got to be kidding," Matt said. "You can even text."

"I mean it, Matt. I'm in my element entering a crime scene for the first time. I can smell and taste and see what's around me. You can't manage a crime scene from an executive office chair. I've always been intrigued by counterintelligence. It's a thinking man's thinking game, oops, person. Finding a way through the intelligence chatter is like working the *Sunday Times* crossword—in ink. You see the mistakes, but can't erase them."

The two were comfortable with pauses in the conversation. Neither bothered looking at the menu. This was a time for drinks and talk. Matt enjoyed his beer, watching Carling sipping on a drink he couldn't identify. "What's that?" He asked.

"Manhattan."

"Who orders a Manhattan anymore?" Matt said. "I bet you had to tell the bartender how to make one. It's an old-school drink for—"

Carling ignored the sarcasm and lifted his glass, signaling the bartender for a refill. He turned back to Matt. "Talk about promotions. You went no-name blogger with hardly any followers to a job as a reporter. *The Toronto Gazette*, no less. What's that all about? Do you have your little notebook for writing this all down?"

"I'm still an outsider," Matt snapped, then softened his tone. "The boys and girls who went to journalism school still don't welcome me with open arms. Some are coming around, but I wear a sweater to work to ward off the chill."

"Seriously, Matt. How *did* you get that job?"

"I lost all of my equipment, computers, and servers," Matt said. "You were there. I had to destroy it all." Matt then took a sip, nursing his drink. "After CleanSweep, I scraped together enough money to buy a decent laptop and started blogging again. I have over twenty-five thousand followers and growing."

"Impressive," Carling said.

"I'm sure some readers are only curious, but I'm serious about blogging now."

"Is that a conflict of interest as a reporter?"

"I'll wait and see. I've been assigned some meaty assignments. I never thought I would end up reporting *and* writing my blog," Matt said. "In the time after I dropped out of university, I headed down so many dead-end paths looking for something meaningful. My blogging career started by accident. I was sure no one bothered reading Verité. Look what happened after Tanner sent me that e-mail about Charles Claussen and CleanSweep."

Carling nodded, signaling Matt to continue.

"The only people I trusted back then were in my online group," Matt said. "Susan didn't take me seriously at first. She was Susan Payne, Hurricane Sue, the famous TV journalist. I was a nobody. But I had the facts and verified my sources. She finally came around." Matt's face clouded in thought. "Look at all we accomplished. It took your help. I needed that, along with the Susan and Remy. I had the heart of the story. Susan uncovered critical pieces with Remy recording it. You helped me stay alive."

Carling finished his second drink and signaled for another. *When did he start drinking like that?* Matt wondered.

"I know you didn't give me any creds at first," Matt said, looking at Carling.

Carling held his fedora and turned it in his hand, looking inside the headband. He pulled a photograph from under the elastic band and held it out. It was a well-worn picture, the four of them holding wine glasses toward the camera, laughing. "Our last time together." Melancholy gave a bass tone to Carling's words.

"I know," Matt said. "We promised to get together. Social media is a poor substitute for real connection. I did get an e-mail from Susan though. They're filming in New Zealand, a documentary of some kind. They were pretty vague about it."

"I got a copy of that, too," Carling added.

"Here we are, at any rate. And you've upgraded your fedora fashion."

They were interrupted by a sullen young woman, her hip cocked to one side. "You guys gonna eat something or just sit there drinking?"

"She must be working on a tip," Matt said, voicing his sarcasm as she walked away with their order.

"Screw the small talk," Carling said. "We both know what we have to talk about: the damned elephant," he said, brandishing an arm around the restaurant. "We need to talk about what Susan said about Claussen in her call."

Matt jerked back at the comment.

"I've never been able to get Claussen out of my mind," Carling said. "I fall asleep visualizing the evidence file and the photograph of the body in Claussen's office." Carling grimaced. "I ordered an enlargement and close-up of the watch. Claussen wouldn't wear a cheap watch if someone held a gun to his head. His idea of a cheap watch was a low-end Rolex. I asked someone about the timepiece he usually sported. They said it was a Louis Moinet."

Matt gave him a question mark look.

"Moinet, a Frenchman, invented the chronograph around 1800. Today, watches made under his name run a cool million. Claussen was wearing a 1970's Louis Moinet Artemis, still made with a mechanical movement. They're rare, so I hear."

Matt flinched at the idea of anyone spending that kind of money for a watch.

"I'm convinced he staged his death. All he needed was another body, a close enough match. That's what we did to stage your suicide, remember?" Carling pulled another photograph from the envelope, placing it on the table facing Matt. "That, my dear friend, is a watch that could take a licking and keep on ticking. If that cost $50, someone paid too much for it."

"You testified about that during the inquest," Matt said. "You kept telling the coroner about the watch."

"A lot of good that did," Carling said. "The police file, the testimony at the hearing, and the coroner's report were all tied with a cute, pink ribbon. Case closed!" He yelled, slamming his hand onto the table.

Patrons and the bartender turned to the noise as the server walked to the table and saw the photograph.

"Gross," she said, slamming their plates down and walking away.

"Then, there was Apalachicola," Matt said. "I'm sure you shot him. I saw the blood and the way he was holding his stomach."

Matt was interrupted when a woman walked to the table. It was the woman listening to Coltrane when he first walked in. She leaned to him and whispered something. She then smiled, dropped a note on the table, and left.

Matt unfolded it and saw her name and phone number. He looked in time to see her walk out the door, looking over her shoulder. Distracted by this good fortune, he turned back to Carling, who was trying to get Matt's attention.

"What?" Matt said.

The elephant is making noise," Carling said. "We need to face the truth, like it or not. Isn't that your tagline? If Susan and Remy saw him..." he started, watching the color draining from Matt's face.

"What if? What can we do about it?" Matt said.

"We damn well can't ignore it."

CHAPTER 23

MICHELLE

att and Carling left the bistro greeted with the sunlight waging a courageous battle with an approaching storm and failing. Furious-looking clouds propelled a sharp drop in temperature. A gust of wind lifted Carling's hat, but he managed to catch it in time.

"Claussen," Carling said. "I can't sleep, knowing he's out there somewhere. It'd be easier chasing that storm than trying to catch his ghost." He clamped his fedora onto his head and held it as he ran to his parked car. He tossed the hat on the passenger seat and ducked his head to get in.

Matt saw Carling's face change. "We have a huge problem, and we both know it. Action's needed, not talk. Is your passport up-to-date?"

Matt watched him drive off as the first swath of rain marched past him. He ran for cover. Despite that, he was soaked heading down the tile steps of the Bathurst subway station. He shivered as the approaching subway thrust a blast of air into the station. The car wasn't crowded, and he had a seat to himself.

Absorbed with Claussen, he reached into his pocket, unfolding the note the woman left. He liked the precise handwriting. *A letter written with care*, he thought, refolding it as the train brakes sighed. Arriving at Davisville station, Matt stood in the casual manner of an experienced subway rider—not too soon, not too late.

Rain stopped by the time he reached street level. It was a short walk to his apartment, only stopping to buy flowers.

East on Davisville and a right at Pailton, Matt reached his apartment building on Balliol, an architectural eyesore left-over from the sixties. He lived on the tenth floor. His view of the mirror image high-rise across the street reminded him to never walk around naked with the drapes open.

With three heavy metal posters around the room, the flowers were a pitiful attempt at decoration. Matt didn't need pretty, only three tables and a chair. He spent a lot of time in his work chair, ensuring it was the best on the market. He never apologized for the lack of comfortable seating, either. No one had ever visited his apartment.

Meals were microwaved dinners, salad, and soda. He used disposable plates and cutlery, standing at the counter or sitting at his computer. The kitchen table was covered with file folders. It looked haphazard, but a system allowed Matt to know exactly where to look, depending on the story.

Matt enjoyed his private life, well, private. He needed a bedroom and space for three tables arranged in the living room. One table held a large screen television continuously tuned to the 24-hour news channel. The second was for his computer and electronic equipment, including a scanner for police, fire, and ambulance chatter.

The third table held his prized possessions: his audio components. Matt practically grew up in the digital age. He was committed to the latest and greatest digital technology in computers, tablets, and smartphones, but there was one difference in his technology craze. Matt was anything but digital when it came to his music.

A devoted audiophile, he was happy to discover a store in the East End. A funny little man with bushy eyebrows showed Matt around the store, touching the equipment as if they were in a museum. "I specialized in vintage analog, high fidelity components," the man said.

Matt gradually built his system. He added a preamp to the amplifier, feeding sound to a Marantz tuner. When it came to speakers, Matt paid dearly for a Klipsch Reference II RF-7. With a speaker as large as his refrigerator, he had enough power to annoy his neighbors within a two-block radius.

He never turned it to blast level, though. For such a large system, it played John Coltrane with delicacy. *It's all about Trane, John Coltrane*, he thought, carefully lowering the arm on his turntable. *Blasting Trane at high volume should be illegal.*

Matt walked back to the kitchen listening to *Ruby, My Dear,* a slow ballad blending the talents of Trane and Thelonious Monk.

His other splurge was a single-cup coffee maker. Waiting for coffee, he almost managed to wipe Charles Claussen from his thoughts. Taking the first sip of his Kenyan roast coffee, he felt the note in his shirt pocket. He unfolded the note.

"Michelle Reagan. 905-318-0999." *She has a Hamilton phone number,* he thought as he taped the note to the side of his computer screen.

Matt looked around. There was no place for Michelle Reagan to sit, he realized.

• • •

Michelle Reagan, with a Hamilton phone number, reminded Matt of his dating shortcomings. First was Darlene Sharpenskin. The two ran out of things to talk fifteen minutes into the date, ending near the punch bowl, watching everyone else dancing.

"Relationship challenged," someone said. Matt knew it was mostly on him.

Sheila lasted the longest—almost six months. The sex was great, but Matt woke the morning after wishing she had gone away during the night. That didn't exactly give the relationship staying power. Worse yet, Sheila was fanatical about ABBA. She played "Dancing Queen" over and over.

Reading the note, it felt different. *She loves Trane, for starters,* he thought. With eyes, he remembered every detail when he saw her at The Twisted Sister. She wore a dark dress, belted at the waist, and a scarf around her neck the color of honey. It framed blonde, leaning more toward brown. *Her eyes,* he thought. *Blue? No. Sapphire.* He remembered a silver bracelet on her left wrist, her only accessory. Makeup was minimal. *Enough to be perfect.*

What is it? He wondered. *There's something about Michelle Reagan with a Hamilton phone number. More than an appreciation for John Coltrane. She touched his heart like a thunderbolt, but Coltrane sealed the deal.* He laughed out loud.

Matt braced himself and entered 905-318-0999, convinced he would make himself sound like a fool. Several rings later, he was about to disconnect.

"Hello, this is Michelle."

"This is Matt. You don't know me, but you gave me—"

"I hoped you'd call," Michelle said.

Matt couldn't believe it.

"I worried I'd been too forward," she said. "I've never done that before. I know I interrupted a tense conversation with your friend."

"It was Trane," Matt stammered. "I recognized a kindred spirit." *I sound like a dufus.*

Thinking back, he couldn't believe how long they had eased into a relaxed conversation over politics, the daily commute between Hamilton and Toronto, and their affection for the golden age of jazz.

"It all started with *Kind of Blue*," Matt said. "His studio album even had Miles Davis."

They argued about the best cut, finally agreeing it was *Flamenco Sketches.* Matt was about to add something about the Modern Jazz Quartet when she said, "It's late. If I oversleep, the train will be standing room only."

Matt felt the air leave him like a basketball deflating. *Did she give me the goodbye signal?* he thought. He took a chance. "If you ever have time—"

Michelle interrupted, "Or, I could always sleep in and catch a mid-morning train." She waited.

This had never happened to Matt, ever. *Is it possible to fall in love this quickly?* All it took was one look at the Twisted Sister, head tilted, listening to the music. Now, he listened to her rich baritone voice, a slight accent suggesting down east, of the Canadian Maritimes.

"Are you still there?" she said. "Did I say something wrong?"

Matt realized he needed to say something quickly. "Still here, Michelle. You didn't say anything wrong. I was trying to think. Where do you work?"

"The Yonge Eglington Centre."

"I know the place," Matt said, in his eagerness. "Café Pleiade, on Mount Pleasant, south of Manor Road. It's perfect for lunch."

"I can walk it," she said.

"It doesn't look like much from the outside. Don't let it fool you. It's like the Twisted Sister. It's totally worth walking in the door." Matt realized he was talking fast and tried to put the brakes on. "The one thing that's made my move to this area worthwhile is Café Pleiade. Wait until you meet Stavros, the owner, and chef."

• • •

Matt had a table at the back, offering privacy. Whenever the door opened, he stood, but no Michelle.

Feeling impetuous, he'd run up Mount Pleasant Avenue as he wanted a chat with the owner. Stavros arranged for John Coltrane playing in the background. When she opened the door, Michelle was surrounded by an aura of sunlight. Matt watched her look around, giving her a slight wave. He was grinning, watching her make her way between tables.

"Those mismatched pillows give the booth a comfy feel," Michelle said, holding out her hand.

Matt held his breath, helping her sit. The chef, Stavros, on cue, brought a bottle of wine, holding it out for Matt. "I happened to have a tasty Amarone in the back."

Matt did the look at the cork thing. In truth, he knew little about wine. He trusted Stavros.

I miss my old apartment on Queen Street, Matt suddenly thought. *It had a proper living room. There's no place for Michelle to sit in my new apartment.* It had never mattered until now.

"Cheers," they both said, touching glasses. Matt was totally in love by the time he helped her into a taxi. Michelle waved as she raised the window.

She's smiling, Matt thought. *Something's gone right.*

CHAPTER 24

SOMEWHERE OVER THE PACIFIC

The next day, Matt was excited to tell Carling about Michelle. He hadn't thought about Charles Claussen since lunch with Michelle. That changed as he and Carling sat at the roof-top bar the next day, Matt's favorite place to watch the Toronto skyline. Not today.

"The elephant's chasing us," Carling said. He held his third—or was it his fourth—Manhattan. Matt wondered how the man could drink so much without showing it.

Carling's hand paused as he lowered his glass. Finally, he said what they both thought. "Charles Claussen's back from the dead, again," he said, almost shouting. He slammed the glass on the table, liquid sloshing over the rim.

Matt saw others turn to look at the disturbance. Mentioning Claussen's name, the elephant in the room gave a final roar, fading away as Matt and Carling talked about the call from Susan.

"I don't get it." Carling pinched his nose. "New Zealand? But they aren't sure. I hope it's just someone who looks like him."

"You don't think it's a look-alike, though, do you?" Matt said.

"Not really," Carling said. "Susan's intuition is bang on. The man was wearing jeans, something Claussen would never do, right? And there was the two-day-old growth of hair. That man was always fastidious. I don't believe in coincidence."

"She really thinks it's him?" Matt asked. "Should we call her, ask her again?"

Matt powered on his tablet, scrolling until he found a page. "They're in the air now, with a two-hour layover in San Francisco. They'll be in Toronto tomorrow morning. It's a brutal flight, almost twenty-four hours all told. I checked the schedule," Matt said. "Maybe Susan will call during their stopover in San Francisco. She said Remy needs his system to analyze the video."

"I intend to be looking over his shoulder," Carling said. "The bastard's alive, I feel it. The worst is not knowing where he is. Now? New Zealand? What's behind that? He's dangerous, Matt. He's a rattlesnake coiled to strike. Except he won't rattle a warning before he strikes. You won't know until the poison is firmly inserted, his fangs deep."

Matt listened to Carling's words, measured and dark with a blend of fear and loathing.

"There's a reason he's there, Matt," Carling said. "He's lulling us to sleep. He'll head here when we least expect him."

"I was going to tell you about something else," Matt said. "I've always been skeptical about coincidence, fluke, luck, or whatever you call it. My editor has been on me to write a follow-up story about CleanSweep. It's coming on three years now. I tried to beg off, but something—my curiosity I guess—got to me. I had a calendar entry with Angela Vaughn's name, a reminder to call her for a follow-up."

"That bitch gave cops a bad name," Carling said. "It still leaves a sour taste." Carling set his jaw. "She was a good cop and detective back in the day. She threw it all away. For what? Look at her now."

"She stepped up at the end. Her testimony was critical," Matt said. "That's why she got off with a three-year sentence, light as a feather for what she did. She told me background details about her involvement, but—"

"No excuse!" Carling shouted. All conversations came to a stop as other patrons ogled in the direction of their table.

"Anyway," Matt said, "I found a new phone number for her. She agreed to meet. I don't know what more she can say, but don't you think it's strange? New Zealand, Susan, Claussen, and Angela Vaughn. We're all rejoined as part of this story."

"I don't like her," Carling said, crossing his arms.

"I know what you think, Carling. She's reportedly been a model prisoner. She's seeking redemption, according to her parole officer. She won over the other inmates, despite being a former cop."

"She's a disgrace to the shield. I don't give a damn how redeemed she feels."

"Think about it," Matt said. "What if she and Carling are...you know... still in touch?"

The detective in Carling took over. "You're right. This is no time for emotions. Find out what she knows. What flight are they on?"

"Air Canada, Flight 1430," Matt said.

"We'll be waiting at the exit," Carling said.

"I'm famished, let's eat," Matt said. He waved to their server, another pouty attitude. She took her time walking over to their booth, earning every cent of the one-dollar gratuity Matt added to the tab, relishing the snub.

• • •

Thirty-one thousand feet over the mid-Pacific, Susan was irate. The sun edged through the overcast, waking her. The pleasant dream faded away, despite her attempt to remember. Her annoyance was quick-lived, however.

Remy's gentle breathing was reassuring. She watched him, head tilted to one side, mouth slightly open, long even breaths. Despite her anxiety about Claussen, she knew he was the professional, already planning the editing job ahead. They wrapped up the shoot in New Zealand, and all the documentary needed now was editing. She sighed, looking forward to being in her own bed.

She leaned back, imagining being home, *The Toronto Gazette* tucked under her arm as she poured the first cup of coffee, black, no sugar.

"I'm awake." Remy took her hand in his. "Where are we?"

She leaned forward and touched the onboard TV display. "Speed, 560 miles per hour. Altitude, 31,550. We're approaching the international dateline," she said.

"Damn," he drawled, "I never know what day it is on these flights. Do we lose a day or gain one when we cross?"

"I think we've passed American Samoa," she said. "It's hours until San Francisco. We should call Matt while we're changing planes. He's talked to Carling by now, hasn't he? I hope so." Susan waved to a passing flight attendant. "Single-malt, make it a double."

"Coffee for me, black," Remy said. "And let me add a please for both of us," he said, watching the attendant smirk.

"Let's look at your video again," she said, pulling the window screen down. "I can't get the image out of my mind."

"It's not going to change without enhancing but knock yourself out." Remy retrieved his camera bag from overhead and handed it over to her.

Susan placed the viewer on the seatback tray. It was like a tablet, a fold out case that acted like an easel. She pushed play as their drink order was served. Susan ignored the attendant, but Remy gave an extra-warm "thank you" to compensate for his partner's rudeness.

Savoring the sharp whiskey taste, Susan leaned forward. "It looks like you're trying to get inside, to be a part of the video," Remy said.

"If only," she said. "Can you slow it down?"

Remy made an adjustment. "Try it now," he said.

She looked closely, her forehead wrinkled with intensity. "It's no use. I want it to be Charles Claussen. Then I'm sure I'm wrong, it's only a resemblance."

"We all have a doppelgänger somewhere," Remy said. "Maybe it's nothing more than that, a double. You told Matt Charles Claussen wouldn't be caught dead in jeans and a two-days-old growth of facial hair." Remy said.

The next eight and a half hours was a mixture of frustration, anger, and boredom for Susan. She turned the viewer off and back on, determined to see something in Remy's video that would prove or disprove it was a man she loathed and feared.

Finally, she told Remy to put the viewer away and leaned back, closing her eyes. She was jolted awake when the landing gear clunked down and locked into position for landing.

Anyone knowing it was Susan walking through the terminal would have been shocked. She had a look all international travelers often have.

"The only time I've ever seen you this raggedy is before morning coffee at my place. That's your get-out-of-bed look. Then it's magic. You go into the bathroom, close the door, and reemerging later like the professional TV journalist everyone sees on their screen."

"No, I don't need to wash my face or comb my hair. I don't give a rat's ass what I look like," she said. Remy had suggested she might want to, as he put it, freshen up.

She stormed ahead until she saw an alcove of chairs. Nobody was sitting in the area. She took out her phone. "Matt? Susan. We need to talk, now."

• • •

Cyberia heard a monitor alarm and turned on a screen. *Susan Payne's on her way back to Toronto*, he thought. The screen turned dark again.

CHAPTER 25

SOUTH ISLAND NZ

"I'm coming for you all!" Claussen shouted over the noise, sounding like a machine gun strafing every hard surface. *When will it stop?* Claussen thought, his head braced between his hands. He couldn't ignore rain bullets peppering the metal roof for the third day straight.

He knew from weather reports it was far from over. Gusts clawed at the oceanside shutters, their thumping adding to his depression. He felt like a scuba diver held down by weights. Four photographs taped to the gap between two windows served as reminders he was hiding, once again, down another rabbit hole.

Stranded in the cabin, he listened to the New Zealand weather service reporting there was no let-up in sight.

• • •

His last safe house was a shabby apartment in Pittsburgh's Hill District. Who would expect to find the great Charles Claussen sharing a building with hookers, drug dealers, and pimps?

Then, the warning call. "The Brotherhood's agents are on the ground in Pittsburgh now. Get out. Use the Greyhound bus. Down the rabbit hole," a man said. "There's a ticket waiting at Cleveland airport. Go to the customer service counter for Delta

Claussen held the phone to under his chin. He pulled a backpack from the closet, looking at the cash and papers he needed.

Claussen looked around the room and gathered his belongings. He put the passport into the back pocket of his jeans and shrugged.

"No computer, no cell phone, and no credit cards except the three you were provided. Got that?" the man said.

Claussen hated being in someone else's hands.

"Whose idea was New Zealand? I don't know anyone there."

"That's your answer?"

Claussen didn't have a response.

"Christchurch's on the South Island. Rent a camper. Take Route 6 south as far as it goes—Jackson Bay. Remember, drive on the left side of the road."

The airport looked like any other, but he was uneasy. Claussen started to relax when he noticed a tall woman with blonde hair. She stood on tip-toe, looking his way.

It can't be, he thought. *Susan Payne? That's insane. I'm thousands of miles away from Toronto.* He lost sight as the woman blended into the crowd. *Impossible*, he thought, trying to reassure himself his imagination was playing tricks.

He turned back as he boarded the car rental shuttle. *No, it can't be her.* He ignored the feeling, clutching his backpack as the shuttle pulled away.

He needed to stay focused. The sight of that woman jarred him. Her looking like Susan Payne rattled him more than he would admit.

He arrived at the rental counter. Lori, according to her name tag, watched him approach. I need to rent a camper."

"You must be a Yank," She said. "

"I have right choice for you. Flexible and spacious bed configurations... exterior slide... shower... a real home away from... your Trailblazer Motorhome from Britz today?"

Claussen handed her an untraceable credit card, theoretically untraceable. He knew better. He'd built an empire on tracing the untraceable.

His nerves on high alert. He couldn't stop thinking about Susan Payne. The *woman at the airport was surely a coincidence, a look-alike.*

• • •

In Moscow, 10,258 miles to the northeast, a man in his early thirties contemplated the second shot of vodka. Cyberia poured, muttering aloud, "????-????," sounding like choot-choot in English. It was a Russian expression meaning only a little more. He poured more than only a little more and was about to put his computer to sleep for the night when the screen unscrambled a message from one of his special tracking programs.

He squinted at the screen. A credit card was used to rent a vehicle at the Britz Campervan Hire and Car Rental on Memorial Avenue outside Christchurch International Airport. The number matched a card used to book a flight from Cleveland to New Zealand, Christchurch International Airport.

In Moscow, Cyberia knew it wasn't a coincidence. Giving the computer a command to keep tracking that number, he tipped his glass to finish off the vodka in one swallow. He wiped his mouth with his sleeve, satisfied. It was time for bed.

• • •

Claussen stopped for groceries. Walking out with his purchase, he saw another store next door, Vodafone, a cell phone outlet.

"Phone's charged and ready to go," the clerk assured him as his untraceable card was swiped.

Walking out with his purchase, Claussen paused to examine the laptop computers on display. His fingers drifted across a touchpad in a gentle caress.

• • •

Each swipe of Claussen's credit card triggered Cyberia's computer program, creating a soft chirp like a bird, possibly a wren, but it wasn't enough to wake Cyberia sleeping nearby. Snoring sounds the same in any language, no translation needed.

• • •

Claussen's last stop was for an altogether different reason. He spotted two mismatched, corrugated buildings. He drove past stacks of wooden pallets alongside one building until he came to a portable office, perched on concrete blocks, a sheet of plastic duct-taped over a broken window.

Cities have places where people of indistinct character blend into the background. Christchurch was no exception.

I always had people who did things like this for me, Claussen thought.

He'd known it would be impossible to lawfully purchase a weapon, but shady characters all seem to have the same look. The seller conveyed danger, wore wrinkled overalls, a filthy shirt, and wasn't on friendly terms with a bath or a shower.

Needs a dental plan at the very least, Claussen thought. He wasn't here to make friends with an underground gun dealer, however, completing the purchase and heading back to the caravan.

• • •

Claussen drove south until he crossed the Haast river. A GPS voice insisted he turn right, then south to Jackson Bay. Reaching the end of the road at Jackson Bay, Claussen parked and stepped out of the van. With a languid stretch, he realized the leg cramps from his long flight had finally abated.

A young couple sat on the back of a car nearby. If they were curious about the rental caravan, they didn't show it.

A man dressed as a commercial fisherman trailed the unpleasant smell of those who gutted and scaled fish, the dirty work on fishing boats. Claussen couldn't avoid the odor.

"You look lost, mate?" the man said. "Don't see many caravans in these parts."

"I'm looking for a place to park. Three or four weeks, maybe longer. Any suggestions?" Claussen said.

"Yank, eh?" It sounded like a question but wasn't. "Your best bet," the fisherman said, scratching his head as if solving a major math problem, "is to drive back a few. A friend rents spaces for caravans. Look for Neils Beach Road. Look for a building with the bright red roof. Good luck, Yank. Maybe see you around?" The man held out his hand. "The name's Trevor, by the way. My friend's name back in Neils Beach is Coulter. His first name's Reggie. Tell him Trevor sent you. Otherwise, he'll have the money out of your wallet without you feeling a thing." Trevor walked away, laughing.

Odd. That voice sounds familiar.

Claussen drove away. Ahead, low-hanging clouds looked like they were mounting an attack on the mountains.

Nearing Neil's Beach Claussen had a nagging thought. *That guy never asked for my name. It's almost like he knew me. I need to get some sleep.*

CHAPTER 26

WHAT IN THE HELL WERE YOU THINKING?

Claussen kept his distance from anyone not considered his equal. His club had a small membership. *Why does he feel approachable?* He thought. *There's something about him.*

With Trevor's advice, Claussen had a place to park the caravan.

"Trevor sent you? That's good enough for me," the man had said. He was short, his back bent over with some bone disorder. He looked at Claussen. "Name's Coulter, Reginald Coulter, and you are?"

Claussen started to say Chuck, one of his many fake IDs. *Fifty-three years old, and I've never, ever, been Chuck*, he thought. *What's my name now?* He remembered. "Samuel. Call me Sammy."

He didn't offer a last name, and Reginald wasn't curious enough to care.

"U.S. dollars?" Claussen asked. He had no idea what the rate of exchange was.

"Suits me fine, mate." The man pocketed the offered money with incredible speed. At the going rate, he'd made a tidy profit on the exchange.

"See that spot at the end of the laneway?" Reggie said. "Stay as long as you like. No call for spaces this time of the year." He coughed, and Claussen watched him pull out a handkerchief, walking back to his office.

He stopped and turned. "Knock me up if you need anything. Oh, you're going to need a long power cord," Reginald said, still coughing. He held the dirty cloth it to his face until he stopped hacking. "I may have a spare somewhere."

After backing into the parking space, Claussen did his best to smile at people walking by, not hiding their curious stares. He felt like he was a circus that recently arrived. He made sure to wave, forcing himself to make small talk, something that didn't come readily to him.

They hid their curiosity behind faces appearing standoffish, but not entirely.

• • •

Four days later, Claussen heard a furious knocking on the caravan door. He reached under the pillow for the handgun, then decided against it. If it was the police or brotherhood agents knocking, it was over.

"How're you doing? I got back a short time ago," Trevor said with a lopsided grin. "Been hauling nets," he said, holding out calloused hands.

Claussen let out a long breath and invited him in. It seemed like the right thing to do.

"You never asked me my name. I'm Sam, Samuel Addison. You guys seem pretty trusting in these parts."

"It's the way we are. Can't think we've ever had a Yank staying here though. This is the end of the road, in more ways than one. It's not like us to pry into someone's reason for being here."

They chatted about fishing and where to buy food. "Looking for nightlife? Won't be finding that in Neils Beach," Trevor said, laughing. "Damn, I'm thirsty," Trevor held his hand like he was holding a glass.

Despite the early hour, Claussen went to the cupboard for a whiskey, Trevor nodding his approval.

"I've been thinking," Claussen paused, then continued. "This," he said, "is already feeling cramped. Do you know if there's a place I might rent if I decide to stay longer? I don't appreciate curious looks I'm getting from neighbors."

Claussen watched Trevor scrunch his left cheek, scratching his head like he was thinking about a solution.

"I may know of a place, pretty remote. Mary owns it. She's visiting family in Scotland, planning to be away for at least a year. It's nothing fancy. The cottage has a good solid steel roof; she's a plain-style woman. Hold on."

Trevor walked out to his truck and came back with a laptop. He fished a satellite dongle from his pocket and keyed in a command. "I'll make a call to ask." The video chat tone sounded.

"Trevor, how are you?" a woman said.

"I'm fine, Mary. With the time change, you must be enjoying break-fast now? I have a proposal for you," Trevor said, not bothering with too much small talk. "My friend here would like to rent your cottage."

Claussen was impressed. His fisherman friend was tech savvy and soon had Mary's okay to use her cottage. Claussen longed to get his hand on Trevor's laptop, despite the warning against using one.

• • •

"I had a whole week off," Trevor said one evening. "What a luxury. Back to my nets now." Claussen realized he would miss talking with his new friend. With Trevor gone, Claussen asked Reginald to help return the caravan. He swapped it for a Hyundai i30 Hatch. Stopped at a red light, Reginald said, "Don't much care for the city." But his eyes gave away his excitement.

"I'm stopping here," Claussen said, looking at the electronics store he'd visited before.

"Will ya look at all this stuff," Reginald said, watching the man he knew as Sammy pull out a credit card to complete purchases. Claussen bought a laptop. "That computer looks snazzy, yep."

Claussen was tired, and tempted to stay over, but he wanted to get back to the cabin and power up his new purchase.

Claussen stopped to buy a bottle, hoping some whiskey would keep Reginald quiet on the ride back. It worked. He dropped Reggie at his place and then drove to his new home.

Mary's cottage was isolated, perched on the side of a ridge. It didn't take long to settle in. Claussen unpacked the computer and plugged in a satellite card. Soon, he scrolled through news websites. No mention of

Charles Claussen or CleanSweep. He was about to check his private e-mail account when he heard a truck struggling to climb the steep laneway.

He saw the popup for an email as he closed the computer. *The truck's getting close*, he thought. The email contained a series of numbers, seemingly in no apparent order. Claussen knew better. He knew the code, sorting the numbers as he reached for his throwaway phone.

"What in the hell were you thinking?" Claussen flinched at the tone. It was a different voice, edgy and angry. "You had two instructions: No phone, and no computer. You, of all people, know how easy it is to monitor... I don't know what to say."

Claussen wasn't used to being talked to like that. He wasn't used to being reprimanded. "I wasn't thinking," he said, knowing how pathetic it sounded.

"New Zealand is one of the Five Eyes partners. They share data with American and Canadian agencies. They had a hit. Your face was a match. They thought it was a glitch, but it won't take long for them to sort it out. Then you have the governments and The Brotherhood on your ass. The Kiwis call the Yanks, and the Yanks call the Canucks. You're in shackles on the next plane home. Treason carries the death penalty."

"What do you want me to do now?" Claussen said.

"Open the sealed courier envelope you have. Use only that passport and ID. Burn everything. Get rid of everything. A ticket for Craig Nelson is waiting at Auckland. Check in at the Korean Air counter. Someone will meet you when you deplane in Seoul. I'd suggest you get to it soonest—"

Claussen listened to the call disconnect, feeling alone.

• • •

A computer in Moscow came to life and recorded the activity. The computer returned to slumber mode as Claussen closed his new laptop in New Zealand.

• • •

Claussen finished hiding the equipment as he heard footsteps on the porch. "Howdy, Sam," Trevor drawled, imitating an American cowboy.

"Thirsty?" Claussen asked. *How can I get him to leave without raising curiosity? It's uncanny, Trevor stopping by as soon as I powered on the computer and made that phone call.*

They sat on the porch, not needing to talk much, both seeming at ease with time together without words getting in the way. That's the way Claussen wanted to look on the outside. Inside, he was on edge.

"I won't be going out on the boat for a while," Trevor finally said. He saw the question mark on Claussen's face. "There's a storm brewing, a big one. We've been monitoring the system. All the models are showing a track taking aim at us."

"Hurricane?" Claussen asked. It was the only frame of reference he had.

"Our version of one," Trevor nodded. "Low pressure moving over this part of the South Island can collect a lot of water vapor. When that happens, look out for torrential rains where it meets the mountains." He looked around and pointed. "See those clouds? Wait until they come in with moisture and, wham, hit those peaks."

"How much rain are you talking about?"

"I've seen rainfall as much as ten inches in 24 hours. You'll think it's never going to stop."

"Will it be here soon?" Claussen tried to hide his concern. He intended renting or stealing a plane at the Neils Beach airport. He thought he could make it to Wellington, from there to Auckland. This weather report was bad news.

"The rain isn't all," Trevor said. "If the following system collects enough cold and moisture near Antarctica, you might see hail—possibly snow. Add strong to gale force winds, you have quite a weather cocktail."

Now Claussen was alarmed. *This is all going wrong. I need to get out of here,* he thought. *Now.*

"It's been said wind and rain hitting the house sounds like bullets from a machine gun."

Claussen tried to hide his alarm and disappointment. He watched Trevor drive away as dusk painted the landscape with patches of dark shadows.

That night, the storm howled ashore.

• • •

The machine gun sound ricocheted from every hard surface.

When will it stop? Claussen thought.

Standing abruptly, he walked to the windows with quick strides. It felt futile, but he pulled the heavy draperies closed to muffle the storm's roar. He looked at the photographs again, the light from the desk lamp casting them with a shadowy quality, which made them look like police wanted posters.

Matt Tremain's photo was pinned to the far left, the person he hated most. Next, a photo of the detective, Carling. He considered Carling a traitor, a double agent, someone who dishonored the police badge he carried.

He sneered at the photo of Susan Payne as if he could transmit disdain directly to her.

"And you're the one who recorded it all," Claussen said, aiming an unsteady finger at Carl Remington's photograph.

"My plan for a perfect world, so close to implementation," he screamed at the photographs.

How did CleanSweep fall apart so quickly? he wondered, a question he had asked himself for three years now. One moment, he was sitting down to a steak dinner only to have it whisked away from the table.

Claussen held a marker and drew a target on the forehead of Matt Tremain. It was only a gesture, but it provided some satisfaction. Charles Claussen wasn't well acquainted with introspection. Instead of looking at his own flaws, he preferred to blame them for ruining CleanSweep, the perfect plan to make the world a better place. The four faces in the photographs mocked him, an embodiment of failure.

"I'm coming for you all, no matter how long it takes or how much it will cost," Claussen shouted at the pictures.

He looked at the expensive watch on his wrist, his thoughts suddenly on pause. The machine gun sound stopped without his realizing it. He could still hear the wind, the door striving to hold it back, so far with success. The gale continued to growl like an enraged brutish creature, puffing its deadly menace.

The staccato hammering has stopped, he realized. *The wind's dropping?*

Claussen pulled the drapery aside, and large, wet globs of snow-flakes blew in a horizontal line aimed at the cottage. Claussen bellowed at the snow and turned back to the photographs on the wall.

To one side, a picture of Angela Vaughn, his former head of security, was taped to the wall. He took that picture and carefully folded it.

Claussen tore the others from the wall, ripping them into small pieces.

He burned every piece of his former identity. He hated destroying the brand-new laptop, but it had to be done. He sat, turning away from where the photographs had been. Gathering his travel knapsack and escape kit, he thought about the images.

"I'll be the last person you see alive."

CHAPTER 27

IS IT HIM?

"They've landed," Matt said, looking at his watch. "Can't you use the siren or something?"

Carling focused on traffic. He knew Matt wasn't serious about the siren; it was simply nerves. "We've got enough time. You know how long it takes them to get through baggage claim, then customs and immigration."

"Brick," Matt said, using Carling's nickname, "Susan sounded... I don't know, apprehensive comes close. She said they were looking forward to getting together, but Claussen is a cloud hanging over our reunion."

Matt watched Carling turn at the next exit. An overhead sign directed them to the cargo terminal. They followed a truck to the security checkpoint. It didn't take long for the truck to be cleared, but it felt too long to Matt. When the vehicle finally drove away, Carling pulled to the kiosk and displayed his badge.

"Official business," Carling said, making it sound like a command.

The security guard looked excited, awe-struck at being part of police business. He waved them through.

"He didn't even look at me," Matt almost pouted.

"He's too busy making up a story to tell his friends."

"And you wouldn't use the siren."

"Too noisy, and this car doesn't have one," Carling said. They made a sharp turn to the left. "The perimeter road takes us to the terminal. Try calling Payne now."

Matt waited for the call to connect. "Hold on, Susan." He turned to look at Carling for further instructions.

"Tell them the door outside international arrivals," Carling said.

Weaving through traffic on the approach to the main terminal reminded Matt of a taxi ride he once had in Moscow—drivers oblivious to any lane markings as they raced to get ahead of rivals. He never quite figured out how it was done without mishap.

Matt watched Carling slither through traffic. "You make it look easy. Anything to do with a flashing red light on the dashboard?" he said.

"I said no siren. You didn't ask about flashing lights," Carling smirked. "Look, there they are. Can you believe that pile of equipment and luggage?"

Susan hugged Matt. Matt wasn't the hugging type, but it felt good. "Let me help," Matt said, starting to lift a large case. "What the—"

"You picked the heaviest," Remy said. "Let's see you swing it into the trunk."

Carling held the trunk open, not offering to help. They all stood, not moving nor talking. "We may not have planned this, but I'm damned glad to see you both," he finally said.

With luggage and equipment finally stored in the trunk, they all started talking at once as the car pulled away from the curb. Finally, Remy yelled. "We can talk about old times later," he said. "I don't know about the rest of you, but I need to get that video to the studio."

• • •

They lapsed into silence, thinking about the real reason for this reunion. With light traffic, Carling turned right onto Rockledge-Hemphill Road. Approaching the studio, the asphalt paving on Cooper Street reflected soft street lighting. A light rain created patterns on the roadway surface, a falling leaf splatted on the windshield.

"Look, a parking place," Susan said.

Carling mumbled something about not needing to have her point it out, but they all knew he wasn't serious.

"Leave our luggage in the hallway. All I need are these two equipment cases," Remy said. He unlocked the office door and held it open for the rest of them. He turned on the lights. "Set my video cases anywhere. I have the card here." Remy tapped his shirt pocket. "It won't take long now."

They watched as Remy turned on the video editor.

"Roland V-800 editor," Remy said, a smug tone in his words. His left hand reached for a toggle switch as Matt looked on.

Matt watched Remy editing before, but only vaguely understood it all. There were labels for things like scaling, input, output, and position. One lever on the lower right corner looked like something from an airplane cockpit. He watched Remy slide it forward as his left hand toggled the position switch. A digital display showed transition, *whatever that is*, Matt thought.

Matt heard Remy's excitement. "I can free-scale and surpass even broadcast quality with the digital output. I have a full range of resolutions at my fingertips."

"Yeah, terrific," Carling grumbled to hide being impressed.

Matt's eyes widened when the TV monitor came to life, a 75-inch hi-def screen. "That set me back over seven large," Remy said. "Damn, I was afraid of that."He sounded embarrassed by the jerkiness of the first images. They knew he made the shot while running. They could hear his voice-over. "I'm sorry," he said to a young woman as he nudged past.

Carling sucked in a breath as they watched the picture zoom in on a crowd leaving an airport terminal. They waited for the video of the man boarding the parking shuttle.

Remy stopped the video and made some adjustments. "This isn't the best shot. Wait. The one we want is coming next." He toggled the video ahead. Now they could see the man.

"Look over your shoulder, damn it," Carling yelled. "I need it to be him," Carling slammed the clenched fist of his right hand into the palm of his left. "There've been sightings, but since he's officially dead, there's no investigative follow through. He was seen in the Bahamas. Then we saw him in Florida. Someone else said he was in Pittsburgh. What's the connection to those places? And now, New Zealand?"

"Quiet," Remy said. "Look at this."

They saw him turn to his right as he boarded a shuttle van. For a moment, his profile was visible.

Remy used the controls to freeze the picture. He tweaked adjustments and zoomed in. The screen filled with the head of the man in profile. "I can use software to enhance the picture," Remy said. "First, I need to transfer the video to the computer." The monitor flickered, the screen went dark, then an image reappeared. "That's from the computer now, instead of a direct feed. Watch this," Remy said. He clicked. The image pixilated briefly, then turned into a high-definition picture. "That's more like it."

All four said it at the same time. "That's Charles Claussen."

"No doubt about it," Matt said.

Carling shushed them. "Now we have to find out what the hell he's doing in New Zealand. He has to be getting help."

"Are you going to report this?" Matt asked.

"Why?" Carling said. "What good would it do now? Nobody wants anything to do with this anymore."

"Isn't anyone interested anymore?" Susan said. She was almost shouting. "It's an international case now. What about Interpol?"

"The riots and CleanSweep are in the past, in a file marked closed. Charles Claussen's been declared dead," Carling said.

"But this is proof," Matt said.

"We know it," Susan said. "You all know it, but Carling's right. What scares me is what he's planning to get even. We spoiled his nice little plan. He knows exactly who's to blame," she said, her arms circling. "He blames us!"

"Can you print pictures from that video, Remy?"

Matt thought Remy looked offended by the question.

Carling turned to Matt. "Grab our passports again."

"What the hell?" Matt said. "I've always wanted to see New Zealand. What's it like there, where you and Remy were filming?"

"New Zealand is two main islands," Susan said. "We were mostly on North Island. We had a contract to film and document sacred sites, places important to Maori culture. We wrapped filming and were scheduled to leave from Auckland, the only airport with a direct flight to San Francisco, but we had to do an extra two days, and our schedule was bent out of shape. We had to leave from Christchurch, on the South Island. That's where we saw Claussen."

"Almost three years and over nine thousand miles. What are the odds?" Remy added.

Nobody had an answer.

"We still have work to do on this project," Susan said. "A lot of money is riding on it."

"At least two more weeks," Remy said. "Susan and I'll be working non-stop to get the project edited. Then, the voice-over."

"Matt and I can go. Can you take time off, Matt?"

"Not a problem. If anyone objects, I'll quit."

"Same for me," Carling said and opened his phone. "Except for the quitting part, that is." Carling placed a call. After a moment, he said, "Sarah, it's Wallace."

The other three looked surprised at him using his first name. "Sarah, darlin', I need two tickets, first-class, to a place in New Zealand. Christchurch." The other three merely listened. "As soon as possible," he said. "She's getting them now," Carling said, holding the phone to his ear. "How much? Holy —"

"How much?" Matt said.

"For both of us? No way. Only one?" Carling said, clenching his jaw. "Are you kidding? No choice, Sarah. Make it happen and text me the tickets. Thanks, sugar." It was a side of Wallace Carling they had never seen.

"There goes my retirement plan if I had one. Only $16,390 each," Carling sighed

"We're a team," Susan said. "Keep track of expenses. We'll settle this at the end. What do you say, Remy?"

He nodded, turning quickly back to the video editor.

"That's settled," she said. "You guys have a long flight ahead of you, and it's smart to be in first class."

Carling looked at his notebook. "We fly from here to Charlotte," he said. "From there to Los Angeles. The long flight is the one to Auckland."

"You can get a short-haul flight to Christchurch if you want to trace him from there," Susan said.

Remy looked around. "No. Rent a car in Auckland. You guys will need a car anyway. It's not a long drive to Wellington, maybe seven hours. There's the Inter-Islander Ferry to Picton on the South Island. It's not far to Christchurch. You even get a boat ride," he said, turning back to the editing.

None of the others saw any humor.

"I wrote down the name of that shuttle company he used at the airport," Carling said. "We'll check that out first. Probably nothing, but we might be able to talk to the shuttle driver."

He turned to Matt. "Our flight leaves in less than thirty-six hours."

Matt nodded. "I'm thinking about another angle," he said. "I've arranged my meeting with Angela Vaughn. It might be interesting to see what she knows about Claussen that she hasn't told us." He walked over to the window, out of hearing. The others watched as he finished the call and turned.

"It's set for tomorrow. Vaughn's one frightened woman. I interviewed her about a year into her prison stretch. She didn't give me much in the way of new but said she'd always be looking over her shoulder for Claussen, or his ghost. She knows first-hand Claussen's thirst for vindictiveness. I remember it sent a chill through me when she said he would even try to reach us from the grave; I didn't doubt her."

"I'm out of here," Carling said and pushed back his chair. "Let's meet tomorrow and finalize details. I want to hear what Matt finds out from Vaughn. Our flight leaves at 11:24 PM tomorrow. We're not going to miss it. Does that give you enough time to meet Vaughn?"

Matt nodded. He put his jacket on and followed Carling. Before leaving, he turned. Remy was hunched over the keyboard of his video editor.

Susan leaned over Remy's shoulder, pointing at the screen. "I knew it was him."

CHAPTER 28

ANGELA VAUGHN

Matt checked the time. He wasn't going to be late for this interview. Her conditions were clear, no room for negotiation, and he intended to follow her directions to the letter.

"Look for a small park half of a block north of the library," Angela Vaughn said. "The one with concrete-slab tables used by chess players. The temperature tomorrow morning will be too cold for them. Do I need to say off the record again? No tape recorder. No Remington hanging around with his camera. I'll be there at 10:30, not a minute before nor after. If you're not there, I'll keep walking."

Matt understood why she was so distrustful. Anything connected to Charles Claussen had that impact on people.

Angela Vaughn had been head of security for Claussen's holding company, Enseûrtech. She was a key player and knew CleanSweep from the inside. Matt was hoping he could get more background about her role. *Maybe there's some small detail she can give me that we haven't thought of*, he thought.

The temperature hovering above freezing, Matt chose a suede jacket, his favorite. A scarf topped off the look he wanted, serious reporter, casual dress, and a disarming smile.

He climbed the stairs from the subway platform. At street level, he was greeted by a gust of cold wind. Matt turned north and raised his collar as a shield. It didn't help. He shoved his hands into pockets, hunching his shoulder to the wind. This was his favorite season, and the walk past the library warmed him. He marched with long strides until he spotted the small park.

The park, laid with flagstone, was sandwiched between buildings. Framed by a brick planter, rose-colored blossoms of Autumn Joy Sedum were the last holdout of the season. There was enough room for three square concrete tables, perfect for chess or checkers. Today, the square was deserted like she said it would be, an empty take-out cup swirling around a back corner.

Matt looked at his phone. *More than enough time*, he decided. He noticed Twin-City Roasters across the street. Coffee in hand, he walked back to sit at a table, wrapping both hands around the cup for warmth. He thought about rechecking the time when a shadow preceded Vaughn's arrival.

She wore a pea jacket over a wool sweater and, Matt guessed, expensive designer jeans. Angela Vaughn didn't say hello. She sat, folding her arms, and gave him a you-go-first look.

"Thanks for agreeing to meet," Matt said.

"We don't have a lot of time. Best skip the chit-chat and get right to it. You want to find out if I know anything about Claussen."

"Do you think he's alive? Do you know if he's alive?"

"Yes, to the first question."

"You're not answering the second," Matt pointed out.

"I never bought the official report," she said. "Claussen would've planned an escape clause. Suicide was the easy way out, holding a gun to his head as the report concluded. He would've planned chess-like moves instead," she said, like the game normally played at the table they were sitting at.

"Detective Carling told the same," Matt said. "When he looked at the crime scene photographs, he saw they overlooked an important detail. Remember that expensive watch he wore?"

"What about it? It cost him more than I paid for my condo."

"Carling noticed the watch on the corpse. It was a cheap watch you could buy on a street corner for twenty bucks."

"Like I said, I've always known he'd have an escape plan. I knew, or know him too well." Vaughn pulled her coat tight. "He would never leave his watch behind. It had some special meaning for him."

Matt opened his notebook.

"I said no notes," Vaughn snapped, starting to stand.

"I'm not writing anything, relax," Matt said as he flipped through the pages. "Here's what I want to ask. Did you know anything about that secret door, disguised as a part of the wall paneling? Carling was there when the investigators found it, but there wasn't any evidence it had been used."

"That's news to me."

"What was it like at the end, your last moments with him?"

Angela Vaughn closed her eyes. The look on her face could have been either concentration or intense loathing; Matt wasn't sure. He waited for her to add more.

"He talked like a man who'd lost everything," she said. "But there was ambiguity in his voice. He sounded like a man still in charge—you know, cold and steady. But there was something else. It was a paradox that didn't register then. In prison, I would lay in bed, trying to clear my mind. I replayed that scene over and over."

She looked at the takeout cup Matt was holding, the steam a memory, the coffee now cooled to the taste.

"Do you want some?"

"No." She waved her hand. "Not enough time. Let's finish this. Thinking back to that gory scene, I'm convinced he wasn't going to choose suicide. He said he loved me. Can you believe that crap?"

They both sat, Matt, absorbing that information.

"You didn't see that coming? He had a wife and children," Matt said.

She looked at him. "I could never understand why he kept letting me off the hook whenever I screwed up. Love? The word never crossed my mind. He kept all feelings well hidden."

"Did you have similar feelings toward him?"

"Here's a tidbit for your notebook you're not writing in. I'm gay. How could he have missed that? He knew background stuff about people working for him. So, no. Besides that, Claussen was menacing. I never felt comfortable around him." She paused. "There's more. He always conducted business as if someone was eavesdropping as if his office was bugged. The last time I was with him, he turned the music volume high and whispered into my ear. He said we would be together soon." Angela shuddered. "When we thought suicide, I figured he'd told me to do the same, to join him, some perverted suicide pact. He really thought I would agree to that? No, my suspicion leads me to the same conclusion as Carling. Claussen's pulled a Houdini act, disappearing behind smoke and mirrors. He'd really told me to wait for a signal to join him.

"I've never told anyone else another thing. His last words were about you—you and the other three. He said you would suffer for what you did to him."

"We only did our job," Matt said. It sounded hollow. "If he is alive, where is he, and why hasn't he made good on the threat?"

"That's why I agreed to meet with you. You asked me the second question. Did I know with certainty if Claussen is alive? He called me three days ago, wanting me to join him. He didn't like my answer. I fear there are five of us on his hit list."

"Did he say where?"

"No," she said. "Caller ID showed a +64 code. Do you know where that is?"

"New Zealand," Matt said.

As if to add an exclamation point, a gust of wind blew Matt's empty coffee cup across the square. Matt told Carling later he could see the temperature falling, matching Vaughn's chill.

Angela Vaughn stood abruptly, Matt scrambling to rise after her. Without a word, she handed him a card with a phone number and started to leave.

"Wait, please. Can we talk again?"

"More than talk," she snapped. "We're in this together, but I'll be well in the shadows," she said and started to leave again.

"Susan Payne saw him." Matt's words stopped her in her tracks. "He's definitely in New Zealand. Carling and I are leaving tomorrow. Can we talk when I know something more?"

"New Zealand. That's about as far from here as he can get. If he's been in hiding this long, he has serious help. Be careful. You won't hear anything until his cobra-like hiss. He won't rest until—" She didn't finish the thought. Vaughn walked to the corner of the square and was gone.

Matt pulled out his phone to report to his team.

CHAPTER 29

THE FOUR DEVILS

Despite a substantial amount of international air miles logged during his career, Claussen had never been to Inchon International Airport. Emerging from the gate, he looked around. He followed multi-lingual directional signs. Once again, he was on the run, looking over his shoulder, fearing capture. Once again, he cursed the reason for his predicament, Matt Tremain.

• • •

Claussen followed instructions to the letter, still bristling from the warning call. He was ready to leave when he got the second follow-up call. *That's the familiar voice from before*, he thought. *It sounds like someone else.*

"A ticket will be waiting," the man said. "Go to the Air New Zealand counter at Auckland Airport. They're code-sharing partners with Korean Air. Make it as soon as you can. Like before, it's a round-trip ticket to avoid red flags with security. Change planes in Hong Kong and take Korean Air to Inchon."

"What happens when I get to Inchon?"

"Someone'll meet you. Walk toward exit 6. There's a kiosk selling bus tickets. It'll be on your right."

"You make it sound..." Claussen said before he heard the call disconnect, his statement unfinished.

Preparing for another change of identity. How did The Brotherhood find where I was hiding this time? This must stop, he thought.

It wasn't the police he worried about. It was The Brotherhood. *They're behind those chasing me, the reason my life's in the balance,* Claussen thought. Claussen was caught between fear of The Brotherhood and craving revenge. It was an uncomfortable place.

I fooled the police. The inquest was a laugh, putting a rubber stamp on the police report. The report stated I was dead. But I didn't fool them, The Brotherhood. He shuddered at the thought back to the meeting with the secret backers. "We have more money than God," one said.

And a long reach, he was to discover.

• • •

Cyberia's computer detected a faint trace of jumbled chatter. He couldn't put this new data into context, but he knew it was about Claussen. *When I get my systems back online, I must give Matt a heads-up,* he thought.

• • •

Claussen met The Brotherhood for the first time in Paris. The first to arrive was the Bosnian, Vladimir Švajgel, a man with eyes that could freeze over hell. Claussen never heard of the man before, but knew he was a man to stay away from.

Next to arrive was the tall man from Argentina. He was always impeccably dressed, preferring a three-piece suit. Claussen always thought Julina Alves looked like a man in search of a tango partner. Alves let slip once that his father had been the favored personal bodyguard to Eva Peron. In the seventies, his father was aide to Jose Lopez Rega, responsible for carrying out 'specific tasks' for the secret police. He'd supervised terror and death squads, targeting groups or individuals with leftist ideas.

"¿Cuántos simplemente desaparecieron, se ha convertido en fantasma?" Arias spoke softly, holding a glass of wine.

How many disappeared? Indeed, Claussen wondered. How many people turned into ghosts during that time?

Charles Claussen thought Alves was a good example of the saying about the apple not falling far from the tree.

The last to arrive was the woman, the most fear-provoking. With a precisely timed grand entrance, she wore a chilly smile. "Rudainah Saja Basar," she said, speaking in English without a trace of native Arabic roots. "Unfortunately, Hsin Shen is attending to other business interests," she added. "He is fully informed of our proposed agreement, however."

Claussen watched the two men acknowledge her authority. It was subtle, hardly noticeable, but it was there. He half expected to see them kneel on one knee. She was clearly in charge. Claussen wondered if she kept a well-honed scalpel handy, ready to neuter any man who dared defy her.

He tried to ignore the fine print details of the agreement he was making, especially the clause about the penalty for non-payment.

"No signatures necessary," Alves said with an uplifted chin.

They became his secret financiers. "*Nacht und nebel*, night and fog," the woman said. Claussen smiled at the German phrase, convinced he would have more than enough to pay them back without difficulty once Cleansweep was in operation.

Faust sold his soul to one devil. Claussen walked out of that meeting with four devils holding a mortgage on his life.

• • •

With CleanSweep in ruins, Claussen was on the run from The Brotherhood. More unnerved than he would admit, a slight tremor of his right hand gave away his unease. *I must get out of this country now*, he thought. *The weather rules out flying to Auckland from here.*

Unfolding and smoothing out a roadmap, Claussen considered his options. He held his finger on the spot that marked Neils Beach. *I need a way to drive to Auckland. How long will it take*?

Claussen made a snap decision and used the throwaway phone one final time, entering Trevor's number. *Voicemail. Damn.* "Sorry, mate. The fish are biting. Off to sea. Leave a message at the tone. Ta."

Claussen didn't like the feeling. This was going wrong, his panic rising. *Why does Trevor's voice sound so familiar?*

He angled his head to one side, listening. *Is the storm abating?* The wind no longer lashed the side of the house with the same intensity. He pulled back a drape. There was enough visibility now to see the top of the trees on the lower slope. Rain bands were sweeping across the distance, leaving a trail of downpour that looked like it was swiped against the sky with an artist's paintbrush.

Looking around the room, he was determined to eliminate any traces. Claussen gathered ashes of burned papers and what remained of the laptop. He placed them outside the rear door. He walked around the room on last time, then took them to a fence line and buried the contents. *The rain should wash away the scrapings*, he thought. He threw the shovel over the railing, hearing it clatter against some rocks.

He gathered his rucksack and began the long hike to the highway. He zipped the collar, walking face into the wind and rain. There was no traffic. He passed a house with smoke curling from the chimney and a warming light from the windows, but this wasn't a time for a friendly visit with neighbors. Claussen kept walking.

Nobody was out and about when he got to Neils Beach. He didn't want to drive the rental in case it was being tracked. He hoped Trevor's pickup might be parked alongside his friend's trailer. There was a pool of water where the truck should have been. Claussen considered asking Reggie for help and decided it was too risky. He couldn't afford to leave a trail or a witness.

It was a long walk to Jackson Bay. Claussen shouldered his bag and started. The wind was still unfriendly, blowing off the ocean. The rainfall was a drizzle, more a nuisance. Claussen was wet, but walking helped maintain body heat. It was an hour's walk along the Haast-Jackson Bay Road. A steep hillside to his left, the ocean to the right, he wasn't in the mood for sightseeing. He was worried about what he expected to find at the end with the vague sense that Trevor left his truck there.

Approaching Jackson Bay, the fog and rain mixture was swept aside by a clearing wind. He saw the T-shaped wharf to his right, and slightly past, he spotted Trevor's pickup, parked alongside the side of the road. Other vehicles were parked haphazardly.

"You're late," a man said.

Claussen jumped, the way people do when startled.

"Sorry, mate. Didn't mean ta frighten ya. Your friends left over three hours ago. They had to go without ya. I'm too old to go anymore. I've finished cleaning the sheds."

Claussen nodded. "They went in this weather?"

"Aye, they're used to it," the man said. "We knew the storm's about to blow itself out. The fish are waiting."

The man rubbed a growth of beard, sounding like he was rubbing sandpaper. "Ya don't look like one of the crew. I know about everyone."

"I'm new," Claussen improvised.

"I'm heading to my place on Murka Island. Need a lift somewhere?"

Claussen heard suspicion in the man's words and chose his answer carefully. "Thanks, old-timer, but I've called someone," he said, holding his phone. "He'll be here as soon as his lazy wife fixes some breakfast. He lives in Neils." *I'm talking way too much,* he thought.

"Don't see many Yanks in this part of the country," the old man said and muttered something as he walked across the road. He opened the door to a two-seater electric car, an import from China. Claussen couldn't hear a sound as the electric motor pushed the car in reverse, then the driver turned to head north.

What did I hear? Carling wondered. *There was caginess.* Claussen was suspicious. *Then again, none of them really trust outsiders.* The encounter only added to Claussen's foreboding. *If the telephone warning's right, I'm in danger. What option do I have? Besides, it was only an old man and his electric car._*

He waited until the car was out of sight to act. Trevor's truck was unlocked, the key in the ignition, a common practice here. He tossed his knapsack onto the passenger seat and slid behind the wheel. Before starting the truck, he checked the contents, making sure the gun was loaded.

I can't take it on the plane, but what if I need it before I get to Auckland? he thought.

The Toyota pickup was eleven years old with more than 675,000 kilometers showing. The engine sounded well-maintained. He checked the gauge. There was enough fuel to make it to Hokitika if he drove with care. Four hours there and then another five hours to the Picton ferry terminal.

His shoulder hurt from tension, driving past the turnoff to Neils Beach. He thought he was unseen and soon relaxed, relaxed, rolling his head and shoulders to ease the stress. Ten minutes later, he approached the sharp turn to the left.

At the T-intersection, he looked right. Nothing.

Claussen looked left; a narrow one-way bridge spanned the Arawhata River and Murka Island. He paused at the intersection. Something was bothering him, and then he remembered. The old-timer said he lived on Murka Island. Nobody lives on Murka Island.

Shaking off misgivings, he started over the bridges. No cars were coming toward him on the one-way bridge. He was almost at the far side of the river when he saw a flash of red and movement to the right. A few meters past the bridge, a side road curled to the right before making a steep spiral down to the river bed. Locals used it for parking and access to the river.

Claussen saw the red SUV accelerating uphill on the steep slope. It happened too fast for evasive action, realizing they intended to block the road. He then saw the two-seater electric car in the rearview mirror, which blocked off the bridge. He saw the old-timer holding an automatic weapon. No escape in that direction.

Charles Claussen had one thing in his favor, and it might save him now: he could be decisive when needed. He might fret over possible outcomes while planning, but if the moment demanded quick action, he was the man.

Gearing down the pickup, he reached for the pistol. He'd seen an opportunity. In his haste, the driver of the Pathfinder SUV didn't completely block the road. It was a careless move and would prove costly. Claussen coasted until the pickup was almost stopped, then leaned out and took aim. He fired shots in rapid succession. The two men hadn't anticipated this.

The driver yelled and grabbed his leg as a bullet shattered bone. The second man, deciding he wasn't being paid enough to be a hero, fled into the brush.

Claussen eased alongside the SUV, aiming at the tires as he passed. Two shots dispatched the tires as the driver pleaded for help.

The two-seater electric car was speeding to catch him but was no match for the Toyota. The last thing Claussen saw was the old-timer standing beside his car, cell phone in hand.

Claussen needed one other mistake on their part. He hoped they intended the next trap in Christchurch. They would be wrong.

If they've anticipated my real choice, the ferry to the north island and the airport in Auckland, I'm caught. Claussen decided to roll the dice, mapping the route in his head.

He needed to refuel before Hokitika, just in case that's a place for an ambush.

The most likely trap's Kumara Junction. If they think I'm heading back to Christchurch, that would be the most promising choke point, he thought strategically.

Approaching the Hokitika bridge, he turned right. A road led upstream toward another bridge. Crossing the river, he reached an intersection and a road to the town. He refueled, careful to use one of his remaining credit cards.

• • •

Rubbing blood stained eyes, Cyberia looked at a computer screen glowing to life. He sipped strong tea, the sound of the latest Russian heavy metal band on the speakers. He took note of the Kiwibank credit card number displayed, a number identified by his monitoring software.

He sipped his tea, holding a sugar cube between his lips, and smiled.

• • •

Charles Claussen skirted the main street through Hokitika. Approaching Kumara Junction, he slowed but didn't see any sign of an ambush. He kept his hand on the gun as he drove. Claussen looked for likely hiding places for an ambush, spotting nothing that stood out. He raced through the round-about, passing the road that branched east in the direction of Christchurch. He drove so fast the truck leaned precariously but didn't tip over.

As the truck skidded, he almost hit a car with two men, their startled looks passing in a blur.

Odd. The two in the car look familiar, he thought. Claussen chalked it off to fatigue and was soon heading north. Four and a half hours later, he approached the ferry terminal at Picton. He was on high alert, his nerves flashing S.O.S. signals to his brain.

He parked and walked into the ferry terminal. He didn't have to wait long. "A departure in fifty-two minutes," the clerk said, handing over the tickets.

"How long will it take me to get to Auckland?" Claussen said. The clerk looked like he was trying to solve an advanced mathematics formula as he thought of the answer. "Including the ferry crossing, about twelve hours."

When the ferry was underway, Claussen found a seat with no one around and was soon asleep.

"Almost there, mate." Someone said, touching his arm, which surprised Claussen, but it was only one of the stewards.

Claussen managed, "Thank you."

Eight hours later, he stood at the Air New Zealand customer service counter. *Auckland airport looks the same as airports all over the world.* He'd left Trevor's pick-up in long-term parking, the key still in the ignition.

"Your boarding passes, sir," the woman said, handing them over the counter. "Your flight leaves in a little over two hours," she said, looking at the computer screen. "Enjoy your flight."

Claussen let out a long sigh of relief.

• • •

"□□□□□□□□; □□□□□ □□□□□□□□□□," Cyberia mumbled. At his desk in Moscow, he examined a printout, using a highlighter to mark numbers. The printout was like he'd said in Russian, "Interesting; most interesting."

He typed an e-mail. "To Matt from Cyberia. Subject: Possible sighting of an old friend."

Deciding to wait a bit longer to see where the trail was leading, he parked the e-mail in the draft file.

"□□□ □□□□□ □□□□□□ □□□□□□□ □□□□□," Cyberia said aloud. "The tea is indeed exquisite this morning," in English.

• • •

Claussen's head pressed against the backrest as the plane hurtled down the runway, the wheels finally breaking free from the concrete. With a steep ascent and slight turn, the plane headed north and west. He looked down at the ticket in his hand.

He tried to be inconspicuous looking around the cabin, ignoring the whining complaint from his seatmate about legroom and space. *Eleven hours next to a woman who must weigh over 300 pounds. If she goes to sleep, she probably snores like a chainsaw.* He guessed right; she did.

Exiting the plane, he looked around the familiar, ultra-modern airport in Hong Kong, a place he'd visited often. He wondered who might be a spotter, looking for him. He imagined someone holding a photo to compare with each passenger deplaning with him.

One more transfer and I should be safe in Korea, he though. Fidgeting during the layover in Hong Kong, Claussen wandered the terminal but didn't see anyone who posed a danger. Then again, he knew he wouldn't likely see danger until it was too late.

Who could possibly follow me here, then to Korea?

Claussen heard the announcement in several languages; fortunately, there was one in English. It was his cue to head to the boarding gate.

He was near collapse when he buckled the seatbelt. *Why Korea?* he wondered again. He fell asleep, snapping awake as the plane descended. "Ladies and gentlemen, welcome to Inchon International Airport, where the time is—"

Bearing the tension of two long flights behind him—along with the interminable wait at customs and immigration—he walked into the terminal at Inchon International Airport. As tired as he was, he looked around at the design, the clean lines of the airport interior. He followed directional signs for Exit 6.

Claussen saw a massive hulk of a man ahead, freezing at the thought he'd been sent by The Brotherhood. He had the exact blank look professional bodyguards have. What Claussen didn't see coming was the man walking from behind the giant. Wearing a well-cut suit and a disarming smile, Trevor, his fisherman friend from New Zealand, stepped forward.

"I'll bet you didn't expect me, did you?"

CHAPTER 30

SEA CRUISE TO VLADIVOSTOK

Now, I'm on a trawler heading to Russia. Can it be any more surreal? Claussen stood next to the captain. *Fourteen hours, over half-way*, Claussen calculated. Surging waves raised and fell coming out of a fog bank, vanishing behind the boat. Whitecaps mesmerized Claussen. He tried to fight off their hypnotic effect, his mind wandering.

How much longer can this go? I've had another narrow escape. How many does that make over the past three years? They're getting closer each time. Now, heading to Russia? My dream of revenge is facing another stumbling block.

Charles Claussen's thirst for revenge hadn't diminished. He was as determined as ever. Still, a feeling of uncertainty nibbled around the edge of his thoughts. He began to doubt his resolve for settling the score, though his loathing for Matt Tremain and partners hadn't abated. They had destroyed his dream as CleanSweep was being implemented. He vowed to get even. *But when? From Russia?* he wondered.

He was exhausted and frightened. He thought about The Brotherhood again. They were more terrifying than the police. The four devils holding the mortgage to his soul had resources that surpassed many governments. They'd been relentless in tracking him down. *Now, I know I've run out of options*, Claussen thought.

The Bahamas worked. Apalachicola was a safe place to hide, but I screwed that up. Then, the cockroach hotel in Pittsburgh didn't last long. New Zealand was a disaster. And now? My life is in the hands of a smiling

Korean, a gigantic bodyguard, and Trevor. Now that's strange. First, Trevor's a fisherman. Then he turns into a tour guide?

"Now I know why you sounded familiar back at Jackson Bay," Claussen said to Trevor. "All those phone calls in the past, warning me. Your voice. I should've known."

The trawler pitched to starboard, interrupting him. He remembered why he was here, fleeing into the unknown. He stood on the bridge of a fishing trawler over fifteen hours now, unable to sleep or eat.

Claussen visualized the map. He'd memorized a line on the chart. It was 344 nautical miles from Ulleung to Vladivostok, roughly 396 statute miles. His engineer's mind loved numbers and problems. It also helped distract him from worrying too much.

A lifetime of self-discipline made Claussen believe he'd mastered his brain, solving problems, multitasking, always functional. While people sought a balance between intellect and emotions, Claussen trained his brain to rule. He considered himself above emotions—except for his passion about CleanSweep, his failed project. And there was Angela Vaughn.

Claussen's body echoed the vibration of the pulsating diesel engine, the steel under his feet rising and falling as each wave lifted the trawler, then lowered into the waiting arms of the next wave.

"Brewed this for you," a voice from behind said. Trevor stepped through a hatchway balancing two mugs. "Unless you'd like something stronger."

The mate stood with his hands on the wheel, eyes on the compass.

"I'm told he doesn't understand English," Trevor said.

Claussen nodded.

"The weather's improving," Trevor said.

Claussen didn't respond at first. "We have a bit over fourteen hours to go," he said. "Choe told me we'll make landfall after midnight. He said the timing was critical."

"This isn't his first rodeo, partner."

"While you were sleeping, I checked out the boat. It looks rough topside, but below it's an engineer's dream, not a speck of grime nor dirt."

Trevor puckered and puffed at the steam rising from his cup, his eyes shifting from the rain-splattered windshield back to Claussen, saying nothing.

"The mechanical equipment's in perfect running order," Claussen said. "I think Choe likes to disguise his trawler's looks."

"It suits his purposes," Trevor agreed.

"I memorized the chart," Claussen said. "Over three hundred nautical miles from Ulleung to Vladivostok. The engineer's English isn't that great, but when I asked, he told me they tow the seine net at speeds less than eight knots. But now we're cruising at top speed, close to thirteen knots. We've covered over half the distance—"

"Vladivostok not safe," The captain of the boat, Captain Choe, interrupted Claussen. "Too many radars and nosey people. Something's wrong." He said something in Korean to the pilot.

"We're changing course," Trevor said, interpreting for Claussen.

Choe motioned Trevor and Claussen to follow him to the chart room.

"We not go Vladivostok," Choe said. "Now Bukhta Pavlovskogo."

"Why?" Claussen demanded. His fluency in Russian didn't include what Bukhta meant precisely. By inference, he guessed it meant it was a bay or gulf. Trevor put a hand on his shoulder, a calming gesture.

"My English not good enough." Choe turned to Trevor, and they exchanged a rapid-fire conversation in Korean.

"Choe got a text," Trevor explained. "Security in the Vladivostok area's been tightened. He's told there're military maneuvers. The navy is looking for a boat like this."

The radio hissed static, and they heard something in Russian. Claussen wasn't fluent, but he caught most of the words. "That's a search team reporting. They say the overcast's clearing," he said.

"Weather much better soon," Choe said, adding something in Korean.

"Our captain speaks Russian," Trevor said.

"Has this happened before?" Claussen wanted to know.

The young mate at the wheel yelled something back over his shoulder.

"Damn," Trevor said. "A plane's coming this way."

The three hurried back to the bridge, staring at two planes approaching. The planes were coming bow on—and fast. Claussen could see they were military. They passed on either side of the trawler with a deafening blowback from the engines.

"They're turning, coming back," Trevor said, sounding calm.

This time, the pass was at a much slower speed, flying so low that Claussen could make out facial features.

A voice in Russian demanded identification. Choe answered immediately, a strained look. "They send two boats to intercept." Seeing the panic on Claussen's face, he said, "We're only fishing boat. Not to worry." The captain leaned and said something to the ship's pilot in a low voice. The young man nodded and turned the wheel a few degrees to the right. "Maybe we reach Pavlovskogo Bay before they find us. No worry. We will get you off the boat first, perhaps."

Perhaps is not a word I like. It's easy for you to say, Claussen thought. He looked at the cup in his hand. The coffee was no longer hot, but warm enough, and Claussen needed a caffeine jolt. He worried about that word, perhaps.

Captain Choe beckoned them aft of the bridge deck. His cabin was a tidy area, enough room for a desk and bunk with a stainless-steel sink in one corner and an aluminum toilet in the other. Choe walked over to the mirror above the sink. He pointed to a small object above the mirror. Claussen thought it was a nightlight until Choe touched it. A panel opened far enough for someone to step through.

He explained it to Trevor, who translated. "The captain said if we're boarded, you and I'll hide in here. He'll have them check the fish and equipment, keeping them away from his cabin."

Claussen saw room enough room for the two of them to stand. His lingering nausea from riding out the storm was still a worry, but he vowed he wouldn't let it get the best of him. He wondered if he should tell someone he was terrified of close quarters, especially in the dark.

The flashback was immediate. He remembered the last time he'd slipped through a false panel, with the police breaking in his office door.

Choe used the intercom microphone, speaking to the pilot. Then he turned to Trevor and Claussen. "Get something eat now."

They followed him out the starboard side and down a companionway to the lower deck. A tall man wearing a white coat gestured to the table. Soon, the cook carried trays with bowls of rice, shrimp, Juipo, and a variety of vegetables. He brought another plate with customary sides of kimchi, spicy bean sprout salad, and fried anchovies with peanuts.

Claussen took chopsticks and started eating. He turned to Trevor. "I'm getting used to Korean food, but what's this?" he said. He pointed to round, beighe-colored, flattened objects, wrapped with something red. "It's salty but quite good," Claussen said.

"That's Juipo. It's like fish jerky." Trevor said something to the cook. "He said it's made from seasoned filefish, then pressed down."

Choe said something. "He says we should get some rest. He'll wake us when it's time," Trevor translated.

Choe gave an order to a crew member resting in a chair. The man stood quickly and bowed. He led Claussen and Trevor to the crew's quarters and pointed out different berths they could use.

Claussen saw Trevor's bodyguard already stretched out with his hands locked behind his head. He seemed relaxed but was very much alert. Wearing denim and a sweater, he looked like another part of the crew, until the shirt was pulled high enough to reveal a handgun tucked into the jeans.

• • •

Claussen couldn't sleep, listening to the groaning sounds boats made when underway and the diesel engine's constant hammering tempo. He looked at Trevor, mouth open, breathing slowly like a man at peace with himself.

Claussen was finally able to sleep until he heard the announcement. "You come up now!" Choe, the captain, announced over the intercom.

Claussen and Trevor stood immediately, both alert. The bodyguard was already standing by the door, ready to go. The three raced for the ladder to the bridge.

"It's like we're a speck in the universe," Claussen said. "I've never seen such an inky black canopy overhead, yet stars create ambient light, almost enough to read by."

He watched Choe point to the left. The remarkable display of stars extended to the horizon where it met other lights.

Trevor translated Choe's Korean into English. "That's Pavlovskogo on the other side. We'll make a slight detour into Bukhta Otkrytaya."

CHAPTER 31

CHANGING COURSE

Claussen watched the young pilot reach for the throttle, slowing the trawler. The captain hurried his three passengers to the deck below, ready to hide if necessary.

"Wait here."

They heard the distinctive sound of outboard motors. "Twin engines," Claussen thought aloud.

The approaching boat came into the light from the trawler. Claussen saw a tall man at the wheel and a short, pudgy man aft. He guessed the length at twenty-five feet and saw twin Yamaha outboards, 250 HP each. *Impressive*, he thought.

Claussen thought he was past surprise. The two men wore Islamic skull-caps and were dressed in waist-length Kurta shirts. *Whatever I expected in this remote part of Russia, it wasn't Muslims*, Claussen thought.

Trevor interpreted for the captain, who was obviously urging them to hurry.

"He'll slow to let them come alongside. We won't have much time. Be ready to jump. It's risky, but we don't have a choice. Once we're in the other boat, Choe will report to officials at the wharf in Pavlovskogo for the official inspection," Trevor said, laughing.

"Uppermost, our next tour guides need us ashore before Fajr," Trevor said, looking at Claussen's confusion. "Fajr—the prayer offered between first light and sunrise. They are devout."

As Trevor said that, the trawler slowed even more. The other boat pulled alongside, almost colliding. The captain judged the time and yelled a command.

His three passengers leaped in unison, landing on the deck of the other boat, skidding on fish scales and sliding to the gunwale on the far side. Their luggage came soaring after them, landing on the deck, bouncing and whirling.

"Any broken bones?" Trevor yelled as they struggled to their feet. They turned to wave a thank you to Choe, but the trawler turned sharply, and all they saw was the transom disappearing into the darkness.

They grabbed a handhold as the twin motors came to life. The boat reached the plane, skimming small waves, as they headed toward the shore. The man at the helm turned and said something in Russian. Claussen responded, and the man nodded.

"He wants to know if we speak Russian. My grandfather insisted I learn it," he said. "He told me to learn the language of the real enemy. Russia would always be the enemy. He says it's almost time for prayer."

The man at the helm judged the distance, stopped the motor, and the boat drifted until it kissed the sand. His passengers stepped out on dry sand.

"That was impressive," Claussen said.

Claussen listened to words in Russian and turned to Trevor. "I got most of what he said. We're supposed to follow that path. Someone will meet us on the road. If no one's there, we wait. There're trees and a hedge for cover."

Trevor and the large bodyguard followed Claussen as they walked along the path. In the faint light, Claussen turned to watch the men from the boat spreading out prayer rugs.

The bodyguard spoke, the first time Claussen heard him talk. "The mats are necessary. They must cover the ground. It has to be a clean surface when they pray." The bodyguard then lapsed into silence.

CleanSweep would have gotten rid of that drivel, Claussen thought. *A clean place to pray, indeed. They would've been targeted. We'd all be better off without Muslims. The very idea that they think a rug offers a clean place to pray. What nonsense.*

• • •

The path led up a hill to a paved road. The huge bodyguard raced ahead, looking both ways. He motioned Claussen and Trevor ahead.

"Does he have a name?"

"Ari Levitsky. Everyone calls him Lev."

"He's a Jew?"

"Israeli," Trevor said, cutting off Claussen's question. "I trust him more than any man or woman I know. If I gave him the word, you'd be dead," Trevor pointed his finger, imitating a pistol. "It might be best not to mention Cleansweep around him," he added, hiding a smile at Claussen's discomfort.

They joined the bodyguard. Claussen looked carefully, almost staring. *I'm in Russia with a Jew as my bodyguard. My nightmare is complete.*

A vehicle approached at a high rate of speed, headlights blinking as it skidded to a stop.

"I didn't expect a Cadillac Escalade," Trevor said. "Talk about subtle and blending in. And, look at her," Trevor added. "Our driver can't be fifteen if she's a day."

"In the back, quick. Duck down if I say so," the young girl said. "I'm Sasha," she introduced herself, turning the Escalade in a tight circle. The tires spun to gain traction, the gravel clattering. Once on the pavement, it was clear Sasha was a skilled driver. *She clearly loves driving fast*, Claussen thought.

At an intersection, Sasha glanced in both directions before turning left. Shortly, they were behind a slow-moving military truck. Sasha flicked the headlights, signaling intent to pass. Two young soldiers leaned out making rude gestures, the sexual implications clear.

Sasha ignored them, passing the truck on the right shoulder. Pulling alongside, Sasha lowered the window and extended her left hand, gesturing, her hand and fingers curled, and her thumb thrust between middle and index fingers.

"It's the Russian version of the finger," Claussen said at Trevor's confusion, "but far ruder."

Sasha pushed the Escalade to ninety km/h on the straightaways, barely slowing around curves. The huge SUV was forgiving, but her three passengers grabbed handholds whenever they spotted a curve ahead.

Claussen looked at his watch. They'd been driving for more than an hour. He wished he had a map to see how long o a ride he was in store for. He hated being at the mercy of anyone, let alone a young Sasha. She slowed, straining to look at something. "Ahead, that road to the right," she said, looking at Claussen in the mirror. *Keep your eyes on the road*, Claussen thought irritably.

Sasha approached the turn-off at a rate of speed that made her passengers cringe. The Escalade leaned precariously as she turned onto a gravel road, swallowed by a grove of trees. After several S-curves rising in elevation, they reached a crest. Once over the top, they descended into a valley and approached a wooden bridge over a swift-running stream. A dacha sat in a clearing, a smaller hut set back to the right.

Claussen wanted to hide his eyes, convinced the bridge wasn't strong enough to support the huge SUV, but it was.

"Welcome to your dacha," Sasha said.

When Claussen visited Moscow, he was often invited to someone's dacha, or summer home, on the outskirts of the city.

"These aren't much more than huts. It's a wild stretch to call them dachas," Claussen said.

Sasha glared at him. "Would you rather have a fucking tent and sleeping bag? You can carry your own luggage," she said, her hands on her hips and pouting.

As soon as they had their stuff out of the Escalade, she didn't wait for them to carry anything to the cabins. She was back in the car, speeding away. Claussen cringed again, watching her drive over the bridge.

"My daughter was like that at fifteen," Trevor said. "Sweet one minute, the next, vinegar."

"My children never behaved that way," Claussen said. "They were taught to respect their elders." He noticed the odd look both Trevor and Ari gave him.

• • •

"We need to talk," Claussen said, a sharp edge to his words.

Trevor tossed his carry-all onto a bed next to the kitchen area. He turned and shrugged. "I know."

"Surprise doesn't even begin to cover it, getting off a plane in Korea and seeing you," Claussen said. "What's the word I'm looking for? I was gobsmacked. Do you know what that means? It means astonished. No, more than astonished, it means utterly surprised. You disappear from the end of the road on New Zealand's South Island, and now, you're in Korea."

Trevor smiled a crooked smile.

"What puzzles me is that I was starting to think of you as a friend, and I don't have many of those in my inventory."

"I've been a part of your life since your vanishing act nearly three years ago," Trevor said simply.

Claussen was looking around the interior of the dacha window and turned suddenly, looking at Trevor, a question on his face. "Who are you?"

"Do you believe in guardian angels?"

"Who are you," Claussen demanded, his voice rising in pitch.

"You arranged it, the way a politician might establish a blind trust, a way to manage something without your involvement." Trevor walked over to a cupboard. "Ah, some strong coffee sounds good to me. Why don't I fix some and we can talk?"

Claussen started a rebuttal, then gave in.

Trevor measured out the coffee, poured in water into the coffee-maker, and turned on the flame. "I need to check the perimeter. This should be finished when I get back. Then, we can talk."

Claussen followed Trevor to the door, watching him walk to the smaller cabin. Lev waited in the doorway, a pair of binoculars hanging around his neck and an automatic weapon in his left hand. He held it casually, in the manner of professionals comfortable with such weapons. Claussen watched the two talking and gesturing. He saw Lev nod and trot toward a row of trees at the top of a nearby hill. The trees shielded the cabins from the road. He watched Lev scan the horizon, then move between two trees, blending in.

Trevor likewise scanned the perimeter. He took a last look and walked back, giving a thumbs-up signal to Claussen.

"Safe from The Brotherhood for one more night," Claussen shouted into the wind.

CHAPTER 32

PRAYER MATS

Something needs to change. This isn't getting me anywhere! Claussen thought as he waited for Trevor.

"Where's our friendly bodyguard?" Claussen asked.

"For a big man, he makes himself invisible," Trevor said. "How are you doing? This must feel like a wild rollercoaster ride."

"It's time to stop the ride," Claussen said, making no attempt to hide his bluntness. "You implied that you're my guardian angel. I'm putting it together. I hear it in your voice. It was you giving me warnings all along."

Claussen watched Trevor nod. "What lengths are you willing to go to help me?"

"You've paid well," Trevor said, then paused as if searching for the right words. "I've even grown fond of you. I cheered for CleanSweep. It should have worked. The police and government are so embarrassed they'll want to keep the truth well buried. It's awkward for them to admit it almost worked. But it isn't the government you have to worry about, is it?"

Claussen's face drained of blood. He knew who Trevor was talking about. He started to say something but realized Trevor wasn't finished.

"The Brotherhood's agents came close to catching you at least twice, too close for comfort. That's not your only problem, however. It's your thirst for revenge that will do you in. Are you listening? That business in Florida was pure nonsense, allowing the detective and the amateur blogger to get the upper hand." He paused and gave Claussen the stink-eye.

"If I didn't have Teddy Roosevelt planted in your crew, you would be gator bait on a river bank in Florida."

Claussen marched in place to warm himself. The temperature in this part of Russia dropped like a lead sinker on a fishing line when the sun went down. "I'm asking again. How far are you willing to go for me?"

Trevor looked down at his shoes, then back, looking Claussen in the eyes. "As my father would say, in for a penny, in for a pound. Guess that about covers it."

"What about your gigantic friend?"

"He'll have our backs, absolutely."

"I admit you've done a good job protecting me, but it won't be long before I'm in the talons of The Brotherhood of Eagles. If I'm caught, I want my revenge first."

"What do you want to do," Trevor asked.

"Toronto."

"You're crazy. Your bloodthirsty craving for revenge is your downfall."

Claussen shrugged. "That may be, but I'll go with a smile, knowing they're all dead. Matt Tremain first. Carling next. I want to do Payne and her cameraman at the same time. Vaughn could have had it all. She'd be here now." Claussen's rage was like molten lava, ready to spew in a volcanic eruption. "I can't help it, Trevor. I dream of strangling Vaughn at the split second of her orgasm," Claussen said, the rage ebbing as he admitted that.

"You do know she's a lesbian, right?" Trevor said.

Claussen shook his head and waved that away. "They're all in Toronto now. They must be. Help me, please." It was near impossible for Claussen to use the word, please.

Trevor started to pace, three steps to the left, three steps to the right, then back again. He stopped, raising his hands in mock surrender. "What the hell. Let's pull a Bogart and go down with guns blazing."

"This means snap planning," Trevor said. "It's getting dark. My guess is the dacha is supplied with some damn good vodka," Trevor said, and the two men began searching cupboards.

• • •

"Another drink, Trevor?" Claussen said, waiting to hear a plan.

"I can get us from here to there. Clandestine border crossings are as old as… Let's just say they've been around a long time. Sometimes the authorities turn the other way; sometimes they don't know."

Claussen and Trevor sat in front of the fireplace that dominated an entire wall of the dacha. The vodka and blaze made Claussen drowsy. "I sat in front of a fire like this at Winston Overstreet's lodge. It was a remote lodge, like this. We were there getting ready to launch CleanSweep," Claussen said.

Trevor wasn't listening. He'd been on his satellite phone for over two hours, gesturing as if the other person could see him. "Here's the plan," he finally said after disconnecting. "I pushed for Alaska, but that's not going to work; too far. Sometimes the best way is the shortest."

"Get on with it, man."

"We've got to meet a plane at the beach where we came ashore. We've got roughly twenty-four hours. The pilot's named Gennady. He has a float plane. Once underway, we'll be flying barely above the waves. One rogue wave, it's over. It's dangerous, but the only way. We need to hope he's sober and make sure he doesn't have a bottle stashed."

Claussen fought off drowsiness and listened.

"He flies a Beriev," Trevor said. It's a funny looking plane, with twin motors attached to the fuselage instead of the wings."

"You mentioned the shortest route. Where're we going?"

"A small village called Rumoi on the west coast of Japan's north island," Trevor said. "The flight's a bit over four hundred miles. We'll land before it gets light. A contact will take us from there to the airport in Asahikawa. It's a small, modern airport with great connections. This is important," Trevor added. "The best cover stories are simple. We're in the Rumoi area visiting old shrines. You got a call your business partner died suddenly. We need an emergency flight back to Vancouver. "

Claussen's face broke into a grin. "One step ahead of The Brotherhood. They're expecting me to go west. I'm heading east."

"They may have a rough idea you're near Vladivostok, but I'm pretty sure The Brotherhood doesn't know about Lev and me yet," Trevor said. "We need to do something about your looks. Governments—and The Brotherhood—use video feeds at airport terminals to match images in their database. Facial recognition programs are hard to fake, and you were flying into Christchurch. Lev and I will pass. We're not in any database. Don't ask me how I know. Your face is known, however."

"What can I do?" Claussen asked.

"We will decide when we land," Trevor said.

• • •

The pilot, Gennady, was mostly sober. The flight was uneventful as was the landing near Rumoi. A guide met them and led them to a small apartment as the sun rose.

Claussen thought about the two Russians spreading their prayer mats.

"You're going to have an accident," Trevor said. "You were photographing the Hokokuji temple when you got the call your partner died of a massive heart attack. You were shocked. In your grief, you lost your balance and fell down the long flight of stairs at the entrance. It'll hurt," Trevor added, handing Claussen a large glass. "Vodka will help some, but it's going to hurt a lot. Drink it all."

Claussen drank until he felt dizzy, his eyes drifting.

"Lev will make it look good — or bad — depending on your point of view. You'll look like had a nasty stumble. Too bad about what the fall did to your face." He whistled, and Lev walked in, ducking under the top of the door frame.

While the large man was pummeling him, Claussen focused on killing Matt Tremain. That, and large swallows of vodka, neat, helped withstand the beating. Lev took no pleasure rearranging Claussen's face; it was simply a task. The right cheekbone of Claussen's head was crushed in, contorting his face into a strange rearrangement. Unconscious, his head leaned forward. He was dead weight when he was lifted from the chair and placed on the bed.

"The sleep will help, but high-dose Percocets will help even more. Either way, we'll have him on the plane to Vancouver."

CHAPTER 33

IT'S HIM

"**A** robust Sumatra blend for my favorite customer," she said, placing a mug on the table. The barista looked over his shoulder as he spread photographs on the table.

Marsha was one of his few friends. "Thanks," he muttered, rearranging the pictures like he was playing three card monte. "Sorry, Marsha. I guess I'm preoccupied."

"Don't fret, Matt. Aren't those photos of Claussen?"

Matt nodded and covered the pictures.

• • •

Looking at the Florida photo of Claussen Tommy, the Ghost, sent that fateful day in Apalach, Matt was deep in thought. *I've never seen him wearing clothes like that. He was always dressed to the nines. That's a camo jacket he's wearing? This other photo, Claussen with a scruffy three-day growth and wearing jeans.*

"Where's he now? Matt said aloud. "That's what worries me; we don't—"

"I know, and we have every reason to be worried," Detective Carling said.

"What's happening?" Susan Payne said, following close behind him. "Remy's feeding the meter."

"I can take orders before you get started," Marsha said from behind the counter.

Carling didn't appreciate chic coffeehouse menus. "Spoiled by cop shop java," he once told Matt. "That and being single." Despite this, he surprised them today. "Marsha, one of your frothy espressos, *por favor.*"

"Italian roast for me, and the same for Remy." Susan and Remy weren't married, but she ordered for him the way longtime married couples did.

"Hey guys," Remy said, joining the group. "I hate this traffic. Makes me think about moving to New Zealand. We should have taken the Red Rocket trolley instead of driving."

They looked at him, knowing he was a committed city kid. He'd never survive rural life anywhere, let alone New Zealand.

"Down to business," Carling said, taking charge. "When you started hearing rumors about Clausen's plan to implement Operation Clean-Sweep, why didn't you take your information to the authorities? I've always wondered about that."

"We tried," Matt said. "They blew me off. The authorities didn't take me seriously. I look back, knowing Claussen already had people on the inside as part of the planning to implement the program."

"The same for me," Susan Payne said. "The station's lawyers told us to back off." She stabbed at one of the photos with a coffee stirrer. "There's Claussen at one of his press conferences with the mayor with a smile a kilometer wide. The same with the Premier. They were like puppies on a leash."

They paused while Marsha brought their orders. "I'll leave you guys alone. Shout if you need anything."

"When the CleanSweep conspirators were exposed, only one eluded capture: Claussen," Matt said. "How did he pull off his escape and manage to elude—?"

"The government preferred it to be suicide and made it official, just like Claussen hoped." Susan interrupted. "Even faced with evidence, they preferred suicide. The whole episode was such an embarrassment for them and their involvement."

"The C word again, conspiracy," Remy said.

Carling listened, knowing the story. "I want us to keep our minds on what we're dealing with," he said. "We're on our own and have the most to lose. The authorities aren't going to help. Claussen has a target on our backs. He could be walking in the door right now."

The other three turned around to look as a reflex.

"See what I mean," Carling said, watching their reaction. "If we don't know where he is, well..."

"New Zealand, of all places," Remy said. "And at the same time we were there. That's creepy."

"It was evident he didn't expect Remy and I to be there at the same time," Susan Payne said. "He may have seen us, but I somehow doubt it. We hardly recognized him." Susan described the airport encounter in Christchurch once more, even though they'd already heard the story.

Then, they told Susan and Remy about their own hurried, futile flight to New Zealand.

"It was a wasted trip. Carling and I went to New Zealand," Matt said. "We followed your advice and rented a car in Auckland. But Claussen eluded us again. All we did was get close, maybe," Matt said.

"We did get close," Carling said. "I saw surveillance video from Auckland. He was boarding a plane to Hong Kong." He grimaced. "Two things. One, he's still listed in the computer as dead. That flummoxed the facial recognition database. That's fixed now, but it's too late. Second. If he ended up in Hong Kong, the airport doesn't exchange data with the Five Eyes."

"What's that?" Matt said. "You keep mentioning five eyes."

"The United States, Canada, Australia, New Zealand, and the UK have a data-sharing agreement," Carling explained. "They call it Five Eyes. They use the information to track terrorists, drug shipments, and the like. It was one of their programs that matched his photo when he entered New Zealand. It was a match. But since he's officially deceased, they chalked it up to a computer glitch."

"Any idea of where he might have gone from Hong Kong, or is he still there?" Susan sipped her coffee.

"That's why I called us together," Matt said. He gestured to the photos on the table. "I've done some research with help from Carling's team."

"Facial recognition programs look for geometrics," Carling said. "When the program scans distinguishing features, it's looking for photometric details, matching them against a database. In this case comparing, against a recorded photo of Claussen. There are attempts to alter appearances, using a mask, hat or makeup, but it's hard to change the eyes. Contact lenses have been tried, but doesn't disguise the photometrics," Carling said, pausing.

"This is Charles Claussen," he said, jabbing at a photograph he placed on the table. I'm betting the farm on it."

"How can you tell?" Matt wanted to know. "It doesn't look like him."

"Look closely, Matt. It's the face of someone who's had an accident, like a nasty fall. It was done on purpose, that ugly purple bruise and swelling change the shape. That bandage adds another level of disguise the face. But..."

The other three stared at the evidence.

"He couldn't change the eyes," Carling went on. "It looks like they tried using contact lenses. I matched this against Claussen's file photo. It's him, alright. He's with two men. The shorter of the two with him isn't tagged; he's flying under the surveillance radar. I don't know who the shorter man is, but that big one," Carling said, "is Ari Lev Levitsky. He's someone to be reckoned with. Trained in the Israeli military, he was recruited by Mossad. He was too frightening, even for them."

"Okay," Susan Payne started. "If it's Claussen, when and where was that picture taken?"

"Vancouver, three hours ago."

The only sound in The Beanery was Marsha cleaning coffee mugs.

CHAPTER 34

PLANES AND TRAINS

His face hurt worse than anything experienced or imagined. Claussen sat back as the Japan Airlines Flight JL-018 began the descent into the Vancouver airport. Each sudden movement made the pain worse.

The transfer at Tokyo International Airport was problem-free. They passed through security and boarded the flight to Canada. As they boarded, a flight attendant looked at his face, her hand covering her mouth. Sympathy or disgust? He wasn't sure.

"Let me help," she said, taking his duffle bag. She motioned him to the alcove where in-flight meals were stored. He watched her looking at the flight paperwork.

Is she rechecking, to make sure I'm not on the no-fly list? He frowned to himself.

"I'm moving you to first class," she said. "Is there anything I can do to make you more comfortable while we're waiting?"

Claussen didn't realize he'd been holding his breath. When he exhaled, a severe pain shot along his jawline. "Thank you. May I use the toilet while we're still boarding?"

"Of course, Mister Stark," she said, checking the name on her paperwork.

The door locked behind him, he turned to the mirror. Claussen was shocked. He carefully touched his right cheek. Even the light touch almost caused his knees to buckle. The right half of his face was a dark purple where it was visible. The rest was covered with gauze. *Lev did an excellent job, making me unrecognizable...I hope*, he thought.

He took his latest passport from his pocket. *How did Trevor arrange it?* He thought. Trevor had someone waiting with new identity paper, passport, driver's license, even a library card.

When he asked how he arranged it, Trevor merely shrugged.

Realizing he'd been in the toilet for a long time, Claussen swallowed three Percocet tablets, extra strength. For good measure, he added a Vicodin, headed back to his seat, and gave do-not-disturb instructions. He was grateful for the window seat and a seat-mate who'd be working on his computer.

He worried about being separated from his guardian angels back in coach. The painkillers worked, however. He slept the entire flight, waking to the announcement, "This is the captain. We've entered Canadian air-space and will be landing soon. Flight attendants, prepare...."

It'd been over nine hours of healing sleep for Claussen.

Later, he told Trevor about vivid dreams, killing his five targets and making sure it wasn't a pleasant death. "Revenge felt sweet indeed," he said.

Claussen felt the lurch as the wheels and flaps lowered, surprised at a depth of his feelings at being back, heading home, despite the pain. He realized he'd been homesick this whole time.

The plane taxied to gate D70 at terminal one. Claussen looked at his phone—almost noon, Vancouver time. The flight attendant handed him the duffle. He tried to walk along the ramp. The Percocet and pain con-spired to upend his balance, and he almost fell against the wall to his left.

"Do you need help," a woman offered.

"Jet lag," he muttered. "Thanks, I'm okay."

Inside the terminal, he waited for the passengers exiting from coach. Claussen felt unsteady, knowing it was mostly drugs and jet lag, but was relieved to see Lev's towering presence. Trevor, walking behind him, leaned around to ask how he was doing.

Claussen looked like it was a silly question.

"You look like you were hit by a truck," Trevor said as if he had no previous knowledge. "Lev did a good job. Now it's showtime—Canadian customs and immigration ahead. Remember your cover story. That's why we don't have luggage. I purposefully asked for a Calgary address for your ID. It's a risk, but you're the one who asked for help getting back to Toronto."

Claussen appreciated Trevor taking charge and nodded.

"We've caught a break," Trevor said as they walked. "I learned The Brotherhood's team found where you were in New Zealand. Lucky for you, the locals they rushed to set up your roadblock bungled the job. I think we bought some time. How much, I don't know. Our detours have created a smokescreen, but we can't assume anything."

"Are we flying directly to Toronto?"

"I know you're in a hurry," Trevor said. "That will be your downfall, my friend."

Claussen raised his hands in surrender.

As they inched ahead in the immigration line, Trevor whispered. "I booked us on a WestJet Flight for Toronto, through Calgary. Wait," he said, stopping Claussen from responding. "It's a trick. We're taking the train, instead. Our highest risk of discovery is at an airport. They use facial recognition and monitor all cell phone calls and text messages. They scan all emails that are sent or received from a terminal."

They were quiet while the line moved ahead.

"No security to get on a train," Trevor said, resuming. "Four nights and three days will do wonders for your healing. We have adjoining berths. What are another few days, eh? We get off one stop before Toronto, in case. There will be a car—"

Trevor was interrupted when a customs officer motioned, directing them to a bank of terminals looking like ATM bank dispensers. They scanned their passports, waiting for a slip of paper to be dispensed. Trevor and Lev were waved through with a welcome home. It wasn't said with any degree of sincerity, but there it was.

When Claussen showed his paper, the agent asked to see his passport again, comparing the passport photo with one on his computer screen. *Is he trying to see through my disguise, my bruised face?* Claussen wondered. He felt perspiration under his arms and tried to appear calm. Finally, he was passed through. "Welcome home," the woman said. She didn't sound sincere, nor sorry about his injury.

Claussen rejoined his two companions. Each footstep he took transmitted a racking pain. He dry-swallowed two more Percocets, his new best friends. "I need water," Claussen said. Lev fetched a bottle, careful to avoid leaving fingerprints. Claussen took it, drinking a long swallow, then took care to deposit the bottle into a recycling bin as he followed Trevor and Lev to the transportation area.

"You're in luck," the cab driver said in Cantonese-influenced English. "Train leaves soon, no wait." In the taxi, Claussen felt his head nod like a bobblehead doll.

At the station, Trevor and Lev helped him out of the cab. If anyone thought Claussen was drunk, his visible injuries dispelled that notion. Boarding the train, he leaned on them for support.

A solicitous porter prepared the bed. Trevor and Lev didn't bother helping Claussen out of his clothes. Lev untied his shoes and took them off, unaware the shoes would have purchased two months of the bodyguard's salary.

Claussen had no sense of time. The train began moving, and he tried to focus. Claussen caught himself drooling and was disgusted. Before he could react, he fell into a deep sleep, the first dreams projected on a movie screen in his mind.

CHAPTER 35

911

Claussen, stirring to the movement and sounds of the train, had no sense of day or night. The window shade was down, and the interior lights of the berth were off. He listened to footsteps. He heard scraps of conversation, but it was only noise to Claussen. He touched the side of his face, the pain indescribable. He was now fully awake. With a sense of revulsion, he realized he had soiled himself.

There was a soft knock. "It's Trevor."

"Wait." Claussen didn't want Trevor to see him like this. *What difference does it make?* He thought as he tried to stand. The agony of trying to push himself up was too much. He stumbled, then fell to the left. His hand against the wall prevented falling. He groped for the light switch. When the overhead light came on, it was like a strobe. He raised his hand to cover his eyes and lurched to the door.

"I've never been so humiliated," he said.

Trevor glanced at the wet stains, offering a sympathetic smile. "How many Percocets have you taken? They'll knock you out. Too many and you lose control like that."

"Not nearly enough," Claussen said, sounding like he had a mouthful of gravel.

"Get undressed and into the shower."

Claussen took off his shirt and began to unzip his pants when the train lurched. Trevor reached to steady him. "Damn," Claussen said. He wasn't given to swearing, but was more surprised he didn't feel awkward undressing in front of Trevor. He stepped out of his dirty clothes.

He was grateful the shower stall was small, making it easier to stay balanced and avoid a fall.

"I have clean clothes ready," Trevor said, holding out underwear and a pair of khaki pants. A plain blue shirt was draped on the bed.

Claussen finished dressing. It was a slow process, every movement creating intense pain. He cursed Lev under his breath, then stopped himself. It wasn't personal. Lev only rearranged his face to avoid facial recognition. *Now I'm on a train heading to Toronto. How can I get to Matt Tremain feeling like this?* he thought. Two more Percocets helped ease his pain.

While Claussen was dressing, Trevor left with the soiled clothes, then returned carrying a carafe and mug. "I figured some coffee was in order."

"Where are we? How long—"

Trevor started to answer.

"I'm sorry," Claussen said, stopping him. "I know you've got a plan. I'm not arguing." He took a sip, careful not to minimize pain. "The coffee is quite good."

"You asked how long," Trevor said. "The trip is four days and three nights. You've been asleep for almost twenty-five hours," Trevor said, looking at his watch.

"What time is it? Where's Lev? I want to thank him for smashing my face," Claussen said.

"Coming on five in the morning," Trevor said. "I need to look at your face. Take the bandage off."

It hurt a lot, but Claussen managed it.

"Yikes, I don't like the look of that," Trevor leaned in to get a closer look.

"The room's spinning... I can't..." Claussen leaned to his right, falling to the floor. Trevor tried to stop him but couldn't. He reached for a radio. "Lev, I need help."

The huge bodyguard hoisted Claussen as if lifting a bag of feathers. "It doesn't look good. Maybe I hit him too hard."

"I don't think so. Something, perhaps a broken bone, is festering. If it doesn't get any better, we may need to get some medical attention."

• • •

Thirty-six hours later, the VIA Rail train slowed, approaching the Winnipeg station. Trevor nodded, and Lev helped Claussen to his feet. Claussen balanced himself on Trevor's shoulder as they started to walk toward the exit steps. Lev followed with the luggage. The conductor gave a sympathetic smile and offered a hand to assist Claussen down.

"We've ordered a taxi," Trevor said. "He needs a doctor."

"Use that door," the conductor said, directing them to an emergency exit.

Claussen tried to talk. His face was swollen to the point he couldn't move his jaw. He felt an urge to vomit and knew that would be disastrous. Trevor tried to hold him from falling, but Claussen suddenly fell in a heap. Passengers gasped as they walked past them, like water flowing around a rock. Most averted their eyes, but some stared the way looky-loos do.

Trevor pulled out his phone and dialed 911. "Too serious for a taxi," he told Lev.

• • •

"That'll help," Dr. Martine said. "We've given him something to stabilize him. He's showing classic symptoms of Percocet abuse. His stomach's sore to the touch; he's sweating like a pig. That's not a medical term, but you know what I mean. Look at the yellowing," the doctor said.

"He was confused when I tried to talk to him. He didn't know who he was. He gave at least three different names. Why would anyone claim to be Charles Claussen? That man," the doctor said and shook his head.

Trevor cringed.

"Now that he's stabilized, I've arranged transfer to the private room you requested. Get some rest. The nurse will let you know when he's conscious."

"What's the cause of that ugly looking bruise?" Trevor asked.

"I didn't see it at first. It took a second x-ray to see a piece of bone, a small fragment actually, had floated upward, and it's pushing on—"

The doctor pointed to the computer screen, explaining the damage to Trevor.

• • •

"Was it my fault," Lev asked. "I knew it would hurt, hitting him like that. Well, hurt him anyway."

Trevor knew the man wasn't making a joke. He'd never heard Lev tell a joke in the seven years they'd worked together. Lev didn't need reassurance, a man who long ago had made peace with violence and his strength.

"He'll either get better, or he won't," Trevor said. That seemed to satisfy Lev. "We're stretched pretty thin now," Trevor added. "We still have resources if we can get to Toronto. You and I can't worry about The Brotherhood. We can take precautions, but we both know what will happen if they catch us. Let's hope the end is quick."

Lev nodded. The coffee mug looked like a small toy in his grip. "We are what we are," he said. "It's been a good run, eh?"

Trevor was surprised. After all this time with Lev, he didn't expect an insight like that.

Trevor reached into his backpack and pulled out his Lenovo Yoga. "At least we've got wi-fi." When he finished, he closed the cover and reached for his phone. He watched Lev sipping coffee. The large man sat quietly, waiting for any orders.

"Trevor, here," he said when the call connected. "I need to know where they are. "Tremain's the primary target. Keep him in sight. Someone needs to cover the detective. Be careful; he can spot a tail. You'll find Payne and Remington together. Do you have the manpower to manage that? Good. I'll wire the money as soon as we hang up." Trevor ended the call without much else.

He looked at Lev. "Claussen's blood lust's our undoing, I'm afraid. That said, are we prepared to follow him? Lord Tennyson comes to mind now. 'Forward, the Light Brigade! Charge for the guns!' Tennyson wrote. I'm afraid we are about to make the charge of the Claussen brigade."

Lev said nothing.

• • •

Cyberia made some headway restoring his systems and watched an icon move along the VIA railway system as far as Winnipeg. Cyberia typed out a text and sent it to the last known number for Matt. "Beware, Claussen on the move and may be on a train. Signed Cyberia."

CHAPTER 36

MAKE MINE SINGLE-MALT

"Now, for today's forecast for the GTA. Currently, it's fourteen degrees and cloudy. Expect a high of eighteen and clearing. Look for a low tonight of thirteen. No precipitation is expected. In other news, oil and mining sectors are leading Canada's latest economic growth..."

Matt Tremain finished shaving, reaching to turn off the radio app. He paid little attention to weather reports, except as a clue on what to wear. Matt was focused on his next blog post. He had a tantalizing lead. During the night, he'd received an interesting call. It was scarcely past one o'clock, waking him from a fretful sleep.

"You the blogger who claims to seek the truth?" a woman said, sounding hesitant.

Matt listened. She claimed a government agency signed millions in contract services without a bidding process. The caller whispered three names, people supposedly behind the scheme, identifying the companies that benefitted.

This's something to get excited about, Matt thought. He thrived on whistleblower stories, his specialty after CleanSweep. Matt looked at the scribbled notes he'd taken in the middle of the night and felt his pulse quicken; it was a story he could bite into. He rinsed his razor when phone chirped.

Matt liked his new ringtone. He picked the spiraling down ringtone used by Wallander, the detective in the BBC series. Matt thought casting Kenneth Branagh was near-perfect.

Looking at the caller display, his thoughts of whistleblowers and ring-tones vanished when he saw who called. "Carling, what's new?"

"I have new intel on Claussen. I called Payne and Remington and left a voicemail."

It stung. "You called them first?" Matt asked, dissapointed.

"It's not urgent," Carling added. At least, I don't think so...yet."

Matt grabbed onto the word yet and couldn't let go. "Want to meet at my place?" He looked around at the mess and regretted the invitation but didn't retract it.

"Good idea," Carling said. "We'd best avoid public places now."

Matt didn't like where this was leading. "It's coming on nine o'clock," he said. "If they get your voicemail, we can meet here at eleven?" He looked at the mess again, figuring he might have enough time to clean.

"I'll handle the details," Carling snapped and ended the call before Matt could ask anything else.

Matt finished a draft of his whistleblower story and started cleaning.

Matt moved two weeks ago and loved this new apartment. It was an old building, an Art Deco architectural senior citizen lacking most, if not all, the modern amenities people expect now. Michelle told him it was on the wrong side of quaint. But his living room cleaned up well, mostly by throwing most of the mess on top of his bed and closing the door. He heard the elevator chunk-chunking its way to his floor and stopping. Two sets of footsteps, he assumed, belonged to Susan and Remy.

He opened the door to a bear hug, Remy clasping him in a grip. Susan followed with a hug a bit gentler, but every bit as sincere.

"Coffee, or stronger?"

"Coffee and stronger," they said, almost in unison, Susan first and Remy a close second.

Matt went to the kitchen counter and started pouring two mugs, knowing they both preferred a dark roast and black. "Beer or Scotch," he asked Remy.

"Beer's fine, mate," Remy said.

"He's been trying to talk like that since we did that shoot in New Zea-land," Susan said, rolling her eyes. "Mate, indeed. Make mine single-malt, please."

They were all startled as the door thumped open. Matt thought about the door at the 10-8 bar, the one Carling nearly demolished, but he looked slightly ashamed at his entrance, a look rarely shown. "Sorry, guess I allowed myself to get carried away. Anyhow, I'm glad we could all make it. If I heard correctly, make mine single-malt too."

They tried their best at small talk. Matt almost told Susan about the one o'clock morning call from the latest whistleblower, but held it in. *Friends maybe, but she's still a competitor,* he thought. "We all know we're here about Claussen. Let's get to it."

Matt didn't notice at first, but Susan claimed the right side of the sofa, and Remy turned a kitchen chair around for a seat. There was cool-ness, couples have, following a fight, something private. *I hope that won't be a problem,* Matt thought.

Matt sat on the floor, notebook at the ready. Carling did what he did best; he paced, claiming it helped him think things through.

"One," he said. "We have surveillance video of Claussen arriving in Vancouver. We all know he was skillful at disguising the foci needed to match his info in the database. Another CCTV camera picked them head-ing toward a WestJet gate. There was a flight to Toronto through Calgary."

"He's here, then?" Remy asked. "What flights are heading here from Calgary?"

"That's what I figured," Carling said. "I back-checked and discovered the name used to book the flight. The problem is, he never boarded the plane. Look at this." He opened a laptop, and they all watched passen-gers boarding.

"Go back to him getting off the plane from Tokyo, Matt said.

When Carling cued the video, they watched closely. "The man iden-tified as Claussen has a misshaped face, wrapped in bandages," Carling said. "I talked to the flight attendants over a conference call. They're probably still in Vancouver. The attendant in charge told me she was sure the injury wasn't fake. He apparently moaned in his sleep, bothering his seatmate. She watched him swallowing pills—Percocets. She said he took them like candy."

"That's one ugly looking bruise, especially with the photo colorized," Remy said.

"It needs medical attention," Matt said.

"Let me get back to it," Carling snapped, then apologized. "I know we're all feeling the tension. If he was out of the country, all we had to do was to worry. He's here. Now, we really worry. Anyway," he continued, "Claussen didn't board the WestJet flight or any other flight. I had someone check all Toronto-bound flights scheduled for the next twenty-four hours. We checked all the CCTV cameras, focusing on those at exit gates. See that," Carling pointed. "That's a Toronto baggage claim and ground transportation coverage. Nothing."

Clausen shut the laptop. "There was one anomaly," he said. "An emergency exit was opened. It was investigated immediately. But nothing."

"It had to be Claussen," Matt said. "He's getting help. He's walking between two men. One was about his size, the other well over six-four."

"I don't like the sound of this," Susan said, the first thing she said since the discussion started.

"Given the way his face looked, I put out an alert to all hospitals and medical clinics in the Vancouver and Toronto areas," Carling said. "We're even checking veterinarian offices, in case."

"What's your best guess, Carling?" Susan asked.

"He's too smart by half. If he's on the move, he has few choices. No reported air charters booked. I asked a friend in Seattle to check. It's down to car, bus, or train. The car rental places have been checked. They have good surveillance. Nothing. *Nada.* He could've boarded a bus or train undetected. Nothing showing. They don't have as much security on buses or trains. A team is checking an CCTV. You asked for my best guess," Carling sighed. "I think he's hunkered down in Vancouver, getting medical attention, legally or otherwise."

"We still need to take precautions," Matt said, stating the obvious.

They all looked at each other and shrugged in unison.

Carling opened the hard-case strongbox he brought with him. Susan started to cry when she saw four handguns resting in protective foam.

Matt forgot about the latest scoop from his early morning whistleblower.

CHAPTER 37

SAFE HARBOR

att stood at the door, watching his friends waiting for the elevator. He saw the worry on their faces, knowing he looked the same. *If Claussen is in the country, he could be close, even on this street,* he worried.

"I'll call when I hear something," Carling said. They stepped in, and the elevator swallowed his friends. Matt stared at the empty hallway, feeling drained. No insights, nothing except dread. He couldn't ever remember all that happened since the downfall of CleanSweep. It was all a blur, a camera out of focus.

Matt looked around. *Is there anything suspicious? Get a grip,* he corrected himself but still made sure the door was locked.

He was carrying glasses to the kitchen when his phone chirped. The sound startled him; he almost dropped the glassware. Matt looked at the caller ID and smiled at Michelle's photo. *Perfect. That's exactly what I need.*

"Hello?" Matt said, suddenly tongue-tied. "Sorry, Michelle. It's great to hear your voice. May I put you on speaker phone while I clean?"

"No problem," she said. Matt loved her rich baritone voice. "Cleaning up after a girlfriend?"

Matt knew she was teasing, wasn't she? He'd told her about Claussen earlier and had an urge to tell her the whole story. *Will it be too much? We hardly know each other.*

"No girlfriend," he chuckled a little too much. "My three friends."

"I hear something in your voice," she said. "Panic? What's wrong, Matt?"

"It's only..."

Hesitating, he knew he needed to confide him her and share the latest developments. "It's the Claussen story. I don't want to say anything and drag you into it." He looked around. "My place is a mess. Carling, Susan Payne, and Remington were here. We... we..."

"Shush." With that one word, he relaxed. "Come to my place," she offered. "I'll meet you at the GO station. I'll have a salad and pasta ready when you get here. We'll pick up some wine on the way back."

Michelle was different. They'd dated; dinner, a movie, and a picnic. This implied an intimacy Matt only dreamed would happen. He'd pictured an apartment with frilly décor, bean bags for chairs, and lots of plants. "No cats," she had said once.

Suddenly, her apartment sounded like a safe harbor, exactly what he needed.

Matt showered and looked in the closet. Khaki slacks and his favorite blue shirt were still in the plastic dry cleaner wrap. He was excited about seeing Michelle, but couldn't shake his apprehension. Leaving his apartment, he looked around; no one was in the hallway. The shadows were only that, shadows. Not waiting for the elevator, he raced down. At the lobby door, he took another look both ways. No sign of Charles Claussen.

Sitting on the GO train, he held a Chianti in one hand and a small bouquet in his other. Well past rush hour, he didn't have to share a seat.

He couldn't stop himself. He twisted around at each stop, making sure Claussen didn't board.

He closed his eyes. *Michelle's gorgeous and she likes me,* he thought. He just had to focus on that.

• • •

"Why you shouldn't have," she said, taking the flowers, a poor imitation of a Southern belle. "Well... maybe you should have," she laughed. "A Chianti. Perfect. Now we don't have to stop on the way. My spaghetti will knock your socks off," Michelle said, slipping her arm under his elbow.

Matt delighted at the touch, the familiarity.

The next morning, Chianti was a dim memory, and a lingering garlic taste reminding him of the best spaghetti he'd ever had. Stretched out with his hands laced behind his head, he listened to the sounds of a city awakening. Twisted sheets held one leg in a snare, the other bare to the chill. *Is this really happening to me?* he thought and smiled as he opened his eyes.

He unlaced his hands and turned. Michelle's funny snore sounded like a helicopter passing overhead. Rolling over, he draped an arm over her shoulder.

"Hmmmmmm." She drew out the sound.

"Good morning, sleepy head." Matt knew it sounded corny, but he didn't have much experience in this department. The only time he'd slept over, it was a woman he'd met at a bar. He remembered grabbing his clothes and was bolting for the door. *This's different, very different*, he thought.

Michelle sat naked, unembarrassed. Matt loved her even more for that.

"Do you believe in love at first sight, Michelle?" He blushed, feeling awkward.

"If you mean an ambush I've planned since the Twisted Sister, then yes. You do remember that day, don't you? I'm on record. I told both my girlfriends that day you were the one."

Matt heard teasing in her laugh. "I've never felt like this about anyone before," he said. "I want to—" he stopped. I want to say something I never—" He stopped again. "I'm in love with you, Michelle." Matt's confidence grew. "We're perfect together." He held out his hand. "Wait. There's more. Will you marry me?"

Michelle was speechless. She was quiet for so long, Matt thought he'd made a huge mistake.

"I thought you'd never..."

Michelle never finished what she was saying. Making love was even sweeter this time.

CHAPTER 38

THE BROTHERHOOD

Rudainah Saja Basar wore a traditional Icelandic coat as she waited in the driveway. She lived near Akureyri, a remote part of Iceland. She ignored the snow, watching the approaching vehicles. She'd expected no less, their arrival precisely timed.

The first vehicle was a Land Rover built to exacting standards. Nothing like it was ever displayed in a showroom of a local dealership. She knew the security team inside was on high alert.

It was followed by a luxury van built on a Mercedes-Benz Sprinter chassis, coal black, in sharp contrast to the wind-whipped snow. The van sliced effortlessly through mounting drifts. It'd been upgraded with a unique suspension system to smooth any bumps.

Another Land Rover followed with the remaining members of the security team.

Rudainah stepped forward as the van stopped. The hydraulic door hissed, unfolding to provide a modest set of stairs. Choosing one of the four seats, she rubbed an approving palm over the fabric. She'd insisted on hand-stitched leather from elephant and stingray skin. The material emitted a pleasant hint of fragrance. Rudainah would never be on PETA's mailing list.

Bulletproof glass protected the windows. The side panels, made of composite steel and titanium metal, served to thwart damage from an improvised explosive device.

Rudainah Saja Basar, Saja to her friends, smiled as she thought about her husband. The native Icelander, Gautur Björnsson, provided perfect cover.

Saja was one of The Brotherhood's four members, a striking woman in her sixties. Her strong Arabic features were a sharp contrast to the pale Viking world she lived in and a climate never fully embraced.

Her Icelandic husband had no idea of The Brotherhood. He'd assumed her income came from one of those Middle Eastern oil pumps. She'd never dissuaded him from his assumptions.

Everything must be perfect, she thought. They were coming; it was her turn to host the meeting. Saja wasn't really concerned. Her penchant for details ensured all was in order.

With a nod to the driver, the convoy headed to a private area at Akureyri airport. She watched through the smoky glass as a turquoise-colored jet approached with a picture-perfect touchdown. At the parking area, the whine of the engines whispered to a stop. A tall man with black hair tugged his cashmere coat tight as he walked down the unfolded steps. Vladimir Švajgel, the Slovenian, was first to arrive.

"You might have arranged better weather, Saja," he said and smiled without really smiling. "Your people certainly know how to do gloomy."

Saja flashed a delicate grin, taking pleasure in flirting with him without modesty. She wore a sea-green dress and a black silk scarf head covering, knowing her appearance was flawless.

"When I heard the weather report, I decided it was too risky to expose my Alfa Romeo to this melancholy Icelandic weather. Would you like some coffee, or...?"

"Coffee would be delightful," he said. "How much did this upholstery cost? I'm thinking of upgrading."

"You had to ask? It was a gift, and I have no idea."

Vladimir felt the leather, drawing in the aroma. "Perfect," was all he said.

They were interrupted by a soft knocking. "Another flight is arriving," a young man said.

Julina Souza Alves joined them in the van. They exchanged polite greetings. "Routine," Senor Alves said when asked about his flight from Sao Paulo. He removed his coat and sat almost daintily, as if ignoring the weather. Julina Alves sported a white guayabera shirt, matching his full head of hair. Senor Alves' deep-set black eyes were inky pools that gave nothing away.

Hsin Shen arrived last. He joked about once posing as a stand-in for Buddha. Joking wasn't commonplace with these four, however. They watched the rotund Shen coming down the steps of his aircraft. "With his size, how does he manage to walk with the grace of a dancer?" Saja asked her companions.

Once, they asked how the large man squeezed himself into a seat. Shen showed them inside his plane, specially configured for his enormous girth.

Before signaling the convoy to start, Saja passed around coffee and a small glass of Björk Liqueur. "Here's to keeping the winter at bay," she saluted.

The convoy pulled out of the airport parking area, the four enjoying their refreshments in silence. The snowfall created artistic drifts, handled easily by the custom-made vehicles.

The first Land Rover led the ways past the Björnsson home. A curving driveway rose to a chalet on a shelf blasted out of the mountainside. The escort vehicles turned to the side as the luxury van stopped at the front door.

"Welcome, madam, and guests." A security guard opened the door to assist them from the van. Two lookouts stood without speaking, their eyes scanning for any dangers.

Their belongings were carried through another door with the utmost discretion. These were the kinds of people who never toted their own luggage.

"Marvelous," Julina said, looking at a buffet table to the right. "I'm famished."

"Traditional Icelandic food and drink," Saja said, indicating the delicacies. "That fish you see were swimming only minutes ago. We have a lot to cover, gentlemen. I propose a meal first. Then, we can get to the business at hand over coffee and dessert. Our security team's in the building next door. Our privacy is safeguarded."

• • •

After dinner, they moved to the den. An entire wall of glass afforded a view to the north, an escarpment curving in an arc that embraced the bay. If the weather cleared, they might see fishing boats swinging at anchor. Two other walls held floor-to-ceiling bookcases.

The fourth wall was stonework built around a fireplace large enough to stand in. Large logs blazed, imparting a comforting warmth. Five chairs were arranged in a semi-circle by the fire. By tradition, an empty chair honored the founder, a priest, Le Père Marmion Auheron Mousseau. He established *La Fraternité de l'Eagles* in 1467, a brotherhood that would long outlast him.

By tradition, membership in the Fraternité was limited to four hand-picked men, each holding vast amounts of wealth, power, and influence. Rudainah Saja Basar was the first woman to receive an invitation. Power, means, and resources were far more important than nationality or gender. Democracy, geopolitics, and morality were mere words. Their wealth was augmented by selling arms. They didn't bother choosing sides, willing to sell to opposing factions—often at the same time.

In comfortable chairs arranged in front of the fireplace, Saja made sure one was designed to accommodate her Chinese guest.

The small table beside each chair held a carafe of strong coffee, along with another small bottle of Björk Liqueur.

"I must say, Saja, this liqueur is the rival of anything we have in Brazil."

"Or Portugal," Vladimir said.

"Enough," Hsin Shen said, sounding like he was out of breath. "Let us talk business. Then we can chat about coffee and drink."

Saja raised her eyebrows. Irritation, impatience, and anger were emotions not permitted, by custom. *Ah, well, this meeting is an exception to the rule,* she thought. She scrolled the screen on her electronic tablet. "This is our agreement with Claussen," she said. She passed it around for the others to see. It was unnecessary. They all knew the contract word for word.

The meeting was called to order when Saja said, "I proposed this extraordinary session to discuss Mister Charles Claussen's contract."

"We all know why we're here," Vladimir said, thumping the table. "He was happy to take our money. When we agreed to back him, we also decided he could be on a long leash. I think that was a mistake. We needed someone inside to keep us—"

Hsin Shen interrupted. "When his CleanSweep operation began to implode, he could have come to us for help and our protection. Instead, he went to ground. Now, our agents can't catch him. We get close, and, poof, he's a ghost."

"I've had enough," Julina said in a smooth, baritone voice. "He continues to elude us. If only Claussen had come to us. If only he explained what went wrong. He owes us an accounting."

Saja raised a hand. "He's an incredibly talented organizer. His plan to start small, to demonstrate success, was brilliant. If it worked, it could be replicated."

The Brotherhood's well-defined rule not to show emotion nor make decisions based on sentimentality was now being tested.

Then, Vladimir broke the rule. "Terminate," he said, slamming his hand on the side of his chair. "Look at the money he's cost us."

"Vlad, each of us alone lost that much with mere changes in the political weather. It's chump change to us," Hsin Shen said, speaking above a whisper. "Wouldn't it be better to see what we can salvage?"

"It's not the money," Vlad insisted. "Claussen didn't come to us with an explanation or ask for help. He went to ground and keeps eluding Harding's surveillance. I'm furious."

Hsin Shen waved his hand. "We have a proverb that if you remain patient in a moment of anger, you will escape a hundred days of sorrow. It doesn't serve us to be angry. If we help him get his revenge, we can salvage the plan. There are other locations he can help create another CleanSweep."

"You're right. This isn't a time for my emotions," Vlad finally agreed. "And you're right, there are other locations."

Shen nodded, sipping the Icelandic liqueur.

Saja felt the slight vibration of her phone. "Excuse me, gentlemen," she said, holding the phone to her ear. "I said we weren't to be disturbed." With a simple nod, she disconnected the call. "I left word we were not to be disturbed," she said, "with one exception. That's Harding. They've located our elusive Mr. Claussen."

CHAPTER 39

IF THE BOSS IS AFRAID

"**D**amn. If the boss is afraid of them?" an agent whispered.

The boss, Javin Harding, owned JH Security. Researching search engines would be a waste of time. JH Security was buried in a holding company with an untraceable link.

Javin Harding was a retired United States Marine Corps colonel. He now headed an international security team comprised of ex-military from around the world. His favored recruits came from El Al Airline. "A focus on security second to none," he'd said. His company also hired the most capable computer whizzes money could buy.

JH Security had one client: The Brotherhood.

With all that talent, it'd been painful to acknowledge the failure to find Charles Claussen. Until now, that is. He could now tell his client he knew where Claussen was. *Will they believe me, after all the failed attempts?* he thought. He was nervous. He turned to his assistant. "Chuck, I'd rather take a bullet than meet with them tonight," he said. "I don't know how, but Claussen had some juice, someone helping him stay one step ahead. The Serbian frightens me the most," he said, opening the door to leave.

"But this is good news," Chuck said. "We're sure this time."

"We've told them that before. Why should they believe me this time?" Harding faced enemies under fire and worked in dangerous locations. "This is more frightening," he said. Military-straight, he put his hand on the doorknob.

He saw two men exchange glances. "He's afraid? I've seen him in action. I didn't think he knew what fear was. If these guys scare—"

Harding cut the agents off with a scowl. The room silent, he took a deep breath and headed out. He leaned into the wind and ran to the chalet.

• • •

Saja motioned him in. "You've interrupted our meeting," she said. "Perhaps you'd like to share what you told me, Mr. Harding."

Harding controlled his breathing. "One of my Canadian agents, Cameryn Martin, was on leave. She's from Toronto and was visiting a friend in Vancouver. Waiting for a flight home, she looked closely at one of the three men walking past her. The man in the middle appeared to be in quite some distress, like he'd been beaten or been in an accident."

Presenting his report, Harding relaxed, sure of his facts.

"Our agents have our proprietary app. She forwarded a picture. Our facial recognition software can match points, but it was inconclusive because of the damage to his face. Then, Claussen made a mistake. He dropped a water bottle into a recycle bin. Perhaps his men were distracted and didn't retrieve it. Agent Cameryn did, however," Harding continued, proud of his agent. "She used plastic gloves and recovered the empty bottle. Filling the bottle with a dark cola, the fingerprints were visible. She sent a photograph of the prints back to our lab. It was a match. The man in bandages was Charles Claussen. We now know he came in on a flight from Japan. Despite all the high-tech evasion, it was old-school fingerprints that confirmed his identity."

"Get on with it! Where is he?" Vladimir shouted as the others motioned for calm.

Unruffled, Harding continued. "We thought we lost him again," he said, watching faces for a reaction. "We didn't have a team in place at the Vancouver airport. There was nothing to indicate the need. If it weren't for Cameryn Martin's chance encounter, we wouldn't have spotted him at all. Claussen eluded us again. This time,we knew where to focus our resources."

Vladimir looked ready to jump out of his chair but waited for Harding to go on.

"We managed to identify one of the men helping him: Trevor Durst. If that's Claussen's shepherd, it explains why he's been so hard to pin down. We have no idea who the large man is with them. The man's a giant. I've dispatched a full team to Vancouver. Claussen is obviously injured. All medical centers—legal and otherwise—were checked."

"What did you find?" Saja asked, holding out a hand to keep Vladimir calm.

"I had a gut feeling he wouldn't stay in Vancouver. He's heading to Toronto. The man can't let go of his revenge. There are five ways he can get from Vancouver to Toronto." Harding said, spreading five fingers, "Air, car, train, bus, or walk." The last was an attempt to lighten the mood. It didn't work.

"Greed is an investigator's best friend," Harding continued. "A passenger service agent at VIA, Canada's rail service, was interviewed. The greedy ticket agent parted with information in exchange for some spending money, describing three men who bought tickets to Toronto. He remembered because one was wrapped in bandages and had to be supported by his friend."

"I'm curious how Claussen got his injuries," Hsin Shen said.

"That not important," Harding said, aware he'd sounded impertinent. "I'm sorry, sir. With our information, it didn't take long to find him. He's in a hospital in Winnipeg. Seven Oaks General Hospital, to be precise. The guard at his door looks like the Goliath that David killed with a rock and slingshot. We haven't been able to get anyone inside the room yet, but Claussen's definitely in that room."

"You're sure," Saja asked.

"I'm sure."

"Leave us."

Harding exhaled slowly, the way a sniper's trained to control breathing. He performed a perfect about-face before he walked out.

• • •

Vladimir started. "I apologize for losing my composure. It won't happen again. I'm the one who brought Claussen's proposal to our table. I feel responsible."

"It's what we do from here that counts," Julina said, sipping his liqueur; the others nodded agreement.

Hsin Shen was quiet. He coughed, covering his mouth with a silk handkerchief. "You thought to terminate him was the only option," he said, placing a reassuring hand on Vladimir's arm. "China's had a long history of martial arts. Shaolin, Wudan, and Emei are well-known examples. Regardless of the name, they all have one thing in common. They recognize an enemy's energy and redirect it." He coughed again. "Instead of an order to terminate, I propose we assist our Mr. Claussen and his quest for revenge. Then we bring him to bay. I still believe CleanSweep is a good concept. Why not help him get rid of undesirables who make no contribution?"

"Then we harvest the world's gene pool to our advantage," Vladimir caught on.

The Brotherhood weighed their options. Saja raised her telephone to her ear. "Mr. Harding, would you come back in, please?".

CHAPTER 40

A PIANO SURPRISE

To Claussen, voices made no sense. They were muted sounds beyond his understanding. *What's that tapping sound?* He thought. Faces floated by, images slightly out of focus, the hallucinatory side effects of an IV tube slowly dripping morphine. He imagined faces of The Brotherhood.

As the tapping sound continued, he recognized the sound—typing on a computer. A doctor was updating a medical chart. Claussen drifted back into deliria.

The drugs told his brain to ignore the pain. Faces of The Brotherhood faded in and out, replaced by an image of Angela Vaughn, his former head of security. The thought of Angela faded, Claussen trying to keep it in focus. The fog of bewilderment and delirium finally cleared. Claussen opened his eyes to see Trevor sitting the corner.

Trevor glanced from his reading when Claussen stirred. "It is good to see you awake, boss."

"What... what..." Claussen couldn't complete the words.

"Water helps," Trevor said, pouring a glass.

"Thanks," Claussen grumbled. He held a hand and tried to motion. He noticed a book in Trevor's hand. "What're you reading?"

Trevor laughed. "Some light reading, *The Epic of Gilgamesh.*"

"I have no idea what that is," Claussen said. "I had hoped for a notebook with Tremain's location."

"Now, I know you're coming out of it. You gave me a fright," Trevor said. He told Claussen about the train to Winnipeg, the ambulance, and the hospital. "You had a brush with death."

"Tell... tell... I can't remember his name. I...don't blame him."

"Lev," Trevor said. "He won't admit it, but he feels guilty."

"I knew the risk. What happened, anyway?"

"A small piece of bone fragment pushed upward, an unintended outcome. It worked, though. We got through undetected. Are you sure you want to go through with this obsession you have?"

Claussen clenched the sheet with both fists, uttering a primal choking sound.

"I'll take that as a yes," Trevor said.

• • •

The human body can withstand a surprising amount of damage and still heal. Surgery on the fractured facial bone succeeded. With two weeks of rest plus intense physical therapy, Claussen was ready to be discharged.

"I wish you the best, and good luck," the doctor said.

"I've never trusted in luck," Claussen snapped. He forced a grin and thanked the medical team for their hard work. Walking away, he whispered to Trevor, "I need a hotel room. We need to begin planning."

Trevor nodded as Lev held a door open.

• • •

The city of Winnipeg below Harding felt the jolt as the wheels dropped into place for landing. However, he had zero interest in the city. Walking through the airport, he barely noticed the sounds. Gift shops, imitation restaurants, and signs for the restrooms all the same worldwide. He ignored endless announcements of "Passenger so-and-so, please report to gate something or other."

Harding never carried his luggage. He strode ahead, reading a text. Two taciturn agents walked behind with luggage, shouldering their responsibility.

As automatic doors separated, Harding nodded in appreciation. A man standing at the curb held a van door open. "As usual, good timing, Scott," Harding said.

Pulling into the exit lane, Scott turned to the boss, sitting in the back. "Claussen checked out of the hospital yesterday," he said. "He looks like crap, his face swollen."

"Where is he?"

"The Freemont." Scott looked at the GPS display. "The Royal Alexandra Suite," he snickered. "He likes spending The Brotherhood's money. The master room has a fireplace and room enough for a baby grand piano in the corner."

"What's the plan?" Harding wanted to know.

"Money talks. It spoke nicely to the concierge. He'll discreetly escort us to the room. We're twenty minutes out, boss. There's a delay, some demonstration protesting who-knows-what."

• • •

Claussen stretched out, his head supported by pillows. He scanned a map of Toronto on his tablet, but looked up in surprise at piano music from the other room.

Trevor stood in the doorway, showing surprise." I had no idea Lev played the piano."

The huge man played with a delicate touch, a melancholy German song Claussen recognized immediately, "Traumirei." Claussen began to weep at the haunting Schumann melody. He couldn't stop thinking about Angela Vaughn as the notes echoed throughout the suite.

Finished, Lev played The Pianos Sonata, number 14 by Beethoven, "The Moonlight."

Partway through another Beethoven sonata, "The Appassionato," there was a soft chime.

Lev stopped, watching carefully as Trevor walked to the door. Before Trevor got to the door, it flew open. Javin Harding walked in as the concierge made a quick disappearing act.

"Relax, Trevor. I mean no harm," Harding started, holding out his hands to show openness.

Lev sat, his hand resting on his weapon inside his jacket, watching Harding walked in followed by two men.

Everyone heard a gasp and saw Claussen, standing at the bedroom door, steadying himself, his terror evident.

"I come in peace, Mr. Claussen. You don't know me, sir. My name's Javin Harding. Keep it simple. Call me 'the boss.' We've never met, but I admired your concept, CleanSweep. I know your friend," he said, turning. "It's good to see you again, Trevor."

"Javin," Trevor said, looking alert.

"Why don't we sit, perhaps enjoy a drink," Harding suggested, motioning Claussen to a chair.

Claussen and Trevor sat. The two agents with Harding were watchful, wary of the huge man towering over everyone. Lev's eyes were mirrors, reflecting the agent's fear.

"Easy, boys," Javin Harding said. His agents relaxed; Lev, not so much. His muscles stretched the sleeves of his black t-shirt.

"I can't tell you how pleased I am to finally meet," Harding said, looking like he enjoyed Claussen's discomfort. "You, Trevor," he said, turning. "You've done an outstanding job. I had my best team on the ground in Pittsburgh."

Trevor didn't respond.

"Yet, you almost get done in by amateurs in Florida?"

Trevor winced, having that pointed out by another professional.

"From Florida to Pittsburgh wasn't hard to track. That move to New Zealand, however, was brilliant. It had us fooled. I had to rush in incompetents. They were no match. What made you pick that place?"

Trevor sat quietly. "No trade secrets, Javin."

"Please, what about a drink? Your whiskey, of course, Mr. Claussen." Harding walked to the bar. "Excellent. Old Pulteney, thirty-year-old single malt. That set you back, eh? I guess over $400," he said, handing the bottle to an agent to pour. "Where was I? It's obvious you're afraid. You've been avoiding The Brotherhood," he laughed. "I'd be terrified too. But it might not be as bad as you think. At least for now."

Claussen began to take a drink when Trevor said, "That's not a good idea with all your medication." Claussen ignored him and swallowed.

"This will rock your world, Clausen, dropping mister to show impertinence. You were scheduled for a come-to-Jesus meeting with The Brotherhood. They were more than a little annoyed with me, not finding you, and all. At the last minute last night, I told them we knew where you were. Right here in Winnipeg. First, the hospital, then here." Harding sipped his drink, continuing. "Frankly, I expected to get sacked...or worse. They're not big on renegotiating. But they surprised me. I didn't hear it all, but they still think you might be of some value. The members are irritated about your obsession for revenge, I tell you."

Claussen sat, blood draining from his face. He felt like a man on the way to the gallows.

"Apparently, your value outweighs their anger for the moment. They've ordered me to help you get even with the blogger and friends. You get your revenge. They have other plans for your talents afterward." He saw astonishment on Claussen's face. "After vengeance is satisfied, they want to meet with you. I'm trying to remember the exact words, something about a pound of your flesh. They want to pick your brain before they pick your bones clean," Harding said and started laughing. It wasn't a pleasant laugh.

"What do you say, Trevor, old man? Work together? And that guy," he said, looking at Lev, "is awe-inspiring, to say the least."

Claussen heard Harding outline a plan and began to weep, something he'd never done in front of anyone, let alone a roomful of strangers. He blamed his medication, but they were tears of joy. It was going to happen. Tremain wouldn't be able to hide from this. *I finally get even with you, Tremain. Best of all, I'll have a second chance at implementing CleanSweep. I have precisely the city and country in mind.*

Feeling expansive, he offered to arrange rooms. "I'll call the manager, personally," Claussen offered but was turned down. Harding said they made their own arrangement.

The real music to Claussen's ears, however, was knowing Harding's scouts were starting reconnaissance in Toronto.

• • •

"I don't like this, boss," Trevor said when they were alone. Lev had slipped out to follow Harding and his team. For a large man, he was exceptionally good at remaining unseen when he wanted to.

Claussen was in a buoyant mood and waved off Trevor's caution.

• • •

Claussen closed the bedroom door for privacy. He looked in surprise at the near empty bottle of scotch. *Was it alcohol fueling my enthusiasm?* he thought. He opened the door to the living room. Trevor was gone, leaving a note was on the counter. "Out for a walk."

Claussen sat by the fireplace, looking at the piano, the memory of Lev's playing still clear.

He leapt from the seat and hurried into the bedroom. He had a phone hidden. The cleaning lady parted with it for a fifty-dollar bill. It was an old phone. No data. No photographs. Only for talking. Best of all—no SIM card.

He dialed a number from memory, hearing the call go to voicemail. "Angela, it's Charles. Can we talk, please?" Please was the least used word in Claussen's vocabulary.

• • •

Light on the Russian's computer screen indicated traffic. To take his mind away from the attack on his computers, Cyberia sat at his desk admiring the view from his window. It was dominated by the central spire on the gold dome of the Novospassky Monastery. The Russian clicked an icon to record the conversation, SIM card or no.

He was frantic. He could record the chatter but couldn't get in touch with Matt. He wondered why not.

CHAPTER 41

SAFE HOUSE

Carling called to warn him. "I can't find a trace," he said. "We haven't spotted his whereabouts for over three and a half weeks now."

"It's what we don't know that frightens me," Matt said.

"I talked to Susan. They're at a farm on the Bruce Peninsula near Owen Sound. She kept it vague. They're treating this seriously and didn't want to give out information over the phone. You should, too," Carling said. "They're smart, heading to a hidey-hole."

"Damn it, Brick. I'm afraid."

"We all are. Be alert for anything out of the ordinary. You'd be surprised at how some details stand out."

Matt sensed Carling's nervousness. "And Matt, make sure to remove your SIM card. The same with the storage card. Dispose of them in different places. Use the throwaway phone I gave you."

Matt followed the instructions. He knew Carling was careful. Matt hated losing photographs of Michelle, but what else could he do?

Matt looked around as he exited the northbound train at Bloor and Yonge station. Head bowed, he pulled the bill of his cap down and walked out to the Street.

The government reassured everyone all secret surveillance cameras installed by CleanSweep agents were removed. Matt was unconvinced. *Why would they dismantle them?* He assumed they recorded his movements.

Matt visualized Claussen or one of his goons waiting in the shadows, ready to spring out as he walked by.

Was that man ducking into a doorway when he caught me looking? He thought. *Is the woman with the red hat following me? Didn't I see her on the same subway car?*

Matt couldn't shake the paranoia-like feeling.

"This is crazy," Matt said aloud, causing a passer-by to glance at him.

He walked east on Bloor Street and suddenly turned around, heading back to the intersection, where he turned right. He walked to the Toronto Reference Library, one of his favorite places. Now, he looked for refuge, a quiet place to concentrate. The library also provided computer access.

He paused at the main entrance, taking in the architecture, floors rising like layers on a cake.

Matt was in luck; computer stations were available. He handed over his library card for the librarian to check and walked to the back row of computers. Matt waited for the welcome screen, entering his library card number and pin. He read a message of a safe house address. *Thanks, Brick,* Matt thought, logging off. He looked around the enormous building. A follower could be anywhere among the nooks and crannies.

He hurried back to his apartment, stowing everything he could think of. He gathered his backpack, deciding it was safest to walk to the address. *What if there's technology to track my transit card usage?* he thought. He thought Carling said the card was safe, but why take the chance? It meant an hour's walk, but Matt was used to long walks.

Bloor Street, east to Church, then south on Carlton. A shortcut took him past the Allan Gardens Conservatory, still undergoing repairs three years after the riots. He remembered a woman who'd helped him expose Operation CleanSweep and put Charles Claussen out of business. He'd written about her in his blogs, calling her the dancing lady. This was the spot of her final, shocking ballet, a dance orchestrated with machine gun bullets. He walked on, his vision clouded from crying.

His zig-zag route went past Orphan's Green. For all his exploring, he wasn't familiar with this part of Toronto. He'd never heard of Corktown Lane until now, though he'd heard of Corktown, north of the Distillery Historic District. This was the area receiving the most damage during the riots.

Matt expected to smell smoke haunting the streets.

Corktown Lane formed a loop from Gilead Place. He looked at the address on the note, continuing past new condos on his right and eventually came to the address Carling provided. It was a plain concrete block building with a door that looked like it hadn't been opened in ages.

"There's a key taped behind the shutter on the window to the left," the note read.

Matt inserted the key and tested the handle. The door opened effortlessly.

"There's a door either side of the hallway. Take your pick. They both have a bed. The toilet's at the end of the hall. Put the bar in the brackets. That'll secure the door," Carling's note said. Matt spotted the large steel bar leaning on the wall and did as directed.

He didn't realize how tired he was until he stretched out on the bed. A sharp pain in the left hip combined with a monster headache, but he couldn't will the pain away. Despite that, Matt was soon gently snoring.

● ● ●

Harding's assistant, Kranshon, was on the phone with Harding when a tech waved for attention.

"I read his email," the man said. "Someone sent it to Tremain, using a spoof address. It's an address on Corktown Lane. I have it on Google maps street view."

"How did you—?"

"Child's play, boss. I placed a trace on anything with electronic data embedded. Tremain's mistake was using his library card and pin number. He accessed a computer at the Toronto Reference Library. From there, it was easy."

"I want all available agents assembled," Harding said. "Find us a location," he ordered the tech.

"On it, boss," the man said, tapping his keyboard. "There's public parking at the corner of Adelaide and Parliament. Practically vacant."

"Make it happen, Kranshon."

CHAPTER 42

CORKTOWN CAPER

att was at the midpoint between deep, slow-wave sleep and awake, dreaming Michelle was in the next room. *Why doesn't she answer her phone?* he wondered. He realized it was his phone. His eyes snapped open. He was in the safe house. He answered.

"Get out now, my friend. Now!" The broad Russian accent left no doubt as to who was talking. "You need to run. Get out, now!"

"Cyberia?" Matt's was speechless.

Cyberia kept his voice calm. "You used your library card." It wasn't a question.

Matt slapped his forehead with his hand, realizing what he'd done. "How long do I have?"

"I think minutes. Get a move on!"

"I don't know what to say."

"Don't try. Get out! Run!" The line went quiet.

Adrenaline fueled Matt like a jolt of strong coffee. He'd been sleeping in his clothes. Grabbing the phone, Matt started to leave by the front door. *Damn*, he thought, *I need to pee*. It saved his life.

Instead of the door, Matt walked the other direction, to the toilet.

When he finished and stepped back into the hall, he noticed a large window to his left. It was covered with plywood. It took effort, but he finally kicked at it until his foot hurt. He put his shoulder into it, using all his strength until it gave way.

Stepping out with the sun burning his eyes, he heard loud banging. It was the door he used last night. They couldn't dislodge the large steel bar. Matt knew it wouldn't hold for much longer, and he started to run. Brick told him running only made him more conspicuous, but Carling didn't know the depth of fear Matt was feeling. *If I'm going to get caught, it'll be trying to escape. Not cowering in some dark corner.*

He sprinted until he ran under the Gardiner Expressway. Matt was almost to Queens Quay when he stopped, hand on knees, gasping for breath. He realized there was a taxi idling at the curb. He got in, still wheezing as he pulled the door closed.

"Where to?" the driver said.

Matt's hands were shaking. It was hard to breathe. When he could open his wallet, he counted. "How far will one hundred and eighty-five dollars take me? Drive."

He leaned back, silently thanking Cyberia.

• • •

Sitting in Claussen's hotel suite, Harding was annoyed by planes taking off and landing. Winnipeg's airport had more traffic than he expected.

Why would anyone pay the price for this suite with noises like that? He thought. *At least we're close to the corporate jet, ready on short notice.*

Harding was switching between Canadian news and CNN when his phone chirped. It was Kranshon.

"Give me the good news!" Harding said.

"I've got good news, and I've great news," Kranshon said. "Tremain used his library card, his only mistake. It was enough. He used a computer at the Toronto Reference Library. My guy got into the library computer Tremain used. He found the email in the history. We know where Tremain's heading. He's there now."

"Next move?"

"We take him," Kranshon said. "We'll hold him until you bring Claussen."

"We'll be wheels up in thirty minutes," Harding said.

"We're covering the airport, train, and bus stations," Kranshon said. "They're looking for the other three. In the meantime, I'm concentrating on Tremain. I have the team assembling now. Hold on, boss," he said with a background of horns honking and brakes squealing. "Asshole. Sorry boss, not you. Some jerk ran a hard yellow and almost creamed us."

"I'm waking Claussen now. Don't make a move until we get there."

"Roger that, boss."

Claussen danced with excitement when he heard. "That's what I've waited for. How soon can we get there? Tell your men not to hurt him. I want that privilege."

"The jet's being fueled now. Pilot says a little under three hours. It's half past eleven now," Harding said, looking at his phone. "We touch down at Billy Bishop Airport around three."

"What's Tremain's location," Harding asked his aide.

"Corktown, sir."

"I'm told traffic won't be a problem," Harding said. "We've rented an entire parking lot on Dockside Drive, near his location."

Claussen beamed an orgasmic smile, he was so animated. "Finally," he muttered, looking out the window. Dark clouds with shades of gray and black sailed by. Claussen's face reflected sunlight, then changed to shadowy as clouds hid sunlight. "Something is bothering me—"

He was interrupted by the ringtone on Harding's phone. "Talk to me," Harding said. His face turned an angry red. "What do you mean? How could you?"

Claussen didn't have to ask. "It's happened again," he said. "Just when you get Tremain in a corner, he slips away. He's a phantom." Claussen was furious and didn't try to hide it.

"Grab the gear," Harding commanded Lev. Lev looked at Trevor for approval, who nodded. "I'll call the pilot. I need to be in Toronto, taking charge," Harding said.

Harding was on another call when Trevor whispered to Claussen. "I've never seen Lev give anyone the stink-eye before."

• • •

Alone in the executive waiting lounge, Kranshon paced, counting his steps. Fifteen steps one way, turn and fifteen steps back. When he'd told his boss about Matt Tremain's escape, the response sounded calm. Kranshon knew better. The wrath in Harding's quiet voice reached through the phone and almost strangled him.

Kranshon stopped pacing when he heard his ringtone. "Ten minutes out." Kranshon wanted to be anyplace other than Billy Bishop airport on Toronto's lakefront. He stepped outside and called his men together. The six agents came to attention, a reflex from their military training.

"Sir, yes sir," they said in unison.

Kranshon walked to the side. "I'm prepared for the blame," he said. "It's my fault." He looked over at his assistant. "You're my likely replacement."

The man looked visibly uncomfortable with that.

To the west, Kranshon watched a plane on its downward slope, veering slightly toward some smokestacks, then aligning with the runway. The wheels smoked as they contacted the tarmac. Reverse thrust slowed the aircraft enough to turn, heading back to the terminal. The plane passed near a Porter Airlines jet taxiing to its take-off point. Kranshon wished he was on that Porter flight, wherever it was going.

Two of Harding's security agents were first down the steps, posing arms crossed with alert glances on the lookout. Trevor appeared in the doorway, looked around, and walked down. The next man filled the entire doorway and had to duck to exit the plane.

"I've never seen someone that large with such grace," a man next to Kranshon whispered. A look from Kranshon silenced him.

Kranshon saw the rage on the next man exiting. *That must be Claussen,* he thought. He guessed his days with the firm were numbered, probably down to one day—today. Claussen looked familiar despite his altered look, a face still healing.

If Kranshon thought his boss looked stony, Claussen's look was like dry ice. He later told a friend that the look could freeze hell over. Kranshon knew Trevor and was surprised to see him following Claussen.

The scared man led Harding, Trevor, and Claussen into the terminal where he'd arranged a private room. Knowing his career was over,

Kranshon decided to go down with dignity. He offered no excuse. That wouldn't do.

He explained his orders to capture Tremain. "They were following my orders," Kranshon reported. "Monitor the building. Keep it under observation until you got here, Mr. Claussen. Kratz didn't wait. He gave the go sign and started breaking down the door. It's still on me," Kranshon said. "I take the heat for what went wrong."

"Where's Kratz now," Harding demanded.

"Fish food."

"What happened next?"

"The blueprint showed one door. We'd checked the back wall facing Gilead. It was nothing but a boarded-up window. Everyone took positions at the door on Corktown Lane. Kratz thought they could break through the door. It turned out to be a thick metal door with a three-inch thick blocking bar. He had set a Semtex charge," Kranshon said. He knew the risk and now accepted his fate. This wouldn't end well for him. "All I found when I got there was that plywood board hanging by a hinge...and Tremain was gone." He didn't wait for a response. He saluted, turned, and started toward the door.

"Stop! Claussen instructed. "We need everyone. Your subordinate screwed up. Not you. This should give you motivation, don't you agree?"

Kranshon let out a long breath and nodded. "I want to get the bastard."

"We've been through a lot together, Kranshon," Harding said. "There's nothing I can say that you haven't already told yourself."

Kranshon's shoulders slumped despite his attempt at keeping his back straight. He still had a job.

"I don't know if you've met him," Harding said, "but there's a man I want you to work with. His name is Trevor. I'm putting you both in charge," Harding ended, signaling dismissal.

Claussen turned to Harding. "That's smart thinking. Now you have someone willing to take a bullet for you. Maybe that's what The Brotherhood sees in you."

They see a problem all right. It's with you, Harding thought grimly.

CHAPTER 43

OUT OF TOUCH

"**I** need an address," the cabbie said. "I have to enter it into the computer."

Matt's breathing still hadn't returned to normal from running. He looked at the driver's dark blue Sikh turban.

"I need to enter an address," the driver said, louder this time.

Matt ignored the request. "What's your name? I'm Matt. I can't see your identification from here."

"Raghavendra Bhandari," the man said.

Matt tried to pronounce the name.

"Rag," the driver said. "Use a soft G, make it sound like Raj. Many have trouble saying my name." Matt saw the driver stare at him in the rearview mirror. "You look familiar."

Matt didn't say anything.

"Ah, I know. You're Matt Tremain." It wasn't a question. "Are you in trouble? I saw you running."

"I need to be far away from here. Someone's after me."

The driver took the ramp to the Gardiner Expressway. Instead of the westbound ramp, he drove east, however, toward Woodbine Beach.

Matt waited for the driver to say something.

"With Operation CleanSweep, my brown skin would be undesirable," Rag said. "My family, my culture, would be..." He let the words trail off.

Matt saw Rag turn off the meter. Waiting for the light to turn green, Rag turned, handing the money back. "Your money's no good with me. Do

"

you need a place to hide?" He lifted the radio handset and announced. "Dispatch, I'm through for the night."

"Sleep well, Dr. Bhandari," the dispatch said with deference.

Rag didn't hesitate when the light turned green. He drove east to Pickering. Turn after turn later, Matt recognized the Cherry Downs Golf Club. Rag drove two more hours, seemingly at random, but Matt thought not. Finally, Rag said, "I have an idea." The driver used his personal phone and clicked a number.

Matt couldn't follow the fast-paced conversation in a different language. He watched Rag gesturing as if the person on the other end could see him.

"I was talking to my wife, Nagina," the driver finally explained.

Matt placed his trust in the man with a regal bearing. Matt wondered what Rag did before immigrating to the land of golden highways, a job for everyone. *Well, it helps if you can drive a cab*, Matt thought.

"Hold on." Rag put the taxi in gear, looked over his left shoulder, and pulled smoothly into an empty lane. "I hope you like vegetarian," he laughed. "We're going to Brampton, the Sikh Ghetto."

"You have something worked out?" Matt wanted to know.

"You need food and rest. Besides, there's a cricket match I want to see. My favorite bowler is Sunil Narine. I like him."

Matt nodded, pretending to understand.

"When the match is over I will teach you how to tie a turban," Raghavendra said. "Nobody looks at me. They only see a turban. It can be your best disguise ever."

Matt looked around as they stopped in the driveway of a duplex, the one to the left. Standing in the doorway was one of the most beautiful women he'd ever seen. *Except for Michelle*, he thought quickly.

Cooking spices and incense produced a reassuring feeling as he walked through the door.

"I am Nagina," she said, making a slight bow and pressing her hands together. "Namaste." Matt knew it was from the heart, not the way Caucasians tossed the word around in Yoga class.

Raghavendra smiled. "Namaste is an ancient Sanskrit greeting. In Hinduism, it means I bow to the divine in you."

Matt started to weep, and his new friends drew him into a heartfelt hug.

"Do you have a landline?" Matt finally said.

• • •

Carling was worried. He'd lost all communication with Matt. As a backup, they had thirty-five-year-old Motorola pagers. Carling called it their ultimate fallback position and didn't laugh. "Funny. Most people think technology has made them obsolete."

"They transmit small bits of data in the way they were meant to since they were called beepers," Carling told Matt. Hoping for a pager message, Carling stood in a bus shelter on Davenport Road. He'd used all his training to avoid surveillance. Scotty arrived in his '54 Peugeot, belching clouds of stomach-churning exhaust. *Not a friend of the environment. It's a car that wouldn't look out of place in Havana*, he thought.

"Brick."

"Scotty."

That was often the extent of their conversations, a relationship established at the police academy. They seemed to know what the other was saying. Scotty was someone Carling trusted with his life, a faith cemented during their long police careers.

Carling had four marriages in his rearview mirror. Each new bride convinced he could be shaped into something he wasn't. He was a cop 24/7, and a 24/7 drinker in his early days. Giving up heavy drinking back then made him cranky. People tended to avoid him. This was old news to Scotty. He was speeding and changing lanes, the car tilting precariously on sharp corners.

"You've become quite fond of the young blogger."

Carling considered that and took a deep breath. "Matt's got balls. I told you what happened in Florida, in Apalach. He had my back."

"That's something you never forget," Scotty said.

"The kid was afraid but pushed through his fear. I underestimated him at first."

"You're bothered."

"Claussen is on his way if he's not in Toronto already. I tell you, Scotty, it scares the crap out of me. He has resources he's coming for us with, I'm certain. Matt is smart and careful, but all it takes is one mistake. You and I know the smallest detail can give someone away."

It was a lot coming from the taciturn detective. Scotty kept driving, nodding to show he was listening.

Brick sighed and brushed back his hair. "We have this," Carling said, holding the old Motorola pager. "I gave him some tips, but you know...." his words trailed off.

Scotty turned north on Yonge Street, east on Davisville, then north on Mt. Pleasant. They bought supplies to take to the safe house, hoping Matt was there. The house was on Corktown Lane. Carling and Scotty bought the place on their own, off the books, and they kept it secret. "Not many people have heard of Corktown Lane," Carling had said when they bought it.

"I need to stop at home," Scotty said, squeezing between two houses that shared a driveway, taking care not to scrape the paint on his beloved Peugeot. The laneway flared out to allow parking. They got out of the car and headed to the door.

"Let's hope for a quiet night," Scotty said. "A night like this calls for breaking the rules. I'm hauling out the single-malt."

Carling couldn't believe his eyes when they got to the safe house on Corktown. The front door was hanging by one hinge. He saw damage from the blast. "No," he shouted and pounded on Scotty's shoulder. "They got to Matt. Fuck me sideways."

He was part way to the door when his pager vibrated, the tone chirping.

"I know it's Matt. What's going on? He sent me a number I don't recognize."

Carling tapped in the number on his cell phone. Hearing the call go to voicemail, he chewed over the implications, putting his phone on auto redial.

CHAPTER 44

You've got Twenty-Four Hours

"What did you find out?"

Kranshon placed his phone on speaker so everyone could hear. The question from Claussen sounded even louder asked in a soft voice. The two men looked at each other. Trevor nodded to Kranshon and took over.

"He was at least a block away," Trevor said. "They ran after him and saw Tremain turn a corner. When they got to the corner, nothing. Not a trace. It didn't take long to comb the area."

Trevor continued the report. "We scoped out every building that was open. Locked cars were intact—nothing to show they'd been jimmied. We also checked under all vehicles in a five-block radius. Nothing. "

Kranshon took a calming breath. "One of my men saw a bus and followed. Tremain wasn't on the bus. What—?"

Claussen cut him off.

"You've got twenty-four hours," Claussen's said, his threat explicit. "I want him by then, or submit your retirement plans."

"Well, we're in it together now," Trevor said.

Harding nodded, and they stepped outside.

"What do you think?" Harding tried to sound calm. It wasn't working. "If you think Claussen's a problem, wait until I tell you about The Brotherhood."

"I've only heard rumors," Trevor said.

"They're more than rumors. Let's go somewhere we can talk. I'll be breaking a confidence, but it's my judgment call. We need to be together on this. You rode down with Powell; let's take my car."

Harding turned onto Polson Street. He drove to the end and pulled into the last parking spot. A high chain-link fence surrounded a collection of old buses, vans, and tractor-trailers. Two tankers were moored alongside, water lines indicating they were both waiting for cargo.

A robust wind blew a flotilla of blustery clouds scraping the top of the CN Tower.

"Neither of us has said a word since we got into the car," Harding said. "Look at that. Whitecaps on Toronto Harbor." He stared. "It's a metaphor."

"You said you were going to tell me about The Brotherhood," Trevor aske.

Harding stared through the windshield.

"*La Fraternité de l'Eagles*," Trevor said. "Fraternity, society, or whatever you call it, is rooted in history. You can guess it started in France. I was curious. Over five hundred years ago, the new French king wanted to marry his cousin's widow, but he had a slight problem: he already had a wife. The Bishop of Vivier, Damien Bussiere, got involved and met with the Pope, negotiating an annulment. The Bishop looked forward to the influence he'd have with the new king, favors returned."

Harding rolled down the window to take in a breath of the cold air.

"It didn't work out. The new king turned out to be a liberal reformer. Father Damien was furious. He wrote to four like-minded intimates, each a man of considerable wealth. Supposedly, their combined fortunes accounted for over eighty-five percent of the country's national wealth at that time."

"That's how the Fraternity got started?" Trevor asked.

"Yes. The membership's been kept to four. When they meet, there's an empty chair, a tribute to Father Damien Bussiere. I tried Google. There's no record of the good Father's end. Like the original Fraternité, these people have money and resources you and I can't begin to imagine," Harding said. "This is breaking all my confidences," he said, looking at Trevor. "I just call them The Brotherhood now, it's easier for me to say.

I suck at French. Anyway, there are still four people, but one's a woman. The four control a significant portion of the world's wealth. The woman lives in Iceland. One man lives in Spain. There's another from Brazil. The last is Chinese, residing in Canada. Who thinks of evil in places like that?"

Harding pulled a face and continued. "They share a common bond, protecting their wealth. Ideas like tax reform, healthcare, and legal and social improvement are threats. They back politicians on the far right. They fund propaganda about the leftist menace. The Brotherhood would like to see the United States and Canada to implement a national identity card system."

Trevor tried to take it all in and didn't interrupt.

"Their ultimate design is far more than Claussen's plan," Kranshon continued as Harding stared at him. "They're putting a lot of money behind uber-nationalism throughout the world, especially in the U.S."

"Harding told me they're considering an embedded radio chip. Everyone would have one. A security agent walking past could scan for identification. The chip would signal an arrest. Illegal immigration would be eliminated. A person with dissenting views could constantly be monitored. Any contrary religious groups would be surveilled. A chip would transmit a code, and the person would be apprehended. Humanely, of course. The Brotherhood is prepared to put serious money behind programs like that."

"I had no idea," Trevor said. "No wonder they were so interested in Claussen's ideas."

"I have to say, Trevor, you did a great job keeping Claussen safe while we were looking for him."

Trevor reddened at the compliment.

"They gave us instructions to capture him," Kranshon said. "Curiously, they hinted we needn't be too diligent. If you and Claussen slipped by us on occasion, well..." He let the words trail off.

Not much surprised Trevor, but this did. "I don't know what to say, Kranshon."

"The Brotherhood has reached the end of their patience. They had a meeting in Iceland recently. That's why you and I are sitting here. If Claussen can get this revenge out of his system, they can put him to work developing the next CleanSweep. They want to help Claussen get revenge out of his system. We now have twenty-one hours. I hope we didn't waste too much time talking."

"Thanks for the background, Kranshon. Let's pull up what we have so far and compare notes," Harding suggested.

They both looked at their tablets, analyzing all the information on record.

A blast of wind rocked the car. "Is that an omen," Trevor asked.

The two men kept reading until Harding said, "I need some coffee," and turned on the ignition. "There's a Tim Horton's nearby." While they waited at the drive-through, an idea struck him.

● ● ●

"I found his weakness," Trevor said. "This photo got me thinking." He indicated a picture on his tablet. "Michelle Lee-Jones, age twenty-eight, works at a tech company in Toronto, commuting from Hamilton. Look how many times they've talked. She's the weak link."

"What's the connection?" Kranshon asked.

"Love, passion, sex. That's our way to him. Tremain's gone to ground. Same for the detective. The TV reporter and her cameraman are nowhere to be found either. Except for the close call on Corktown Lane, they've eluded us. They haven't left any electronic footprints, except using that library card, and now this, calling his girlfriend." Trevor smiled. "His Achilles heel, he's vulnerable."

"I like where this is going," Kranshon said.

"We're running out of time, and you told me how ruthless The Brotherhood will be with failure." Trevor sipped his coffee, thinking. "We can't get to them, so let's get Tremain to come to us. We use Ms. Lee-Jones as our bargaining chip."

"I don't know," Kranshon said. "I've done my duty, what I've been asked. I've never hesitated when it was necessary to kill—but this is sleazy."

"Will The Brotherhood accept our apology if we fail?" Trevor said. "This isn't the time for debating ethics. I don't want to face the repercussions of failing The Brotherhood, do you?

Kranshon was quiet.

"I say we tell Harding," Trevor said. "Let him decide. Will that let you off the ethical hook?"

• • •

The project stalled. It wasn't going well. For Michelle, today was garbage in-garbage out, GIGO. No matter how much she tried, her programming kept ending with the wrong code.

She decided to sign out early. "Catching the train before the rush hour," she said, passing the front desk.

"It's turning cold," the receptionist said.

"Thanks," Michelle said. She put on her bulky grey coat, taking a hat and scarf from the pockets. She waited for the elevator, wondering again why Matt wasn't answering his phone. He hadn't called or attempted to contact her since that last cryptic call. *Was it his words? Did his mood sound wrong? No, it's what he did say that bothers me*, she thought. *Is he breaking up with me*? Michelle quickly squashed that thought. *He loves me.*

On the commuter train to Hamilton, Michelle tried to replay that last phone call. Her apprehension followed her as she walked along Victoria Avenue. She tried another call, but it went straight to voicemail.

Mid-afternoon, the sidewalk was uncrowded. Nearby a green van pulled into a loading zone to her left.

Retail therapy will help, she thought, stopping to look at a window display. Michelle saw reflections in the window of two men walking in her direction, who stopped abruptly behind her. Michelle turned when one of the men asked a question. She didn't understand because of his accent. "What did you say?" Michelle said as a cloth covered her face.

It was over in less than a minute. Michelle felt euphoria, faintly aware of being lifted gently into a van, the side door closing without a sound.

"Did anyone see us?" the man in the passenger seat asked.

• • •

Something's wrong, a woman thought. She was walking on the other side of the street. She wasn't sure what she'd seen but she called 911 anyway. "I can't be sure. Maybe I'm mistaken," she told an arriving police officer.

CHAPTER 45

THE CHECHEN

Why *am I floating on an inflatable raft, waves rocking it back and forth? Maybe that explains the nausea*, she thought. *Am I seasick?* The mildly pungent, musty odor was no more than a curiosity. Aware of the taste, she had no context for it.

Michelle had a growing sense of alarm. She couldn't comprehend her irregular heartbeat and diminishing breathing capacity. She was going into respiratory depression, her body lacking the ventilation to perform a full extension of the lungs to provide the needed gas exchange.

It felt as if she was clamped in a large vise, slowly compressing her chest, constricting her breathing.

It wasn't terror; Michelle felt impending death.

• • •

"Are you sure she's okay?" the passenger asked.

"See if she's breathing," the driver said, looking over his shoulder. "I gave her a larger dose than usual."

"Pull over, let me check," the passenger said. When the van came to a stop, he jumped out and opened the side door. "Her eyes are fluttering. It looks like she's trying to talk."

"She's breathing then. Get back in," the Chechen said. "We have to transfer her to the ambulance before we cross the border."

"Where is it, the ambulance?"

"A garage on a farm south of Grimsby."

"Where did you learn how to, you know, knock her out like that?"

The Chechen glared at his passenger, then turned his attention back to driving. "You ask too many questions. Ridge Road takes longer It'll be faster taking the QEW expressway. This is slower, but if anyone saw us grab her, the cops will be checking the QEW, for sure."

The passenger nodded, rebuked for asking questions.

"I used a veterinarian."

"What," the passenger asked.

"You asked me how I sedated her. The vet allowed me to practice on some dogs. Don't tell PETA," the Chechen said, laughing. "I already knew what to do but didn't want to burst his bubble. I needed a test run to refresh my skill."

"Chloroform?" the passenger said.

"Nah. That's not used anymore. There's Halothane in liquid form. You need a syringe, and it's hard to get that right on a moving target. It looks good in the movies though; a quick thrust is all that's needed." The Chechen man swerved to avoid a pothole. "Fluothane's better. It's administered by inhalation. That's what I gave her. Controlling heart rate and breathing is critical, why I asked you to check. That's what worries me."

A car sped past the van, nearly clipping the front-left corner of the vehicle. The Chechen shouted something, a language the passenger didn't understand. The context was obvious, however.

"Son of a whore," the Chechen said, this time in English. "That's what I called him."

"The vet sold me Forane," the Chechen continued. I learned to use in Russia." He lifted a can from the drink holder. "This is an aerosol anesthetic. It was quick, eh? She didn't feel a thing."

"But you did use a syringe later?" the passenger said.

"When we had her in the van, fluothane to keep her asleep. Want me to try some of this spray on you?" The Chechen said. It wasn't a pleasant laugh.

They rode in silence. The passenger turned on the radio. "*Nyet*," the driver said. "No radio and put down your smartphone."

Ridge Road made a slight zig on Mountain Road, then a zag to the east. The Chechen turned into a driveway, driving a short distance past the house. A large shed had a door opening to the side.

"Open the door. Use this key," the Chechen said.

Inside was the ambulance, white with blue and green striping.

"Close the door quickly!"

As he closed the door, the passenger heard a shout he didn't understand. He guessed it meant trouble, however. "She's scarcely breathing. I gave her too much. I told you to check. All you had to do was turn around and look," the Chechen said, his anger clear.

"She's barely breathing." The Chechen had a look of panic as he talked.

"You've always seemed so calm," the passenger said.

"Shut up, fool." The driver switched to a language the passenger had no way of translating.

"Quick, get my bag," the Chechen said.

The Chechen withdrew a vial, pushing a new syringe through the seal. Without explanation, he threw the syringe and vial down in frustration. "I have a better idea," he muttered. "A nitroglycerin spray. I should have considered it earlier."

Using the spray, the Chechen began compressions, a light thrusting on Michelle's chest until he felt steady breathing again.

"She's breathing," the driver said. "Now, we can transfer her into the ambulance. There's a compartment, top right. Get the ventilator. That will even help us at the border, having her face covered. There." He pointed at two garment bags. "We need to wear uniforms. When we get to the border, let me do the talking. Keep your mouth shut."

Waiting to shift Michelle to the ambulance, the passenger didn't realize he'd been holding his breath. "How did you know to use that spray and stuff?"

"I was in my last year of medical school in Moscow. It wasn't a friendly place for a Chechen, like me. I got the bad news. The Russian bastards used rockets, wiping out my town. I'm all...." He gathered himself. "I'm all that's left of my family. Grandparents, my parents, a brother and three sisters, aunts, uncles, cousins, all dead. Not to mention friends. I hate Russians."

As they transferred Michelle to a gurney, she let out a sound. It wasn't a groan; it sounded like a question. The passenger gave a questioning look.

"It's nothing, let her sleep. You keep this mask on her face." The Chechen took out a paper and unfolded it. "This address?" he said, opening the app on his phone. "The address is on the New York side. The driver squinted at the street level view. "It looks like an abandoned factory of some kind." He put the paper away. "It's safe to use the freeway now. We're using the Lewiston-Queenston bridge."

CHAPTER 46

BORDER CROSSING

"**W**hose number is this, Matt? Is it safe? I'm using Scotty's phone."

"How would I know if it's safe," Matt shot back. "I think it's safe. I hope so. It's a landline. I got here by pure chance, and I know not to use my phone, Brick."

"Calm down, Matt," Carling said. "Tell me where you are."

Matt told him about the taxi and ending up in Brampton.

"There's more. That's why I contacted you. Michelle's phone goes straight to voicemail. She always checks messages." Matt couldn't keep concern from his voice.

"How long has that been going on?"

Matt looked at the time on his screen. "Over fifteen hours. What's happening?"

"I'll call back. Hang on and try to stay calm."

Carling had good instincts. Something was terribly wrong about this development.

Matt ended the call and turned to the taxi driver and his wife, who saw his pain. Nagina Bhandari went to the kitchen, walking back with a pot of tea. Perhaps it was the tea, but Matt suspected it was more due to the calm radiating from the couple. Their soft way of speaking helped him relax.

He imagined the privations they've endured, ghettoized and under-valued. As a journalist, Matt wrote a story, interviewing people like them.

Sipping tea, Nagina said, "I trained as a nurse. I've waited over five years for my training to be recognized."

Raghavendra leaned back. "I'm a Botanist, a doctorate in Apiology, the study of the humble honeybee." Rag laughed. "Good preparation for driving a taxi in Toronto, eh?"

Rag was interrupted when their phone chirped.

"It's for you, Matt," Rag said.

"What'd you find out?"

"Easy, lad. Your lady friend left work and hasn't been seen since. She used her transit card, heading back to Hamilton. She's not at her apartment, and the neighbors couldn't add anything. There was an anomaly, a 911 call reported two men helping a woman into a van. The witness described a tan Nissan Quest and a partial plate number. Odd," Carling said. "That's only two blocks from Michelle's apartment. When officers responded, they didn't have anything to go on. They finally put out a broadcast describing the van. Nothing."

"What do you make of it, Brick?" There was a long pause, leaving Matt wondering if his friend heard the question.

"I don't believe in coincidence," Carling said. "I'll call if I hear—"

Matt slammed down the receiver.

"I'm sorry about your phone. He doesn't know anything for sure," Matt said to his hosts. "I need to think." Nagina refilled his cup, Matt watching the steam spiraling. It reminded him of smoke signals in old westerns. That always spelled trouble for the cowboys. He walked onto the back deck, closing the door behind him. He looked up at the stars spreading like a celestial tapestry. A man not given to prayer, his mind began to formulate one, a plea, begging for Michelle's safety.

• • •

The Chechen was careful, staying within the speed limit. Passing motorists glanced at the ambulance traveling toward the border between Canada and the United States.

"Stop fidgeting," he told the passenger. "Border guards are trained to smell fear. It's the same the world over. Let me see your passport."

"Right here," tapping the pocket of his uniform jacket.

"Show it to me, damn it." Satisfied, he told the passenger to move back with Michelle. "Don't say a bloody word."

The Chechen followed green signs overhead, suddenly rattled. "Which is the right one," he mumbled. He followed a line of trucks when he was motioned into another lane. The woman wore a dark blue uniform, shoulder patches of U.S. Customs and Border Protection Officer.

Stopping the ambulance, the Chechen lowered the window. As a man who had crossed many borders during his lifetime, he knew to remain quiet, answering questions and volunteering nothing beyond information requested. He hoped his passenger, now sitting back with the patient, remembered instructions to do the same.

The officer examined the document detailing the destination medical center. The phone number would trigger a spoof number. The person answering would verify the paperwork as legitimate.

Two officers used mirrors to look under the truck. A third opened the back door, the passenger expressing concern for his patient, an oxygen mask over Michelle's face. She was breathing so slowly it was hard to see any movement of her chest.

"She's sedated, officer."

The Chechen clenched his jaw, vowing to smack the passenger for offering unnecessary information once he got the chance.

It didn't matter. The ambulance was cleared. The Chechen's phone indicated a text. After reading it, he adjusted the GPS before pulling onto I-190, merging with the flow of the traffic.

"Now they've texted an intermediate stop," he said over his shoulder.

Fifteen minutes later, he crossed the Niagara River to Grand Island, taking the off-ramp onto West River Parkway. "There's Whitehaven Road," the Chechen said, starting to laugh. "It's a funny place to take someone in an ambulance, there's a sign Assumption Cemetery."

"Huh," the passenger said, sounding like he was sleeping.

"Why did they have us circle like this," the Chechen said, venting his frustration. Arriving, he drove back until they were shielded by trees.

The headlights swept past a man by a black Sprinter van, a sinister looking vehicle with dark tinted windows. Nobody said a word. The three moved Michelle to the van. Placing her onto a mattress, the Chechen was relieved to see breathing, slow but steady lung movements.

The stranger handed over a key fob and drove away with the ambulance. The transfer took less than four minutes.

The Chechen didn't see any observers as he turned left and headed toward the interstate. He had a new address in Lackawanna, south of Buffalo. With light traffic, they drove past the city, turning onto Route 5, the Buffalo Skyway.

"See those wind generators," the passenger said. "They're kinda sorta neat."

"Like ghosts standing guard over the old steel mills," the Chechen said. "If you listen, you can hear them sigh."

It was getting dark when the Chechen parked at a construction trailer.

"I'm glad she doesn't weigh much," the passenger grunted.

"There's supposed to be a bed inside."

The two men carried her in and placed her on the bed. "She's soiled herself," the Chechen said with tenderness. He didn't want his assistant to see her undressed. "Wait outside."

The Chechen checked Michelle's vital signs. He did his best to clean Michelle, then covered her with a blanket before calling the other man in. "There's a coffee maker. And I have vodka in my bag. We can rest now after I make my call."

• • •

"It's all arranged," Harding said. Claussen sat in the back. Trevor stood at the open door. "Tremain has to take the bait. We've got his girlfriend. As soon as he hears, he'll come charging like a raging bull."

Claussen clapped his hands. "Brilliant, let's go."

"All I need are the GPS coordinates," Trevor said.

"I want eyes on her. There've been enough screw-ups," Claussen said. "I intend to micro-manage now."

Harding's jaw clenched. His men knew he was pissed, seeing him walk away, clicking a speed dial on his phone.

Trevor watched him. "He's not happy about something, boss."

"Screw him! Let's get going."

Trevor never heard Claussen utter such an inelegant phrase, another indication the man was close to a meltdown. "We need to trust his team," indicating Harding. "They're doing the heavy lifting on this."

Claussen was silent, a smirk on his face.

Harding walked back with a taut expression, almost hissing words between closed lips. "We're doing it your way, Claussen." With that, he opened the front passenger door and got in, slamming it to make a statement.

The driver rushed to get into the SUV, slipping on loose gravel. Trevor sat behind, reaching to give Harding a calm-down pat on the shoulder. It worked. Calmer now, "Here's the address," Harding said. I'm assuming we have our passports."

The driver, taking pride in providing a smooth ride, was soon negotiating the afternoon traffic on the westbound expressway. "According to the GPS, we'll be there in two hours. It depends on backup at the border."

CHAPTER 47

SWIMMING UPSTREAM

It felt like swimming upstream against a strong current. One arm overhead then the other, each stroke draining energy. Michelle wanted to stop, to let the water embrace her, to feel like a leaf floating on a lazy summer day. As she fought a sense of detachment, helplessness, Michelle turned her head to the side to take a breath, like her swim team coach had taught her.

Instead of air, she gagged, as if water was filling her mouth, triggering panic.

"Don't worry," someone said. "You're dehydrated. Take small sips. I'll hold your head so you won't choke."

The words implied an accent. *My coach doesn't have an accent*, she thought. She quickly realized she wasn't swimming, and this wasn't her coach. With a mind struggling to make sense, Michelle felt her body go rigid, an intense pain was like her head was in a large clamp.

"Relax, it will help," someone said. A hand stroked her forehead. "It will get better."

Work...?

I was... looking... at, what... a window display?

Matt, I must call—

Her eyes opened to a terrible reality, and Michelle tried to raise her arm, to touch her sore lips.

"I'm truly sorry," the Chechen man said. "My comrade put duct tape over your mouth." The voice suggested compassion. "It was a stupid thing to do. It could have killed you, drowning in your own vomit."

Michelle struggled to understand. Her headache lessened when a cool cloth was placed over her forehead.

"I had to remove the tape quickly. I'm afraid it still hurts."

Michelle felt tape being removed from her arms, the last wrenching the skin, and her wrists felt like they were on fire.

"Would you like to sit now?"

Michelle felt an arm under her shoulders, lifting her to a sitting position.

"More water," she heard the man say, trying to make sense of his accent. There was a slight inflection, the nuance escaping her, but it seemed important to identify it. She didn't know why it mattered.

Slowly, Michelle tested her five senses. *Touch?* She rubbed her hand over a mattress, maybe a blanket. *What's that taste?* There weren't words to describe the taste. It was appalling. *The smell?* she thought. *An odd hospital smell mixed with the unpleasant odor of the garage where I get my car serviced.*

Sight? Something held Michelle back from opening her eyes. She imagined the face of evil. She couldn't resist. Squinting, she slowly opened her eyes.

It was like being tossed by a tornado. Michelle looked at discolored ceiling tiles, one with an odd-looking stain Michelle couldn't identify, and cringed at the dirty windows. Clean windows were an obsession of hers.

She turned to a man sat next to her, his arm held her head, placing a pillow behind her, but it was strange; she wasn't afraid of him.

Without thought, Michelle screamed. It started as a primal gut reaction from the inside. The scream reached outside, hurting her throat as she shrieked liked the man in the painting by the Norwegian artist, Edvard Munch.

I'm in a horror film, and I don't know the plot or my lines, she thought. Michelle heard soothing words from the man sitting next to her but wasn't pacified. This wasn't a friend, no matter how reassuring he sounded.

"It's about Matt, isn't it?" Michelle said. With that, the dam holding back her tears gave way, streaming down her cheeks. When the man tried to wipe her face, she slapped his hand away. "Don't touch me!"

"You should eat something," the Chechen man whispered. "You need water and food."

Michelle glared, rebuffing his words. She'd always thought she was good at stink-eye. "What's this place? It's filthy."

"It's a trailer used for a construction site. Who cleans, eh?"

Suddenly, Michelle was horrified at a dominating odor—urine. *It's coming from me.* The ammonia-like odor was even more potent because she was dehydrated. "I pissed myself?"

"You were sedated. It couldn't be helped. I tried to clean you and removed your—"

Michelle instinctively reached under the covers as she stifled another scream.

"Don't worry," that slight accent again. "I mean you no harm. Your honor is intact."

For some reason, she believed him.

"I've cleaned your clothes, and there's a toilet," the man said. "You can finish cleaning yourself."

Michelle wanted to make sense of it all.

"I'll give you privacy. I'll wait outside."

When he walked out, Michelle tried to stand, the blanket dropping to the floor. *Oh my god, I'm naked,* she thought, steadying herself as she walked to the toilet. The water was cold but soothing on her face.

She looked at her clothes, draped over the back of chairs. She blushed, realizing she had been wearing her sexy best in case Matt—

What have I gotten into?

• • •

Her clothes were damp, but it felt good to get dressed. Michelle felt the back-right pocket of her jeans. Her phone was still there. Michelle ignored trendy, flashy smartphones, preferring her compact device. She tiptoed to the window and saw the man standing next to a van. *He's smok-*

ing. How'd he fail to find my phone? He would've found the phone when he washed my clothes, she thought. *Did he leave it on purpose*?

She turned it on, realizing prompt action was needed. *Damn, only nineteen percent of the battery.* Michelle saw the service provider icon of an American company. *Can I call a Canadian number?*

She called Matt first. Voicemail. She scrolled her contacts and called Carling. No answer. No voicemail. Feeling desperate, she couldn't remember Susan Payne's phone number. Watching the man flick his cigarette stub over his shoulder, he stretched back, his hands on his waist. She didn't have much time.

Why didn't I think of it sooner? My call history, she thought. Susan called her last week. There it was. She pressed the call icon and held her breath. Susan answered at once. Michelle whispered her situation. "I have to hang up now, he's coming back. Can you locate me from this call? Contact Matt. You have to help—"

Michelle slipped the phone into a pocket as the door opened.

CHAPTER 48

A Chance We have to Take

"**I**t's Michelle, Remy." She's been kidnapped," Susan yelled.

"What? What did you say, Susan?"

"She whispered, but I filled in the blanks."

Susan stared at the phone. "It's creepy," she said. "Michelle was whispering; it was hard to hear clearly. She tried to call Matt but got his voicemail. Do you still have an emergency contact?"

Remy ran over to the desk, unzipping a pocket of his messenger bag. "We're using this," he said. "It's a Motorola knockoff. We used these when we were investigating CleanSweep. They're old-school, almost impossible to monitor. Where's yours?"

"I'm too rattled by the call. Make contact, please."

He sent a numerical message. The device immediately vibrated a return message. Remy looked at the number. "I don't know that number," he said. Opening a drawer, he took out a phone.

"Where'd you get that dinosaur?"

"Funny thing about these old phones," Remy said. "They don't send a GPS signal." Susan watched him enter an unrecognizable number. "Matt? Hold on. Susan needs to talk to you."

"Here!" Susan grabbed the phone. "Michelle called. She's in trouble, Matt."

"Her phone goes to voicemail. I tried," Matt said.

"She's been kidnapped. That means Claussen," she said. Susan turned on the speakerphone for her and Remy to hear Matt screaming. "She managed to tell me she's being held on the the American side."

"Where?" Matt shouted.

"I've told you all I know."

"He cut me off." Susan looked at the phone. "Claussen's behind this."

• • •

"What did you say, Matt?" Carling said. Slow down and say that again."

"Kidnapped," Matt said. "It's Susan. Michelle's tried to call me, but I left the phone in my apartment. That's what you told me to do. She tried you, then contacted Susan. Michelle's been kidnapped, and they've taken her across the border."

Carling watched the blood drain from his friend's face. "That's your weakness. They've found a way to get to you. I should've anticipated a move like that."

Matt squared his jaws, looking determined. "We need guns. If they hurt her," he managed to say before breaking into tears. "Not Michelle!"

"Hold on, partner. Claussen's trying to get in your head. You can't let that happen. No one's contacted you yet. You don't know their plan. If she phoned a warning, they might have been behind the call," Carling said. "Both of us need to stay calm, especially you. You're smart. Use that."

"We've no idea what's happening, where Michelle is. They've taken her across the border."

"We can't rush headlong. The hard part is waiting to hear something."

"That's easy for you, Brick. She's not your girl," Matt said, instantly sorry.

"Knock it off, Matt. They need to show proof of life. Until they reel you in, they can't afford to..."

"You were going to say kill her," Matt shouted.

They were interrupted when the French doors opened. Nagina Bhandari was holding a tray. "I was about to offer tea." Matt and Carling lowered their voices and thanked her as she placed the tray on a side table, backing away. They waited until she left, closing the door.

"There's another issue," Carling said. "The longer we stay here, the riskier it becomes for the two of them—Rag and Nagina. Claussen likely doesn't know about them yet, but we don't want in danger."

"You're right. I know. I'm sorry I bristled like that."

"Let's pack and get moving, now," Carling said. "We have to get your other phone."

"I'll explain to Rag when he gets home," Nagina said. "I know you're in danger. I will light a candle." She kissed each man softly on the cheek. They were speechless when she pulled a car fob from a pocket. "My Kia," she explained. "It's in the garage. Take it and find your girl, Matt."

• • •

"Can you believe those two, Carling? Nagina gave us her car just like that."

"If Claussen had his way, CleanSweep would've targeted them for elimination. Persons of color were high on his hit list."

Turning east, they saw a string of red brake lights. "What can we do? Look at the traffic jam," Matt groaned.

"If there's an accident, turn off, and work your way to Derry Road until it becomes Rexdale. It's not direct, but it'll get us around this traffic.

"Do you really think she's okay? Did you mean that, or saying it to calm me down?"

"I won't lie to you, Matt. If these guys are professionals, they won't let emotions take over," Carling said. There." He pointed. "Take a right."

"What if they have eyes on the apartment?"

"A chance we have to take," Carling said. "They won't know about Nagina's car."

Matt changed addresses so often he had to think. *What's my address?* He fought panic and drove to his building. A parking space was open on a nearby side street. Locking the car, Matt and Carling walked to the apartment building. Carling scanned the street, tapping his impatience with his foot while Matt fumbled with the key.

"It doesn't look like I've had any visitors. The tell I put there is still in place." Carling didn't tell Matt that a pro would have circumvented it with ease.

Matt saw Carling draw his weapon, holding it alongside his leg.

Opening the door slowly, Matt leaned in. "I don't see anything."

Carling followed, closing the door, and sliding the deadbolt into place. "Where's the phone," he asked.

"It's attached to the charger cord." Matt powered his phone on. "Look at all these messages. It'll take hours to go through them all."

"Check those from Michelle's number first. You can go through the rest later."

Matt nodded in agreement. "I'm sorting by name. Look, Michelle's called me over thirty times. I feel guilty. Maybe I could've warned her."

"Time for *mea culpa* later." Carling checked for signs of intruders.

Matt put her voicemail on speakerphone, so Carling could hear as well. "Listen to that pleading in her voice," Matt said. "She's more frantic with each message."

Finally, only two voicemails were remaining. In the first, Michelle sounded like she was drugged. Her mumbling words were incoherent until they heard her say Susan Payne's name.

"One more message," Matt said. "My intuition's telling me not to listen."

His fear was confirmed. It was Claussen. "If you want to see your precious little Michelle alive, it's simple. You'll get a text with an address. You have six hours. Follow instructions or your bitch is dead."

Matt felt his legs turn into rubber. He threw the phone at the wall. Carling moved to catch it in time. "Partner, we need that contact."

Matt flopped back on the sofa, straining to keep from crying. "What can I do, Brick?"

Carling watched his friend trying to move a mountain of feelings. Finally, he reached into his jacket pocket and took out a cigar. "Partagas. I got this in Havana." He went through the lighting ritual, then exhaled, smoke signals puffed toward the ceiling. He was trying to signal Matt to slow down.

It didn't work. Both men flinched when the ringtone signaled a text message.

Reading over Matt's shoulder, Carling had his notebook ready. He wrote down the address and opened a map on his phone. "It's south of Buffalo, Tonawanda? No, Lackawanna. Let's get going, partner."

He saw Matt walk to a closet, retrieving a box from the top shelf. "This might come in handy," Matt said, holding a handgun. Carling hadn't been paying attention, his phone to his ear. He covered the phone when he saw the gun.

"No way, Matt. You can't get that across the border. Scotty's heading to Buffalo. He'll arrange weapons for us after we clear customs and immigration."

"I have something else, too, Brick. He went into the bedroom and came out with a roll of cloth. "Nagina showed me how to turn this fabric into a turban. Will this work as a disguise? Do you think they will be expecting someone wearing that?"

"That's crazy... Grab your passport and let's get the hell on the road. Bring the turban if you want something to hang onto."

CHAPTER 49

GRIGORI

"Passports ready?" Kranshon said, easing the Escalade toward the inspection booth, an unnecessary prompt for men experienced in border crossings. "It's going to rain," he said, glancing at the rearview. "It's getting dark." His passengers weren't interested in a weather report.

The officer's neon-red hair shone in glaring contrast to her dark cobalt-blue uniform, Customs and Border Protection patches on each shoulder. Her gold badge reflected sunlight, blinding Kranshon momentarily.

Handing over his passport, Trevor muttered, "She sucks lemons for breakfast. What a sourpuss."

Lightning flashed as she asked the usual questions. "Destination? Citizenship? How long do you intend to stay—"

A dazzling flash was quickly followed by deep thunder. She flinched, handed their passports back quickly, and waved them on.

"She didn't even welcome us to the USA," Trevor said.

"Turn the radio off and drive," Claussen shouted. "I need to think. I'm savoring Matt Tremain standing in front of me."

Javin Harding sat in the front passenger seat. He leaned over, pretending to reach into the console, and gave Kranshon a warning look. Kranshon replaced the original driver at a rest stop. *If it weren't for The Brotherhood's order, I'd cut Claussen free. Calling him a loose cannon doesn't come close. He's going to take us all down*, Harding thought.

Kranshon nodded, acknowledging to the warning.

"Trevor's with us. He's a pro," Harding said. "If it goes sideways, well—"

Driving on I-190, the tires made a sound like bacon sizzling on a grill. The weight of the Escalade kept it from hydroplaning, spraying water pooled on the highway.

"There's an E-Zpass transponder in the glove compartment," Kranshon said, keeping his voice low. He didn't want to risk Claussen's annoyance. "We'll need it when we get to the Grand Island Bridge."

Harding stuck it on the windshield.

"How will that work? We don't have New York plates," Trevor leaned forward to ask.

"E-Zpass recognizes a Virginia transponder. We're good to go,"

After crossing the second bridge, Kranshon considered bypassing downtown Buffalo. Instead, he stayed on I-190, alongside the Niagara River. The fast-moving current was challenging a small powerboat fighting its way upstream.

"Who'd want to eat fish from this filthy river?" Claussen said.

The other three men remained quiet.

Kranshon appreciated the light traffic of the early Sunday morning. He kept the speedometer under the speed limit, thinking there was no need to give the police a reason to pull them over. With the skyline of Buffalo to the left, the GPS showed a turn onto the Skyway. "Fifteen minutes out, boss."

Harding sent a text ahead, thinking Claussen's smile could have turned water into ice.

• • •

"They'll be here in fifteen minutes," the Chechen said. He told the other man to wait at the gate. "Let me know as soon as you see an Escalade."

He watched the chubby man walk out and turned to Michelle. "The man's elevator doesn't quite reach the top floor," he said, a moment of candor unusual for him. "I'm sorry," he said.

Michelle was surprised but kept from showing any emotion.

"□□□□□□□□ □□□□," his voice sounded weepy. "That's Russian for tethered goat. They're using you to get to your boyfriend. This isn't right. I'm not... I don't like what I'm doing."

Is that a teardrop? It looks genuine, she thought, her spirits suddenly rising. *Maybe this man with the strange accent might let me go.* She glanced at a large clock on the wall. It was hanging crookedly. Michelle felt an urge to straighten it. "There's no time, is there? Whoever it is will be here in less than five minutes now."

"I'm sorry," the Chechen said again.

Michelle didn't feel like accepting his apology.

• • •

"Look at that fat little idiot, waving his arms," Claussen said, as the GPS voice announced, "You've reached your destination on the right." Kranshon didn't stop at the gate. He raced toward the trailer, leaving the chubby man to run after them.

They heard him gasping for breath. "She's inside," the man said needlessly. Trevor waved his hand as if wafting a bad odor away.

Claussen dashed ahead and shoved the door open, straining the hinges.

Michelle looked at him, recognizing the man from pictures. She sat on the side of the bed, a pose suggesting composure. She wore a light touch of makeup, her hair tied neatly back, clothes unwrinkled.

Claussen expected a terrified hostage, one that was disheveled and crying. This woman looked almost defiant. Claussen turned to the Chechen, who was standing with arms crossed like a bouncer at an upscale nightclub—which he was when he wasn't kidnapping Michelle.

Claussen saw flexed muscles straining the sleeves of a black T-shirt and arms wrapped with large tattoos, unable interpret their meaning.

The Chechen told Michelle they represented his prison history, along with some chilling Russian-Mafia affiliations. There wasn't a tattoo of his medical school transcript.

Claussen turned back to Michelle as if making a purchase. "I see why Tremain's attracted to you. But whatever do you see in a gimp like Matt Tremain?" He didn't expect an answer.

Michelle sat calmly.

"You can go now, Grigori," Trevor said, gesturing toward the door.

That's his name, Michelle thought. She hadn't yet heard it and was starting to think he didn't have one.

The Chechen gave Michelle a brief parting look as if still hoping for absolution. He walked out, softly closing the door behind him.

"Stop!" Claussen yelled. "Come back."

Harding stopped Grigori. "The boss wants you."

"I'm not malicious," Claussen said when the Chechen returned. Trevor closed his eyes at Claussen's remark. Risking an eye roll was sure to land him in hot water. "Grigori, you have taken excellent care of, what's her name?" Claussen said. "What's your name," he asked Michelle.

She kept a steady gaze, maintaining her poise and her silence.

"It's Michelle," Grigori the Chechen said.

"Let's go outside. We have a lot to do, preparing for Mr. Tremain," Claussen said to the others. "Leave the fetching Michelle in Grigori's care." They started for the door. "And somebody," Claussen added, "please tell that dithering fat man outside he's no longer needed."

• • •

Michelle and Grigori were alone again. It was like the sound was vacuumed from the room. Grigori watched her slowly breaking apart as she fell back onto the bed, sobbing quietly, more forceful in the softness.

"Thanks for letting me clean myself before they got here, Grigori."

That offered Grigori, the Chechen, comfort as he looked down at □□□□□□□□ □□□□, the tethered goat.

CHAPTER 50

WELCOME TO THE UNITED STATES

"**P**ull off at the rest stop, now!" Carling said. "Driving like that'll..." letting the words trail off. "Now, damn it. I need to pee."

Matt swerved into the right lane, braking hard. He slammed on the steering wheel with frustration, annoyed at a car well under the speed limit. A gap opened at the Casablanca Boulevard exit. Matt accelerated into the exit lane. He considered flipping a finger as he passed the slow driver but let the annoyance pass. "I've got Michelle to worry about," he said.

"What?" Carling had been thinking, not paying any attention to Matt's driving drama. He looked right. "That's a good place to stop," he said. "I can use something to eat. Maybe a coffee."

Matt slammed on the brakes. "We don't have time. Men's room, and we're back on the road. We're so close, and we only have two hours," he said, looking the GPS display.

"Matt. Claussen's using Michelle to get inside your head, and it's working. Slow it down and think. We also have a stop in Buffalo."

"I can't think. Everything's swimming around in my head."

"While your thoughts are swimming, I'm taking the wheel. Your driving's erratic and dangerous," he said, holding a hand to stop Matt from talking. "I'm trained in high-speed driving. Okay, training was back in the day. But I can drive while you focus on what to do when we get there."

"Brick, you're always telling me to come up with a plan, when all the time you've thought of a better one."

"Change sides while I run inside. I won't be long, promise."

Matt got out. He put his hands on his hips and leaned back to stretch his spine. Jogging in place to help the circulation in his legs, he looked to the south, staring at the face of the escarpment. *Saving Michelle's going to be like scaling that wall,* he thought, *something that looks easier from a distance.*

His phone chirped. Matt fished the phone from his pocket. It was a text from Michelle's phone. Excited, he hesitated. *Do I really want to?* he wondered. *I must.* It was a blurry photo, Michelle on a bed, her hands and legs bound with rope, looking like she was unconscious.

Another text arrived with instructions. He made sure the address was programmed, and checked an app showing wait times at the border.

Carling dropped behind the wheel, the car rocking.

"We have some luck, Brick," Matt said. "The wait time on the American side of the bridge isn't long."

Back on the QEW expressway, Carling looked over his shoulder, signaled, and merged left. He pegged the speed at five over the speed limit. "Stop doing that," he said. Matt was drumming his fingers on the dashboard.

Matt reached for his tablet. Powering it on, he clicked on Google maps. "This's easier to see than the phone," he said. "When we're across the border, there's a turn right, across an intersection, then a quick left paralleling Hamburg Turnpike," he said. Squinting at the screen, Matt saw a satellite view of the address. "Okay, Carling. Do you have a plan, or do I go first?"

Carling slowed as they approached the Peace Bridge, driving past Canada Customs booths on the left. A long line of cars was backed up, waiting to enter Canada. Once past the crown of the Peace Bridge, Carling slowed to the speed limit on the American side. "I can't believe it," he said, "an open lane."

He couldn't help it. It was nerves. His hand shook as Matt handed over his passport, confident he would be stopped, questioned, and turned back. "Welcome to the United States, and have a nice visit," the officer said as he returned their passports.

Carling accelerated, then surprised Matt by making an unexpected turn. Instead of following the sign to the interstate, he made a sharp right, almost a U-turn.

"What the—" Matt was almost out of his seat, "Why aren't you taking the expressway?" looking at the direction he expected. "Where are we going?"

"I told you back in Toronto. We need serious firepower. We couldn't risk bringing anything across the border."

"What, you've got another contact like Panama City?"

"This is personal. I've known him for over twenty-five years. We've worked cases that overlapped both cities. He's stand-up, Matt. Scotty's there now, making necessary arrangements."

"Scotty helped during CleanSweep. I don't think I've seen him since—" Matt didn't finish. He sat back as Carling sped down the access ramp to Sheridan Terrace, then a quick right onto Massachusetts Avenue. Passing through the roundabout and driving north on Richmond Avenue, Matt lost track. At last, Carling pulled into a quiet neighborhood and slowed.

A porch light came on, and a man stepped out, Scotty behind. "That's Jess," Carling said. Jess waved them into the driveway. Jess and Scotty followed them. Jess opened the garage door with a remote.

It was quiet. Matt heard the motor pinging, a dog barking in the distance, and a baby crying somewhere. They were all soothing sounds, at odds with his state of mind.

"Thanks for this, Jess. You have no idea what this means," Carling said.

"Who's your partner?"

"Matt. Matt Tremain."

"You're kidding? You're the guy? Brick's talked my ears off about you. You didn't mention that, Scotty."

Shaking hands, Matt realized Carling and Jess were almost doubles. "Where's your fedora?" Matt asked. He couldn't resist it.

"Yeah. Matt has a lame sense of humor," Carling said. "I think that's why he limps," he said, slapping Matt on the shoulder. "Relax, partner."

Inside, Jess pressed the remote. The door closed as Jess turned on overhead lights. "What do you think you might need?"

"Something for closeup, if we manage surprise. What do you think, Matt?" Carling asked.

"Like I'm an expert now?"

"Look at the map again, Matt. Does it give you any ideas?"

Scotty and Jess simply stood by a cupboard and listened.

Matt showed Carling the screen. "See? This looks like a wooded area between the Skyway and this huge building. If we get through there without being noticed. If the address is right. If they're in that trailer," he said. "I don't have anything but ifs."

Jess looked over Matt's shoulder. "That's near an abandoned factory," he said. "That whole area is being leveled. They're getting rid of derelict buildings, sad reminders of steel mills and factories in full operation. Until it's rehabbed, it's a great place to dump bodies. I landed two cases there, both times someone 'happened' to trip over the bodies," Jess said, using air quotes. "You know how it is. No suspects. No leads. Nothing. Pros, likely."

"Copy that," Carling said. "Take care walking there. Tall grass and weeds, scrap metal and sharp objects carrying germs defying identification. Add to that, it'll be getting dark."

"I don't care," Matt said. "Let's go. They've got Michelle."

"You didn't tell me much," Jess said to Scotty. "What's the deal, Wallace?" he was obviously one of the few people allowed to use Carling's first name.

"We're still trying to sort out the details. We know they have her and where. What we lack is intel. How many? The landscape? My guess is they're keeping a low profile, but who knows?"

Jess unlocked the large cupboard and took a weapon off the top shelf. "You can't beat this for close quarters. It's a Desert Tech MDR. You can swing this big-assed boy around and cover a wide area. The forward-mounted ejection spits your casings away to the front. What do you think, Scotty?"

Scotty smiled. "What about throwing in a couple of automatic weapons and handguns to go with it?"

"I happen to think this is the best handgun, a Sig Sauer P226."

"Do you have one for each of us," Carling asked.

"And, more. Do you need backup?"

Matt thought Jess sounded hopeful.

"No, this is personal," Carling said. "It's his show. We're not putting anybody else in harm's way."

"You might like this," Jess said. "An Intratec TEC with a 32-round magazine."

• • •

They loaded enough ammo to start a small war. Goodbyes and thank-yous over, Carling and Matt strapped on the seatbelts. "You have a plan yet, Matt?"

Matt powered the nav system again. "Forty-five minutes. Let's go. I'll tell you on the way."

"Aren't you going to wrap your turban?" Carling said. He meant it to tease Matt but stopped when he saw his friend was crying.

CHAPTER 51

WHAT LUNACY

"**M**ichelle? Kidnapped? I can't believe even Claussen would stoop that low," she said. Susan Payne paced with her hands locked behind her back. "Michelle's in trouble. Matt's in distress. You and I both know Matt will take the bait, running right into Claussen's pile of shit." Hurricane Sue was about to become a category five storm. "This isn't going to end well for Michelle, for us, unless he's stopped. We did once, but this is different. How can we finish the job?"

Three years ago as newsmaker for Action 21 News, she was a household name with countless awards for investigative journalism. Reporting from war zones, she knew the danger, ready to risk it all to get a story.

This wasn't a story, however; it was personal. "I can smell it, Remy. It's intense, palpable."

"We're back on the job," Remy said. "I've been your cameraman for over fifteen years now. Whither thou goest."

"This has Claussen written all over it," she said. "We can't get rid of him."

Susan scrolled through her phone calls, shaking her head. "We don't have any way of contacting them. We agreed to throwaway phones. What good are they if nobody answers?"

"What if Claussen's already has them all?"

Susan didn't answer. Walking to the kitchen, she opened a bottle of wine. Susan carried two glasses in one hand, the bottle in the other. On the sofa next to Remy, she leaned her head on his shoulder. They enjoyed moments like this in the past, but this was different. Lives of their friends were at stake.

"I'm restless. I can't help it. Claussen's using Michelle as bait, drawing Matt into a trap," Susan said.

Her Bluetooth connected with concealed speakers, and she picked Maja Milner from her playlist. The singer's high-range vocals anchored the Swedish quintet, Makthaverskan. The band's booming post-punk music sounded like a car wreck to Remy, but Susan loved it.

Competing with the soundtrack, Susan almost didn't hear the throw-away phone ring. She raced to the pass-through to the kitchen.

Remy saw her face turn a deep crimson as she grew increasingly agitated. He muted the music as she reached for her notebook. Ending the call, she finished writing and turned to Remy.

"Our favorite detective. He confirmed it. Michelle's being held hostage. The confirmation text came directly from Claussen," she said, hissing words through a clenched jaw. "Carling gave me this address," she said, holding the phone for Remy to see. "He's saying Matt wants to go it alone, only the two of them. Carling says it's a stupid thing to do. He asked how long it'll take us."

Remy stood, looking at the time. "Under three hours, depending on the border crossing. This time on a Sunday shouldn't be a problem."

Payne was already packing her gear bag. "Grab your cameras. Let's get going. The M & M's need help."

Remy followed Hurricane Sue out the door. He didn't tell Hurricane Sue about the weapons he had in a duffle bag. *No sense in her worrying at the border,* he thought.

• • •

Angela Vaughn held the overhead strap as the subway gained speed. She held her breath, trying to ignore the heat and unpleasant body odor around her. She remembered driving with a revolving blue light on the dashboard, traffic pulling to the side as she sped through Toronto and missed it.

An overweight woman lurched, the corner of her handbag stabbing Angela in the back. Angela repaid with a sharp elbow, both trying to pretend it was accidental.

Looking at the transit map without really seeing it, Angela mulled over her current life: days watching a computer screen, on the alert for shoplifters. Sitting in a small, dark loss-prevention office was grim. She regarded it as penance, striving to atone for her fall from grace. Angela remembered a young, eager graduate from the police academy, vowing to serve and protect.

Her fall from grace began with a seduction. For Charles Claussen, it wasn't sex. No, power was far more seductive. Claussen knew that better than anyone. He glibly seduced her, recruiting her to be head of security of his holding company. It turned out to be a job enticing her to step over an ethical line. Once taken, there was no retreating.

What's even worse are the extra pounds I'm carrying. I'm gasping for breath walking up, she thought. *I kept in top shape while I was in prison with a regimen of healthy food and exercise. Now, greasy burgers, cheesy fries, and high-calorie snacks.*

She heard the ubiquitous transit's tri-tone signal. "Mind the doors, the doors are closing," the announcement said. A last-second passenger squeezed through closing doors. With a shudder, the subway continued north to Davisville station. *One more stop,* she thought.

Vaughn was depressed and didn't need a shrink to tell her that. She had had it all. Now, she felt she was on a journey to her own Judas Tree, carrying her thirty pieces of silver.

A seat was available. Angela sighed. It wasn't worth it, only going to Eglinton station, the next stop.

Starting up the escalator, she shoved a young man to the side. "Get off your phone," Angela muttered. He gave her a finger salute. She returned that with a upturned chin. *That'll show him,* Angela thought. *Do I have a dinner date with Judy tonight?*

On the escalator, reaching the top, her phone buzzed. Cell service underground was spotty. Now, almost at ground level, Angela heard a ringtone.

The phone vibrated, followed by a special ringtone—morse code for SOS. That meant the one thing she dreaded. Horrified, Angela stopped while the escalator was still moving. At the top, passengers pushed, sending her sprawling onto the tiled floor. Angela scrabbled to a wall, ignoring offers of help. Knees to her chin, Angela tried to make a small profile, flushed with embarrassment. *Who the fuck cares*, she thought, struggling to her feet.

Angela put a hand on the wall, using the other to key an icon for text messages. SOS meant the one person she never wanted to see again: Charles Claussen.

"My plan is working, at last," the text read. "I'll have Tremain and the others soon. Come to this address. I love you."

Angela vomited. *He loves me?* she thought. *What insane asylum am I living in? He's the last—*

On the sidewalk, Angela rushed to make the walk sign. Gasping for breath, she raced to Dunfield Avenue; she didn't hesitate. At her building, Angela took the elevator to level two and her parking place. Angela bought the 3-year-old Volvo because it looked sedate and uncomplicated. The only after-market addition was a gun safe bolted to the floor in the trunk. She checked her inventory of weapons. Angela knew there was a risk crossing the border with them, but it was a gamble she was willing to take.

On the freeway, Angela set the cruise control and tried to think. Claussen's words of endearment were disturbing. *After all this time, he expects me to join him? What lunacy. The man truly is crazy*, she thought.

"I'm coming to the address, Claussen, but you won't like it when I get there," Angela shouted at the windshield.

CHAPTER 52

NO SIGN OF LIFE

"I've thought this through," Claussen said, returning to the trailer. "It's brilliant, Tremain like a bull charging a red cape." He looked around the construction trailer, choosing stage props for his theatrical scene. "Tie her to that chair," he ordered.

Michelle's calm gave way, her eyes filling with tears.

"Don't worry, my dear. It's only for dramatic effect."

He ordered Grigori to place Michelle in a chair. It was a well-worn chair many contractors used and abused. It tilted to one side, the left armrest leaning down at a precarious angle. Michelle started to resist but realized it was useless.

"Hand him the duct tape, Trevor." Claussen then instructed Grigori, "Tape her to the armrests. Perfect. Now, take this rope and tie her to the back of the chair."

Finished, Claussen stepped back like he was directing a play, which in a way he was. Wetting his hands in the rusty sink, he wiped his hands on the filthy countertop. He rubbed dirt onto Michelle's face until he was satisfied. "She looked quite disheveled, eh?" he said.

With a wicked chuckle, he filled a glass and poured water over Michelle's head. "That's it. Dramatic effect," he said. He stepped back, caressing his chin as he thought. "Tearing her clothes will make it look even worse."

Michelle drew back when Claussen ripped her shirt open, but she was restrained by the rope and tape. "Nice tits," he said with an unpleasant sneer.

"An even better idea," he said, taking out his phone. "Turn off some lights." He made a video of Michelle squirming in obvious distress. "I think this makes a nice attachment."

"What's his number, bitch?" Claussen said. I know you have it."

Michelle shook her head no. His slap came so quickly she didn't see it coming. Claussen hit her, then again, blood streaming from a cut on her lower lip.

Michelle, realizing it would only get worse, gave him Matt's number. Claussen took another photo, the dripping blood adding dramatic effect.

"That should rattle him," Claussen said, as he sent off a text, photo, and video to the number Michelle gave him.

● ● ●

Matt and Carling were both startled when a large plane passed over the interstate on its approach to the Buffalo airport.

"I think I can cut back west—"

"That's Michelle's number," Matt said, interrupting Carling. "Wait, it's a text."

Matt read the text, then opened the attachment. He looked closely, refusing to believe what he saw. "It's my worst nightmare... Look at this," he said, holding the phone so Carling could see.

Carling's look was one of pure rage. Matt's head snapped back as Carling accelerated. Matt leaned to see the odometer, moving past the hundred mark, one hundred and five, one hundred and ten, still rising.

Carling's phone chirped. He took the call on the car's Bluetooth connection.

"We've cleared the border," Susan said.

Matt wasn't mad or surprised. He welcomed all the help he could get now. "Thanks, guys," he said. "There's a park slightly north of the address Claussen sent," Matt said. He scrolled through the map on his tablet. "It's called Tift Nature Preserve. Here're the coordinates."

"Did you get that? Meet us there," Carling said and disconnected the call.

• • •

Carling pulled in at the sign for the nature preserve. A blast of cold wind blew from Lake Erie. A line of dark rain clouds marched from right to left and flashed of lightning outlining the swirls. "It'll be dark soon. Where are they?" Matt asked.

"Relax, buddy."

It wasn't long before a car approached from the north without stopping. The next set of headlights blinked as a dark red Jeep Grand Cherokee turned in. Susan raced to give Matt a hug. It was a special gesture coming from someone not one to comfort others.

"What's the plan?" Remy asked.

"Matt thinks it'll fool them if he wears a turban. Then he can knock on the door shouting surprise," Carling said. "C'mon guys, some levity."

Matt didn't laugh, let alone smile.

"There's no way of knowing how many we're up against," Carling said. "We have to assume they're dangerous and professional. And, they're on high alert. Looking at a map, I think Matt's plan is good. It's simple. Simple is best at a time like this." Carling pointed at the map. "Here's the trailer. That has to be where the photo and video came from."

Matt started pacing.

"Stop. That's not helping," Carling barked. "We can't simply drive up, jump out, and shoot. Michelle's safety comes first. We've got extra weapons. Do you need some, Remy?"

Remy shook his head no. He opened his jacket to reveal a holster and handgun. "Plenty of ammo, too."

They all turned when Susan Payne said, "I'm qualified. I can handle guns. Shooting's been my way to let off steam, a hobby—until now."

Carling opened the trunk, handing her an automatic. "That makes us four, against how many?" he said. "When the shooting starts, don't take time to aim. I told Matt in Florida, noise can be unnerving. Point your weapon in the general direction and hope for the best."

"I know what to do," Remy shot back. "Once a Marine, always a Marine."

Carling nodded in approval. "Your training will kick in when the shooting starts. Hang back, Susan. Look for any visible target, okay?" Carling said.

She nodded and pushed the cartridge into place with a practiced move.

"Let's get to it," Matt said, showing the other two the photo of Michelle tied to the chair.

"Good lord," Susan said. "That's..." her words trailing away, not knowing what to say.

Carling took charge of Matt's idea. "Follow me. I'll look for a parking spot alongside the highway. It's Sunday, so there shouldn't be much traffic. We must get across the highway and the railroad tracks. If, and it's a big if, we do that without being seen, we can make our way to the woods. Thanks to Jess, we know they provide cover. It may not be much, but it's better than a frontal approach."

Carling and Matt got into their car and drove south, the Grand Cherokee following close behind. The spot Carling had spotted on the map was a vacant lot. They pulled both vehicles alongside an abandoned restaurant, away from any lighting. Nobody talked while they checked weapons and ammunition. Stepping out of the shadows, they waited for two cars to go by. Nobody in the passing cars seemed to take notice of two vehicles parked in a deserted area. Between organized crime thugs and gangs, people in this area were programmed to mind their own business.

"Let's get going before any other cars come by," Carling said.

They followed as he ran across the highway and stopped at a fence. "I didn't expect this," Carling said. "Throw your weapons to the other side and help each other over."

They saw headlights in the distance coming from the south. "Flatten yourself on the ground," Carling yelled.

"What about snakes," Susan panicked. Nobody answered.

Watching the car's taillights disappear, they scaled the fence to face another obstacle. Three parallel rows of coal cars stretched in both directions. They were exhausted by the time they ducked under the couplings.

"Hurry," Carling whispered as if he might alert someone in the trailer. They made it to the woods, walking until they were at the far edge, the trailer in sight.

"Can you use this?" Susan said, handing Carling binoculars.

Scanning the trailer, he lowered them. "Peculiar. There's no sign of life in the trailer," Carling said, immediately regretting his choice of words.

Matt jumped and started running. Carling held his hand for the others to stay put, then changed his mind. "What the hell," he yelled. "Let's go."

The near-silence at the trailer was creepy, the only sound the whisper of wind.

"There's a note taped to the door," Matt yelled as they gathered at the trailer. Matt tore the note from the door window and read the message out loud.

"If you want to see Michelle alive, here's the address. Feel free to bring your detective friend, along with Payne and Remington. I know you're all reading this."

Matt showed the note. "How's this for insulting? He even drew a smiley face."

Carling looked at the address on the note. "I need to make a call." He dialed and waited. "Jess, what's the location of this address?"

Carling made notes while he listened. He disconnected and looked up.

"Jess says it's an area of abandoned buildings, old factories that were closed years ago. It's dangerous. Rats, people squatting, and who knows what germs if somebody scrapes old, rusty parts." Carling looked at his phone again. "It's north of downtown Buffalo. Jess and Scotty will meet us. We can use their help."

Matt started running back through the wooded area, his limp not slowing him. Almost through the trees, he tripped on a discarded car door, falling to the ground. Blood started oozing through a large rip in his jeans, then spreading down his right leg. Carling knelt and held Matt flat. "Stay put," Carling said. He pulled out a knife, cutting the bloody pant leg to expose the wound. "That's nasty. It needs immediate treatment. That door's rusty and who knows what crud is nearby."

"Wrap something around it," Matt said, trying to stifle a grimace. "I'm going with you, not some hospital."

Remy quickly assessed the problem, taking his shirt off, then stripping off his t-shirt. "Here. Wrap it tightly," he said. "Wait! I forgot I had this in my pocket." He pulled out a coil of wire. "It's a cable for connecting my equipment. It'll make a good tourniquet." When he finished, Remy looked at Matt. "Can you make it over the fence?

Matt took Carling's hand, scrambling to his feet. Born with a limp, it was more pronounced than usual, dragging his foot. "Let's go!"

• • •

Angela Vaughn parked next to a low building and took a pair of binoculars out of the glove box. She watched Carling make a call, turning on a scanner, hoping to listen in to his conversation. The scanner was left over from working for Claussen. It was a gift from a friend in the intelligence community. It could snag chatter from nearby phones.

Frustrated, Carling finished before she could use the scanner. Vaughn ducked down as the two-car convoy sped past her, heading north. Vaughn relied on police training and experience to follow, keeping them in sight.

Carling spotted out the tail right away. He stared at the mirror. *How many are there? Only the driver,* he thought. Carling didn't share his concern.

He placed a call to Remy. "I'm slowing," he said. "Pass me and take the lead. In case we're separated, you have the address, right?"

Remy flicked his lights and swerved out to pass, nearly driving an oncoming car off the highway.

Matt watched Carling ease off the accelerator and adjusted the rearview mirror.

CHAPTER 53

NIGHTMARE COME TRUE

Men gathered around Claussen, waiting. The wind gusted through the abandoned building, creating a low-pitched moan. A man looked over his shoulder as if expecting an apparition flying from the rafters. "Relax, Mark, it's only the wind," the man next to him said, not sounding all that convincing.

When a piece of metal blew against the side of the building, everyone was startled except Claussen. He stood like a commander, ready to lead troops into battle.

"I want you back in the shadows," he finally said. "Trevor, you're with me. Kranshon. You and your men find cover here. When they arrive, let them through. I know how to get them upstairs. They'll head for the stairs. That's exactly what I want. A scream from our lovely Michelle should work magic."

Claussen walked over to Georgi, standing to the side, supporting Michelle. Her arms were wrapped behind her back with duct tape, a piece of tape covering her mouth. "Take her upstairs. There's a room that used to be the manager's office. Wait until Trevor and I get there. "It's simple," he continued. "Tremain and friends won't be thinking straight, especially Tremain. I want them charging in. I've left enough indicators; they'll be like a fox following the scent. You, Kranshon, that was brilliant, leaving that video cam at the trailer. Some army, eh? Any questions?"

The men muttered acknowledgment.

"Whatever happens, don't panic," Claussen said.

Harding looked at Kranshon when Claussen told him not to panic. He knew Kranshon's professional pride was tweaked, but nodded, keeping his wounded pride hidden.

"I've waited too long. It ends tonight," Claussen said, determined. "I'll look Tremain in the eye. He'll know it's me ending his useless life. Then, the detective's turn," he spat. "He's a traitor."

Claussen, Harding, and Trevor joined Michelle and the Chechen upstairs. The abandoned building groaned, displaying its age and vulnerability. Lightning strobed, revealing a surreal scene before darkness returned.

Harding looked at Kranshon below. *I hope The Brotherhood didn't make a grave error in judgment, helping this idiot with his revenge*, he thought.

• • •

"I don't like this at all, but what choice is there?" Carling whispered as Susan and Remy joined them. "Matt and I did some scouting. We'll walk from where we park. Are you okay with that?" he said, turning to Susan.

"You should ask Matt, not me," she said, her words laced with sarcasm. "Look at that blood."

Matt gave her a look, and she quit talking.

They looked ready when Carling dropped the bombshell. "Someone's followed us from the trailer. There's only one person, and I took evasive action," he said. "He's damned good, but I lost him. Any questions?" he said, looking around.

The other three shrugged.

"We'll park in that building across the street. Park as far back as you can. Be as quiet as you can."

Nobody needed that reminder. They parked and began walking, Matt leading the way, using the map on his phone.

Wind, gusted between buildings, trying to claw at them.

• • •

Angel Vaughn watched the blip on her phone, showing where they parked. *He thinks he lost me,* she thought. *I could see he didn't check for a tracking device in the wheel well.*

• • •

"Single file," Carling said. "Look for my hand signal. It's getting dark, so hurry slowly." They knew what he meant by that.

The building was a two-story structure, brickwork crumbling away in places, I-beams exposed. A door, once used for trucks to load and unload, dangled at an odd angle. It provided an opening to squeeze through.

• • •

Watching them approach, Kranshon and four men spread out, well back in the shadows, waiting. Kranshon heard approaching steps, holding his hand to signal absolute silence.

Squeezing through the door, Carling whispered to Matt. "Something's wrong." He stopped suddenly, Matt almost running into him. "Where did Remy and Susan go?"

Matt started to say something. Carling put a finger to his mouth. A warning. No talking.

Remy's a Marine, Carling thought. *He's made a tactical decision to split away. They won't expect that.*

Squinting, Carling tried to see if anyone was waiting. When it looked clear, he motioned Matt to follow. Then, they heard a sickening noise. Horrific screaming came from overhead. They both knew it was Michelle.

Carling knew he couldn't stop Matt. Limping ahead, the leg of Matt's jeans drenched in blood, crimson fluid leaked down, leaving a trail of blood-red ruby droplets. Carling, his weapon ready, raced after.

They reached the top of the stairs when Claussen fired the first shot. It was joined by a rattle of automatic weapons firing from the opposite direction.

What the fuck, Kranshon thought. "I screwed up," he yelled to Harding. "They've got back up." Intent on Tremain and Carling, he'd ignored his back. His team went down quickly, barely time to raise their weapons. He saw them drop one by one. Then, a man stepped into the light. "Who the hell are—?"

He watched Jess, realizing he carried a big ass gun. Jess held the trigger until the cartridge emptied. Kranshon was nothing but bloody pulp when the firing stopped.

Harding ran to the top of the stairs in time to see Kranshon's death dance. Richocheting bullets carved fragments from the brickworks. He dropped to the floor, trying to see who was below. He couldn't see anyone. Trevor joined him and pointed. "I see someone there." Trevor took aim, steadying one arm with the other. Taking a calming breath, Trevor pulled the trigger, watching Jess drop.

"I think you got him."

"Yeah," Trevor said, rolling over on his back, struggling to stand.

Matt and Carling were standing with their arms out, letting weapons drop to the floor. Claussen held a rifle in one hand and a handgun in the other hand aimed at his two victims while Grigori tied their hands. Matt saw Michelle in the office and started to speak when Claussen smashed the butt of his automatic rifle into the side of Matt's face.

Trevor said, "They're all dead. How the hell—"

Suddenly, more bullets from below silenced him. Scotty found Jess and knew his injury was serious. He took the weapon from Jess, reloaded, and started firing. Off to the side, Jess saw Remy wave a signal as he and Susan climbed another set of stairs in the back. "They look like friendlies, Scotty," Jess managed to say.

At the top of the steps, Remy dropped to the floor in a firing position, firing as he fell. Kranshon's man standing next to Claussen took the hit, his face disappearing into a red mist. The remaining Harding agent turned toward Remy, raising his weapon too late. The man clutched his abdomen, blood gushing through his fingers.

Everything suddenly seemed to be in slow motion, Claussen grasping that his advantage was gone. In desperation, he was still determined to get revenge. He leveled his handgun at Matt's head.

It's the vision from my nightmare, Matt thought, waiting for the shot.

Before Claussen could pull the trigger, Angela Vaughn stepped into the open. As she shot, casings rained around her, showering to the floor.

She kept firing blindly until the bullets were expended. One bullet shattered the bone in Claussen's right arm, his handgun rotating unhurriedly as it fell from his grasp. A second shot hit him in the chest, sprouting a blood blossom.

Trevor was a pro. He reacted and fired. Three shots hit the target, Angela Vaughn.

Claussen leaned back against a pillar. He tried to aim with his left hand. He pulled the trigger, Matt falling back, his head hitting the floor with a thud.

Claussen tried to move. *Someone has tied my hands*, he thought, the feeling in his arms and legs gone.

Harding aimed at Michelle, his face a mask of rage. Remy and Susan both fired at him as Grigori raced forward to shield Michelle. *An act of atonement?* Michelle wondered as Grigori's face turned to mush.

The odor of cordite flooded the building, now almost in total darkness, the lightning storm over.

Carling dropped alongside Matt. "I feel his pulse, but it's weak. We need an ambulance."

Susan rushed to Michelle, carefully removing the duct tape.

"Headcount?" Remy shouted as an odd silence flooded the building. Then the storm returned, rain pounding on the bricks and skylight, wind howling like an angry animal.

There was a loud scream when the tape was removed from Michelle's mouth. She raced to Matt, appalled by the amount of blood pooling around him.

"I've called it in," Jess yelled from below. "I'm hit, but I have a working radio."

Order replaced the chaos of battle. Carling, unhurt, was in control again. He told Remy to watch Matt. "There's not much we can do until the EMTs get here. You know what needs to be done." They saw the stony look on Carling's face. "Matt will live or he won't."

Susan was consoling Michelle as best she could, lacking mothering skills, but keeping Michelle in a tight hug, her head turned away from the sight of Matt's body.

Carling noticed Angela, trying to raise an arm for help. He knelt alongside. He knew blood oozing from the side of her mouth signaled death. He counted at least three fatal gunshot wounds.

"I was a good cop," she said, then settled back.

Carling knew she was dead. "Serve and protect," he murmured, closing her eyelids.

"What the hell," he yelled. He looked around. "Where did Claussen go?"

They heard approaching sirens as his question floated around the room like a hot air balloon.

CHAPTER 54

THE VET

Trevor supported Claussen, the injured Harding doing his best to help. Claussen's head flopped to the left, his feet dragging through the dust. "He's in bad shape," Trevor said. "I've contacted Lev. He stayed behind as a lookout. It was a bad decision on my part. This wouldn't have gone south with him there."

"I'm losing it, Trevor. Gutshot." Harding's ardvoice was shaky.

"Let me carry him," Trevor said. "You take care of yourself." He lifted Claussen over his shoulder in a fireman's carry. Harding tried to follow. Finally, he said, "No more." He sat on the ground and handed Trevor a satellite phone. "Look at the contact list," Harding said. "There's only one number. It's a direct call to The Brotherhood. Tell them everything. Don't sugar coat anything. I can't believe it's ending like this, making a rookie's mistake."

Trevor watched the man dying, a pale blank stare replacing the color in Harding's eyes. Trevor left him sitting against a brick wall. "Nothing more I can do, friend."

He picked up Claussen's body and started toward the Niagara River.

Taking rest stops, Trevor headed toward the intersection where he was to meet Lev. The big man broke into a run and lifted Claussen off Trevor's shoulder as if the injured man was a rag doll.

"It doesn't look good," Lev said, loading Claussen into the back of a Mercedes SUV.

Trevor sat on the passenger side, taking slow calming breaths. He motioned Lev to wait while he dialed a number on the phone Harding had given him. "I have no idea who The Brotherhood is," he said. Harding told me some, but..."

"I'm calling for Harding," Trevor said when the call was answered. He explained all that happened. "I have Claussen. He's badly injured and needs immediate medical attention." *I don't think he'll make it. If you ask me*, he thought but didn't say.

"Tremain's dead. I don't know about the detective. It was a freakin' bloodbath." He didn't say that Claussen's thirst for revenge cause it all. Trevor listened and motioned for the paper to write. "Yes, sir," he said, writing. "I've got it. Count on it!"

"You and I have new bosses," Trevor said. He gave Lev the paper. "It's the address of some veterinarian, about two hours from here. Floor it."

The SUV headlights stabbed at the asphalt stretching into the distance. The hypnotic effect of the white lane divider nearly put Trevor to sleep.

"We're almost there, boss." At the sign for Dr. Benson, Veterinary Clinic, Lev pulled into the driveway. "The farm's dark, not even a security light."

Light over the barn door came on. A man who looked like he'd spent over eighty years guarding the barn door stood under the light. White hair, whiskers framing his face, wearing a plaid shirt tucked into bib overalls.

"I didn't know you could still get bib overalls," Trevor noted.

Lev drove the van inside as the old man closed the door behind. He led Trevor and Lev as they pushed the gurney through a door to an operating room rivaling any modern emergency room. The sign said "veterinarian" but this was a place for humans. "Can't bring me to retire," the old man said, talking as they carefully lifted Claussen onto an examining table.

With deft hands, the old man cut clothing away. "Horses, dogs, cats, and humans, are more alike than you think," he said, running a hand over Claussen's wounds. "Hmm," he said. "It's not good."

"The shoulder is a through-and-through. That can wait. This other isn't too bad. But this one's a killer," referring to Claussen's chest. He chatted as he prepped Claussen's body, asking Trevor and Lev for assistance from time to time. "He's unconscious, but I gave him more than enough to keep him under."

Waiting for the anesthesia to take effect, the veterinarian kept a running dialogue. "My practice was hemorrhaging money. It wasn't hard for them to convince me. I started subsidizing my vet practice with a lucrative side gig. You'd be surprised how much mobbed-up guys pay for my kind of help," he said, laughing as he tied the loop on a final stitch. "Yep, they come from as far away as Des Moines and Atlanta."

"It's time to operate," the vet said. The three lifted Claussen on a gurney. "Through that door, fellas."

Concealed to look like part of the barn, Trevor said, "Your facilities aren't intended for animals, for sure."

"No sense in advertising that fact," the vet said. "Your man will need at least a week before he can be moved. When I finish, I think he'll come around in six to eight hours. Would you guys like something to ea—"

A high-pitched alarm sounded. The veterinarian turned back to the gurney.

"We've seen that before, haven't we Lev," Trevor said. "We didn't need an alarm to tell us that."

"Yeah, dead is dead."

• • •

Michelle sat in the ambulance, holding Matt's hand, wanting to yell at the driver to slow down over bumps. At the same time, she wanted him to drive faster.

"I know it's hard," the attendant said. "We've stabilized him. We'll be at the hospital soon. On cue, the driver turned the siren off as they pulled under the porte-cochere, bright light flooding the ambulance when the door opened. Michelle lost count of the people around Matt, attaching tubes, wires, and stabbing him with needles.

"It's in their hands now," a man said, leading her to a private room. "It's the chapel. Wait here, ma'am."

The wait was unbearable without a phone, no way to contact anyone. *Carling,* she thought. *What happened to him? Where are the others?*

A woman carried in two Styrofoam cups. She handed one to Michelle. "Sugar? Cream?" Michelle shook her head and sipped on the coffee. It tasted better than expected.

"I'm the chaplain," the woman said. "I'm here to keep you company. It sounds like you were in a stressful incident."

Michelle looked at the steam rising from the cup. "May I borrow your phone?"

"Of course."

Michelle dialed and talked to Carling. "I don't know. It's been hours now." She looked at the clock on the wall, shocked. "I'd swear it seems like hours, but it's only been…"

She called Susan's number too, but the call went to voicemail. "Susan. Please. I need you here," she moaned, giving the phone back to the chaplain.

The door opened, and a doctor wearing scrubs stepped in. "I'm Doctor Wilson. Are you Michelle?" He asked. "Mr. Tremain had a card in his wallet granting you the medical power of attorney. I'm sure you have questions."

"Will he live? Will he pull through?"

The chaplain put an arm around Michelle's shoulder for comfort.

"He's in an induced coma," the doctor said. "His head took a dangerous jolt. It's far more concerning than his other injuries," the doctor said, looking at the tablet he held. "Let's go to a room near the patient."

The chaplain walked alongside Michelle, not talking, but offering a reassuring touch. They followed Dr. Wilson into another room.

"We've treated two gunshot wounds. You were lucky to get this guy when you did. He lost a lot of blood. That wire tourniquet saved his life."

"He lost a lot of that when he fell over that discarded car door," Carling said, walking through the door. Michelle thought Carling was crying.

Dr. Wilson's phone chirped. "We can go to his room now. I can talk on the way. The gunshot wounds weren't serious. The head injury is. The leg is badly infected," the doctor said. "It complicates the treatment plan. We've started aggressive treatment. The infection is more than serious. He might lose his leg. Any questions?"

"When will he wake up? When can I talk to him?" Michelle said.

The doctor rubbed his forehead, trying to avoid the answer. "It could be now, tomorrow, next week, or..." He shrugged. "It's always hard to tell in a case like this."

Carling and Michelle looked at each other, filling in the blanks for themselves.

Walking into Matt's room, Carling and Michelle each drew a gasping breath. He was unrecognizable, wrapped in bandages with tubes dripping fluids into him.

"He's getting the best care possible," a new doctor said. He walked into the room, pulling off a scrub mask. "I'm Doctor Millerson, the chief neurologist. This is the room we use for the complications your friend's battling." He walked over to a computer and ran the cursor over an icon.

Four images appeared in split frames on a large, hi-def screen. He maximized one and pointed to a dark spot. "That's my worry. If we see that starting to shrink, I'll bring champagne."

Michelle and Carling sat quietly after the doctors left. The lighting was low, the hum of the ventilator the only sound. Michelle held Matt's hand, willing a response from the man she loved.

"I'm glad you're here for him," Carling said, his voice sounding like it was being filtered through a mouthful of marbles. "I have something I have to do and needed to know Matt's in good hands."

Michelle realized Carling was leaving. She stood, wrapping her arms around him. She rested her head on his shoulder, the tears dampening Carling's shirt.

"I won't stop until I find out what happened to—"

"Quiet," she whispered. "If the bastard's still alive, I want you to kill him, Brick."

It's in her eyes. She wants her revenge, now, he thought. "You know what you're asking of me?"

She nodded.

Carling turned on his heels, and Michelle watched the door close behind him. She sat down, holding Matt's hand. *What did I hear about reading to someone at a time like this? Will it really penetrate Matt's coma?* Michelle wasn't sure she believed it, but she wasn't going to take any chances. She held his hand, watching the rhythm of nurses and doctors coming and going. *No matter how long, I'll be here, waiting for you to come back to me, Matt.*

• • •

The room was dark, the only light coming from the hallway. Michelle reached into her handbag for her phone. Using her music app, Coltrane's music filled the room. She couldn't stop crying during the ten minutes of pure soul, "Blue Train," from the album of the same name.

She closed her eyes and remembered their argument. Matt demanding that the 1957 album was Trane's favorite—and his. Nobody asked her to turn down the music.

• • •

"Matt. I'm back online. It was a train wreck, but I fought off the attack. Claussen's laying another trap." Cyberia's message went to a computer in Toronto. Matt's computer screen lit up for a moment, then went dark again.

CHAPTER 55

NEED A WINGMAN?

Carling kept his temper in check as he raced into another hospital. When he got to the floor he wanted, a police officer stood guard at room 434. He gave Carling a no-nonsense look. Carling flashed his badge. It didn't work. "That's a Toronto shield. This is Buffalo."

"Let him in," Jess yelled from his bed.

"I can tell you're gonna pull through," Carling said as he came in. He looked sheepish, holding a small plant from the gift shop. "The bullet with your name is still out there."

"I'm a friend, I tell you." It was Scotty, trying to get past the officer posted outside.

"What's with all the Canadian shields?" the office said. "I suppose Jess knows you too."

"He's my other friend," Jess said. "Don't worry, George. There won't be more. I only have two friends."

The officer smiled at the joke and closed the door as he left.

"He thinks I'm kidding," Jess said. "It's closer to the truth than I care to admit."

"Ah, but damned fine friends we are," Scotty said. "Do they have a camera in here?" Scotty asked. He pulled a bottle out. "Old Pulteney. Not the cheap stuff."

Pleased as he was, Jess waved the treat away. "Some other time," he said. "It hurts like hell, and I'm sore and tired. "The doctors say I have a long road ahead. More surgery and rehab."

Scotty raised his glass. *"Slàinte mhòr agus a h-uile beannachd duibh.* That's Gaelic," he said. "Great health and every good blessing to you."

"Roger that," Carling said. "We'd better let Jess rest." They turned to wave goodbye, but their friend's eyes were closed, though he was smiling.

"We might as well get it over," Carling whispered. "Let's get a drink somewhere and talk about the interview coming. Interview hell, it'll be an interrogation."

• • •

"Is this our only choice, mate?" Scotty said. "Where did all the neighborhood pubs go? We'd belly up to the bar and talk. Look," he said. "There must be at least twenty hi-def screens. It's almost impossible to keep from looking. It's a bloody distraction. Not a single dartboard in sight. I miss the Bar Maid's Arms. Remember on Yonge Street?"

Carling knew Scotty wanted to move the clock back forty years. He also knew Scotty's nerves were raw as his own. Carling sipped his beer, thinking. "The lead detective is smart," Carling said. "Bullshit isn't going to baffle his brains. I could tell by the way he checked us out on the scene."

"I know, mate. They all know Jess. He told us to tell the truth. Straight, no chaser. Does that mean we can't embellish our story? You know, mix facts with the truth."

"Embellish?" Carling said, his voice above a whisper. "They want an explanation for at least nine people dead, enough blood to start a blood bank, and a shit-load of illegal weapons. Yeah, let's embellish that," Carling said.

"Yeah, there's that," Scotty said.

"I saw two men leave with Claussen," Scotty said.

Carling nodded. "This is the second time I've seen Claussen's shot, pulling a Houdini both times. I know he was hurt, bad," Carling said. "I saw Claussen sitting on the floor, holding his stomach. The next moment, he was gone. He's our only explanation for being there, but he's officially a dead man. How we explain defending ourselves from a dead man?"

"What do you think we should say?" Scotty asked.

"It's all about Michelle's kidnapping. Claussen pulled us into his spider web of hate and revenge, using her as bait. I gotta pee, back in a sec."

When Carling returned, he didn't sit. "I got a text that Remy and Susan made it back across the border, planning a long vacation in New Zealand."

"What's the latest on Matt," Scotty asked.

"Wait and see," Carling said, his face turned a deep red.

"The way I see it," Scotty said, "I'm going to say we got a call that Michelle was kidnapped. We took matters into our own hands. It wasn't the right thing to do, but that's how it was. We didn't set out to break any laws. Well, maybe bend them a bit. We'll know if we're in deep if there's an FBI agent in the room."

"Simple explanations are always the best," Carling said and laughed. "I was thinking about retirement anyway. Florida sounds better than a jail cell in Buffalo. Let's get it over with, and see what it'll be, Florida or Buffalo."

"Copy that," Scotty said. They left a tip on the table and left.

● ● ●

Carling and Scotty walked into Buffalo police headquarters. It was like a freeze frame on television, everyone stopping to watch them, the Carling-Scotty version of a perp walk. They were led to an interview room. "Funny to be sitting on this side of the table, Scotty."

"Ha-ha is for funny. This isn't ha-ha, Carling."

"It's strange though, Scotty. They're not splitting us. That's protocol in any police department."

The door opened. Two men walked in. One was four, maybe five inches over six feet, wearing a tailored uniform with an array of medals. The man following him wore a rumpled suit and the weary look of a detective who'd been on duty for eighteen hours straight.

The detective turned on a recorder, and the four of them danced through two hours of embellished truth. Then Carling nudged Scotty and pointed with his chin. The recorder was actually turned off. "We're off the record," he whispered.

The officer in the uniform stood, pulling his jacket smooth. He paused before beginning.

"You two are an embarrassment I didn't need. I've dedicated over thirty years to this police force. Add to that, my utmost regard for Toronto Police Services. If it weren't for Jess Wilson, one of my best detectives,

I would've thrown you both under the bus. How will I explain this story when we're trying to say Buffalo's a good place to live and raise a family? I had to assure everyone it's not an act of terrorism. We finally decided, gang-related activities explain what happened."

The detective sat, not giving anything away as the Chief of Police continued.

Seeing Carling about to ask a question, the officer said, "Shut up and listen. You'll both enjoy our escort to your side of the Peace Bridge. I spent quite some time talking with your chief. That sound you're hearing? Your careers flushed down the toilet."

The chief then made an impressive about-face and left the room.

"What can I say, guys?" the detective said. "Jess said you guys did a helluva job. That's why I'm giving you this."

Carling looked at an enveloped the detective slid across the table.

"Jess said you earned this."

Carling stared at the photo and showed it to Scotty. "No doubts now. Claussen's dead."

"The Angola Travel Plaza, a rest stop on the Thruway. The cleaning crew found his body propped in a toilet stall. Your perp had medical grade stitchery if you ask me."

• • •

The car was hot. Carling rolled the windows down and turned on the A/C. Scotty sat in the passenger seat.

"It's not over for you, is it, Brick?"

"I always suspected Claussen had hidden resources," Carling said. "How did he stay out of sight all this time? I heard one of the men helping Claussen. I couldn't hear it clearly, a lot of noise, eh?" Carling rubbed his eyes. "He said something about CleanSweep. He also said Claussen had secret backing from something called The Brotherhood, The Brotherhood of Eagles. Did you ever hear of The Brotherhood?"

Scotty shook his head no.

"What aren't we seeing? I intend to find out. After all, I'm retired, and...I owe it to Matt."

"Need a wingman?" Scotty asked.

CHAPTER 56

ANOTHER LIMP

Michelle sat with her eyes closed, savoring the Miles Davis recording, "Flamenco Sketches," the fifth track on *Kind of Blue*. She wanted to believe Matt was listening, her left hand rested on the bed holding his. Her other hand tapped the slow, bluesy rhythm.

She felt a small movement. It sent a surge of electricity through her. It was the smallest of movements. *Did Matt's fingers contract?* she wondered.

She jumped from the chair. Michelle stared at Matt, still looking like someone very much in a coma. His vital signs were unchanged, a steady beep-beep for a soundtrack. Several lines of various colors scrolled across the screen, rising and falling in steady waves.

Heart rate, normal, she thought, reading numbers on the monitor. *Blood pressure, nothing different. No alarms. Did I feel it, or did I only want to feel it?*

Michelle reached for the call button to summon for help and stopped, her finger poised. *Someone's behind me,* she thought. *I feel it.* Turning, she almost fell back into the chair in disbelief.

Matt stood in the doorway, outlined by backlighting of fluorescent lighting.

It can't be, Michelle thought, looking back at the man on the bed. *Who is this? The same height? The same build? The same age?* She watched a man walk in. *He even has Matt's limp. It must be Matt's twin,*

Michelle thought, shaking her head, skeptical. *Matt didn't have a twin. Whoever this is...is limping with the wrong leg.*

Michelle stepped back, her panic rising.

"*Uspokoysya,*" the man said in a soft baritone voice. "Be calm, Michelle. I mean you no harm."

He even sounds like Matt, Michelle thought. "Who... who are you?"

"□□□□ □□□□□ □□□□□□□," the man said. "My name is Alexei."

"How did you get in here? This is a secure area, nobody allowed without permission," Michelle said, her voice strident. "I'm calling security."

"Cyberia and I walk through walls," Alexei said. "We're one and the same," and smiled.

Michelle raised a hand to her mouth. "You? You're Cyberia? Matt's... Matt's—"

"Friend," Alexei said, finishing for her. "Yes, I'm Matt's friend."

Michelle eyes flooded with tears, staring at Matt's doppelgänger. Cyberia, Alexi, stepped to embrace her. *This's the man who saved Matt's life, throwing an electronic flotation device to his drowning friend,* she thought.

Michelle felt something for the first time since Matt's surgery: Hope.

Michelle watched as Alexei walked to Matt's bedside. There was sadness in Alexei's eyes. But she also saw tenderness, the way he took Matt's hand in his. Alexei stared at Matt for a long time. He pulled a chair alongside and sat, holding Matt's hand again.

"□□□□, □□□□ □ □□□□□, □□□ □□□□," he said.

Without understanding, Michelle recognized the gift in those caring words.

"In my language, I asked God to be with him," Alexei said. "I wish that for you, as well."

"That's a good blessing in any language," Michelle said. "Thank you."

A moment ago, I thought I felt his fingers move. He hasn't moved since... I'm so afraid, Alexei."

"I'm not leaving Matt, or you," he said.

"But how? You live in Moscow. How?" Her question hovered between them.

"It will help me to tell the story," Alexei said, his eyes wet with tears. "This shouldn't have happened," Alexei said, looking pained. "I thought I had Matt's back. How will I ever come to terms with this? We Russians wallow in guilt and deep depression like hogs rooting in the mud. The truth? I let my guard down. I'm not given to hubris, but I thought I was invincible. Hiding behind my skill and training, I imagined ample layers of electronic protection keeping me safe.

"My limp, you may have noticed, the same as Matt. Except we don't limp with the same leg," Alexei said, almost smiling. "I first saw him in a video, walking with a limp. It was like watching myself. I had the advantage, knowing what Matt looked like. Yet when he wanted personal details about me, I handed out specifics as if they were precious diamonds. I wasn't secretive; it was a game, egging him on to ask more."

Michelle sat quietly. "I want to hear," she said.

"I knew Matt's limp was genetic. I told him I had a limp too, but didn't say mine was a different leg. Hah, it was the same kind of limp though. I told him mine was a skiing accident. "*Nyet*. It was no accident. In my final year at Moscow Technological University, I joined a student protest group. The police were quite zealous about stopping us. Two strong *politseykiey*, policemen, tossed me. I skied down a flight of concrete steps."

"Why Cyberia?" Michelle said.

"When it comes to the police, Russians have a built-in distrust and aversion. Specifically police of a secret kind. I think we're born suspicious. It's hardwired into our collective DNA. That's perhaps how survived everything Czars and Soviets. They came and left. Somehow it feels the same with whoever's in charge now."

"Is that why you hide in the darknet?" Michelle said. She saw his shock. "Matt told me about it," she explained. "If you checked me out, you know I'm savvy around computers."

Alexi blushed. "You are getting to know me too well," he said, laughing. His laugh broke the gloom. "I'm no recluse. I don't like to be around people. I prefer hiding behind my computers, you might say, and you would be correct. Okay, I admit I was close to becoming a recluse. I shopped for necessities, went to the doctor and dentist, things like that. But more and more, I sat in my chair. It was only my computers and me."

Alexei stood and stretched, his hand covering a yawn.

"Even with your education and experience, you might be surprised to know what my computers can do," he said. "Computers, plural. Better to call them servers. I hid each of the seven in different locations, most inside the Third Ring Road. It was easy. Five went into unused rooms of different technological universities and institutes."

A doctor came in to check Matt's condition. Michelle and Alexei looked at him, hoping for any change. He shook his head. "It'll take time," he said. He typed notes on the bedside computer and left.

"Is that what I think you're doing? Michelle said, smiling.

"Born to hack," Alexei said. "I downloaded his chart to my tablet. Fancy a coffee?"

●●●

Hospital cafeterias have a certain rhythm. At three in the morning, the lights are lower. Doctors and nurses sit in a group. Family members look like they don't have a clue why they're there. Michelle looked around and found a table where no one would hear the two of them talk. "What's the chart say?" she said, leaning forward.

Alexei finished reading. "You can read it. There's nothing they haven't told you. The surgeon uses the word hope and prayer a lot."

"Finish your story, Alexei. Coffee is helping me stay awake."

"Following Matt wasn't stalking. It was like keeping tabs on an old friend. I was certain it was impossible to find a trail back to me. I used a different server for each person in our group. In addition to Matt, Ubari logged in from someplace in Africa. Lake Devil lives somewhere in South Florida. The one calling herself Chin is from Chengdu, the capital of Sichuan in China. How was anyone going to break into the networks the four of us guarded?"

Alexei yawned again. "It was a long flight," he sighed. "What was I saying? Oh, the group. All humans have a need to connect with other people. The five of us had a common bond, hiding from people, in the world, not of the world, eh. Did I mention that in real life I am beyond extremely reclusive?"

Cyberia, Alexei, doesn't seem to notice how his Anthropophobia—a fear of people—keeps looping around, Michelle thought.

"I was uber-selective about people I connected to. I mined data-banks to check out anyone I befriended. I divided online contacts into three groups: fun and games, curiosities, and real friends. Matt was in the latter," Alexei said, "Sorry I didn't mean past tense." He paused, sipping coffee. "I goofed around with the first two groups, but I was serious about my real friends. We grew close and protective. Except for Matt, the rest had computer skills you can't begin to imagine. Matt wasn't all that computer savvy, but I, we, admired his tenacity about the truth. That's a rare commodity these days, eh?"

Michelle nodded.

"I was the only one who knew Matt's identity. To the others, he was Verité. No surprise why he picked that nickname. Then, Charles Claussen came crashing into our world," Alexei said. "When the conspirators came out of the shadows, I called on every technological trick I had. Matt told me I saved his life. That may be, but I was able to feed him information, some of it, how do you say it, in the nick of time. I was proud of Matt. I was proud of being able to help. Ubari, Lake Devil, and Chin stepped in, and between us, we made sure Matt had all the information we could—" Cyberia stopped and sipped on the bottle of water. He was crying.

"Go on," Michelle said, softly encouraging him to continue.

"Sadly, after CleanSweep was exposed, we all went our different ways. We maintained occasional contact, but it eventually became less and less. We promised to stay in touch but didn't." Alexei took a deep breath. "Then my computers and I took a wrong turn. We went to a dark place. I don't have a need for money. But it became an obsession to see how much I could accumulate. I have no idea how it happened, but it started to border on greed."

"What happened?" Michelle asked.

"Enter Bratva. In Russian, братва. Bratva means brothers. Americans call it the Russian mafia, but it's nothing like the Sicilians. Ours is more a collective of gangs and thugs, not known for subtlety. They made me an offer I couldn't refuse like the movie line goes."

"That's a lot of talking for a recluse," Michelle said with a smile, clinging to every word.

Alexei finished. They stood and embraced, holding on to each other for a long time. Then, Alexei took Michelle's hand, leading her to the elevator. "We check on Matt. Yes?"

●●●

Trevor's phone chirped. He read the text: *We've attached a letter from a lawyer, along with our offer. If you're interested in the offer, text yes.* "I need to download these, Lev," he said. "Is your bag packed?" Trevor asked, knowing it was.

Trevor read the first of the two attachments, a letter from the Miami law firm of Rodriquez, Pineda, and Wilkins.

In the event of my death, I, Javin Harding, bequeath JH Enterprises, all assets, and personnel, to David Kranshon and Trevor Allison. Signed, Heiler Rodriguez, Esquire.

The second attachment was short and clear, the offer from The Brotherhood.

Lev waited, incurious.

Trevor grinned, typed yes, and hit send.

He got an immediate response. "Here're the coordinates. A plane's waiting at Niagara Falls airport. Bring your large friend."

"Lev," Trevor said. "Have you ever been to Iceland?"

CHAPTER 57

KEFLAVIK

Michelle sat next to Matt's bed, trying to remember how long it had been like this. Alexi walked in with more coffee and bagels. "What did your boss have to say?"

"He wasn't happy," she said.

"What about your job?"

"They asked for password access to my project," she said. "I thought about asking to work from here, but knew I wouldn't have the concentration. My severance package isn't too bad, I must say. You're practically retired. Carling's retired. Scotty's retired. I might as well be, too."

"Any change? What did the doctor say?" Alexi asked.

"I was going to ask the same thing," Carling said.

She looked sad. "No change."

"Michelle, you look prettier every day," Carling said. "Matt's going to wake up to your smile. What a lucky guy. Good to have you around, Alexi. I know both Michelle and Matt need it."

"What about you?" Michelle asked. "Do you have your condo in Port Saint Lucie yet?"

"Last on my bucket list," Carling replied.

"You look like you have something to say," Alexi said.

"I do, but first, what about Jess?" Michelle asked.

"Yesterday was his first day back on full duty," Carling said, sounding pleased. "I'm surprised they still let me across the border; I drove down to fill you in. Scotty and I've been building up frequent flyer miles. Alexi, what do you call those dolls inside of dolls things?"

"Matryoshka dolls. Russian nesting dolls. Why?"

Scotty and I have been trying to dig up information about The Brotherhood. You told us even you couldn't get in via computers. We're doing it the old school way, one interview at a time. But each time we open a doll, we find another inside. We must be ten dolls in by now." He paused. "What we've learned scares the hell out of us. There's no allegiance to politics, nationalities, or religions. When it looks like they back the extreme right on the political spectrum, we found they're also funding the extreme left. Is there any water?"

Michelle poured him a glassful.

"I understand why they put all that money behind CleanSweep," Carling said. "I suspect they like the idea of destabilization. The feds in the U.S. have suspicions that The Brotherhood's funding extreme right groups, especially neo-Nazis."

"They have ties to Russian intelligence," Alexi said.

"I booked a flight to Bulgaria," Carling said. "We have a name, someone who can fill in some gaps."

"Be careful, my friend," Alexi said. "Those are some dangerous hackers in that country. They can be ruthless."

"Always—"

Carling was interrupted when the door opened.

Dr. Millerson, the neurologist, walked in, hands behind his back. "I'm glad you have their support, Michelle," he said, looking around at the small crowd. "She's like a soldier, standing guard on young Mr. Tremain."

Michelle picked up something; Dr. Millerson had a strange look on his face. *This is going to be bad news,* she thought. Matt had another scan a few hours ago, and she braced herself for the worst.

"I'm going to break the rules," Dr. Millerson said. "I left word at the nurse's station for some glasses." He was holding a bottle. "Okay, it's not champagne like I promised, but the scan's good... Good news, indeed. It will take time, but we're going to wake him up. That's the good news. The not-so-good news? Rehab will take months."

• • •

Trevor enjoyed Saga class, Iceland Air's version of first class. The food was outstanding, and the wine perfectly matched. Trevor watched the screen on the seatback display. *I've never been to Iceland.*

The announcement came in Icelandic first, then English. "Ladies and Gentlemen, welcome to Reykjavik and Keflavik International Airport."

• • •

The End

Thank you for choosing The CleanSweep Counterstrike, by Chuck Waldron. If you missed book one in the series, it's not too late:

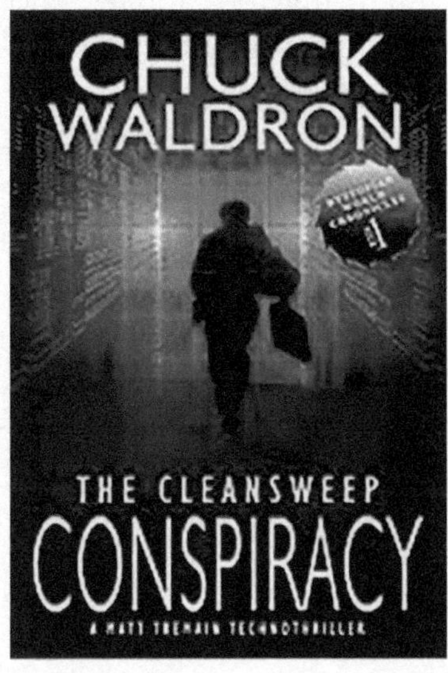

In this riveting technothriller, investigative blogger Matt Tremain is covering devastating riots in Toronto when he learns of a plot to rid the city of "undesirables." The operation is called CleanSweep and appears to be led by billionaire Charles Claussen, who want to sweep Toronto clean of all street people and any citizens who don't match his restrictive screening matrix. Matt questions whether he has the courage, skill, or influence to take on Claussen, but the murder of one of his sources convinces the blogger to put his life on the line. He gambles on the loyalty of a Toronto police detective and a local TV reporter for help. If his trust is misplaced, Matt will become yet another victim of CleanSweep, and the truth will be buried with him forever.

ABOUT THE AUTHOR

Chuck Waldron is the author of four riveting mystery, thriller, and suspense novels and more than fifty short stories. Inspired by his grandfather's tales of the Ozark Mountains and local caves rumored to be havens for notorious gangsters, Waldron was destined to write about crime and the human condition. Those childhood legends ignited his imagination and filled his head with unforgettable characters, surprising plots, and a keen interest in supernatural and historical subplots.

With literary roots planted in the American Midwest and South, and enriched by many years living in the fertile cultural soil of metropolitan Ontario, Waldron now resides on Florida's fabled Treasure Coast with his wife, Suzanne. While keeping an eye out for hurricanes, alligators, and the occasional Burmese python, visitors will find Waldron busy writing his next crime thriller.

Chuck's always delighted to hear from readers.
Chuck@chuckwaldron.com

And on the web: www.chuckwaldronauthor.com

Visit Chuck's site at Amazon Central here:
Chuck Waldron@Amazon Central

CHECK OUT OTHER NOVELS BY CHUCK WALDRON

Tears in the Dust.

"I was a party to two murders; therefore, I do not particularly trust in fate…I have given you, my last and only friend, my confession."

So begins this gripping historical suspense novel set against the backdrop of the Spanish Civil War in 1937. It is with a heavy pen that a reporter, Michael, fulfills his promise to tell the complicated story of his departed friend Alec, who volunteered to fight in the International Brigade but didn't realize the true price he would pay for his patriotism. Returning from Spain to his home in Vermont, Alec seeks healing but is instead accosted by Samuel T. Harrison, a dark, twisted investigator with a deep hatred of communism. Confronted with the unspeakable, Alec flees and assumes a false identity. But no matter how far Alec goes, he cannot outrun Harrison, who pursues him through the years and across countries only to catch up with him in a stunning conclusion.

Remington and the Mysterious Fedora

In this supernatural mystery, we meet Josh Cody—a smart, young, aspiring author who has challenged himself to write a complete novel in one month. Looking for inspiration, Josh stumbles into a run-down thrift shop and buys a classic Remington manual typewriter and a dusty old fedora. When inexplicable coincidences start to occur and the story of a frightened young woman begins pouring out of him, Josh wonders if the typewriter and fedora are somehow channeling an unsolved mystery from the past. Thus begins Josh's story within a story and the journey of a lifetime. For readers—and writers—looking for a unique, fast-paced read, *Remington and the Mysterious Fedora* is an entertaining choice.

I hope you're waiting for more about
the adventures of Detective Carling,
Matt Tremain, and his friends. It's time to
go nose-to-nose with The Brotherhood,
and the clock is ticking. An email to
chuck@chuckwaldron.com is all it takes
to stay tuned.

Book Three

The CleanSweep Consequences
By Chuck Waldron

CHAPTER 1

The first bullet shattered the passenger-side window. Glass, flesh, and bone sprayed the side of Carling's face. A red mist bathed the car's interior. A short-lived void of terrifying silence was broken by a soft moan, the sound of sucking air until Scotty's breathing was close to inaudible.

With a second shot, the windshield exploded, a slug lodging in the driver's side door panel.

To Carling, it seemed like ultra-slow-motion, and he was unable to grasp what was happening.

The third shot hit Carling, passing through muscle and soft tissue below the shoulder joint. The pain was immediate and intense as if he'd been touched with the burning end of a cigar.

Instinct saved his life. He pushed the door and rolled out. The next shot lodged in the headrest where he'd been sitting. He spun onto his left side, eyes watery from the pain. Carling reached for his weapon. *Still in the hotel safe. We were just driving out to—*

His thoughts were interrupted. The last burst of gunfire seemed like it would never end.

Carling hoped it was over. *How long since the last shot?* He wondered. *Shag me sideways,* he thought. *What's dripping? Crap, it's gasoline!*

Ignoring the pain, he pushed up and sprinted around the car. Carling clutched Scotty, hauling him as far away as he could. He confirmed there was a pulse. Scotty was alive, but Carling knew the signs. Scotty needed immediate medical attention.

Out in the middle of bloody nowhere, he thought, surprised when his emergency call was answered. *Damn, she doesn't speak English.* His call was transferred to another operator, English without a trace of an accent.

"We're in middle of nowhere. How would I know where?" Carling shouted, breathing deeply to calm himself. "How long? We left Reykjavík after breakfast. I drove the speed limit," he said, looking at his watch. "We've been driving three hours, or so.

"No, I don't see any landmarks. Wait. There's a sign. I can't even begin to pronounce the words. There's a turnoff," he cried. "Sorry, I'm in a lot of pain. There's a sign in the shape of a seal. There's an arrow pointing up, with 6 km to something islands. Some touristy looking sign."

At least the car's not burning.

Carling dropped next to Scotty, checking for a pulse again. Carling was close to unconsciousness himself. He touched his shoulder, using the pain to stay awake. *There's no way they can get here in time,* he thought. The faint sound of an ambulance siren almost made him forget his pain.

"Hold on Scotty," he pleaded.

•••

The sniper and spotter were dressed in white, perfect camouflage for landscape inside the Arctic Circle.

"What do you see?" the shooter asked.

"Your first shot hit one of the targets. You got the passenger in the center of the chest, below the chin," the spotter said.

"I know that. It's the other target, the driver."

"Your second shot took out the windshield. The driver didn't have time to react. I'm pretty sure you got him with the third shot. If not, when you emptied the magazine on automatic, you couldn't have missed."

"I'm going to send it in," the sniper said, taking her phone from a sleeve pocket. "Time to send the boss a text.

SNIPER: "Targets eliminated."

TREVOR: "Confirmed?"

SNIPER: "Visual. Spotter has video."

TREVOR: "Make sure!"

SNIPER: "Sirens. Must rely video. Out."

"Let's get the hell out of here," she said to her spotter. They eliminated evidence of their presence and started jogging toward a Land Rover in the distance.

•••

Carling sat on the rear platform of the ambulance. For some reason, he didn't expect the level of sophistication, communication and medical equipment on display.

Two EMTs attended Scotty, while a young woman sat poised at a computer console.

Carling couldn't understand the language but heard the same tone EMTs back home used, soothing, calm, urgent.

He didn't hear a man approach. "The team only speaks Icelandic. I apologize. The woman's a nurse. She's connected to the trauma center in Reykjavik. A satellite link allows real-time communication," the man said. He cautiously put a hand on Carling's shoulder. "Everything is being monitored." Carling inspected the man in a black uniform with checked markings, sporting a patch, *Lögreglan*, Icelandic for police.

Carling detected a sense of urgency from the nurse at the computer. *Damn, what's she saying? What's with this language? It sounds like it's all consonants, and no vowels.*

What's she saying? Carling asked the officer.

"The helicopter is five minutes out. They're taking the victim to Reykjavik." Anticipating Carling's question, he said, "only room for your friend. I know you're worried. They're doing all they can. My name's Police Constable *Árnþórsson*, first name Páll. I have some questions while we wait. May I?

"First, the EMTs need information. What's your friend's name?"

"Brogan McGregor," Carling said. "We call him Scotty. His mother moved to Canada from Kilmarnock in Scotland, his father from Glasgow."

I'm rambling. Too much unneeded stuff, Carling thought.

"He's Canadian?"

"We left our passports at the hotel front desk."

"How old is your friend?"

"We're the same age, 68."

"Is Mr. McGregor employed?" the Constable said.

"Retired," Carling said. For some reason, Carling held back mentioning they'd been detectives with Toronto Police Services.

"*Kanadíska. Brogan McGregor. 68 ára. Eftirlaun,*" Constable Árnþórsson, said to the nurse at the computer.

"I gave them Mr. McGregor's details. May I have your name, sir?" the Constable asked. "Then, if you don't mind, one or two questions."

"Carling, Wallace Carling. Also, Canadian. Also, retired. Also, 68," Carling said, prickliness in his answers.

The first question he'll ask is what are Scotty and I doing here. He's following the same playbook all cops use, Carling thought. *It won't be long until questions turn into an interrogation.*

*Árnþórsson and Carling squint*ed into the sunlight. The whop-whop sound of helicopter rotors signaled a halt in the questioning.

Carling knew the pause was temporary.